A

CANDLELIGHT REGENCY SPECIAL

CANDLELIGHT REGENCIES

Infamous Isabelle

Margaret Summerville

A CANDLELIGHT REGENCY SPECIAL

Published by
Dell Publishing Co., Inc.
1 Dag Hammarskjold Plaza
New York, New York 10017

Dell ® TM 681510, Dell Publishing Co., Inc.

ISBN: 0-440-13867-1

Printed in the United States of America

First printing—June 1980

Chapter 1

Lord Biddleton was reading the newspaper when his butler entered the library in an apologetic manner. His lordship reluctantly pushed the newspaper aside and looked questioningly at the servant.

"Yes, Mills, what is it?"

The butler replied hesitantly, "I am sorry to disturb you, my lord, but Lady Ambrose is here and wishes to see your lordship immediately."

At this intelligence a slight frown appeared on Lord Biddleton's face. The frown was quite understandable to his lordship's butler. Mills had been in the Earl of Biddleton's employ for almost eight years and was well acquainted with his lordship's sister. Lady Ambrose, he knew, was a most difficult woman.

"Very well, Mills," replied Lord Biddleton in a resigned voice, "send my sister in immediately as she wishes."

The butler gave a perfunctory nod and hurried out of the room. He returned in a few moments followed by a rather formidable-looking female.

Lady Ambrose was a tall, large-boned woman of two and forty who walked with a rigid posture. She gave the impression that it pained her to look anywhere but straight ahead, an unfortunate circumstance for her acquaintances of short stature. Lady Ambrose's whole countenance spoke of an inflexibility of character. Her features were severe and disapproving and she very seldom smiled. Indeed, her smile was more like a grimace, so that many could not recognize it on the rare occasions when it did appear. Her brother, familiar with his sister's countenance, saw that it was particularly grim that morning and wondered what catastrophe she was about to put before him.

"Lydia," he said, primly pecking her on the cheek. "What brings you here at this early hour?"

His sister sat down stiffly, giving him a critical glance before she answered.

"Good morning, Lucius. I have come to see you about a very important matter. You know I rarely ask anything of you, Lucius," she continued. "I have seen fit to shoulder my own burdens in this life." She paused to give this statement some effect. Her brother, whose features now appeared as severe as her own, made no reply.

Lady Ambrose's voice became bitter. "God knows the burdens I have had to carry . . . with Mother and Father dying, leaving me to raise you." Her brother's frown deepened, as always, with this familiar speech. "And then, of course," continued her ladyship, "there was George."

Their marriage had been a misery and Ambrose's death five years earlier had no doubt been, as one of his friends remarked, "a great relief to both of them."

Lady Ambrose's voice became bitter. "God knows the but always sufficed it by saying, "And then, of course, there was George." She looked at her brother, who showed no sign of sympathy. However, Lady Ambrose seemed unperturbed by her brother's lack of response. "As I said, Lucius. I do not like to ask anything of you but I really do need your help in this matter."

"Yes, Lydia?" asked Lord Biddleton who felt a good deal of reluctance in offering his help but was also firmly ingrained with a sense of familial duty.

"It's Cuthburt," said his sister curtly.

"Cuthburt?" said his lordship, blankly repeating his nephew's name.

Lady Ambrose made a stiff gesture with one hand. "I do not know what to do with the boy. He has fallen in with

6

the most . . ." She sought briefly for the appropriate word. "Unacceptable. The most unacceptable people."

"Oh?" said her brother, finally showing a flicker of interest.

"Yes, he has become fast friends with Robert Clairemont. Cuthburt met him at school and Clairemont has been a dreadful influence."

"Clairemont," murmured Lord Biddleton, trying to remember where he had heard the name.

His sister saw his puzzled expression and said impatiently, "Surely, Lucius, you've heard of the Clairemonts. Robert's father is the Duke of Fothingham."

"Fothingham! Oh, yes, of course," said Lord Biddleton. "The infamous line of Fothinghams. As I recall the Fourth Duke was a rather shocking fellow. Married a young kitchen maid when he was in his dotage."

"And his grandson the Sixth Duke is no better." She added knowingly, "It's in the blood, and bad blood it is."

Lord Biddleton shook his head. "And Cuthburt has become friends with the present Duke's son?"

His sister, seeing that he was of the same mind as she was in regard to such an unsuitable friendship, continued in a more animated fashion. "Yes, and the Clairemont boy is a wild one. A gamester just like his father. I tell you, Lucius, the Clairemonts are a disreputable family and I don't want Cuthburt associating with any of them!" She craned her head toward him and said in a dramatic whisper, "And I haven't told you the worst of it yet."

Her brother sat down and eyed her curiously. "What is the worst?"

"Cuthburt thinks himself in love with Isabelle Clairemont."

Lord Biddleton again looked puzzled. "And who is she?"

His sister gave an exasperated cry. "Isabelle is Robert's eldest sister, one of the daughters of the Duke! I am surprised you have not heard of her, Lucius, she is quite notorious."

"Indeed?" replied her brother, lifting an eyebrow. His sister gave one of her rare grimace smiles.

"Don't expect me to go into details, Lucius. All you need to know is that Lady Isabelle is quite unsuitable for your nephew."

"But Lydia," returned her brother, "has Cuthburt told you about her?"

"Hardly!" snorted her ladyship. "He knows I would disapprove. I was in his room and found some drivel he had been writing about the 'fair and divine Isabelle.' "

Lord Biddleton stared disapprovingly at her.

"You needn't look at me like that, brother," she said quickly. "I'm his mother and I had a right to know what mischief was afoot. And a good thing I found out before it was too late."

"Too late?" queried her brother.

"Why, Isabelle Clairemont is scheming to marry my Cuthburt! Everyone knows that Fothingham has been gaming away what fortune he has. Lady Isabelle sees my Cuthburt as an easy means to a fortune. She has been unable to snatch a rich husband yet and must realize that her time is fleeting. Why the girl is six and twenty if my reckoning is correct."

Lord Biddleton frowned. It was difficult to imagine his young nephew in the claws of some mercenary female. But his sister's account sounded convincing enough. Certainly his nephew would be a great prize for this scheming Clairemont woman. The Earl knew that fortune hunters were not restricted to his own sex and this Lady Isabelle had reason to seek a rich husband. No doubt she was one of those extravagant females that abounded in London society, overspending their means on lavish gowns and jewels. The Earl of Biddleton had no intention of seeing his nephew married to such a female.

"You are quite right to bring this to my attention, Lydia. Cuthburt can't think to marry the woman." His sister nodded, pleased by her brother's grim look of determination.

"What shall we do about it?"

Lord Biddleton stood up and paced a few steps. He stopped and looked at her. "There is nothing to be done except to face Lady Isabelle with the truth."

"What?" cried Lady Ambrose in considerable astonishment.

"Yes, Lydia. I will go see her and tell her I know her intentions." On observing his sister's dubious look, he shrugged. "Oh, she will no doubt act shocked and cry out protestations, but the point is, Lydia, she will get my message quite clearly. There will be no mistaking it. Lady Isabelle will see that her ambitious scheme has no chance and will seek out some other unfortunate prey."

"Perhaps you are right," replied Lady Ambrose thoughtfully. "I have always believed in candor but it is something that I fear Lady Isabelle has little experience with."

"Do not worry. I shall not be deceived by the lady," replied Lord Biddleton. "And I think I should also speak to Cuthburt. He has, I am sure, only been temporarily led astray by this unfortunate acquaintance."

"Oh, yes, I am sure of that. It is that dreadful Clairemont family I assure you. Once he is away from their influence . . ."

"Then he must be made to understand that the Clairemonts are not the sort for him to associate with."

"Yes, he must be made to see that, Lucius," repeated Lady Ambrose nodding. "Cuthburt needs an example to follow, brother. A noble example. Like yourself. Yes, what better example than his uncle? For the most part, Lucius, you are a very prudent and sensible man."

"Thank you," replied Lord Biddleton without enthusiasm, for although he was willing to save his nephew from a misalliance, he was not eager to involve himself further.

"Cuthburt has never had any male guidance," continued Lady Ambrose. "You know how George was. Never one to discipline the boy. I have done my best, but there's only so much a mother can do." This was a rare admission for Lady Ambrose to make and her brother regarded her warily. "You really don't see enough of Cuthburt, Lucius. I know he has been away at school a great deal of the time and you have been away so often . . ."

The Earl cut in rather abruptly. "I know, Lydia. The boy and I have never been on the best of terms. But I shall attempt to take him in hand on this matter."

9

"Then I am satisfied," replied Lady Ambrose. "I am certain you will not fail me."

"I sincerely hope not," murmured her brother.

His sister regarded him for a moment and smiled. "Now tell me about yourself, Lucius. I have not seen you since Lady Frampton's dinner party."

"There is nothing to tell, Lydia. I go on as usual."

Lady Ambrose's smile disappeared. "Really, Lucius, you must begin thinking of the future. You are nearly thirty years of age." Her brother again knew what speech was coming and frowned. "You need a wife, Lucius."

"But Lydia, you seem to forget that I am engaged to be married."

"I haven't forgotten, brother, but sometimes I fear you have. You have been betrothed to Eudoria Waxwood for over a year now, yet you won't set a date for the wedding. How long do you expect the girl to wait for you? If you're not careful, you'll lose her. That odious Garfield Chalmers has been paying her quite a lot of attention of late."

"Oh?" said the Earl indifferently.

"Yes. Of course, it's obvious he's after her fortune. That Chalmers is a cunning one."

"Cunning? Chalmers?" asked Biddleton in surprise. He had only recently become acquainted with the man, but cunning was certainly not the word he would use to describe Garfield Chalmers.

Lady Ambrose nodded. "I warn you. That Chalmers is a man that needs watching, although I'm quite sure Eudoria can see through his gallantry. She is such a sweet girl. I do look forward to calling her my sister."

Lady Ambrose again stood up to take her leave. "Well, I must go now, Lucius. I shall be waiting to hear of your talk with Lady Isabelle."

"Certainly," said her brother. He rang for Mills who quickly appeared for instructions. "Please escort Lady Ambrose to her carriage," said his lordship. The butler nodded, relieved at the short duration of her ladyship's visit. Lady Ambrose bid her brother a brief farewell and marched out after the butler. Lord Biddleton watched her retreating form and then returned to his newspaper.

＊　　＊　　＊

The notorious Lady Isabelle Clairemont was unaware that morning of the furor she had aroused in Lady Ambrose. Indeed, she was not even acquainted with that lady. Isabelle was concerned at the moment with settling a dispute between her sister Harriet and brother Lindsay.

"Belle," her twelve-year-old sister was wailing, "would you please scold this detestable child?"

Isabelle shook her head as she looked at her brother and able to snatch a rich husband yet and must realize that sister. They were eying each other as if they were knights ready to do battle. "What is the trouble with you two now?" Isabelle asked with some amusement.

Her brother Lindsay burst in before his sister could say a word. "Oh, Harry is having the fidgets over nothing."

"Nothing!" shouted Harriet. She added as an afterthought, "And don't call me Harry!"

"Oh, all right, Lady Harriet," he replied, making a sarcastic bow.

"Lindsay, you are a little toad!"

"And you . . ." began her brother.

"Lindsay!" cried Isabelle. "You must remember that a gentleman doesn't say uncivil things to a lady."

"A gentleman. Hmpf!" muttered Harriet. Her brother glared at her.

"Nor does a lady say uncivil things to a gentleman, Harriet," continued Isabelle. "Now, not another word from either of you. Here comes Mama."

The Duchess flounced into the room followed by her daughter Anne. "Harriet, there you are!" said her Grace in her fluttery voice. "You must hurry and get ready. Lady Samuels expects us at twelve o'clock."

"Oh, Mama," cried Harriet, "must I really go to Lady Samuels's?"

"Of course, dear. She would be very upset if you didn't go."

Harriet shook her head. "But Belle's not going and Belle is a favorite with Lady Samuels."

"When you are older, Harriet," said the Duchess, "you may choose your social engagements as Isabelle does."

"What's that, m'dear?" questioned a jaunty voice as a large good-natured-looking gentleman entered the room.

"Oh, Giles dear. We were just discussing Harriet's reluctance to call upon Lady Samuels."

The Duke of Fothingham laughed loudly. "Poor Harriet. But we all must do our duty, what?" The Duke looked contentedly at the faces around him. His gaze fell on his youngest son, who was watching him eagerly. "Something on your mind, my boy?"

Lindsay replied excitedly, "Rob said you were going to Jim Crowley's bout today."

"By God, you don't think I'd miss it do you?" said his father grinning.

"Please, Papa, may I go along too?"

"Really, Giles," interrupted the Duchess, "don't you think Lindsay is too young to attend bouts of fisticuffs?"

"I'm not too young!" said Lindsay emphatically. "I'm almost eleven."

"Almost eleven," sniffed Harriet. "A mere child."

Lindsay shot her a wrathful look.

"Come, come, m'dear," said the Duke, patting his wife's cheek. "I'll take care of the lad."

Lindsay gave an excited shout. "Thanks awfully, Papa!" Harriet gave a cry of protest.

"He gets to have fun and I have to see Lady Samuels!" Her father laughed.

Isabelle watched the scene with both amusement and some concern. She was well aware of her father's weakness for gaming and knew he risked large sums on the outcome of boxing matches. Isabelle thought Lindsay too young to attend such affairs and worried that he would soon follow in his father's footsteps. She was already worried enough about her brother Rob.

Harriet was still sulking. "Mama, must I really go to Lady Samuels's? She will be quite content with you and Anne."

"What about Belle?" asked the Duke, looking over at his eldest daughter.

"Belle's not going," replied Harriet. "She said Charles Fensbrook is paying her a visit this afternoon."

12

"What?" cried the Duke. "Fensbrook ain't going to the Crowley bout? My girl, the fellow must be damned serious about you to miss that."

"Nonsense, Papa," laughed Isabelle. "Have you ever known Charles to be serious about anything?"

The Duchess listened to this exchange and sighed. She did not think Charles Fensbrook good enough for her daughter, but if Isabelle was in love with him. . . . Her daughter was by most reckonings already beyond the age of eligibility and she must marry soon or be labeled an un-marriageable spinster. Indeed most unmarried females of six and twenty were already considered as such, but one could hardly think it of her beautiful Belle.

"What is this gathering of the clan about?" cried a voice which sounded very much like the Duke's.

"Rob!" cried Lindsay rushing over to his brother. "Papa is letting me go to the bout."

"Is that so?" smiled Rob, winking at his father. "We must watch this rascal, Papa, or he will try to fight Jim Crowley himself."

Lindsay beamed. His admiration for his older brother Rob was equaled only by his admiration for his father and his idolized eldest brother, George. George, the Marquis of Burwicke, had taken on heroic proportions to Lindsay since he entered the Navy and was off fighting the French.

"Well, we all have places to go, so this group had best disperse," said the Duke. He kissed his wife on the cheek and said jovially, "Do have a good time at Abigail's, m'dear."

"Yes, Giles," said his wife sighing. "I don't suppose I have to tell you to have a good time."

"That is quite unnecessary, Mary," laughed the Duke. "Come, sons," he said in a voice which betrayed as much excitement as Lindsay's, "we best get ready and be off."

As the three of them walked out of the room, Isabelle tried to catch Rob's eye, but he seemed to be avoiding her. She noticed that Anne was also watching him with a worried expression and wondered if she knew what trouble he was in. But there was no opportunity to ask because her mother was shepherding Anne and Harriet out of the room.

"Come now, girls," said her Grace, "you know how Lady Samuels insists on her guests being punctual."

Anne, as was her nature, left obediently. Harriet lingered. "Mama, do I really have to go?" she whined.

"Yes, miss, you do!" replied the Duchess in an unusually firm voice. Harriet frowned at Isabelle and hurried out of the room. The Duchess looked at her remaining daughter.

"You are sure that Mr. Fensbrook is coming, my dear?"

Isabelle smiled. "One can never be too sure about Charles, can one, Mama?"

"Yes, that's true," replied her mother sadly.

"Do give my regards to Lady Samuels, won't you, Mama?"

"Of course, dear," replied the Duchess. She suddenly remembered she had to give some last minute instructions to Marston and spying the butler in the hallway, hurried away. Isabelle smiled and walked over to the window seat to watch the departure of her family.

Lady Isabelle was in the drawing room awaiting Charles Fensbrook that afternoon when Marston noiselessly entered the room. She was somewhat surprised when the butler announced not Fensbrook but another visitor, the Earl of Biddleton.

"The Earl of Biddleton?" asked her ladyship, puzzled.

"Yes, my lady," replied the butler who was as curious as her ladyship but restrained himself from showing it.

"But, Marston, I don't know the Earl of Biddleton. Surely he can't mean to see me?"

"Yes, my lady," replied the butler, nodding slightly. "His lordship expressly said he wanted to see you."

Lady Isabelle smiled. "Well, Marston, it is a mystery to me, but send his lordship in." The butler quickly retreated out of the room. He returned a few moments later followed by an extremely tall gentleman.

The Earl's height was the first thing most people noticed about him. Lady Isabelle, who was rather tall herself,

14

found she was looking up curiously at the mysterious Earl. She discovered an unsmiling face distinguished by a rather prominent forehead, large angular features, and a pair of cold blue eyes that seemed to be regarding her disapprovingly. Lady Isabelle almost laughed at the expression on his face. Instead, she smiled and held out her hand.

"My lord, I fear we are unacquainted, for I am quite sure I would remember if I had met you before."

Lord Biddleton took her hand briefly and gave a stiff bow. "Please excuse the impropriety of my visit, Lady Isabelle, but it was quite urgent that I speak with you."

Lady Isabelle motioned to the sofa. "Now I am intrigued. Please sit down, Lord Biddleton."

The Earl of Biddleton took a place on the sofa and seemed to hesitate, giving Lady Isabelle further opportunity to study him. The Earl was not really handsome, she thought, but rather imposing. He appeared unconcerned about the opinion of others, almost arrogant in his bearing. His clothes, though tasteful, were somber, and his dark hair was clipped neatly in a modest style. When he turned toward her, Isabelle was amused to see him frown at her. She could not imagine what she had done to fall so quickly into disfavor with the Earl of Biddleton but she had a feeling she was about to find out.

The Earl had already formed his opinion of Lady Isabelle from his sister's comments about her. "The notorious Lady Isabelle" his sister had called her and when Lord Biddleton saw her he could well believe it. Lady Isabelle Clairemont was considered one of the beauties of society. She had dark golden hair set in ringlets about her face and a pair of mischievous blue eyes fringed by dark gold lashes. Her features were sculpted on classical lines, flawed only by a too generous mouth which some gentlemen viewed as no fault at all. Her height seemed to make her even more striking and her figure was most becoming. She wore a simple blue dress which by its very simplicity accentuated her beauty. Lord Biddleton detected a frivolous nature in those blue eyes and smiling lips and could well see that she was the descendant of the infamous Fothinghams.

"Lady Isabelle," he finally began in a grave voice, "I have come to see you about my nephew Lord Ambrose."

"Oh, of course!" cried Lady Isabelle suddenly. "You are Cuthburt's uncle. He and my brother Rob are great friends."

"Yes, I believe so," murmured the Earl.

Isabelle smiled. "Cuthburt is quite different from Rob, of course, quiet and so polite. But they do get along so well. I think," she confided, "that your nephew is a good influence on Rob."

The Earl of Biddleton could not restrain an ironic smile.

Lady Isabelle suddenly asked in concern, "Oh, dear, I do hope nothing has happened to Cuthburt."

"I'm afraid, ma'am, it has. He thinks himself in love."

At this startling revelation Lady Isabelle burst into laughter and Lord Biddleton frowned. "Please forgive me, my lord, but really I was expecting something quite serious."

"I assure you, Lady Isabelle, it is quite serious." The Earl was somewhat surprised by the severity of his own voice. It had sounded very much like his sister Lydia's.

Lady Isabelle was also surprised by the Earl's tone and answered coolly, "Forgive me, sir, I see that you are concerned about your nephew but I can't imagine why you came to see me."

"You, Lady Isabelle," said the Earl accusingly, "are the object of my nephew's infatuation."

Lady Isabelle stared at the Earl in amazement. "Cuthburt?"

The Earl shook his head. "Come now, Lady Isabelle. I am well aware of your intentions."

"My intentions?" echoed a startled Lady Isabelle.

"Yes. Your intentions to marry my nephew. But it won't work, you know. Cuthburt is still under age and under my authority. I would never allow such an unacceptable match to occur. You shall not lay your hands on my nephew's fortune."

Lord Biddleton observed an angry flush appear on Lady Isabelle's face and her eyes flashed menacingly. Never had she been more insulted. She was about to say something

16

when she appeared to check herself. The flush slowly left her face and was replaced by what seemed to Lord Biddleton a more dangerous expression. To his surprise she laughed abruptly.

"So, my lord, you have found out my scheme. What a pity!"

Lord Biddleton appeared shocked. "You admit it then?"

"Of course," replied Lady Isabelle lightly. "I see I cannot fool you, my lord. I admit it all." The Earl eyed her suspiciously. He had expected outrage and denials, not a confession. Lady Isabelle laughed again.

"You see, my lord, I did plan on marrying Cuthburt. Such a charming boy, and of course I've heard that his fortune is enormous."

Lord Biddleton replied sharply, "I am amazed, ma'am, at your admitting such a scheme. Trying to bamboozle a mere boy into matrimony!"

"Ah, but he is near one and twenty, is he not, Lord Biddleton? Not a mere boy. I find youth much more diverting, you see. I was planning to marry a gentleman much advanced in years before I met your nephew. Albert was a dear man, you understand, but a dreadful bore."

Lord Biddleton looked at her in disbelief. "I do not wish to hear any more, ma'am. I can well see how you earned your reputation."

A flush reappeared on Lady Isabelle's face, but she merely smiled. "You appear to be well informed about me, my lord. But let me give you one last piece of information. I shall marry whomever I choose and you will have nothing to say about it."

"We shall see about that, Lady Isabelle," replied the Earl angrily.

They were glaring at each other when Marston entered the room. The butler was quite surprised by the hostile scene and looked curiously at her ladyship.

"Yes, Marston?" she asked, anger still evident in her voice.

"Mr. Fensbrook to see you, my lady."

"Send him in please, Marston." The butler glanced at her uncertainly and left the room. When he returned he

17

was followed by a dapper gentleman who strolled lazily toward Isabelle.

"Belle, how perfectly charming you look." He took her hand and held it what seemed to the Earl an improperly long time.

"Charles," said Isabelle, "are you acquainted with the Earl of Biddleton?"

Mr. Fensbrook glanced over at the Earl and lifted his quizzing glass. "I do believe we have met, haven't we, my lord? It was at Lady Hemsted's last year."

"Yes, quite," mumbled Lord Biddleton. He did not remember the fellow at all but had seen many of his stamp. Fensbrook, Biddleton immediately deduced, was one of those men of fashion who aped the exalted Brummell. No doubt Fensbrook with his modish attire and insolent manners was a member in excellent standing with the Carlton House set.

Fensbrook was highly amused at seeing the priggish Lord Biddleton, or "that old bore Biddle" as Fensbrook's friends at the club called him. Although he had only met the Earl once, he had often heard stories about Biddleton and his dragon of a sister, Lady Ambrose. He wondered how the Earl had found his way to the Clairemont house. It was really quite astonishing. Old Biddle having a *tête-à-tête* with Lady Belle Clairemont.

An amused expression had appeared on Lady Isabelle's face as she viewed the two men together. The Earl was looking sternly at Fensbrook while that gentleman eyed him with a comical expression. "Lord Biddleton and I have just become acquainted," she explained to Mr. Fensbrook, "but already I feel as though I know him quite well." She smiled over at the Earl, who answered her smile with a scowl.

Fensbrook looked closely at the Earl, an enquiring expression in his sleepy eyes. "Don't tell me, Biddleton, that you have become another of Lady Belle's suitors?"

"I hardly think, sir, that the lady needs anyone else dangling about her," said the Earl testily. Before anyone could reply he announced his departure, gave a curt bow, and stalked out of the room.

18

Fensbrook gave an astonished laugh. "Good God, Belle, what was that prig Biddleton doing here?" Isabelle laughed with him.

"Oh, Charles, it was funny. Lord Biddleton thinks I'm a most brazen fortune huntress out to capture his poor nephew Cuthburt."

"The devil!" said Charles Fensbrook, sorry he had missed such a scene. "Biddleton came here and accused you of that?"

"Oh, yes. He said he was quite aware of my 'reputation.' "

"My dear girl," said Fensbrook, "I fear I shall have to call the fellow out." He looked relieved when Isabelle chuckled.

"Gracious no, Charles. There is no need for that. I simply told his lordship the truth."

"I see," replied Fensbrook.

"I admitted to him," continued Lady Isabelle, "that I was out to snare poor Cuthburt."

"You what?"

"Yes, I quite shocked his lordship. I told him how I had heard his nephew's fortune was enormous."

"I'll be damned," laughed Fensbrook. "That must have upset solid old Biddle."

"I have never seen such an odious man. Do you really know him, Charles?"

Fensbrook took out a snuff box and flipped it open with a practiced air. "Oh, I've met him. However, as you could see, I did not make much of an impression on the Earl."

"But I have never seen him."

"He ain't one for society. If you think he's odious, you ought to see his sister, Lady Ambrose. Never been so unfortunate myself as to have had to meet her but I've heard about her. A most ferocious female."

Isabelle laughed again. "Well, she could be no worse than he is. You know, Charles, I think it would serve the Earl right if I did marry his nephew."

Charles Fensbrook smiled. "Well, my dear, I do hope you invite me to the wedding. It should be the event of the season." He leaned back on the sofa in his usual indolent

19

fashion. "But tell me, Belle, who is this puppy that is so unfortunate to be related to Lady Ambrose and old Biddle?"

"Cuthburt Ambrose. He's a friend of Rob's and really a nice young man in spite of his relations. Surely you've met him?"

Fensbrook shrugged. "I find it impossible to remember all of your brother's friends. Except, of course, the ones that owe me money."

Isabelle frowned slightly. "Charles, I have been meaning to talk to you about that."

"What, Belle?"

Lady Isabelle seemed embarrassed. "About Rob and, well, Charles, I know he has been running up quite a few debts. He won't talk to me about it, but I feel he might be in trouble."

Charles Fensbrook studied her a moment and then answered casually. "Really, Belle, must you coddle that young cub so? I'm sure he's old enough to take care of himself."

Isabelle answered angrily, "I am glad you are so unconcerned. It is quite reassuring."

Fensbrook smiled. "My dear girl. Do you expect me to rescue Rob from all the little scrapes he gets himself into? I assure you it would be a full-time occupation."

Isabelle looked dejectedly at the floor. "No," she finally replied. "I can't expect you to get entangled in my brother's affairs."

Fensbrook retained his smile, but his expression showed a trace of irritation. "Belle, your sisterly concern is quite touching but unwarranted. Now do try to look more cheerful. Shall I tell you about Sir Bingley?" Without waiting for a reply Fensbrook began an amusing anecdote concerning the irascible Sir Bingley. Although Lady Isabelle smiled at Fensbrook's account, her usual gaiety had deserted her. Fensbrook, sensing her mood, cut his visit short, leaving an uncharacteristically glum Lady Isabelle.

Chapter 2

Lord Biddleton was far from pleased with the outcome of his visit with Lady Isabelle Clairemont. He had never met such a woman before. A strange restlessness seemed to take possession of him as he reflected on their meeting. For once his lordship was glad that his sister, Lydia, had come to him for help. He could not have his nephew marry that brazen Clairemont female. As he strode impatiently around the room, the Earl decided he should waste no time in speaking to his nephew. He ordered his phaeton and quickly departed for his sister's house.

When he arrived, Lord Biddleton was informed that Lady Ambrose was not at home but his nephew would see him in the library. Biddleton entered the room and received a shy greeting from the youth.

His lordship did not have a close relationship with his nephew. His sister had very early impressed on him the necessity of raising children with a stern hand. As a result the Earl had taken an attitude of cool formality with the boy despite the fact that he was less than ten years his senior. Cuthburt, a quiet and somewhat timid boy, always felt that his uncle was somehow displeased with him. Now a young man, Cuthburt still felt uncomfortable in his uncle's presence.

"Uncle Lucius, it is good to see you, sir," said Cuthburt, somewhat hesitantly putting out his hand. The Earl took the youth's hand and mumbled an appropriate reply. He was suddenly embarrassed by his mission and stood looking awkwardly around the room.

"I am sorry, sir, that Mother is not at home. She is visiting the Waxwoods."

"I see," said the Earl, frowning.

Cuthbert stood uncertainly before his silent uncle. "Would you like to sit down, sir?" he asked politely.

"What?" asked the Earl brusquely. "Oh, yes, of course." He sat down on a sofa and his gaze rested on his nephew. Lord Biddleton was always surprised at seeing how much the boy had grown. Although he was not as tall as his uncle, Cuthbert had reached a rather impressive height. Indeed, there was a resemblance between the two. Cuthburt had the same large angular features shared by his mother and uncle. However, he had a gentle expression to his countenance, no doubt due to his nature and the dark, rather melancholy eyes he had inherited from his father.

Cuthbert was becoming uneasy under his uncle's scrutiny. "Would you care for anything, sir?" he asked.

"No, thank you," replied his uncle. "Actually, Cuthburt, I came to see you about . . . er . . . a matter that has been brought to my attention."

"Yes, sir?"

Lord Biddleton paused and then continued. "I have heard that you have become friends with Robert Clairemont."

"Yes. I met him at school and he's a dashed fine fellow."

"Hmmm," replied the Earl. Cuthbert suddenly became worried.

"Is something wrong, sir?"

"Well, yes. You see, Cuthburt, the Clairemonts are . . . they're not the sort of people your mother and I want to see you associating with."

Cuthbert flushed and stammered a reply. "I don't think I understand, uncle."

Biddleton sighed. "The Clairemonts have a reputation for recklessness and, well, eccentricities."

"Eccentricities?" repeated Cuthbert.

The Earl was finding his task very unpleasant, but his

22

duty pushed him on. "Why, take the present Duke's grandfather. An odd fellow. Married a servant when he was in his dotage."

Cuthburt, despite his anxiety, almost laughed. "But Uncle Lucius, I don't see what that has to do with Rob and his family."

"I just mention him to illustrate the Clairemonts' unfortunate ancestry."

Cuthburt shook his head. "But it's not fair to judge them by some crusty ancestor, uncle."

"I believe," continued the Earl sternly, "that one may judge the behavior of the present Clairemonts to be nearly as shocking as that of their unfortunate ancestors."

Cuthburt remained silent. "You must know," continued his uncle, "that the Duke is a notorious gamester. I've heard the family is on the brink of ruin due to the Duke's excesses. And his children are a wild, unruly bunch. I met one of the daughters . . . Lady Isabelle . . . and I never met a more ill-behaved female." Lord Biddleton had been watching his nephew closely and saw the youth's face redden.

"Lady Isabelle?" stammered Cuthburt. "She is most gracious and . . . and beautiful."

"Yes," said the Earl ominously, "beauty often covers a shallow, selfish character."

Cuthburt's timidity departed him at hearing such words spoken about his beloved Isabelle. "You cannot know the lady, sir, or you would not slander her with such words!"

"Ah, nephew," said the Earl sadly, "then it's true that you've become enamored of the woman."

"I . . ." began Cuthburt, confused. He finally managed to blurt out, "I don't think that is any concern of yours, uncle."

"You are wrong, Cuthburt. It *is* my concern. I won't have that fortune huntress in my family and I told her that too! I have a duty to my sister and—"

He was interrupted by his nephew. "Fortune huntress?" he choked. "You told her that? My God, uncle, I won't tolerate this."

"Oh," said the Earl, surprised by his nephew's vehemence. "I think you will. Your mother and I can't allow you to ruin your life. You're young. This feeling you have for that woman is just a boy's infatuation. You will realize it in time."

Cuthburt stood staring at him with an expression of astonishment and rage.

Lord Biddleton stood up. He disliked scenes and having performed his duty, was eager to leave. "I must go now, nephew, but mind what I have said." He attempted a rather unsuccessful smile. "An intelligent young man like yourself will, I'm sure, realize the folly of such an attachment." His nephew did not reply but stared sullenly away. Lord Biddleton shrugged and left, grateful that his sister had not returned.

When the Duchess of Fothingham arrived home from her visit with Lady Samuels, she complained of a headache and immediately retired to her room. Harriet, happy to have the ordeal of the visit over, was eager to meet a couple of her friends in the park. Neither Anne nor Isabelle felt up to chaperoning their sister and her chatty friends, so Isabelle's maid, Mildred, was dispatched to accompany the young Lady Harriet.

Isabelle and Anne smiled at each other as they watched their sister depart. She was talking rapidly to the maid and her talk was interspersed with high-spirited giggles.

"Poor Millie," said Isabelle, "she will be worn out after a mere hour with Harriet and her friends."

Anne smiled but there was some concern in her expression. She had observed the dispirited look in her sister's eyes when they had returned from Lady Samuels's. "Is something wrong, Belle?" she asked.

"Dear Annie," said Isabelle smiling, "always so observant."

"Perhaps too observant? I didn't mean to pry, Belle, if it's about Mr. Fensbrook . . ."

Isabelle shook her head. "No. Well, only partially. I have been a little worried about Rob lately."

"Oh," said Anne faintly.

"Anne, do you know what trouble he's in? I feel there is

something wrong. Something more serious than his usual scrapes."

Anne seemed reluctant to speak. "Did he say anything to you?" asked Isabelle, wondering if her sister had pledged silence.

"Oh, no. Rob acts quite unconcerned. But, well, I heard a gentleman say something to Mr. Fensbrook two days ago."

"To Charles? Something about Rob?"

"Yes. He said Rob owed him fifteen hundred pounds and if he didn't get his money soon . . ."

"Yes?" asked Isabelle, her face turning quite pale.

"Well, then Mr. Fensbrook noticed me and hushed up the gentleman."

"I see," said Isabelle quietly.

"Oh, Belle, I didn't know what to do. This is the first opportunity I have had to speak to you about it. I tried to talk to Rob but he just laughed and put me off. And Papa . . . Papa doesn't really seem to understand."

"Yes," said Isabelle sighing. "I daresay Papa would not become concerned until he entered the very gates of debtor's prison."

"Belle!"

"It's true, Anne," said Isabelle, laughing at her sister's shocked expression. "Papa is hardly one to lecture Rob." She shook her head sadly. "I had hoped that Charles . . ."

Anne waited and Isabelle laughed. "Oh, Anne, I was foolish enough to ask Charles for help. He did not like the idea at all."

Anne remained silent. She had developed no great fondness for her sister's elegant suitor. A shy young woman of twenty, Anne always felt ever more awkward in the presence of Charles Fensbrook. She disliked the man's mocking tone and his indifferent attitude toward everything and everyone. She realized that striking such a pose was the fashion, but she wondered if Mr. Fensbrook's pose revealed much of his true character. Anne was constantly reprimanding herself for her harsh thoughts of the gentleman. She feared her sister was in love with him and she felt guilty for hoping that it was not so.

"Anne, I'm afraid you look as glum as I do now," said Isabelle smiling. She squeezed her sister's hand. "I'm sure everything will be all right." She suddenly laughed. "Perhaps I should marry Cuthburt Ambrose. His fortune would come in quite handy."

Anne looked stricken by her words. "Marry Cuthburt?"

Isabelle laughed again. "Oh, Anne, I was only joking." Seeing Anne's perplexed expression, she smiled. "I didn't tell you of my visitor. The Earl of Biddleton."

"Cuthburt's uncle?"

"Why, yes. Don't tell me you know him?"

"No, but Cuthburt has mentioned him."

"Poor Cuthburt. To be plagued with such a relation. The man is insufferable. Do you know, Anne, he came here and accused me of scheming to marry his nephew? I could not believe his audacity. To come to this house, a complete stranger, and insult me so."

"Oh, no!" cried Anne. "He thinks that you want to marry Cuthburt?"

"Yes, he believes I am after his nephew's fortune and am trying to ensnare poor helpless Cuthburt. His absurdity was matched only by his pomposity. And I know I shouldn't have done it, but I'm glad I did."

"What did you do?" asked Anne nervously.

"I told him it was the truth. I was after his nephew, or more to the point, his nephew's fortune." She laughed at the memory of Lord Biddleton's shocked face. Anne merely stared horrified at her.

"Oh, Belle, you didn't!"

"Indeed I did. The noble Lord Biddleton was quite taken aback I assure you." Anne herself looked rather taken aback and that made Isabelle laugh all the more.

Her merriment was interrupted by Marston, who entered the room and delivered a letter to her. Isabelle looked at it and smiled at the familiar handwriting. "It's from Aunt Agatha." She quickly opened the missive and began scanning it. "Aunt Agatha wants us to visit her next week at Winterhaven. Such short notice! But quite like our aunt!"

Anne smiled. "It would be nice to visit Aunt Agatha,

but I'm afraid I can't go. I promised Lucy Cummings that I would spend a few days with her at Lyngate."

"Oh, dear," said Isabelle. "Aunt Agatha will be so disappointed."

Anne brightened. "Perhaps Harriet could go instead."

"Yes," said Isabelle, "instead of being disappointed, Aunt Agatha will be aghast!"

"Belle! You know Aunt Agatha adores Harriet."

"Yes, she adores her . . . from a distance. We both know Aunt Agatha has little patience where children are concerned. Except, of course," she added with a chuckle, "her own Hector. Though, I daresay Aunt Agatha was much relieved when Cousin Hector left his childhood behind."

"Well, yes," laughed Anne, "I suppose you are right."

"And you know how Harriet would react to being packed off to Aunt Agatha's. I would rather not be subjected to such melodrama!"

Anne laughed again.

"No," continued Isabelle, "I will go to Aunt Agatha's alone. But I do wish you could go with me."

"So do I, but I did promise Lucy . . . She is quite anxious for me to come."

"Ah, two old friends sharing confidences?" smiled Isabelle.

"Well," replied Anne sighing, "no doubt Lucy will do most of the confiding."

Isabelle laughed. They both turned suddenly toward the door at the sound of a commotion in the hall. Their youngest brother bounded into the room followed by his father and brother Rob.

"Belle! Anne! What a fight it was!" He began mimicking the match, dancing about the room and flailing his fists. One of his punches almost knocked over a vase and Anne and Isabelle both let out cries.

"Come now, you scamp," said his father, placing Lindsay in a firm grip. "Stop before you break your mother's china."

Rob picked up the ornate vase which had almost fallen

victim to his brother's enthusiasm and studied it with a comical expression. "Really, Lindsay, you should have been a bit more accurate in your aim. I myself would be delighted to see this monstrosity in pieces."

"How can you say such a thing?" said Isabelle in mock indignation. "That was a present from Cousin Lucretia."

Rob put the vase down reverently. "Well, what do I know about vases? I submit to Cousin Lucretia's superior judgment," and he gave the vase a ludicrous bow.

"Well, daughters," said the Duke of Fothingham, ignoring his son's antics and settling his rather large form comfortably into a chair, "since you have gotten an account of our afternoon, how about telling us of yours?" He suddenly looked around the room. "By the way, where's your mother?"

"She went to bed with a headache, Papa," replied Anne.

"Ah," said the Duke thoughtfully, "so now we know how Lady Samuels was." He directed his gaze at Isabelle. "And how was Fensbrook, my girl? Did the fellow propose yet?"

"No, Papa," she replied lightly, "but I did not know you were so eager to have Charles as a son-in-law."

"Well," replied the Duke frankly, "I ain't so eager."

Anne thought a new topic would be wise. "Oh, Papa, Aunt Agatha wrote and Belle is going to visit her next week."

"Well, I can't say I envy you, daughter."

"Now, Papa," said Isabelle smiling, "you know you always have a splendid time at Aunt Agatha's."

"What?" cried the Duke, and his children all laughed. He looked at his eldest daughter and shook his head. "I see you're joking, Belle. You know I always have a miserable time at Agatha's. Why, do you remember last spring when I visited her? She had that one fellow there . . . Hemmings or Hastings or something like that."

"Heppelworth, Papa," corrected Isabelle, "Leopold Heppelworth."

"Heppelworth. Yes, quite. The fellow was mad. Always talking some damn nonsense. No, Belle dear, I repeat, I do not envy you your visit to Agatha's. But tell me, when do you plan on leaving?"

"Next Thursday, I suppose. It's not very much time is it? And Anne is going away too."

"And where are you going, Annie, my dear?" asked the Duke.

"To Lyngate, Papa, to stay with Lucy Cummings."

"Ah," smiled the Duke, "I saw Lucy the other day with her mother. A right pretty thing she is too."

"Do you mean Lucy or her mama?" asked Rob mischievously.

The Duke, who had an appreciative eye for the ladies, smiled. "Both of them are pretty creatures," he decided. "Of course, they can't compare to the Clairemont women."

"Dear Papa," said Isabelle, "praise from an unprejudiced eye!" She turned to Anne. "Well, Anne, I do hate to go in the midst of flattery, but I think we should leave this masculine company and make some plans for our upcoming journeys."

Anne nodded and they both got up to leave. Their youngest brother jumped up, ready to follow them.

"And where might you be going, Lindsay?" asked the Duke.

"I wanted to tell Peter about the fight, Papa." Peter Spencer was a neighbor of the Clairemonts' and Lindsay's best friend.

"All right, my boy, but don't be making a nuisance of yourself. And watch out for the Spencers' china!"

As the Duke smilingly watched his three children leave the room, Rob looked over at him. He hesitated a moment and then spoke.

"I say, Papa, this is rather fortunate, because I wanted to talk to you."

The Duke looked at his son and nodded. "Well, Rob, what is the problem?"

His son was a little disconcerted by such a direct question. He favored a more roundabout approach to the matter himself.

"Oh, it's nothing serious," he assured his father.

"Good," replied the Duke who seemed relieved. He suddenly began looking around him. "Now what did I do with that blasted pipe of mine?"

Rob smiled. "Didn't you leave it on the mantel?"

The Duke stopped and pondered a moment. "By God, I think I did." He lumbered over to the mantel and gave a shout of triumph. "Here's the rascal!" Rob watched him as he proceeded to fill the pipe and light it.

"You know, Papa," Rob finally ventured, "a fellow has a lot of expenses these days."

"Eh, what's that?" asked the Duke, looking over at his son.

"I was just saying how expensive things are, Papa."

"Damned expensive," agreed the Duke nodding his head.

Rob, heartened by this response, continued. "Well, Papa, I seem to be a little short of blunt these days. You see I played cards with Sir Lipton at the . . ."

"Old Lippy?" broke in the Duke. "I ain't seen him for ages! A jolly fellow, Lippy."

"Yes," said Rob ironically, "a jolly fellow, old Lippy."

"Why, I remember," said the Duke, a nostalgic gleam in his eye, "when Lippy and I were young blades like you, Rob. We had some wild times, by God. But you're a young 'un," he said winking at his son, "you know what I mean."

Rob smiled. "I think I do, Papa. As a matter of fact . . ."

"Old Lippy," muttered the Duke, smiling at some memory.

Rob was becoming frustrated. "Papa," he said loudly, shaking the Duke out of his reverie.

"What?" asked the startled Duke.

"The thing is, Papa, I am short of money and wondered if you could loan me some?"

The Duke looked at his son a moment and shook his head. "Sorry, Rob, but I am a bit short myself right now. Been having devilish bad luck you know. You'll just have to get by on your allowance."

"But, Papa, that's just it. I don't have any allowance left. I've overextended myself, you see, and some of the

30

fellows I owe money to are getting a little anxious about getting paid."

The Duke shrugged. "They'll just have to wait. Don't worry, my boy, your credit is good. Just do what I do."

"What's that, Papa?"

"Avoid the fellows you owe money to," laughed the Duke.

Rob, who had already been practicing this suggestion without much success, shook his head.

"Come, my boy, you can't spend your time worrying about a few measly debts."

Rob smiled weakly.

"Now, how's Old Lippy doing?" continued the Duke. "Did I ever tell you about the time Lippy and I climbed Netherfield Tower?" With that the Duke proceeded with a colorful tale about his youthful adventures.

Chapter 3

Lord Biddleton was sitting at his desk staring vacantly into space when Mills entered the room. The Earl seemed unaware of his servant's presence, causing Mills to regard him with a slightly puzzled air. He had never seen the Earl of Biddleton in such a preoccupied mood. The butler gave a discreet cough that brought Lord Biddleton out of his trance.

"A gentleman is here to see you, my lord. Sir Ralston Keith."

The Earl seemed surprised but delighted by this news. "Send Sir Ralston in, Mills."

The butler soon returned followed by a handsome red-haired gentleman.

"Rolly!" cried Lord Biddleton, jumping up and grasping the gentleman's hand. "I didn't know you were back."

"Yes, Lucius, I am back," replied the baronet warmly shaking his friend's hand. "You are looking at a civilian now."

Lord Biddleton stood back and observed his friend. "You are looking well, Rolly."

"Well, you know the healthful effect sea air has on one."

Lord Biddleton smiled. "Especially when that sea air is filled with French cannonballs." They both laughed. "It is so good to see you, Rolly, but . . ." The Earl hesitated and then continued, "I am sorry about your brother. He was a fine man." Sir Ralston nodded. They stood in silence for a moment, then the baronet spoke again.

"Tell me, Lucius, what news do you have? Have you and Eudoria set a date for your wedding yet?"

"No, not yet," said the Earl noncommittally.

"Well, just don't forget to inform your best man, old fellow."

"I shan't forget, Rolly."

"And how is Eudoria?"

The Earl hesitated. "She has not been very well, I fear."

"I do hope it's nothing serious," replied Sir Ralston somewhat surprised by his friend's apparent lack of concern.

"Oh, no. Nothing serious."

Sir Ralston decided that his friend did not wish to discuss his fiancée, so he asked about the Earl's sister and nephew.

"Oh, they are fine. Lydia has been a little concerned about Cuthburt, though. He has fallen in with a most unsuitable crowd. He has developed some unfortunate friendships with members of a certain unruly and unacceptable family."

"Your nephew Cuthburt?" replied Sir Ralston in surprise. "I know I haven't seen the lad for years, but I remember what a nice, quiet fellow he was. Who are these wild fellows he's fallen in with?"

The Earl frowned. "The Clairemonts, of the infamous Fothingham line. Perhaps you are familiar with them?"

"I should say so!" replied Sir Ralston in considerable astonishment. "Lord Burwicke was my captain!"

"Burwicke?"

"George Clairemont, the Marquis of Burwicke and the Duke of Fothingham's son. And I daresay, Lucius, you could not find a better man in all of England."

"He was your captain?" It was now the Earl's turn to look astonished.

"Yes, and a damned good one, too."

Biddleton looked embarrassed. "I didn't know the Duke had a son in the Navy."

"Burwicke is the Duke's eldest son. Unusual for the eldest son to go into the service, but Burwicke is a headstrong fellow. But what's this about the Clairemonts and Cuthburt?"

Lord Biddleton gave a slight shrug. "Cuthburt has become friends with Robert Clairemont. The Clairemont boy is a wild one . . . a gamester and an ill-mannered youth. Quite an unfit companion for my nephew."

"I am really quite amazed, Lucius. His brother, Captain Lord Burwicke, is a fine fellow and an excellent officer, none better in fact. I am sure you would like him."

Lord Biddleton sat regarding his friend and finally commented. "It would appear then that this Burwicke is a white sheep among a family of black ones!"

Sir Ralston laughed. "I see, my friend, that you quite disapprove of them. But I must say that I never was that well acquainted with the family. I do remember that one daughter, Lady Isabelle, was quite a beauty." He noticed a strange look come on his friend's face and asked in some surprise, "Do you know her?"

"I have recently become acquainted with the lady," said the Earl, frowning.

"And is she still a beauty?"

"Yes," said the Earl indifferently, "she is beautiful." He had no desire to discuss his meeting with the infamous Lady Isabelle.

Sir Ralston controlled a smile. It was quite evident that his friend did not approve of any of the Clairemonts, even the beautiful Lady Isabelle.

"I say, Lucius, I almost forgot. My aunt, Lady Dumbreck, is having a party this Friday and I wanted you to go. I have been out of society for a time, you know, and could use your help."

His friend shook his head. "I fear, Rolly, I am not the one to provide help on that score. You know I am not one for society."

"Oh, come, Lucius. You must go."

"Well . . ." said the Earl uncertainly.

"Good! I knew you wouldn't disappoint an old friend. But I really must be going now. I promised my aunt I

34

would visit her this afternoon. I'll see you Friday night, all right?"

"All right," replied Lord Biddleton, now resigned to attending Lady Dumbreck's party.

Sir Ralston stuck out his hand and the Earl again shook it warmly. "Now don't forget my aunt's party Friday night," said Sir Ralston.

Lord Biddleton shook his head. "You seem to think I have become frightfully absentminded, Rolly."

His friend laughed. "I'm sorry, Lucius. I know you have a remarkable memory. It always amazed me how you could remember all those dreadful Latin phrases in old Professor Thomas's class. Old Professor Thomas. Do you remember how we called him the Old Centurion? Oh, yes," he laughed, "of course, you remember, Lucius." He looked at his friend and smiled. "I should like to stay and reminisce about the old school days with you, but duty compels me to my aunt's." With that, he gave his friend a cheerful wave and hurried down the walk to his phaeton.

Lord Biddleton was happy to see his friend Sir Ralston Keith again. He and Sir Ralston had known each other since childhood and were the best of friends. The Earl, who did not make friends easily, had sorely missed Sir Ralston while that gentleman was in the Navy. Having him back in town put the Earl in an exceptionally good humor. However, his good mood was somewhat darkened by a letter delivered by his butler. The Earl quickly detected the flamboyant handwriting of Lady Samantha Waxwood, his future mother-in-law, and he frowned. He reluctantly opened the missive and read Lady Waxwood's brief note.

The note informed Lord Biddleton that his betrothed had been indisposed but was feeling somewhat better and would be happy to receive visitors. Lord Biddleton guiltily threw the note down. He had given little thought to Eudoria over the past few days. The Earl grimly decided he had best make amends for his inconsiderate behavior and instructed Mills to have his phaeton readied.

A short time later Lord Biddleton was ushered into the

Waxwood's sitting room where he found Lady Waxwood, his fiancée, and Mr. Garfield Chalmers. As he looked at the stout, red-faced gentleman, Lord Biddleton suddenly thought of his sister's warning and eyed the man curiously.

"Oh, Lucius," cried Lady Waxwood in a shatteringly loud voice, "how wonderful of you to pay us a call." Lady Waxwood was a very slight pale lady whose stentorian voice never failed to shock those making their first acquaintance. Unlike her mother, Miss Eudoria Waxwood seemed far from pleased by the appearance of her fiancée.

"Lucius," she said in a sarcastic voice, "how good of you to come." Lord Biddleton dutifully approached her and kissed her hand.

"How are you feeling, Eudoria? You are looking quite well."

This remark did not at all please the lady. "I am a little better, thank you, but hardly well."

Lord Biddleton realized his error. "Of course, Eudoria. I meant to say you are looking better . . . but hardly well."

"Lucius," said Lady Waxwood, observing her daughter and future son-in-law with some concern, "do you know Mr. Chalmers?"

Lord Biddleton turned to that gentleman and nodded politely. "Yes, we are acquainted. How are you, Chalmers?"

"Only fair, I fear, only fair," said the man in a brisk voice. "A stomach problem, I think."

"Oh?" replied Lord Biddleton with a disconcerted expression on his face.

"Yes, but you look very healthy, sir." Mr. Chalmers said this in a somewhat accusing tone. "Yes, extremely healthy, I think." He continued rapidly. "I was just paying my respects to the ladies, yes, very charming ladies they are, too." He looked at Miss Waxwood as he gave this compliment and she smiled gratefully at him. Lord Biddleton felt strangely compelled to laugh, but his strict upbringing held him in good stead. Lady Waxwood again entered the conversation.

"Mr. Chalmers is such a dear man. We have known him only a short time but he has been most kind, inquiring about Eudoria's health every day." Lord Biddleton felt this remark was aimed at him and he frowned slightly.

"That was good of him," murmured the Earl.

There was an awkward silence which Eudoria ended with a sigh and a rather abrupt announcement. "I really don't think I am quite up to attending Lady Dumbreck's party after all."

The Earl looked at her with some degree of surprise. "Were you planning to attend the party, Eudoria?"

"I was, but I fear it was rather silly of me. I really do not think I am quite well enough yet."

Mr. Chalmers nodded sympathetically and Lord Biddleton looked somewhat relieved. Since he himself was attending the party he would have felt obliged to escort his fiancée and her mother. However, if she was not going, there was no need to mention his own plans to attend.

"Dear Lady Waxwood," said Mr. Chalmers, suddenly standing up, "I really must go now." He turned to Eudoria. "I hope you are better soon, Miss Waxwood."

"Thank you, sir," she said with an expression that caused Lord Biddleton to look at Mr. Chalmers suspiciously.

"Lord Biddleton, good to see you. Yes, very good to see you." The Earl gave a slight nod.

"I will show you out, Mr. Chalmers," said Lady Waxwood, strategically leaving her daughter and Lord Biddleton alone. When she and Mr. Chalmers had departed, Lord Biddleton sat feeling rather uncomfortable. He had always found it difficult to converse with his intended bride and now vainly sought for a suitable topic. However, Miss Waxwood was the one to break the awkward silence with a rather sharp rebuke.

"I am glad, Lucius, you were finally able to visit me! I suppose you were quite busy, though."

Lord Biddleton stiffened at her quarrelsome tone. "Yes, Eudoria, I have been busy, but I am sorry for not coming to visit you sooner."

Miss Waxwood did not seem placated by his stern apology. "You spend too much time on matters that don't need to concern you, Lucius."

"What do you mean?"

"I mean," she replied angrily, "that you could have that secretary of yours look after things. What are you paying the man for?"

"My secretary is worth every penny I pay him," returned the Earl frostily, "and I don't need you to tell me how to manage my affairs, ma'am. What would you have me do? Become one of those idle fellows about town?"

Eudoria sniffed. "You might at least spend more time with your fiancée. And don't you think it's time we set our wedding date, Lucius? There are a lot of preparations to make."

Lord Biddleton remained silent for a few moments but finally replied evasively, "We will discuss that when you're better, Eudoria. I fear you are upset and we mustn't have that. I will leave you now to get some rest."

She watched him disapprovingly as he kissed her hand. The Earl, finished with his unpleasant obligation, quickly departed the Waxwood house. His good mood had been replaced by a black depression as he reflected that he could not forestall his marriage much longer. The prospect of a future with Eudoria Waxwood seemed particularly grim to him that afternoon.

Chapter 4

Lady Dumbreck, a most amiable and discerning woman, was extremely pleased with the way her party was progressing. Although the evening was still young, a great number of distinguished personages had already arrived. Lady Dumbreck counted three dukes, five duchesses, an Italian princess, and a glittering assortment of lesser peers and peeresses among the guests. Never had an evening started more propitiously.

Lady Dumbreck greeted all the guests with her well-known charm, performing her duties as hostess with practiced skill. She had been slightly disconcerted by the arrival of Mrs. Fairfield Livingston, a lady whom she counted among her greatest enemies, but managed to mask her surprise with a cool look of indifference. However, it was even more difficult to hide her amazement at the arrival of the Earl of Biddleton with Sir Ralston Keith.

Good heavens, thought her ladyship, I do have a success if Biddleton condescends to put in an appearance. I thought he never attended such things.

Lady Dumbreck managed to put aside these thoughts quickly as her nephew and the Earl approached.

"Ralston," cried her ladyship, taking her nephew's hands in her own, "how wonderful that you are here and to have brought the Earl of Biddleton! My goodness, sir, it has been too long since you have honored my house."

Lord Biddleton managed a stiff bow over Lady Dumbreck's hand. "Indeed, ma'am, far too long."

"Of course, aunt," said Sir Ralston with a grin, "Lucius does not often attend parties, but I persuaded him to come."

"And I am grateful to you, Rolly."

Lord Biddleton peered across the room and noted the large number of guests. "It seems, ma'am, that my appearance here would scarce have mattered. Indeed, there are a good many people here."

Sir Ralston laughed. "I should hope so. My aunt gives the best parties in London. No one would want to miss one."

The Earl, who never enjoyed such events, reflected that he knew at least one person who would have preferred to miss the affair. Yet for Ralston's sake he smiled in what he hoped was a gracious manner.

"Then we'll move on, aunt," said Sir Ralston. "We won't monopolize our hostess any further. It looks like a smashing success, Aunt Clara." He said the last words in a low voice and squeezed his aunt's hand. Lady Dumbreck smiled warmly, reflecting what a good and charming boy was her nephew, Ralston.

The two gentlemen moved on and Lord Biddleton noted with disapproval the presence of a number of frivolous and unsuitable people. Sir Ralston, however, seemed delighted to see them all and kept assuring his friend that this party could in no way be a bore.

The Earl was not so convinced, for suddenly he saw Mr. Garfield Chalmers standing with Lady Waxwood and his betrothed Eudoria. Lady Waxwood, who prided herself on her quick eye, spied his lordship and motioned to him.

"Oh, dear," said Lord Biddleton, "I didn't know Lady Waxwood and Eudoria would be here."

Sir Ralston, who had not been listening, said, "What is it you say, Lucius?"

"Lady Waxwood and Eudoria, my betrothed."

Sir Ralston looked across the room.

"Of course. Eudoria looks charming. I haven't seen her in ages, old boy."

"Well, you will see her now."

Sir Ralston looked at his friend with some surprise, noting that the Earl expressed no joy at the thought of greeting his fiancée. Indeed, his manner seemed cold and his voice reluctant. But the Earl said no more and the two friends proceeded over to Lady Waxwood.

"Lucius!" she cried in a voice so loud the Earl was sure everyone in the large room had heard it. "How surprising to see you."

Sir Ralston regarded Lady Waxwood with undisguised wonder. He had never heard such a loud voice coming from such a small woman.

Lord Biddleton bowed gravely. "Lady Waxwood, Eudoria." He paused. "And Mr. Chalmers. I believe you ladies know my dearest friend, Sir Ralston Keith." The ladies acknowledged the acquaintance. "Though I suspect that you, Mr. Chalmers, have not yet met Sir Ralston."

Garfield Chalmers nodded glumly as if this were indeed an unfortunate circumstance. "I fear so, Lord Biddleton, I fear so. Never have had the pleasure. Sir Ralston Keith is it?

"I know all about you, sir, I think. I follow all the naval battles. Count myself an expert on Trafalgar. Know just about everything about it, I think. Perhaps not everything, but a great deal. I think. Would have liked to be a naval man myself but for my health. I've been plagued with poor health, sir. Worst luck, I think. Never been entirely well, I think."

Lord Biddleton glanced over at his friend and was relieved that Sir Ralston was listening politely without a trace of the incredulity he must have felt.

Eudoria Waxwood then spoke for the first time. "Oh, yes, Sir Ralston, Mr. Chalmers has suffered a great deal." She cast a sympathetic look at that gentleman. "I, of course, can sympathize with him, for I too have experienced the miseries of an infirm constitution."

Sir Ralston expressed his sorrow at this unfortunate news and noted that Miss Waxwood was very small and thin like her mother, and did indeed have a pale unhealthy look about her. Indeed, thought Sir Ralston, but for that wilting flower look, she'd be a fine-looking girl.

Lord Biddleton was not thinking at all about his fiancée's appearance. He was too busy wishing she would cease her incessant discussion of her health.

"It is extremely nice to see you ladies again. And an honor to meet you, Mr. Chalmers."

"The honor is mine, I think," said Mr. Chalmers enthusiastically. "So good to meet a former officer of the King's Navy and one with such a gallant record, I think. I do hope we shall see more of you now that you are returned to London. So good to meet you. So good."

"Yes, indeed," said Sir Ralston embarrassed by Mr. Chalmer's exuberance. "And if you will excuse me, I must greet some of the other guests. Since I have been gone so long I have so many people to see."

And with these words Sir Ralston was off, retreating, thought Lord Biddleton, like a fox before hounds.

"A fine young gentleman, Sir Ralston," proclaimed Lady Waxwood loudly.

"Yes," agreed the Earl, wishing his future mother-in-law could better modulate her voice.

"And now, Lucius," said Miss Waxwood, looking at his lordship with her large dark eyes, "I do hope you will explain why you did not inform us you would attend this party. Surely you could have escorted us."

The Earl looked slightly uncomfortable. "I didn't plan to attend. You see, I only agreed to come after seeing Ralston. He persuaded me to come and I did not think that you ladies would be attending."

Miss Waxwood looked reproachfully at the Earl. "I am certain I told you about this party, Lucius. I remember I told you because I said that I was not sure whether I would attend. I have not been feeling that well lately. You know how sensitive I am and I believe I caught a slight cold."

Lord Biddleton made no reply, but Mr. Chalmers replied solicitously, "My dear Miss Waxwood, I hope you take great care about these things. I myself am afflicted with many such ailments, I think, and they are nothing to be taken lightly. Especially, I think, by a lady of your delicate constitution."

Miss Waxwood looked gratefully at Mr. Chalmers. "How kind you are, sir."

Lord Biddleton was finding it hard to remain civil and stared glumly from Miss Waxwood to Mr. Chalmers.

"I do think we should all sit down now," said Eudoria, "for I am feeling a little faint. Perhaps it was not prudent to attend tonight feeling as I do."

"I think we should sit down then," cried Mr. Chalmers. "Oh, dear lady. Take my arm. This way, I think. Come, come."

Eudoria took the arm that was so eagerly extended and, in Lord Biddleton's opinion, leaned too heavily upon it. The Earl frowned but could do nothing but offer to escort Lady Waxwood and follow Chalmers and Eudoria across the room.

The Clairemonts always arrived late at parties and this fact was so well known that it became popular among the fashionable set to lay wagers upon their arrival time. Thus the arrival of the Duke and Duchess was always awaited with great eagerness.

When the Duke arrived with his Duchess on his arm, all heads turned. All, that is, save those of Lord Biddleton, Mr. Chalmers, and Lady Waxwood and Eudoria. They were still sitting in an inconspicuous spot discussing the unfortunate state of Miss Waxwood's health.

What most of the guests were eager to see was the appearance of Lady Isabelle Clairemont, whose beauty had dominated all manner of assemblies for many seasons. However, it was common now for guests at such gatherings to comment upon Lady Isabelle's advanced age as well as her remarkable beauty.

When Lady Isabelle entered with her brother Rob and sister Anne, all eyes fell upon her. No one was disappointed, for never had her ladyship appeared lovelier. Her pale blue gown showed off her trim figure and her blond hair was piled atop her head in a fashionable style accented by pale blue flowers that matched her gown. Several young gentlemen were struck dumb at Lady Isabelle's appearance and stood open mouthed until they were at last brought to their senses by their disapproving mothers.

A few of the ladies, while acknowledging Isabelle's beauty, shook their heads. "Six and twenty if she's a day," confided one distinguished-looking matron.

"Yes," replied another, "though it's hard to imagine she's not yet married. A pity, too, for she's a nice young lady despite being a Clairemont. A wild bunch, those Clairemonts."

"Yes," replied a very stout gray-haired lady. "They are wild and the Duke has squandered the family fortune from what I hear. I also hear Lady Isabelle refused many offers in her younger days and now has no prospects."

"They say she's in love with Charles Fensbrook," said still another lady. "And he's not about to offer for her." The ladies shook their heads and regarded Lady Isabelle sympathetically.

Although unaware of what the guests were saying about her, Lady Isabelle knew that her appearance always prompted a good deal of talk. She hoped that no one would notice that the gown she wore that evening had been refashioned from one several seasons old. Thank goodness, thought Lady Isabelle, that her maid, Mildred, was such a talented seamstress.

Her ladyship had no cause for worry on that account, for the gown was stunning and no one would suspect its humble origins. Yet Isabelle was finding it increasingly difficult to keep up appearances. She did not like to ask her father for money, for he could refuse her nothing and would only go further into debt.

Instead, the Clairemont women had become increasingly frugal and skillful at making what money they had last longer. Isabelle noted with satisfaction that Anne's gown looked quite lovely. It, too, was a piece of Mildred's handiwork, and although Lady Anne was not nearly so stunning as her sister, she was a most attractive picture in her simple green dress.

Lady Isabelle looked around the room and recognized

44

many of the guests. A number of young gentlemen rushed to the Clairemont sisters.

"At last," cried one young man who was dressed in what he hoped was the latest mode. "Lady Isabelle and Lady Anne. At last you two beautiful ladies have come."

Lord Robert, who had a sister on each arm, shook his head. "Good God, Webster, don't pounce upon my sisters. We have only just arrived."

The young man looked slightly crestfallen.

"Come now, Clairemont," said another young gentleman, "can you blame us if we are so eager? Lady Isabelle, you look beautiful."

"I give up," said Lord Robert in mock despair. "Sisters, I will leave you to these scoundrels."

Isabelle smiled graciously and looked at the crowd of adoring young men. Suddenly she felt very old and very weary. The gentlemen flocking about them seemed younger all the time, and their artless flatteries were growing increasingly hard to bear.

It was some time before Isabelle was finally able to extricate herself from her throng of ardent young admirers and retreat across the room toward her parents.

The Duke and Duchess and her brother Rob were engaged in an animated discussion with a handsome young gentleman with red hair and a rather military bearing. As Isabelle approached, they stopped talking and the Duke greeted his daughter merrily.

"Belle," said his Grace of Fothingham, "here is the naval hero that Burwicke has told us so much about. Lieutenant Keith. He is no longer in His Majesty's Service, of course, but has been telling us much about Burwicke."

"Oh, yes, Isabelle," said the Duchess. "Sir Ralston has been so kind to answer all of our questions. Such a dear man and from Burwicke's account so very brave."

Sir Ralston looked embarrassed. "Your Grace is too kind, but I assure you I am not at all courageous."

All of the Clairemonts looked approvingly at the modest young man.

"Of course, I did not want Burwicke to be a naval officer," said the Duke. "I told him, 'You're my eldest son.

45

You're needed here. It won't do for my eldest son to be out upon the high seas.' But Burwicke pleaded, and I confess I am an indulgent father."

"And His Majesty's Navy is glad of it, your Grace," said Sir Ralston, and the Duke glowed with pride.

Isabelle studied Sir Ralston in silence. He was a most likeable and charming man. "Now, Mother and Father," said Lady Isabelle, "I think the lieutenant must be growing weary of so many questions."

"Not at all, ma'am," said Sir Ralston. "What man would not relish the opportunity to tell of his exploits to such attentive listeners. Indeed, it is their Graces who are doubtless weary of my conversation."

"Nonsense, dear Sir Ralston," cried the Duchess. She looked fondly at the lieutenant and then at her daughter. "Oh, dear," she said, "I think we have not yet presented our daughter Isabelle to you, sir."

Sir Ralston took Lady Isabelle's hand and bowed low. "I am charmed, Lady Isabelle. Would you do me the honor of dancing with me? If, of course, their Graces would excuse us?"

"Of course, of course," said the Duke.

Isabelle smiled at Sir Ralston, made a graceful curtsey and the two of them walked off.

"Don't they make a handsome couple?" said the Duchess wistfully. The Duke nodded enthusiastically.

"A good sort of a young fellow, ain't he?"

Lord Robert and the Duchess agreed, the latter wondering about the extent of Sir Ralston Keith's fortune.

"As I would expect," said Sir Ralston Keith as he and Lady Isabelle began to dance one of the newly fashionable waltzes, "you are a wonderful dancer."

Isabelle smiled. "As are you, though one does not expect it of a naval lieutenant who has been so long at sea. You must have kept up with society."

"Well, ma'am, we are not always aboard ship."

Isabelle laughed. "And do you think you will like civilian life?" she said.

"I don't know. I shall miss the Navy of course. I had

expected to spend my whole life in the King's Service, but I had little choice when my brother died and I came into the title and property. There was no one to see to the estates and so here I am." He smiled at Isabelle. "And I am beginning to enjoy myself immensely."

Isabelle smiled and realized that she could say the same thing.

"I can see, my lady, that returning to civilian life has its advantages."

"You, sir, have a gift for flattery."

The baronet laughed and was about to reply when he spied Lord Biddleton.

"Oh, there is Biddleton and my cousin Fanny."

Lady Isabelle looked in the direction of Sir Ralston's gaze and saw the tall form of the Earl of Biddleton.

"Good heavens," she said, "do you know the Earl?"

"He is my dearest friend. We've known each other from childhood. He's a dashed fine fellow."

"Is he?" said Isabelle genuinely surprised.

"Of course he is, though I know some think he's something of a cold fish. He's not at all."

"I am slightly acquainted with the Earl," said Isabelle noncommittally, wondering at how a charming man like Sir Ralston Keith could have such a friend.

When the music stopped, the dancers applauded politely and Sir Ralston's cousin Fanny waved at them.

"Do you mind, Lady Isabelle, if I present my cousin to you?"

"I should be honored to meet your cousin." Lady Isabelle made no further reference to Lord Biddleton, for suddenly she thought that meeting the dreadful Earl again might prove amusing.

Sir Ralston Keith's cousin Fanny was daughter to Lady Dumbreck and newly married to Lord Easton, a Scottish noble. A vivacious young lady of nineteen with fashionable dark locks and a wide smile greeted them warmly.

"Rolly! How wonderful to see you this evening."

Lord Biddleton looked extremely uncomfortable at the approach of his friend and the infamous Lady Isabelle. He had not thought that any of the Clairemonts would be in attendance and he was not eager to renew his acquaintance with a lady he knew to be a shameless fortune huntress. He noticed with disapproval that Sir Ralston was looking quite delighted and he suddenly feared that his friend had succumbed to Lady Isabelle's fatal charm.

"Fanny," said Sir Ralston, taking his cousin's hand and kissing it warmly. "You look so lovely. I believe married life suits you. But where is your lord and master?"

"I'm afraid Easton is engaged with a certain French marquis who is a dreadful bore. I escaped and was lucky enough to see dear Biddleton."

Dear Biddleton? thought Lady Isabelle and a slight smile appeared on her lips as she beheld the Earl's sour countenance.

"Now, Fanny, I want to present Lady Isabelle Clairemont to you. Lady Isabelle, this is Lady Easton."

"How good to meet you," said Isabelle, shaking Fanny's hand. "I believe I know your husband's sister, Lady St. Clair."

"Oh, of course. My sister-in-law is a delightful woman. But I am thrilled to meet you finally, Lady Isabelle."

Lady Easton smiled ingenuously and Isabelle liked her immediately. The orchestra struck up another waltz and Lady Easton looked at her cousin. "Now, Rolly, I have wanted to dance with you all evening. I insist you dance now." Lady Easton took her cousin's arm firmly.

"Fanny!" cried Sir Ralston, amused and at the same time dismayed at losing sight of Lady Isabelle.

"Oh, it is only one dance and Lady Isabelle will promise to wait here with Biddleton. Pray do, Lady Isabelle, for I never get any opportunity to see my cousin."

"You know Lord Biddleton, of course," said Sir Ralston reluctantly.

"Of course," replied Lady Isabelle now thoroughly amused.

"I must apologize for my impulsive cousin," began Sir Ralston, but Fanny cut him off short and pulled him toward the dancers.

Lord Biddleton was quite dismayed at finding himself facing Lady Isabelle Clairemont. He promptly concluded that Lady Dumbreck's party was one of the most unpleasant social occasions he had ever faced. First he had been obliged to sit and speak with the Waxwoods and dreadful Garfield Chalmers for nearly three hours. Now, after finally seeing a means of escape in the form of his best friend's cousin, Lady Easton, that lady insisted upon leaving him alone with the infamous Isabelle Clairemont, a lady who disliked him as much as he did her.

Lord Biddleton was completely at a loss for words and Lady Isabelle said nothing, obviously waiting for him to say something uncivil. His lordship could think of nothing to say and it was becoming dreadfully awkward to stand there in silence. "Would you care to dance?" he said finally.

Lady Isabelle looked at him in astonishment. The Earl's face looked grim as he said these words and her ladyship was sorely tempted to laugh. She controlled herself with some difficulty and managed a slight curtsey.

As they joined the dancers Lady Isabelle noticed that the Earl looked as though he was engaged in a most unpleasant task. What a dreadful prig, she thought and as the absurdness of the situation came to her, she began to enjoy herself. Never, thought Lady Isabelle, had she danced with a more reluctant gentleman.

He took her hand and placed his arm about her waist with grim stoicism. He proceeded to dance in a mechanical way that seemed to disregard entirely the rhythm of the music. He stared straight ahead, never looking once at his partner's face and never speaking a word.

Lady Isabelle was by this time having a very hard time controlling herself. The situation was so ludicrous that she feared she would suddenly collapse into a fit of laughter. She bit her lip and looked down at the dance floor.

They continued to dance in silence and finally the Earl spoke. "Sir Ralston is a good friend of mine," he said.

"I beg your pardon," said her ladyship, startled at the Earl's abrupt statement and fighting desperately to keep from laughing.

"Sir Ralston is a good friend of mine."

"Indeed."

They danced on in silence and Lady Isabelle wondered what prompted this break in what seemed to be the Earl's vow of silence. Then suddenly the realization came to her—he's worried about his friend falling victim to my treachery. It was too ridiculous, but a look at the Earl's glowering countenance confirmed it.

Lady Isabelle grew suddenly angry. The insufferable puritanical old toad, she thought. Her blue eyes blazed ominously for a moment and then her face took on a mischievous look.

"I find Sir Ralston to be a very charming man," she said softly. "I do hope to see more of him."

The Earl looked down at his partner for the first time and found the look in the attractive blue eyes very irritating and yet at the same time disconcerting.

"Yes, Sir Ralston is so very charming." She paused and looked up into the Earl's face. "I've heard that Sir Ralston is very rich. I do hope that it's true."

The Earl stiffened and a look of horror came to his face. He could not believe the brazen manner of this female and he was so taken aback that he could only stare at her. He looked, thought Lady Isabelle, like he had just seen the Medusa and she again found herself fighting the urge to laugh.

Fortunately for the Earl the waltz ended and he was able to release his infamous partner. Soon Sir Ralston and Lady Easton returned, and to the Earl's dismay, Sir Ralston smiled eagerly at Lady Isabelle, his expression confirming the Earl's worst fears. His friend had already fallen victim to the lady's scheming ways.

Sir Ralston, unaware of his danger, offered his arm to Isabelle and they were off for another dance. The Earl watched them go, a strange look upon his face.

Lady Waxwood had watched her future son-in-law dance with Lady Isabelle Clairemont with undisguised incredulity. Her mouth dropped open and when Miss Waxwood noticed her mother's odd expression she too looked across the room.

There to her horror was her fiancé dancing with the stunning Lady Isabelle Clairemont. Never had Miss Waxwood been more astonished. Her thin hand flew to her mouth and she gasped.

Mr. Garfield Chalmers, who was still in attendance, followed Miss Waxwood's stricken gaze. I knew it, he thought. Biddleton's a cad, I think, a sly dog, I think. Poor Miss Waxwood.

Poor Miss Waxwood looked extremely pale. "He knew I was not well enough to dance," she said weakly, "so he found another partner."

Garfield Chalmers glared indignantly across the room at Lord Biddleton.

"I feel quite unwell," said Miss Waxwood. "Oh, Mama, please let us leave."

"If you would be so good, Mr. Chalmers," said Lady Waxwood, "to escort us, sir."

"With infinite pleasure," cried that gentleman. He took Miss Waxwood's arm, patting it gently with one large hand and led the ladies from the room.

The evening was growing quite late when Mr. Charles Fensbrook finally had the opportunity to speak to Lady Isabelle. After dancing with Lord Biddleton, Isabelle danced two dances with Sir Ralston Keith and was then so besieged by her young admirers that she finally agreed to dance with all of them.

After dancing a series of country dances, three waltzes, and two energetic mazurkas, her ladyship was ready to sit down for a time. Pleading her advanced age Lady Isabelle retired to a chair and was joined by her sister Anne and later Mr. Charles Fensbrook.

"Lady Anne," said Mr. Fensbrook with a slight bow. Anne, who was never happy to see that gentleman, nodded coolly. Although not encouraged by the response of either of the ladies, Charles Fensbrook sat down and began to regale them with an amusing anecdote about a particular Scottish baron who was spending the season in London for the first time.

Isabelle listened without enthusiasm, for although Charles was in fine form and his tale very amusing, she was not in the mood to hear his witticisms. Lady Anne laughed in spite of herself, but Isabelle merely smiled.

Mr. Fensbrook shook his head. "That story, my dear Belle, is one of my best. The Prince Regent laughed for the longest time when last I told it. Really, Belle, I am quite offended."

"Forgive me, Charles, but I fear I am too tired to appreciate even your stories. I am getting too old I suppose. In my youth I could dance until dawn but alas, those days are gone."

Mr. Fensbrook smiled but regarded Lady Isabelle curiously. He had never seen her lack energy and he felt slightly puzzled.

"I suppose it is exhausting dancing with a man like Sir Ralston Keith."

"Very much so." Lady Isabelle looked at Charles closely. Did she detect a trace of jealousy in his voice? No, she knew Charles too well for that.

"And my poor Belle, you even danced with the Earl of Biddleton."

"Yes, poor Belle," chimed in Lady Anne, "he was not a good dancer and he is so grim."

"Grim?" said Lady Isabelle. "He is perfectly odious to be sure."

"But he seems quite enamored of you," said Fensbrook.

Lady Isabelle burst into laughter and her sister joined in.

"Oh, Belle, that is famous. Lord Biddleton enamored of Belle? Really, Mr. Fensbrook, you are awfully silly."

"Perhaps, Lady Anne, but it's said that the Earl almost never dances and it was noted that he had a faraway look in his eyes as he danced with Lady Belle."

"Faraway look? Oh, Charles, he looked as though he had acute indigestion. The poor man."

They all laughed.

"But he is dreadful. I should be happy if I never see him again."

Mr. Fensbrook was surprised at her ladyship's vehemence and looked thoughtful for a moment.

* * *

Sir Ralston Keith glanced at his watch and noted the late hour with surprise. The time had passed very swiftly and his aunt's party was a resounding success. What had made it so successful from Sir Ralston's point of view was the fact that he had danced three dances with the most enchanting lady he had ever met.

As he stood musing about Lady Isabelle's charms he was interrupted by a tall figure.

"Lucius," he said. "By God, it's late. I thought you'd have been gone by now. It looks as if most of the guests have gone."

"Yes," said the Earl of Biddleton, a slightly haggard look on his face. "Even the Clairemonts are gone and some dashed odd fellow, name of Claxton or Claxmore or God knows what said, 'When the Clairemonts go, we might as well all go.' I think he was drunk, but it seems everyone agreed and left."

"Oh, I know what you think about the Clairemonts, Lucius. Of course, the Duke is a bit of a wild one still, but the whole family is so charming. Of course I am favorably disposed toward them because of Captain Lord Burwicke. He's a brilliant officer. You'd like him."

"You keep telling me that, Rolly," said his lordship sullenly.

Sir Ralston laughed. "But it is true. And have you seen a more lovely creature than Lady Isabelle? She is the most beautiful woman in the kingdom and so delightful."

The Earl frowned. "It's said she's after a rich husband."

"Lucius," cried Sir Ralston, "I am amazed that you should say such a thing. And what's so dreadful in that after all? I daresay most unmarried ladies would prefer rich husbands to poor ones. It's only logical. But it's amazing a woman like that hasn't got a husband, rich or otherwise. God, what it would be like to be married to a woman like that!"

Lord Biddleton frowned at his friend's exuberant praise of La Belle Clairemont but wisely refrained from commenting further. It had been an especially miserable evening and he had no wish to make it worse by offending his best friend who was obviously infatuated with the dreadful Lady Isabelle.

"I will bid you good night, Rolly," said the Earl, giving Sir Ralston a friendly pat on the back. "Late hours do not agree with me. Promise to call on me. We have not had much time to talk."

"Certainly, Lucius."

The two shook hands warmly and the Earl of Biddleton went on to bid farewell to his hostess.

Chapter 5

On the morning of her journey to Winterhaven, Lady Isabelle Clairemont was sitting in the parlor waiting for her carriage. She looked up as the butler entered the room.

"Oh, is the carriage ready, Marston?"

"No, my lady," replied the butler. "Lord Ambrose is here."

Isabelle appeared surprised. "Cuthbert? Please send him in."

The young Lord Ambrose seemed upset as he walked into the room but he smiled when he saw Isabelle.

"Cuthburt," said Lady Isabelle, "it is nice to see you again."

The youth mumbled a reply as he took her hand and made a polite bow. Isabelle motioned him to the sofa and Cuthburt obeyed and sat down.

"And how have you been of late?" inquired Lady Isabelle, smiling. "You have not visited us in some time. Have you been keeping that brother of mine out of trouble?"

Lord Ambrose smiled, but words failed him and he simply gazed stupidly at her. Isabelle smiled encouragingly at him and his courage was somewhat restored.

"Lady Isabelle," he suddenly blurted out, "I felt I had to come and apologize for the unpardonable behavior of my uncle. He told me he came to see you and I have been most upset. I could not believe his . . . his foggy old notions and his rude and unjust remarks. I fervently pray that you are not too offended and might forgive me."

"Forgive you? Why surely, sir, there is nothing to forgive. I can't say I find your uncle a very endearing man, but truly, I do not feel any prejudice toward you on his account."

"Oh, thank you," said Cuthburt, impulsively taking her hand. "Lady Isabelle, may I tell you of my great affection and devotion to you?" He ended this fervent speech by kissing her hand.

Isabelle was both amused and embarrassed by the youth's sudden ardor. Apparently his uncle had been right on at least this point. She controlled a smile and said kindly, "Thank you, Lord Ambrose. It is flattering for a woman of my age to have such a handsome young man express himself so."

"But you are not that much older than I!" cried Cuthburt. "You mustn't let my uncle influence you!"

"I assure you I would never allow that."

"Then you must believe me . . . I am in love with you."

Isabelle shook her head. "Thank you, Cuthburt. I am truly flattered, but I fear we really aren't suited for each other."

Lord Ambrose flushed. He stood up stiffly and Isabelle was somewhat amused at his stern expression. It made him resemble his uncle even more.

"I do beg your pardon, Lady Isabelle. And I hope you have a safe journey to your aunt's." With those coldly spoken words he quickly strode out of the room.

"Members of that family do make the most abrupt exits," decided Lady Isabelle shaking her head.

Cuthburt Ambrose left the Clairemont house in a decidedly bad humor. He was angered by the rebuff he had received from Lady Isabelle. Their meeting convinced him that she viewed him as a mere boy, a friend of Rob's and that was all. However, as the youth walked down the street, his anger soon departed and he was left with a feeling of despair. Why had he been so foolish to think Isabelle could care for him? He must have lost his senses! How could he ever face her again? How could he face any of the Clairemonts?

He was soon to find out as a familiar voice hailed him. Cuthburt looked up and saw his friend Rob hurrying across the street. A small groan escaped from his lips, but he stood his ground and even managed a half-hearted wave.

"I say, Burt, old boy," said Lord Robert Clairemont as he clapped his friend on the shoulder. "What the devil's the matter? I was nearly hoarse trying to get your attention."

"I'm sorry, Rob, I was thinking."

"My dear fellow," said Rob, "we musn't have that. Thinking is dashed unhealthy! I mean walking around in that distracted state you might have been run over by a wagon!"

Cuthburt gave a strange laugh. "That does not sound like such a bad thing at the moment."

"Burt!" cried Lord Robert, beginning to look truly concerned. "What is it, old man? I've never seen you so blue deviled before."

Cuthburt looked at his friend and then looked away. "I really don't want to talk about it, Rob."

"I see," said his friend, shaking his head in sympathy. He continued talking to himself. "Of course, I can't imagine what it could be. I meant it ain't like Burt Ambrose to get himself in a muddle. I'm always the one doing that." He gave his friend a long sidelong glance "Hmmm . . ."

"Really, Rob, must you stand there studying me like some damned specimen?" said Cuthburt, smiling in spite of himself.

"Sorry, Burt. But I just want to help. Come on, tell your old school chum what's wrong."

"Oh, all right. I might as well. I'm sure your sister will tell you in any case."

"My sister? Annie?"

"No. Isabelle."

Rob looked at his friend with a perplexed expression. "What about Belle? She ain't trying to get your help in seeing that I walk the straight and narrow is she?"

"No, no, nothing like that."

"Well, that's a relief! But really, Burt, what's this about?" Rob watched his friend's face redden and a flash of insight hit him.

"Oh, no, old fellow. You haven't lost your head over Belle?"

Lord Ambrose stared miserably at his feet and Rob patted his friend sympathetically on the shoulder. "I'll be damned!"

Cuthburt burst out, "Oh, Rob, I made a complete ass of myself. I told your sister how I felt and . . ."

"And she gave you one of her set downs."

"Oh, she was very kind, or she tried to be," said Cuthburt sadly.

"Well, buck up, Burt. Belle has sent many a fellow on his way. I keep telling her to find a rich husband, but she don't take my advice! It would help me out, you know."

Cuthburt looked indignant but soon laughed at the ridiculously mercenary expression on his friend's face.

"That's better, Burt. It ain't so tragic now is it?"

"I suppose not."

"Burt! I've got a jolly idea. Let's go to Fothingham."

"Fothingham?"

"Yes. It would do you good. And I must admit I am quite anxious to be out of London for a time myself!"

Lord Ambrose hesitated for a moment and then replied, "Well, all right! Why not? When shall we go?"

"Why not right now?"

"Now?"

"Yes, I'll go get a few things packed and then I'll drive by your house and pick you up. Oh, I just remembered. Belle's going to Aunt Agatha's today. We'll have to take the old carriage that Papa refuses to part with. Can you imagine being sentimental over an ancient, creaking carriage? It's a dreadful lumbering old thing, but it should get us to Fothingham all right." He looked at his friend. "Well, don't you think you had better get going, Burt?"

"Right! I'll be ready!" Cuthburt turned to leave but hesitated. "Thanks awfully, Rob."

"Don't be foolish, old boy. Now hurry!"

Cuthburt smiled and quickly departed for his house. Rob shrugged. Think of that. Steady old Burt losing his balance over Belle. Poor old fellow.

As Lord Robert began walking home, he spied a gentleman walking toward him. He muttered an "Oh, damn!" but kept up his pace.

The gentleman, a large swarthy man in his forties, shouted out to Rob as they approached each other.

"I say, Clairemont! Now, ain't this fortunate!"

"Damned fortunate," muttered Rob under his breath, but he answered jovially. "Tilden, old fellow, how are you?"

"Oh, I'm fine, Clairemont. And how are you? I haven't seen you for weeks. In fact, not since we shared the gaming table at the White Ox."

"Well, yes, I fear it has been a frightfully long time, but do forgive me, old man. I really am in a hurry."

"I'm sure you are, Clairemont," said the man, putting a firm hand on the young man's shoulder.

"I say, Tilden," said Rob, still smiling, "would you remove your hand from my shoulder? It's a bit uncomfortable."

"I'm so sorry," returned Tilden sarcastically. He tightened his grip and said in a stern voice, "I want that money you owe me."

"You'll get it."

"When, by God? I ain't planning to live forever, you know."

"Oh?" replied Rob hopefully.

Tilden released his grip roughly. "I'm telling you, Clairemont, I want my money. And I hear I'm not the only one."

Rob tried hard to retain his composure and smiled at Tilden good-naturedly. "I swear, Tilden," he said, "one would think you needed the money."

"It ain't that, you young rascal. I won that money fair and I expect to get it."

"I tell you, you'll get it."

"Well, I better get it—and soon. 'Cause if I don't, Clairemont, I'll be sending a certain person to collect. And he ain't as sweet tempered as me, my boy!" With that warning Tilden continued his journey down the street. Rob watched him go and then resumed his own walk.

I really am most eager to see dear old Fothingham, he thought, as he quickened his pace.

When Cuthburt Ambrose arrived home he was glad to discover his mother was away on a round of social calls. He hurried to his room and deciding not to bother any of the servants, packed his own case.

As he lugged the case downstairs, he was met by a rather shocked servant. "My lord," cried the man, "your lordship should not be carrying that."

"Oh, that's all right, Simpson. I didn't want to disturb anyone."

Simpson merely looked curiously at his young master.

"Listen, Simpson, I'm going away for some time with . . ." Cuthburt hesitated. He remembered his mother's displeasure over his friendship with Robert Clairemont. "Tell her ladyship I'm going away to the country with a friend."

"A friend?" repeated the butler raising his eyebrows.

"Yes." There was a knock at the door and Cuthburt quickly added, "I haven't time to explain now, Simpson. I'll send my mother a letter."

"Very well, my lord," replied the butler with a look which indicated it was not well at all. Simpson went and opened the door to a young footman.

"I'm to get Lord Ambrose's luggage, sir," said the footman. Simpson looked out and saw a vehicle in front of the house. He thought he could detect the Fothingham crest on it.

"Here," said Cuthburt, hurrying toward the door with his bag. The servant took it from him and, glancing at the disapproving Simpson, hurried out the door.

Cuthburt was quick to follow the footman, turning back only briefly to the suspicious butler. "Tell her ladyship I'll write. Good-bye."

As he watched his master depart, Simpson frowned. Lady Ambrose, he knew, would not be pleased by her son's mysterious departure.

Lady Ambrose was, in fact, already rather displeased that day. She had had an indigestible luncheon at Mrs. Cyril Lesley's house. The meal was bad enough in itself, but Mrs. Lesley gave an endless monologue on her new son-in-law, Sir Ashley Creighton, on top of it. Even Lady Ambrose's most chilling looks did not quail Mrs. Lesley, whose incessant chatter soon gave her ladyship a headache.

However, Lady Ambrose had felt remarkably better driving away from the Lesley house. As the phaeton traveled down the street, a carriage drove by in the opposite direction and Lady Ambrose got a quick look at one of the carriage's occupants.

Lady Isabelle Clairemont had been looking out the carriage window and had also observed Lady Ambrose. The women's eyes met for only a moment as the two vehicles passed each other, but it was long enough for Lady Isabelle's eyes to register a slight shock of recognition. She had never met Lady Ambrose but the woman bore a striking resemblance to the Earl of Biddleton.

Lady Ambrose, who had never been introduced to Lady Isabelle but had seen her several times, frowned at that lady. A chuckle escaped from Lady Isabelle and she found it impossible to resist sticking her head out the carriage to get another glance at Lord Biddleton's formidable sister.

"Where is Lord Ambrose?" she asked her butler, Simpson, as she entered the house.

Simpson looked uncomfortable. "I am sorry, my lady, but his lordship is not at home."

"Not at home?" she repeated irritably. "Did he tell you where he was going?"

"No, my lady, not exactly."

Lady Ambrose looked at the man and frowned. "Well, Simpson, what is it?"

Simpson looked at her fearfully. "His lordship left ear-

61

lier, my lady. He had packed a case and said he was staying with a friend in the country."

"What friend?"

"He . . . he didn't say, my lady. He said he would send your ladyship a letter."

"Send me a letter?"

"He said he was in a hurry."

Lady Ambrose was incredulous. "He was in a hurry? He couldn't even say where he was going or with whom?"

Simpson shook his head. He was hesitant at first but then spoke. "My lady, there is one thing."

"Yes, Simpson?"

"A carriage came to pick up Lord Ambrose and I think I could detect the Fothingham crest of the door."

"Fothingham!"

"I have seen the crest many times, my lady."

Lady Ambrose stared at the butler. So he's gone off with that Clairemont boy, she thought angrily. An even worse possibility suddenly occurred to her. Why, she had seen the Fothingham carriage on her way to her townhouse! Lady Isabelle Clairemont had peered out at her! With a horrified expression on her face, Lady Ambrose remembered that brief moment as the two vehicles passed. The Clairemont woman had looked at her rather strangely. She had had a look of surprise on her face. But why would she be surprised? Why indeed? muttered Lady Ambrose to herself and she then turned to her butler. "Simpson, I must go and see my brother immediately. Tell James to get the phaeton ready."

"Yes, my lady."

James, who had just about completed unhitching the team from the vehicle, was somewhat perplexed to hear that Lady Ambrose intended to go out again. What business is this! he thought curiously, well aware that capriciousness was not a part of Lady Ambrose's character. He was even more perplexed by his mistress's peculiar behavior on the ride to her brother's house. She was usually cautioning him against driving too fast, but now she was constantly urging him to go faster.

Mills, Lord Biddleton's butler, was not only perplexed

but a trifle alarmed by Lady Ambrose's behavior. She had hurried into the house like a madwoman, not even waiting for him to announce her.

She found her brother with his secretary, Mr. Galbreath, in the library looking over some papers. Galbreath quickly excused himself and Lord Biddleton, who was alarmed by his sister's appearance, demanded to know what was wrong.

"Lucius! It is dreadful! I don't know if I can believe it but I don't know what else to think."

His lordship escorted her to a chair and pulled another one close to her. "Now what is this all about, Lydia?"

"It's Cuthburt! He has eloped with Isabelle Clairemont!"

"What?" cried Biddleton in a shocked voice.

"Yes, you see, Cuthburt left with luggage and wouldn't tell Simpson where he was going, just that he was going to the country with a friend. He said he'd write me a letter!"

"Well, Lydia, that was rather inconsiderate of the boy, but what makes you think . . ."

"Oh, it is not at all like him to sneak off like that. And Simpson said the carriage that came to pick him up had the Fothingham crest on it."

"But, Lydia, couldn't he have been going off with that school friend of his, I forget his name?"

"Robert? That's what I thought at first but then I remembered that I saw the Fothingham carriage myself when I was driving home from Mrs. Lesley's and Lady Isabelle was in it. And what's more, Lucius, she looked at me so strangely . . . as if she were shocked to see me."

Lord Biddleton considered this rather grimly. "She said she meant to marry Cuthburt," he muttered.

"What?" cried Lady Ambrose.

"Well, Lydia, I went to see her last week and she admitted that she planned to marry him. I should have told you about it. Then when I danced with her . . ."

His sister looked at him in disbelief. "When you did *what*?"

"I danced with her at Lady Dumbreck's party."

Lady Ambrose, for once, looked dumbfounded.

Lord Biddleton continued. "Oh, it's a long story, but

when I saw her last week I told her I would not stand for her marrying Cuthburt."

"And what did she say?"

Her brother frowned. "She said she would marry whomever she wished."

Lydia stared at her brother and finally shook her head.

"I am sorry, Lydia, but I never expected her to do something like this. When I danced with her, and I must say I had no choice in the matter, for we were thrust together in an abominable manner, she led me to believe that she was now interested in Sir Ralston Keith rather than Cuthburt."

"Yes, she led you to believe that! And now she and Cuthburt are on their way to Gretna Green!"

"Don't worry, Lydia," said the Earl grimly. "I will find them. How much of a start do they have?"

"I saw Lady Isabelle's carriage not more than an hour ago. To think that my son was with her!"

"Don't think of it, Lydia. There is only one way that they could have gone and I'll catch up with them."

Lady Ambrose seemed unconvinced of this but nodded. Lord Biddleton hurried to the door to give instructions to his butler to have his horse saddled. Mills, who had been wondering about the cause of Lady Ambrose's strange behavior, was even more astonished by his master's abrupt command.

A few moments later the Earl of Biddleton strode into the stable, followed by his sister Lydia. A groom had just completed saddling the Earl's horse and led it over to him.

"Very good, Jim," said Lord Biddleton to the groom. He turned to his sister, speaking in a low voice so the servant couldn't hear. "Don't worry, Lydia. I will get Cuthburt back." He then mounted his horse and set off at a furious gallop.

"What in heaven's name!" exclaimed the startled groom as he watched his master's wild ride down the street.

Chapter 6

The carriage clattered noisily along the rough road and Lady Isabelle and her maid, Mildred, were jolted constantly.

"Oh, heavens!" cried Mildred after the carriage hit a large rut. "Oh, my lady, I thought these roads was improved. Mr. Marston said he read they was improved."

Lady Isabelle laughed. "Obviously not all the roads have been improved. But remember, Millie, that the road to Winterhaven is not precisely the most traveled road in the kingdom."

Mildred sighed and pulled her cloak more tightly around her. She had not looked forward to the trip to her ladyship's aunt's house. She had attended her mistress on previous trips to Winterhaven and had told the other servants upon her return that the country house would have been better named Loonyhaven.

Still it was good to leave the congestion and dirt of London and the weather was still quite good in spite of the appearance of some rather ominous-looking clouds.

Lady Isabelle, unlike her maid, was eager to join her aunt. They got on extremely well and Isabelle was always amused by her aunt's inevitable collection of unusual houseguests.

Aunt Agatha, or Lady Balderston as she was known to society, was a lady of strong will and independent spirit. A formidable-looking lady with piercing blue eyes and unruly graying hair, she had definite opinions about everything and was disdainful of London society.

She preferred to stay at Winterhaven, her late husband's ancestral home, with her son, Sir Hector, the Sixth Baronet. Isabelle smiled as she thought of Cousin Hector. He was a dear young man, though he thought himself a poet and wrote the most lamentable verse.

One never knew who might be staying at Winterhaven. Aunt Agatha welcomed Alsatian counts and Prussian theologians. She delighted in freethinkers and utopian philosophers and she loved poets and artists. One could always expect the unusual, like the time Lady Balderston entertained a dowager Austrian princess who wrote epic poems and a self-taught Scottish sculptor whose crude manners only delighted the company.

Isabelle smiled more broadly as she speculated upon the guests who would be at Winterhaven this season. Suddenly there was another jolt and the two women nearly were thrown from the carriage seat.

"My lady!" called Mildred. "What is Jock doing? He's going far too fast!"

The carriage had indeed picked up speed and her ladyship looked out the window and shouted, "Jock, what is it?"

Jock, a burly Scotsman, heard his mistress's shout and hollered in return.

"Highwayman, m'lady!"

Mildred's eyes grew wide. "My lady," she cried.

Lady Isabelle looked out the small oval window in the back of the carriage and saw a figure on horseback galloping toward the carriage.

Good Lord, thought Isabelle, it is a highwayman!

The carriage continued to bounce and jolt as Jock whipped the horses furiously. The ladies were thrown against the back of the carriage seats and Mildred clutched the leather upholstery in terror. Finally there was a loud cracking noise and Lady Isabelle and Mildred found themselves thrown sideways against the carriage door as the vehicle tipped precariously to one side, bounced again and was still.

"Are you injured, my lady?" cried Mildred hastening to help her mistress back onto the carriage seat which was now tilted at a severe angle.

"I'm fine, I believe," said her ladyship getting up from the carriage floor. "And you, Millie?"

"Oh, I am bruised, I expect, but not so bad."

"Can you get the door open?"

"Aye, my lady, I think so."

Mildred pushed the door open and climbed out and then turned to help her mistress.

"Jock, where is Jock?" cried her ladyship after climbing out of the carriage and seeing the coachman's seat empty.

"Here, m'lady," said a voice and Isabelle saw the coachman at the side of one of the horses, a pistol in his hand.

Isabelle turned to see the rider advancing upon them. "Don't ye fear, m'lady, I've got a clear shot."

The Scotsman raised the pistol and leveled it at the approaching horseman.

Suddenly her ladyship's mouth fell open in astonishment as she recognized the horseman. "Biddleton!" she cried.

Jock pressed the trigger just as Isabelle said the name and the approaching horse reared up at the pistol's violent report. The rider managed to maintain his seat and shouted, "What the devil!"

Jock was no marksman and his shot was far wide of his target. "Damn!" he cried in exasperation and Lady Isabelle felt tremendous relief and thanked providence that Jock was a poor shot.

"Jock," she cried, "it's no highwayman. Stop, please!"

By this time Lord Biddleton had arrived at the side of the waylaid carriage and he glowered at the coachman.

"What are you doing? You could have killed me, man!"

"Perhaps that would have been best," cried Lady Isabelle her relief turning to fury. She approached his lordship's horse, her blue eyes blazing with murderous rage.

"I demand to know the meaning of this, sir!" she cried. "Why did you descend upon us like a demon from hell? By my honor, Lord Biddleton, we thought you a highwayman and were all nearly killed. You had better explain, sir!"

Biddleton was momentarily stunned by the fury in her voice and the wild picture she presented with her long blond hair falling wildly about her face and her lovely face flushed with anger.

"Where is Cuthburt?" demanded the Earl finally.

Lady Isabelle stared up at Lord Biddleton as if she did not comprehend his words.

"Cuthburt?"

"My nephew, Lord Ambrose."

Isabelle shook her head in disbelief. "You thought Cuthburt was with me? Then you thought he and I were . . ."

"Eloping! Of course, and where is he?"

Isabelle burst into bitter laughter. "My lord Biddleton, you have been misinformed. Cuthburt is not with me. As you can see I am accompanied by good Jock here," she nodded at the burly Scot who was looking at his lordship with a most insolent, threatening expression, "and my woman, Mildred."

Mildred was at her ladyship's side pulling her cloak tightly around her and regarding the Earl with suspicion.

"Then he is not here?"

Isabelle laughed. "You may want to search the carriage."

The Earl looked at the carriage which was tilted at the side of the road. A wheel was smashed badly, the spokes lying in splinters on the ground.

"Oh, dear," said Lord Biddleton suddenly aware of his mistake. He jumped down from the horse. "Oh, I have been a fool. But I had good reason to believe . . ."

Lady Isabelle pushed a strand of blond hair from her face. "Oh, I know what you believed, sir, but look at our predicament." She looked over at the carriage. "It's a dreadful mess, all right. What do you think, Jock?"

Jock glared at Lord Biddleton and then examined the wheel.

"This will nae travel nae more, m'lady. Aye, bad it is."

"I hope you are pleased with yourself, sir."

Lord Biddleton stared awkwardly at the ground. "Lady

Isabelle, I am sorry but I thought . . . I know I was a fool."

Isabelle obtained little satisfaction from this confession but continued to stare at the wheel. "So what is to be done?"

"There's a place down the road where I could fetch help," said Jock.

"Of course," said the Earl. "You can take my horse."

Jock looked at Biddleton and then at the horse. It was a fine animal but its coat was flecked with foam. "That one would nae make a mile," said Jock. "He's winded. You'd best walk him down."

Lord Biddleton looked at Jock in surprise, for he was not accustomed to having servants tell him what to do.

Lady Isabelle nearly laughed despite her anger when she saw the insulted look on his lordship's face.

"You had better do so, my lord."

The Earl looked at her icily and turned to Jock, "Then take one of the coach horses and be quick. I'll stay with the ladies until you return with a vehicle to convey them to lodgings."

Jock ignored the Earl and turned to his mistress.

"I think the gentleman is right, Jock. You could take one of the coach horses and return."

"But will your ladyship be safe here?" He turned and looked distrustfully at the Earl.

"Of course, Jock. I assure you this is no highwayman. This is the Earl of Biddleton."

Jock seemed unimpressed by this information and shrugged. "If your ladyship is certain."

"Yes, yes Jock. Do go on."

The coachman touched his hand to his forehead to bid his mistress farewell and ignored the Earl. He quickly unharnessed one of the lead horses and was off down the road.

"That's an insolent fellow," said the Earl. "I'd have him horsewhipped."

"How dare you, sir!" said Lady Isabelle. "Do you expect him to fawn over you? You nearly killed him!"

"And didn't he nearly kill me?"

"Oh, I had forgotten that."

"Well, I have not. I am not accustomed to pistol balls whizzing past my head."

"Shouldn't you see to your horse?"

The Earl bowed curtly and returned to the nearly spent animal.

"Is he really a gentleman?" whispered Mildred.

"He purports to be one," replied her mistress, "though at the moment I have reason to doubt it. But gentleman or no, he is the Earl of Biddleton."

Mildred frowned. "It grows cloudy my lady, and cold too." The maid shivered and Isabelle looked up at the sky. The clouds now appeared rather ominous and the wind had picked up speed.

"Don't worry," said her ladyship encouragingly. "Jock will return shortly and we'll soon be in some snug inn for the night." She looked at Lord Biddleton who was walking his horse up and down the road. "That man," she said. "That man."

That man finished walking his horse and returned to Lady Isabelle. He tied his mount to the carriage and stood glowering at her.

Her ladyship, who usually made the best of uncomfortable situations, found the Earl's sour expression infuriating.

"Must you glare at me like that, sir?" she said finally. "You act as if this predicament were my doing."

Lord Biddleton folded his arms. "You must admit that you gave me good reason to believe that you wanted to marry Cuthburt. You told me as much and what was I to think when I was told Cuthburt went off in Fothingham's coach?"

"So you thought I had spirited away your precious nephew. By my honor, sir, I am not so eager to become your relation."

"But you said . . ."

Isabelle shook her head and looked disgusted. "Do you not recall how you barged into my house with that insufferable pious air of yours and demanded I cease scheming to marry poor defenseless Cuthburt. I have never suffered such an insult. How did you expect me to react?"

"Then you had no designs on Cuthburt?"

"You are too absurd. I had no designs on poor Lord Ambrose. He is a very nice young man, but I had never given him a thought."

"Then you said those things to aggravate me."

"How perceptive you are, my lord."

The blue eyes regarded him with contempt and the Earl seethed with rage. Never had he met a more difficult female. Isabelle too was furious. A lady of a friendly, cheerful disposition, Isabelle's feelings toward the Earl at that moment were most uncharacteristic.

"And I thought that you knew I had abandoned my pursuit of your nephew since we saw each other at Lady Dumbreck's party. Alas, poor man, you had the misfortune to dance with me."

"I don't know what you mean," said the Earl, embarrassed by the reference to Lady Dumbreck's party.

"I mean, of course, that you saw how I had chosen new prey and was scheming after your dear friend, Sir Ralston Keith."

The Earl reddened as he saw the mockery in her eyes. "So that was for my benefit too? Really, ma'am, I find that quite . . . quite unseemly. I should not think a lady would act so shamelessly."

"Oh, you," cried Isabelle now, so angry that she was momentarily at a loss for words. "You are so infuriating, such a self-righteous, bigoted, conceited . . ." She paused searching for an appropriate term, ". . . old fossil." And not trusting herself any further she turned her back on him and walked off.

Mildred had watched this exchange with alarm and fascination. She had never seen her mistress so angry. Certainly Lady Isabelle had bouts of moodiness and temper but she was not subject to such outbursts. Indeed, members of the household thought of Lady Isabelle as the diplomat and peacemaker of the family.

Yet, reflected Mildred, the Earl of Biddleton was obviously a dreadful man. She was greatly insulted that he dare speak to her beloved mistress in such a manner and thought that if she had been a man, she would have punched him soundly, Earl or no Earl.

Mildred was lost in these unpleasant thoughts and stood glaring at Lord Biddleton when suddenly she heard a noise and turned toward the grove of trees at the side of the road.

"My lady!" cried Mildred as a man stepped out from behind the trees. He was carrying a heavy pistol and Isabelle gasped. The Earl was quite startled and could only curse the fates that had brought even more ill luck to him that miserable day.

The man brandished the pistol menacingly. "Well, what have we here? The gentry come upon bad luck it looks like. Stranded here quite defenseless."

He looked at Biddleton. "Join the ladies if you will, guvnor."

Biddleton moved across and stood next to Isabelle.

"I hope none o' you will try anything foolish. 'Twould be a pity to see such fine clothes rent by a pistol ball."

The man looked them over with an insolent eye. "My, ain't she a beauty," he said regarding Isabelle with great interest. "A good-looking wench indeed. I've a mind to take you with me, my girl. Aye, I might. But don't worry, my pretty. If you're good to me, I'll not be so hard on you."

Lord Biddleton was astonished by the man's impudence. "Look here, fellow," he said, "you are addressing a lady!"

The man cocked his pistol. "I'll advise you to keep your mouth shut, guvnor, or I'll not be so easy on your lady here."

Lord Biddleton clenched his fists and Isabelle thought for an instant he would do something rash. She put her hand upon his arm and looked up at him, her expression warning that he be careful.

"And now, my lady," said the footpad, "I'll have that ring from your pretty finger."

Isabelle hesitated.

"I want the ring," he shouted. "I'll not wait long."

Her ladyship took the ring from her hand.

"Bring it to me, my girl."

Isabelle moved slowly toward the man and extended her hand. The outlaw took the ring and as her ladyship withdrew her hand, the man grasped her wrist and pulled her to him.

"How dare you!" cried Isabelle struggling to free herself from the man's grip.

"Villain!" cried Biddleton suddenly leaping upon the footpad. The two men struggled and the pistol went off.

Lady Isabelle cried out in terror and Mildred covered her face with her hands. The shot went wild, but the footpad, who though shorter than his lordship was stocky and very muscular, was able to plant a firm punch on the Earl's midsection. The Earl doubled over in pain, gasping for breath.

The outlaw landed another punch to the Earl's shoulder and his lordship fell to the ground. The outlaw pulled a long knife from his belt. "Don't think I wouldn't kill you, my fine gentleman. Now give me your money."

Lady Isabelle rushed to the Earl's side. He was still gasping. "Oh, do as he says," she whispered. The Earl reached for his purse and threw it toward the footpad, who picked it up and felt its weight with satisfaction.

"I've plucked a fat partridge I see. Now I'll take those boots."

The Earl looked at the man in surprise.

"You, pretty lady. Get his boots."

Isabelle exchanged a glance with the Earl and moved over and knelt in front of him grasping one dusty boot and pulling it hard. She took the other boot and tossed the pair at the outlaw.

"The finest, of course," he said.

"And now your watch." The Earl handed it over.

"And your ring."

The Earl looked down at his hand. It was the Biddleton ring given to the First Earl by a grateful monarch nearly three hundred years ago. His lordship made no move.

"Would you rather I take your ring or your lady, guvnor?"

Lord Biddleton glared at the man and removed the ring and tossed it to the outlaw.

73

"And finally, good sir, I'll have your coat. Lady, help his honor with his coat." Isabelle did as she was told and handed the robber the Earl's coat.

"A fine one," said the footpad. "You, sir, have been a very cooperative gent and I'll leave your lady be."

He kept his knife poised in the air and walked to the Earl's horse. He untied it and got into the saddle. Still holding the knife in a menacing pose, he rode over to the carriage horses and leaning over cut them away from the traces. He shouted and the three remaining carriage horses were off.

"You'll pay for this, you blackguard," said his lordship, his fists clenched tightly.

"Will I, my fine gentleman?" The robber laughed, kicked his lordship's horse roughly, and was off.

Lady Isabelle grasped the Earl's arm. "Are you hurt, sir?"

"I do not think so."

His lordship tried to get to his feet and had to lean heavily on Lady Isabelle. He finally rose and stood shakily.

"I think you should sit down, sir," said Lady Isabelle with a look of concern of her face.

"No, ma'am, I shall be fine, I assure you."

Isabelle turned to her maid. "Millie, there is water in the carriage. Fetch it for his lordship." Millie did so and Isabelle poured a glass for Lord Biddleton who drank it with an unsteady hand.

"I want to thank you, Lord Biddleton."

"You have nothing to thank me for," he said curtly and Isabelle looked at him in surprise.

"But I do," she said.

His lordship frowned. He had never felt more humiliated and was sure that Lady Isabelle considered his efforts on her behalf quite ludicrous. Surely she was mocking him, standing there looking at him with those infernal blue eyes, her dress covered with dirt from his boots.

Lady Isabelle frowned. He was a difficult man, the Earl of Biddleton. One minute he was trying to save her from an outlaw and the next he was very sullen, refusing to accept her thanks and regarding her with those cold blue eyes of his as if everything were her fault.

"My lady," said Mildred drawing Isabelle's attention away from the Earl. "It looks like rain. Oh, my lady, what shall we do?"

No sooner had the faithful Mildred said these words than large drops began to fall. "My lady," cried Mildred, "what shall we do?"

Isabelle looked at the Earl, who was staring down at his bootless feet and then at the carriage. "I daresay we cannot stay in the carriage. It looks as if it could topple over."

"I think there was cottages," said Mildred. "I remember seeing one from the road not too far back."

The rain began to fall harder. "I think we should try to find one of these cottages," said her ladyship. "Can you walk, sir?"

"Of course I can walk," he said petulantly.

"Good heavens, sir," cried Isabelle, the rain streaming down her face. "Why are you acting so angry? We are all miserable. This is hardly the time for bouts of temper."

"Temper! And you think it is no small thing to have almost been killed by some blasted scoundrel and now soaked to the bone in some godforsaken desolate place."

"Do not forget," cried Isabelle, "that you chose yourself to follow me like some madman with your ridiculous fears. Mildred and I are going to find some shelter. I do not care whether you come with us or choose to stay here and lament your miserable fate. Come, Mildred."

With that, she and her maid hurried on down the road.

The Earl stood in the rain which had become a fearful downpour. He debated for a moment as to the best course of action. He looked down again at his bootless feet and then at the road. It was one of the new macadamized roads made up of tiny stones and it was passable in all kinds of weather yet extremely painful to walk upon in bare feet. The Earl gingerly made his way to the side of the road and reluctantly followed the retreating forms of Lady Isabelle Clairemont and her maid.

Chapter 7

Lady Isabelle was very wet and very miserable as she walked along the road with Mildred by her side. However, she told herself that things could have been much worse. Isabelle kept thinking of the footpad and the memory of him made her shiver. She prayed that he had left the area and would not pounce upon them again.

"He's coming," said Mildred, looking over her shoulder.

"Who?" said Isabelle quickly thinking of the outlaw.

"His lordship, I mean," whispered Mildred.

The Earl, it seemed, had chosen to follow them and his long strides soon allowed him to catch up.

Isabelle looked over at him. He looked quite ridiculous. His face was set in his usual grim arrogant expression and his clothes and hair were dripping wet. He was stepping gingerly along the roadside trying to avoid stones and Isabelle found herself staring at the way his shirt clung to his body. She noted with surprise that he was well formed and muscular. She had not realized how broad his shoulders were and that his arms looked very strong. When she realized she was thinking about the Earl's physique, Isabelle blushed and looked away quickly.

Her ladyship would have been surprised to learn that the Earl, too, was glancing over at her and could not help noticing that the wet and dripping traveling dress was revealing a very shapely figure. His lordship, ashamed at his interest in Lady Isabelle's figure, forced himself to concentrate on his task of avoiding the many sharp stones that were dangerous obstacles to his stocking-clad feet.

All three of the wet and weary travelers were overjoyed to see a cottage up ahead. It had seemed to Isabelle that they had been walking for miles.

When they arrived at the cottage, Mildred's teeth were chattering and she pounded eagerly on the door. After what seemed like an interminable time, the door opened and a burly young man with tousled sandy hair surveyed them with suspicion. He seemed particularly interested in Biddleton's lack of footgear.

"Don't just stand there gawking, man," cried Biddleton testily. "Let us in before we drown."

The man scowled at the Earl, who started to reply angrily, but was stopped by Isabelle's warning look.

"I am Lady Isabelle Clairemont and this gentleman is the Earl of Biddleton and this is my maid, Mildred. Forgive us for disturbing you, but we have had some difficulties."

Despite Isabelle's bedraggled appearance, the famous Clairemont smile was dazzling and the man at the door softened and ushered them all inside. It felt so good to be out of the pouring rain and Isabelle thanked the man with her usual charm. Lord Biddleton only frowned and looked around the cottage. It was a small but clean place and the fire looked very inviting.

"What is it?" asked a feminine voice and a rather short stout young woman appeared at the man's side.

"These folks be wanting shelter, Maude."

The woman surveyed the newcomers curiously. Despite their rain-soaked appearance, they were obviously quality and Maude was not accustomed to being visited by the gentry.

Lady Isabelle flashed her famous smile again. "As you can see, ma'am," she said, "we have had some very bad luck. The carriage wheel broke and then a footpad came upon us."

"Footpad!" cried the burly man suddenly interested. "It be Black Sam! Were he small and red-headed?"

77

"I think he was indeed," said Isabelle.

"Aye, then it be Sam or I am not Will Potter. Oh, he be a bad one."

"Aye," said his wife, "Black Sam be the cause of much grief in these parts."

"If the fellow is known," said his lordship irritably, "why the devil isn't he arrested?"

"Black Sam be too clever," said Will Potter, and the Earl was more irritated to note that the burly young man seemed to have great respect for a despicable criminal.

Lady Isabelle noticed the Earl's increasing discomfort and thought it best to divert the conversation from talk of the footpad.

"I am sorry to trouble you people, but there is little else we could do but try and find shelter."

Mrs. Potter, who found herself liking Lady Isabelle from the start, ushered them to the fire. "So wet you are, ma'am," cried Mrs. Potter. "Stand nearer the fire."

Isabelle was grateful for the fire's warmth, for her rain-soaked clothes were uncomfortable and she was chilled to the bone.

"The fire feels so good, my lady," said Mildred, trying valiantly to keep her teeth from chattering.

"My poor Millie," said Isabelle, "I do hope you do not catch cold."

"Don't worry about me," replied the faithful Mildred. "It's your ladyship I worry about. You're soaked and in need of dry clothes."

Mrs. Potter could not fail to notice Isabelle's title. "Aye, m'lady," she said. "Both you and your woman be needing dry clothes."

"I'm afraid our boxes are on the carriage, and we have no other clothes. But I pray you do not worry about us."

Isabelle looked over at the silent Earl, who was staring sullenly at the fire but made no move to come closer to it.

"Come, sir," said Isabelle, a trace of a smile appearing on her face. "You too are soaking wet and cold. Do stand nearer."

His lordship hesitated and then moved up to the fire. The cramped area made it necessary for him to get into a

position of unfortunate proximity to Lady Isabelle Clairemont and the Earl felt very uncomfortable.

Isabelle noted the Earl's grim expression and whispered,
"I pray, sir, that you will make the best of this and cease
your scowling."

Biddleton frowned down at her and made no reply and
Isabelle felt that she had never met a more exasperating
man. She moved away from the fire and turned to Mrs. Potter, who was now holding a small sleepy child in her arms.

"And who is this little one?" asked Isabelle.

"My son, Jeremy," said Will Potter with obvious pride.

"A brave looking little fellow," said Isabelle. "I fear our
arrival has disturbed his sleep."

The little boy yawned and looked at her ladyship with
large brown eyes. Isabelle laughed. "Yes, little Jeremy
must wonder what all this commotion is about."

"Aye," said Mrs. Potter. "He heard the voices and he's
always been a curious one." She put the boy down and he
stood and stared up at the visitors.

"It be unwise to stay in wet clothes," said Mrs. Potter.
"Come with me and I'll find something. I know 'twill be
nothing fine or what's fit for a lady, but 'twill be dry."

"You're very kind," said Isabelle. "I should be very
grateful."

Mrs. Potter went over to her husband and whispered a
few words to him and then led the two women into another room. It was a small dark bedroom that contained a
bed and a crib for little Jeremy and an ancient chest of
drawers.

Mrs. Potter opened one of the drawers in the ancient
chest and pulled from it a faded dress. "I know 'tis not
what a lady should wear."

"Nonsense," said Isabelle with a smile, "you are kind to
loan it to me."

Maude Potter pulled another garment from the drawer
and handed it to Mildred who murmured her thanks.

"And I'll get some supper ready," said Mrs. Potter.

"I do hate to intrude upon you like this."

" 'Tis nothing at all, m'lady, though I wish I could
offer more. 'Twill be meager fare for a lady and gentle-

man." Mrs. Potter reached into the drawer again and took out some other garments and then smiled at the two women and left them.

While Lady Isabelle and Mildred were changing their wet clothes, the Earl of Biddleton was silently cursing his fate in front of the fire. Mrs. Potter came back into the room and handed a bundle of clothes to her husband and then vanished into the cottage's tiny kitchen.

Will stared at the bundle of clothes in his hands and shrugged. He then approached the Earl of Biddleton.

"M'lord," he said and his lordship turned around.

"Yes?"

"My wife thought your lordship would have want of some dry clothes." Will looked rather embarrassed and extended the bundle toward the Earl. His lordship took the bundle and stared at it.

" 'Tis my best shirt," explained Will, "worn only to church and my other pants and clean they are. Maude's one for cleaning. And here be my shoes, m'lord. New from the cobbler just last week. 'Tis no good to be without shoes."

"Indeed," said the Earl coldly, embarrassed by this reference to his bootless state. Will appeared quite crestfallen.

Despite his reserved and often arrogant manner, the Earl of Biddleton was not totally insensitive and he felt suddenly ashamed of his ungracious behavior. "I do thank you," he said, "most heartily. Indeed, I shall be most happy to be rid of these wet things."

Will Potter was somewhat heartened by these words but he could not help notice the Earl's distaste for the humble garments.

"Your lordship's own clothes will dry by the fire soon enough," said Will. He then took his son's hand and left the Earl alone.

"I daresay, Millie," laughed Isabelle looking down at the faded dress. "Mrs. Potter and I are not very similar in size. But it is good to be dry."

Mildred tried to hide her dismay at seeing her mistress so humbly clad. " 'Tis not so bad, my lady," said Mildred loyally. "I've always said there's not a dress made that don't look tolerable on my lady."

"Stuff and nonsense. And how do you like your dress?"

Mildred looked at the poor green garment she had just put on. " 'Tis good to be warm again," she said.

"Spoken very diplomatically, Millie. Then let us rejoin our kind hosts again."

They entered the main room of the cottage and Isabelle grinned as she beheld a most ludicrous sight. The haughty Earl of Biddleton stood by the fire clad in the clothes of a yeoman farmer. He wore a rough shirt that had been carefully mended several times and a pair of ill-fitting trousers, like those worn by laboring men.

"My lord," said Isabelle, a mischievous smile on her face, "how different you look." She came up to him and whispered, "You have changed your tailor."

The Earl scowled. "I think levity is misplaced under the circumstances."

Isabelle shook her head. "If you could recognize the humor in the situation, you would be far less miserable."

"Unlike you, my lady," said his lordship, "I do not think everything is one amusing joke. You seem to be enjoying this. Doubtless you think it fun to dress below your station and socialize with your inferiors. I do not."

Isabelle looked astonished. "Good heavens, sir! This is no place for your arrogance. Pray do try and take off your coronet for a time. Indeed, all of us would be less miserable if you would do so."

The Earl seemed startled by this rebuke and before he could reply, Isabelle gave him a disgusted look and walked across the room and sat down on a crude bench beside Mildred.

Mrs. Potter did her best to provide her unexpected and exalted guests with a suitable supper. However, since there was little in the house, she had to make do with some cheese and brown bread and the remains of the midday stew. Isabelle was so hungry by the time supper was ready that she had no complaint with it and praised the stew very highly and attacked the bread and cheese with relish.

His lordship was less enthusiastic and ate silently, directing disapproving glances at Isabelle. He thought she was treating the Potters with excessive courtesy and seemed unconcerned with the impropriety of sitting down to supper with persons of such inferior status.

Isabelle, meanwhile, was angered by Biddleton's manner and found the only way to keep from losing her temper was to ignore him completely. She questioned the Potters about their son and then about their farm. It took little time for Maude Potter to get over her awe of Lady Isabelle and she answered the questions eagerly.

Lord Biddleton, despite his distaste for sitting at a table with such persons as the Potters and Mildred, had found Maude Potter's stew palatable and felt much better after eating. When the meal was completed, Mr. Potter ushered the guests back to the fireplace while Mrs. Potter, assisted by Mildred, cleaned up. Lord Biddleton had glumly followed his host from the kitchen and had sat down near the fire. He sat there staring at the flames.

Lady Isabelle glanced about the room looking for a place to sit. "You'd best sit by the fire, m'lady," said Will Potter. Isabelle hesitated for a moment, but then sat down beside the Earl. He said nothing and seemed to be doing his best to ignore her presence.

The rain continued to beat down upon the cottage roof and Will Potter shook his head. " 'Twill be bad for us if this rain don't stop," he said. "I fear for the crops as is and if it don't stop there will be no crops at all."

"Surely it must stop sometime soon," said Isabelle.

"I pray so, m'lady," said Will, "but could be like in seventy-five when these parts was flooded. Sore bad it was, so they say."

"Aye," said Mrs. Potter, who had by now finished her washing up and joined her guests. "Many a story they tell about the flood. But 'tis not as bad as that."

Will looked grim. "Nay, 'tis not so bad."

Lady Isabelle was finding the discussion of the flood to be a most unpleasant topic. She thought suddenly of Jock, her groom.

"I do hope no harm has come to Jock, my man, who was driving the carriage. He left us to summon help."

Lord Biddleton, who had been staring at the fire, turned and looked at Isabelle.

"No need to worry about the fellow," he said.

Isabelle was surprised at his encouraging words. "Do you think so?"

"I've never met anyone more capable of looking out for himself than he is. Don't doubt that he is sitting in some inn at this moment."

Isabelle looked at the Earl. She was slightly puzzled at his change in tone, but she was grateful for his words of encouragement.

Little Jeremy, who was sitting on his father's lap, had been fascinated by the visitors. However, the hour was growing late and the four-year-old boy finally rested his head against his father and fell asleep.

Isabelle smiled. "It seems as though young Jeremy has gone to sleep."

"Aye, m'lady," said Will, smiling fondly at his son.

Mrs. Potter looked from her son to her husband and then at Isabelle and Biddleton. " 'Tis getting late," she said and then hesitated as if unsure of what to say next. "I know m'lady and m'lord and Mildred, too, must all be sore weary and though this be a humble place, we can offer you a poor bed. I thought that your lordship and your ladyship could take our bed."

At these words the Earl looked quite horrified. "How dare you suggest such a thing!"

The Potters were quite astonished at the Earl's reaction. " 'Tis clean, I swear," said Will defensively. "You and your wife will have no complaint of that."

Isabelle looked from Will to Biddleton and burst into laughter. "Oh, dear," she said, "I fear there is a misunderstanding." She laughed again at the look on his lordship's face. "Pray do not be offended. You see, Lord Biddleton's sense of propriety is easily shocked. We are not husband and wife. Indeed, we are scarcely acquainted."

"Oh, no!" cried Maude Potter. "But we thought you and his lordship . . . Oh, I am sorry."

Isabelle looked at the Earl again and was even more amused by his grim expression. "Do not look so serious, sir. I know the thought of being married to me would be very upsetting, but indeed, my lord, the thought of being Countess of Biddleton is rather unnerving, too. I expect we must count ourselves fortunate that the Potters are mistaken."

"I did not . . ." began his lordship.

"Do not say a word, my lord," said Isabelle with mock seriousness. "I understand your horror at the very idea. You should have seen your face, sir. I must say I was not very flattered." She broke into laughter again.

"I'm glad you find things so amusing," said the Earl testily. "A lady of greater sensibility would have been shocked."

"Indeed, sir?" said Isabelle. "It does not take a lady of great sensibility to be shocked at the idea of sharing your bed."

"Lady Isabelle!" He looked at her in amazement and then shook his head, got up from the bench, and retreated across the room. It was a very small room and his lordship could not go far, yet he was anxious to separate himself from the infuriating Lady Isabelle.

Her ladyship smiled and looked at Mrs. Potter, who seemed dismayed by Lord Biddleton's ill temper. "Do not worry," said Isabelle, "Lord Biddleton does not have a sense of humor, you see."

Mrs. Potter leaned toward Isabelle and whispered, "Glad I am that your ladyship is not married to such as his lordship. A proud gentleman he is and though it be not my place to say it, 'twould be a hard lot for any lady to be married to him. Does he have a wife?"

Isabelle smiled and whispered in return, "No, he is a bachelor and I believe that if he had his wish, he would remain so."

Will Potter shook his head. He could not understand a man who would be incensed over the idea of being wed to a woman like Lady Isabelle. He was an odd one, thought Will.

" 'Tis a different case, now," said Mrs. Potter. "Your ladyship and Mildred could take our room then. And his lordship could have the bench by the fire."

Isabelle, who was growing weary sitting on the hard

84

bench, reflected that the Earl of Biddleton would have a most uncomfortable night.

"You are very kind, but where will you sleep?" asked Isabelle.

"Do not worry, m'lady. Maude and me will be quite cozy in the kitchen, won't we?"

"Aye, and we'll bring Jeremy's little bed out here, too."

The sleeping arrangements thus completed, Lady Isabelle and Mildred bade the Potters good night and left. Will Potter pulled Jeremy's small bed into the area between the kitchen and the living room, placed weary Jeremy in it, and then retreated into the kitchen.

Finally alone, Lord Biddleton stood by the fire and reflected on his miserable condition. He silently cursed his fate and then he cursed his sister Lydia for sending him on this ridiculous mission. Finally he cursed Lady Isabelle for being so infuriating. She was enjoying plaguing him, shocking him with outrageous statements, and then turning those enormous blue eyes upon him. God, she was the most exasperating female!

The Earl sat down on the bench and then lay down upon it. "Damn," he muttered. "How am I to sleep on this?" He rose in disgust and settled into a large and uncomfortable chair. He stared into the fire and to his great irritation he could not get the picture of Lady Isabelle Clairemont from his mind. She was probably sleeping soundly by now, he thought, while he was sitting there thinking about her. It was quite abominable.

However, Lady Isabelle was not yet sleeping soundly. Instead, she was lying in the Potters' bed smiling as she remembered the look on Biddleton's face when Maude Potter had offered them the bed. It was too funny, she thought. "How Annie will laugh when I tell her."

Isabelle pulled the blankets up around her neck and concentrated on the sound of the rain. It would seem to slacken for a moment, but then it would come pounding down again with great force. Oddly enough, Lady Isabelle's last thoughts before drifting off to sleep were of the Earl. I hope he can get some rest, she thought, too tired to wonder at her charity and soon fell into an exhausted sleep.

Chapter 8

Somehow the Earl of Biddleton did manage to get some sleep despite the fact that he usually found it impossible to sleep sitting up in a chair. He awoke several times during the night but soon fell back into a restless slumber. At dawn his lordship awoke to notice that the rain had stopped. It seemed strangely quiet and he was relieved. He had seen the ravages of flood and knew that there could be great danger in such low-lying areas.

He suddenly felt very sore and got up and stretched and went over to the window and peered out. The wet grasses glistened in the newly risen sun and a few birds flitted about. Biddleton returned to his chair and closed his eyes again. It was no use. He could not sleep any longer. When he opened his eyes again, he was surprised to see a small nightshirted figure standing in front of him. It was four-year-old Jeremy looking tired and slightly disoriented.

His lordship had little experience with children and felt uncomfortable as Jeremy gazed up at him. "You're up early, are you not?" said the Earl in a soft voice. "You'd best get back to bed."

Jeremy stared at the Earl as if transfixed.

"Or why don't you find your mother?"

Jeremy made no move but continued to stare at the Earl with a sad expression. His lower lip began to quiver and his lordship feared that he would burst into tears.

"Come now, young fellow, Jeremy, is it not? Yes, Jeremy. You're not going to cry, a brave fellow like you?"

Jeremy shook his head.

"Good," said Biddleton. As he said this the rain began to fall again, softly at first and then harder. "Damn," muttered the Earl as it grew dark again. Suddenly there was a flash of lightning and then a crash of thunder and before he knew what was happening, a small form was clutching his knees.

"Come, come," said his lordship, trying to extricate himself from Jeremy's grip. "Don't be afraid. Come here."

The Earl lifted Jeremy into his lap. "Now, don't be afraid. It is only thunder, after all."

Jeremy did not look convinced and buried his head on Biddleton's chest. The Earl could do nothing but pat the boy awkwardly on the back and wish that his old nurse could be there to take the lad. His old nurse. Biddleton smiled a little. His lordship was not given to nostalgic reminiscences, but the thought of his old nurse brought back many pleasant memories. "Yes," he whispered to Jeremy, "if Nurse were here, she'd tell you about thunder. She had many stories to tell."

Jeremy looked up at the Earl with wide eyes. "Stories?" he said.

His lordship was surprised to hear the boy speak. "Yes, of course, many stories."

The little boy was suddenly eager. "So you like stories?" said the Earl, a rare smile crossing his face.

"Aye," said Jeremy.

The Earl stared down at the boy and was somewhat perplexed. He was not a storyteller or a nursemaid. He was the Earl of Biddleton and by some ill luck he was sitting in a peasant's hut with a four-year-old brat sitting upon his knee.

"There was once a very clever fox," began the Earl of Biddleton.

Lady Isabelle was an early riser by nature and when she saw a trace of light coming through the shutters she rose from the bed, careful not to rouse the sleeping Mildred.

The rain was still coming down, a fact that her ladyship noted with concern. At least it was daylight and surely Jock would find them. With this optimistic thought Isabelle left the bedroom and crept silently toward the living room. It was very quiet and perhaps the Potters were still asleep. She thought she heard a voice and decided that the Potters had indeed risen.

When Isabelle looked into the small living room, a look of amazement came to her face. There was the Earl of Biddleton sitting in a chair with little Jeremy Potter in his lap. "And the hound sat down upon his haunches," his lordship was saying, "and shook his head. He was outsmarted, you see, and he knew it. And so the clever fox hid among the briars and he laughed and laughed and that is how the story ends."

" 'Twas a good story," said Jeremy enthusiastically.

"Thank you," replied his lordship.

Isabelle nearly burst into laughter at the look of satisfaction on Biddleton's face. Jeremy looked over and spied Lady Isabelle.

"You could tell another," said Jeremy. "That lady may want to hear it."

"That lady?" The Earl looked over and saw Isabelle, and although he tried to appear nonchalant, he knew his face was turning quite red.

"Good morning to you, my lord," said Isabelle, "and to you, young Jeremy."

"Good morning," said Jeremy. The Earl remained silent.

"So his lordship was telling you a story?"

"Aye, ma'am."

"And a good one?"

"Aye, ma'am, He tells good stories!"

A smile came to Isabelle's face. The Earl lifted Jeremy down from his lap. "I think you had best find your mother now," he said. Jeremy seemed rather reluctant but finally scurried off to the kitchen.

"A very nice little boy," said Lady Isabelle watching him go. She then turned to Biddleton. "You amaze me, sir," she said.

"I?"

"I would never have thought you were fond of children."

"No doubt you think I eat them for breakfast."

Isabelle burst into laughter. "I knew it."

"Knew what?"

"That you do have a sense of humor. Ah, my lord, perhaps there is a very different sort of person hiding beneath that gruff exterior. To think that the great Earl of Biddleton would be telling stories to a child. Everyone would think it quite remarkable."

"And you shall doubtless inform all of society."

Isabelle laughed. "Do not fear. Of course, I am a shameless gossip but I can be persuaded to keep your secret if you will be civil to me and the Potters."

Biddleton frowned as he gazed into Isabelle's blue eyes. "You enjoy mocking me," he said.

Isabelle grew suddenly serious. "I do not. Well, perhaps I do, but it is only because you are so disagreeable to me and to everyone. Though I daresay little Jeremy seems quite impressed with you and it was kind of you to tell him a story. No, I am serious. I think it very kind and though I smile, it is not to mock you. I find your kindness to little Jeremy very sweet and affecting."

"Come now, madam."

"I swear I am serious."

The Earl relaxed slightly. "I know I am not an easy man to get along with."

Isabelle was amazed at this admission.

"I am serious and humorless by nature. You must understand that is how I am."

Isabelle smiled. "And you must understand that I am seldom serious. It is my nature to be frivolous, and so it would be very odd if we did get along with each other. Still, it is refreshing to speak without bickering, is it not?"

Biddleton nodded. "It is indeed."

Her ladyship smiled again and marveled at the amicable conversation they were having. But before it could continue, the Potters entered the room with Jeremy.

"Did he bother your lordship?" said Mrs. Potter. "He's usually such a good boy."

"He did not bother me, Mrs. Potter. He is a very polite young man."

The Potters were amazed at his lordship's civility and Will Potter regarded him curiously.

"The rain continues," said Biddleton to change the subject. "I think some of the roads may wash out."

"Aye," said Will, "and the crops are sure to be lost."

Suddenly there was a furious pounding on the cottage door and Lady Isabelle looked at the Earl in alarm. Maude Potter's face grew pale. "Whatever could it be, Will?" she said.

Will hurried to the door and opened it wide. There stood a very wet and agitated young man.

"Trouble at the sluice," cried the young man. "You're to come, Will."

"What be the problem, Jack?"

"'Tis the river! There's been flooding upriver and there's worry about the gates. We have been working all night, but Bobby Lynch wants every able-bodied man to help. I've got others to fetch, Will, and so I must be off. Hurry now!" With these words the young man turned and was gone.

Through the open door Isabelle could see the rain coming down with increased force and the young man's words filled her with foreboding. She looked over at Biddleton and saw that his face had taken on a grim expression.

"Never did I see Jack Higgins in such a state," said Will Potter taking his coat from a hook near the door. "I'd best hurry."

"Be careful, Will," said Mrs. Potter, her face filled with concern. "'Tis no place for any man to be out in such a storm as this!"

Lord Biddleton rose from his chair. "Wait, Will, I'll go with you," he said.

Will Potter looked surprised. "You, m'lord? 'Twill not be the place for a gentleman."

"Nonsense, man. The boy said every able-bodied man, did he not?"

"Lord Biddleton," said Isabelle. "Is it wise for you to go?"

The Earl paused and looked at her. He was unsure whether the question was prompted by concern for his safety or the lady's opinion that he could do nothing to help. He thought the latter more likely.

"I'm going," he replied curtly in a tone that precluded any further discussion.

"Take my coat then, m'lord," said Will. "I'll wear me old one. Don't be afraid, Maude. We'll soon be back."

Maude Potter nodded and pulled little Jeremy closer to her as the two men left. She looked over at her ladyship. " 'Tis nigh on seven years since last this land flooded, and nigh on thirty since the great flood. Since the new sluice gate and the dam on the Old Carne River was built, we thought there was little to fear."

"I am sure there is no need to worry," said Isabelle, managing to smile in spite of the uneasiness she was feeling.

"I pray so, m'lady. Though never have we had such rain as this. I don't like my Will out in it and it is certainly no place for a gentleman like his lordship."

Isabelle frowned. "His lordship," she said, "is a stubborn man." She looked over and saw Mildred had come into the room and was looking at her mistress with a questioning expression.

"Don't worry, Millie," said her ladyship. "We shall all be fine."

The maid smiled at her mistress but found the relentless pounding of the rain against the cottage roof to be a most unsettling sound.

It was raining so hard that the Earl and Will had some difficulty walking. The sluice and dam were less than a mile from the cottage and they soon arrived, soaking wet and very cold.

There were a number of men there already and they rushed here and there in what seemed in Biddleton's eyes a disorderly and purposeless fashion. His lordship wiped the rain from his face and surveyed the scene.

The river was extremely high and it battered against the sluice gates which his lordship could readily see were of inferior and weakened construction. The men were working to shore up the gate with timbers and earth, but Biddleton could hear the wooden gates creaking from the great burden.

"Good God!" cried the Earl. "Will, who is in charge here?"

"Bobby Lynch be the gatekeeper, m'lord."

"And where is he?"

Will looked around the confused scene. "There, I think, though it be hard to see. Aye, 'tis Bobby in the green coat."

Lynch was shouting directions and pointing and gesticulating wildly. Biddleton rushed over to him. "Lynch," cried the Earl, and the gatekeeper looked up and was surprised to see a stranger.

"Good God, man," cried the Earl, having to shout to be heard above the roaring of the water. "It will never hold! You'd best open the gates."

"Are you daft?" cried the gatekeeper. "Open the gates and Fenwillow be flooded with ten foot a water!"

Will Potter, who had followed his lordship, looked over at the men struggling with the gate.

"It do look bad, Bobby," he said. "If the gates stay closed the Old Carne will overrun its banks. Aye, if this rain don't stop."

"I don't think your gates will hold much longer. Egad, man, this could go at any minute and these men would all be killed!" cried Biddleton.

Lynch looked at the Earl and then at Will Potter. "Who is this fellow, Will?" he said angrily. "I don't think we need strangers at times like this."

"Mind your manners, Bobby. This gentleman is the Earl of Biddleton and guest at my house he is, and I think his lordship is right in what he says."

Bobby Lynch, who had no use for the gentry and even less for the nobility, scowled at Biddleton who despite his simple attire had the bearing of an aristocrat.

" 'Tis no place for such as you," he said. "Now come, Will, there's work to be done."

His lordship looked again at the sluice gates. He had a long-standing interest in such structures, for his estate at Huntbridge-Lee was set in lowlands subject to flooding. The Earl had worked closely with an engineer who had designed a very modern and successful flood-control system.

His knowledge of such things was extensive, but the Earl knew that one did not have to be an expert to realize that things were very wrong at Hanley Sluice. The rain continued to fall and the river hammered against the sluice gates, encouraged by a gusty north wind.

One of the other men hastened over to Lynch. "Bobby," he cried breathlessly, "it won't hold. I know it won't and young Jack Higgins has just come from Wexter and he says the Old Carne has begun to come o'er the banks. We'd all best get to our homes and get the families to St. Peter's Church. 'Tis the only high ground."

Bobby Lynch looked from the breathless man to Will Potter.

"By God, Bobby!" cried Will. "Call the men out and open the gates or we'll not have time to get our families out."

"But Fenwillow. There be forty or so there and they've had no warning."

The Earl studied the gate for a moment. "They'll hold a bit longer, I think. If you can hold them until someone can get to this Fenwillow and get the people out. Will, how long will it take?"

"An hour if we be lucky."

"Then you, Lynch, have most of the men return to their homes and get the people evacuated immediately. Have someone go to Fenwillow and warn them there. Wait with a handful of men for about an hour, then open the gates. If you don't, this whole structure will be torn away and it will be even worse for everyone."

Bobby Lynch knew he was defeated and though the Earl's commanding tone irritated him, he nodded.

"Then I will go to Fenwillow myself," said Will. "Let's hurry back then, for my horse, m'lord."

"Yes, hurry," agreed the Earl striding off quickly.

When they neared the cottage the rain had begun to slacken and it was a little easier to see where they were going. Will Potter did not like the look of the creek that passed under the footbridge near the cottage. The creek that was usually no more than a trickle now reached up to the bottom of the bridge and threatened to go higher. It was moving with surprising rapidity, sweeping a great many twisted branches and pieces of refuse toward the river. Will stopped upon the water-slick bridge. Grasping the hand rail firmly, he paused and looked downstream.

" 'Tis never been so high, m'lord. Never. Soon 'twill be over this bridge. 'Tis hard to see . . . What is that floating?" Will looked curiously into the waters of the creek and leaned against the bridge railing.

Suddenly the aged wood of the handrail snapped and Will Potter found himself plunging headfirst into the swollen creek.

"Good God!" cried the Earl as his companion hit the water with a great splash. Biddleton watched in horror as Will vanished beneath the water.

The Earl did not hesitate but leaped into the water. It was chest high and rushing very swiftly. Biddleton could not see Potter and he flailed about in the water attempting to locate him. He found nothing and, taking a deep breath, plunged into the creek. The water was cold and murky and it was also quite dark, and the Earl could see nothing. He searched the area with his long arms and after what seemed an eternity his hand touched a solid object.

He grasped Potter by the waist and raised him to the surface. He then dragged him laboriously out of the water. Mercifully, the rain had become a gentle drizzle and the Earl pulled Will Potter away from the creek. There was a cut on his head and the man was unconscious.

His lordship was unsure what to do and feared that his companion was dead. He slapped Will's face with a gentle tentative slap and when this brought no response, he pulled Will's arms above his head and then back again.

"Will," he cried. "Come on, man." There was still no response and the Earl looked helplessly at the stricken man. Suddenly there was a slight movement and Will began to cough. "Thank God!" cried Biddleton as Will opened his eyes and continued to cough. It was some time before Will could stop his coughing, for he had swallowed much water.

"Come on, Will," said his lordship, helping him to sit up. "The cottage is not far if you can walk. There's still work to be done!"

He helped Will to his feet, but the man could not stand on his own. He leaned heavily against the Earl and his lordship shook his head. "I can see that this will never do and there's no time to waste."

He grasped Will's arm and then hoisted him onto his shoulder. Will Potter was a big man and although the Earl was quite strong, it was a rather difficult maneuver. Still, he was able to carry Will to the cottage door and once there, kicked the door open.

Mrs. Potter and Lady Isabelle jumped as the door was suddenly flung open and in stepped the Earl of Biddleton with Will's inert form on his shoulder. Maude Potter let out a shrill cry as she recognized her husband and Mildred, who was playing with little Jeremy, pulled the child to her.

"He will be all right," said his lordship entering the room and hoisting Will down onto the floor near the fire. "He fell into the creek and hurt his head."

"Will," cried Maude, leaning over her husband and taking his cold hand in her own. "Will!"

"No need to holler, woman," he said weakly.

"Yes, he'll be fine, but he's soaked. The fire feels wonderful."

Isabelle regarded Biddleton in amazement. "What on earth happened? My lord, you are as wet as he!"

"The railing on the bridge gave way and Will fell in."

"And you pulled him out?"

"I suppose I did. I didn't really think. I'm not even sure what happened."

"You are soaked through. Come stand by the fire."

His lordship looked at Isabelle curiously, surprised at the concern in her voice. "I'm afraid I cannot stay long, nor can any of us."

Isabelle frowned. "The sluice gates?"

The Earl replied in a low voice. "I do not want to alarm Mrs. Potter. God knows she has enough to worry about, but the situation is grave. You must all get to the church. Take what food there is and use the cart. I saw it outside. I think the road will be passable for a little while longer. You must hurry."

"And you, my lord, must put on dry clothes. Your own are dry now."

Biddleton smiled. "I fear there would be little purpose in that, for I will only get wet again. I must go to Fenwillow and right away. There is not a minute to spare."

"But . . ."

"No, my lady, I must. And you must get yourself and your woman and the Potters to the church and quickly." The Earl turned to Mrs. Potter. "Please do as Lady Isabelle says and tell me how to get to Fenwillow."

Maude Potter looked puzzled but answered without question. "Down the road south one mile and then go right at the crossroads and then two miles more."

"How many horses do you have?"

"Two."

"Good. I'll take one and you'll need the other. Tell Will I've gone to Fenwillow and will see you all at the church." With these words he began to rush out.

"Wait, my lord."

"Lady Isabelle?"

"I wanted to say . . ." Isabelle paused. "Be very careful."

Biddleton was slightly disconcerted by the expression of admiration in the lovely blue eyes. He smiled slightly and made his way into the storm.

Will Potter was in no condition to object when he found the Earl had gone and directed Lady Isabelle to see the family got off to the church.

"His lordship is a man accustomed to giving orders,"

said Isabelle, "and though I am not accustomed to obeying them, I find it wise to do so in this case. Now we must hurry and make ready. Mrs. Potter, you must get everything ready to go and Millie and I will see to the cart."

"You, m'lady?"

"Yes, though I'm counting on Millie to know what to do."

"I do, my lady," said Mildred, happy to be useful. "I've hitched many a pony to a cart."

Fortunately, this proved to be the case, for Millie's rural upbringing in a house full of girls with no brothers to do the masculine chores had given her great facility in handling ponies and carts. The horse was soon hitched and ready to go. The rain had now stopped and Isabelle prayed that it would not begin again. However, the sky was still filled with ominous gray clouds.

Everyone got into the cart, and although there was little room to spare, they were not uncomfortable. Mildred took the reins and they were off. Although the road was very bad, they reached the church without incident.

St. Peter's Church was an old and venerable edifice and the pride of the community. By the time Lady Isabelle and her companions arrived at the church, it had grown very dark again and she was in no mood to appreciate the magnificent gothic architecture and the great bell tower that was the pride of St. Peter's.

The bells were pealing, as they arrived, in warning of the impending flood. They called everyone to the safety of the ancient structure and it seemed that all the residents of the area were heeding the call. People were everywhere and there were carts and horses and children and dogs. Everyone was restless and excited. Yet, because there had been no news of calamity or loss of life or property, a merry holiday spirit prevailed and the people greeted each other warmly, exchanging stories of rising waters and flooded land.

The Potters and Lady Isabelle and Mildred entered the church and Isabelle was struck by its great size and the beauty of its interior. It was a masterwork of medieval craftsmanship and Isabelle was much impressed by its high, beamed ceiling and the multitude of carvings to be found inside.

Mildred was more interested in the number of people who were filling the church. She was glad to be in a place of safety and found her spirits rising as she noted the cheery atmosphere.

Will Potter was by now well recovered but for a slight headache and some dizziness, and when they made their way into the nave of the church, a number of people called out greetings.

The Reverend Alexander Fairborough, Vicar of St. Peter's, noted their arrival and wondered who the very attractive blond lady could be. The vicar recognized a lady of quality when he saw one and was quite surprised to see a gentlewoman accompanying one of his less prosperous parishioners.

"Will Potter," said the vicar, hastening to the Potters. "I am so glad you were able to get here. I've been worried about you since you are so close to the river." He turned to Isabelle. "And welcome to you, ma'am. It seems ill fortune has somehow overtaken you. You were traveling, were you not? Ah, this dreadful weather, but then we are safe, so we must thank providence for it. I am Reverend Alexander Fairborough."

Isabelle smiled at the vicar, who was a slight, pleasant-looking man with graying hair and cheerful gray eyes. He looked very much the country parson and seemed especially animated by the disaster.

"I am Lady Isabelle Clairemont and this is my maid, Mildred," said her ladyship shaking the vicar's hand. Mildred curtseyed politely. "The Potters have been very hospitable. I was on my way to my aunt's house and our carriage broke down. My man went to summon help and we had some further trouble from a footpad."

"Oh, dear."

"And then the rain came and we took shelter at the Potters' who have been very kind. The Potters beamed at the praise, for they knew many of their neighbors were listening, and praise from a fine lady was praise indeed.

"You have a lovely church here, sir," said her ladyship.

98

"I do hope there will be room for all those needing shelter."

"Have no fear of that, my lady," said the vicar. "And I insist you come to the vicarage. Mrs. Fairborough will be thrilled to have a lady of your standing as a guest."

Isabelle smiled. She had completely charmed the vicar who was eager to escort her to the vicarage. He knew that his wife would be overjoyed to have a highborn lady at the house, for Mrs. Fairborough was herself the cousin of an impoverished baron and was fond of mentioning her illustrious connections with the nobility. The Reverend knew that his wife would appreciate some diversion, for she was none too fond of having all the residents of the parish taking up even temporary residence at her doorstep.

Before the vicar could spirit his noble prize off to the vicarage, a group of very weary men entered the church. Their arrival caused a good deal of commotion, for it was Bobby Lynch and the men who had remained at the sluice gate.

"Bobby," cried the vicar, "what is the state of the flood gates?"

Mr. Lynch was not accustomed to being the center of attention and he relished this rare moment when all heads were turned in his direction and all waited eagerly for his words. "She's holding," he said, after waiting for the suspense to build to a satisfactory degree. "We held her an hour or so and then opened the gates. I think the flooding upriver will not be so great though that below will be bad. 'Tis Fenwillow that will get the worst of it."

The parishioners seemed relieved, for no one from Fenwillow was among them and they thought that their own cottages and crops may be spared. Bobby Lynch looked around the church and spied Will Potter. "Will," he said, "did you warn the folk at Fenwillow in time?"

All eyes turned to Will. "Nay, not I," he said. " 'Tis his lordship, Lord Biddleton, that went. I was near drowned myself and could not go, and his lordship went, but has not returned."

An ominous silence descended upon the church as Mr.

Lynch shook his head. "The Lord help them that's caught in Fenwillow."

Lady Isabelle looked at the man in horror. Lord Biddleton had gone to warn them there and she thought of him caught in the worst of the flood. Of course, she did not like him, but she felt somehow responsible. And he was, she told herself, terribly courageous.

Reverend Fairborough noted the stricken look on Lady Isabelle's face, and not being well versed in the family trees of the nobility, thought that this Lord Biddleton must be a relation of some kind. "Who is Lord Biddleton?" asked the vicar, looking kindly at Isabelle.

"He's a right one, sir," said Will Potter. "He saved me life. I nearly drowned, I did, and his lordship pulled me out. And he's a smart one, too. He told Bobby here what to do with the gates."

Mr. Lynch looked insulted. "I know me job," he said petulantly.

Isabelle listened to Will's words with great interest and wondered that the Earl, who had been so uncivil to the Potters, now was in Will's eyes a great hero.

"Is he related to you, Lady Isabelle?" asked the vicar.

"No, indeed not," said Isabelle. "I am only slightly acquainted with the Earl. We met upon the road, you might say."

The Reverend Mr. Fairborough was slightly puzzled by this statement, but before he had time to question Isabelle, there were some new arrivals who prompted as much interest as Bobby Lynch.

"Sally Little," cried Mr. Lynch, "Sally Little and some folk from Fenwillow."

Sally Little, who was leading a child by the hand, was eager to tell the tale. "We was spared, sir," she said. "We'd be gone now if the gentleman hadn't warned us. A stranger he was, but a proper gentleman by his way of talking. And he said the sluice gates was going to be opened and we'd best leave everything and come here." Sally's face grew suddenly grave. "We did and it's all gone. All we had though that be little enough, but all of us was saved though and I fear many animals were swept away. No time to get them away."

"We must thank God you escaped with your lives," said the vicar.

"Aye," agreed Sally. " 'Tis a sad thing to lose all we had but—" she looked down at the small child who was clutching her hand "—could have been worse. Me family be safe and all the neighbors at least from the look of it."

"But what of the gentleman who warned you?" asked Isabelle, who had noted with concern that the Earl was not among the new arrivals.

Sally Little frowned. "He asked if there be any other families nearby not in the village. I told him just the Weavers and he rode off. I don't know what became of him or the Weavers, for just as we was upon the higher ground, there was a thunderous noise and Harry Miller said it be the gates of Hanley Sluice. From the high point on the hill we could see the water sweeping across the land. A fearful sight it was."

Bobby Lynch shook his head. "Then I don't think there be much chance for the gentleman and the others."

Everyone seemed to share this opinion and Isabelle grew more fearful. If Biddleton were dead, she would feel responsible. It was too horrible to imagine, and she tried to force these thoughts from her mind. She was glad when the vicar changed the subject.

"Only time will tell," he said, "and we must go on here. Everyone must get comfortable as best they can. There will be soup for everyone. Come, find a place to sit." The church was quite spacious and there was room for all the families. Isabelle thanked the Potters and hugged little Jeremy. Then she and Mildred were led from the church across to the vicarage.

The vicarage was a roomy, pleasant place and Lady Isabelle felt guilty knowing the discomfort of the parishioners. Yet she took tea with Mrs. Fairborough to that lady's great delight.

Mrs. Fairborough had shown her ladyship to a very comfortable room where she was able with Mildred's help to make herself presentable. Mrs. Fairborough also loaned

Lady Isabelle an afternoon dress which fit tolerably well and looked quite attractive on her ladyship.

As they sipped their tea, Mrs. Fairborough thought how envious her sister Emma would be when she told her about entertaining a duke's daughter. Mrs. Fairborough knew all about the Duke and Duchess of Fothingham and was acquainted with the Duke's wild reputation. Still, a duke was a duke.

Isabelle engaged in small talk with Mrs. Fairborough, but found herself thinking only of the people in the church and, of course, Lord Biddleton. Many of the people had lost their meager possessions and Biddleton, Isabelle shuddered at the thought, may have lost his life. These thoughts made small talk difficult and after tea Isabelle begged her hostess to excuse her. She felt very tired and needed some time to rest, and Mrs. Fairborough insisted she retire to her room and take a nap.

However, Lady Isabelle soon found that it was impossible to get any rest with the thought of Lord Biddleton being missing, so she soon returned downstairs and informed Mrs. Fairborough that she wished to go out to the church again and see if the Potters were well and if there was any news of the flood victims.

Mrs. Fairborough, though a vicar's wife, did not enjoy philanthropic endeavors and abhorred the plight of needy people. Therefore she tried to persuade Isabelle to stay put, but when this failed she reluctantly accompanied her ladyship to the church, but retreated hastily at the sight of so many noisy, hungry people.

Lady Isabelle was more accustomed to noisy groups of people and she made her way to the Potters. After seeing that they were fine, she found the vicar and offered her services.

"How kind, my lady," replied the vicar, "but do return to the vicarage. There is little you can do here. We are bringing in some soup and my servants can handle everything."

Isabelle looked at the crowd and then at the vicar. "Perhaps it would be best if you served the soup from this area."

The vicar looked thoughtful. "I think you are right. I shall have them move everything."

"I think it will be much more convenient." Isabelle made some other suggestions that the vicar gratefully accepted. Soon the soup was being dispensed in an orderly fashion.

"Thank you for your assistance," said Reverend Fairborough, much impressed by her ladyship's good sense. "I think everything is well under control now, thanks to your sensible advice. And now, dear lady, please return to the vicarage. You will be far more comfortable there."

Lady Isabelle saw that there was little more she could do and left. The rain had stopped and showed no sign of starting again. The air had cleared and Isabelle was glad that it looked that it had finished for a time. Everything was very wet, and although the ground surrounding the church was higher than most, water was everywhere. The fields beyond the churchyard looked like vast lakes.

Her ladyship stood looking around the grounds. The air was cool and it was very damp. She folded her arms in front of her and looked from the flooded fields to the church and then to the vicarage. She was not so eager to return to Mrs. Fairborough's drawing room, so she walked about the church grounds trying to avoid the mud and puddles as best she could.

It was very quiet now save for the noise coming from the church. After a time Isabelle shrugged. I'd best go in, she thought, but just as she was turning toward the vicarage, she saw something move. Someone or something was coming down the road. She strained her eyes to see. It was a man walking along the flooded road with uneven shaky steps.

As he neared, she thought she could detect something familiar about him. Suddenly a smile came to her ladyship's face. "Biddleton!"

Lady Isabelle felt tremendous relief and was off down the road, oblivious to the puddles and the mud that was splashing on her borrowed dress.

"Biddleton!" she cried again. "It is you!"

The Earl was walking very slowly and stopped when he heard Isabelle's voice. "Lady Isabelle," he said weakly.

When her ladyship got close enough to see the Earl clearly, she gasped in horror. He looked dreadful. He was wet and dirty and he was holding his arm gingerly as if it hurt to move it.

"My lord!" she cried, "You have been injured."

"Lady Isabelle, don't look so horrified. I am well when all is considered."

"Can you make it to the church? I shall run and get some men to help you."

"No, I assure you I need no help."

He took a few more faltering steps and stopped. Lady Isabelle feared he was going to fall over, so she reached out and put her arm around his waist to steady him. The Earl of Biddleton then found himself with his arm around her ladyship's shoulder leaning against her for support. "Lady Isabelle," he said in embarrassment, "forgive me. I'm so dirty, I'm ruining your dress."

"Never mind about that. Lean on me and I'll help you to the church." It was not very far, but even so, Biddleton was leaning very heavily on her, and Lady Isabelle had little chance to think how odd it was that her unusual closeness to the Earl of Biddleton did not seem at all unnatural.

As they neared the church, Biddleton motioned for her to stop. "May I rest a moment? There, let me sit there for a moment. He was pointing to a large white block of marble that was the burial marker for the grave of one of the parish's wealthiest merchants. Isabelle helped Biddleton over to it and he sat down heavily.

"It is only a few more steps," she said, unsure as to the propriety of sitting upon tombstones.

"I would like to rest before I see the others."

Isabelle's relief at seeing the Earl had made her forget their old animosity. "You don't know how relieved I am to see you."

"And why is that?" The Earl rubbed his shoulder and regarded her curiously.

"We thought you were dead."

"And I daresay, I don't see why that should have caused you such concern."

Isabelle was shocked and hurt. "How could you say such a thing? I should not wish such a fate on anyone."

"Even the Earl of Biddleton?"

She looked at him and shook her head. "How could you say that to me? I should have known better than to worry all evening about you."

"Did you?"

"Of course I did. I know we do not get on very well, which I hasten to say is your doing, my lord, for everyone will tell you that I am a very easy person to get along with. Of course, I admit you do bring out the worst in me. But it is absurd to be arguing at such a time. You are hurt and in need of rest. Let us call a truce for now until you are better. We can argue and insult each other as much as we want when you are well."

His lordship smiled in spite of himself. He was tired, hungry, cold, and miserable. Lady Isabelle was being very kind and he was tiresome and insulting. He looked into her face and saw those magnificent blue eyes staring at him with concern. He had been through a dreadful ordeal and throughout it all, he had thought only of those blue eyes. He suddenly felt incredibly tired.

"Truce," he said weakly. "Yes, a truce."

"Good. Now, I must get you to the vicarage, my lord Biddleton. Do stay awake a bit longer. You shall insult me greatly if you fall asleep in my presence. I assure you no one has ever done so, though a few have probably stifled a great many yawns. Come, sir, get up."

With a great deal of difficulty, Isabelle helped the Earl to his feet and somehow was able to get him to the vicarage door.

Mrs. Fairborough could not believe her good fortune in having two noble houseguests at one time. Although the arrival of both Lady Isabelle and the Earl of Biddleton had been somewhat unorthodox and she did think the Earl looked dreadfully common, covered with dirt and dripping wet as he was, he *was* the Earl of Biddleton.

Mrs. Fairborough knew that the Earl was very wealthy and his title was one of the oldest in the kingdom. So what if he had a reputation for being an unsociable bore? He was an earl and a hero besides.

Unfortunately, the illustrious Earl was physically exhausted and had to be carried to bed. Mrs. Fairborough thought distastefully of the mud that had been tracked into the vicarage. Yet, the carpet had cleaned up quite nicely and the Earl also. He looked far more presentable after her husband's manservant had done his work and after the physician had looked at his arm. How fortunate that the wound was not at all serious. Still, it had to be watched.

Lady Isabelle's relief at seeing the Earl of Biddleton was matched only by Will Potter's. That worthy man had been in despair to think that the man who had saved his life was killed doing his own job. In addition to the knowledge that he would not have to feel guilty, he realized that he respected the Earl enormously and was very glad to know he would be well. Will's opinion of his lordship was expressed so fervently to his neighbors that the Earl became quite a hero in the parish, and it became popular for the local people to discuss his exploits and hope that he made a speedy recovery.

The Earl, unaware that his health was a matter of much public discussion, slept throughout the day following the flood. The vicar thanked divine providence that the Earl had been spared, though he had not been able to find out about the Weaver family since his lordship had gone to sleep immediately and was not to be disturbed.

The sun came out that day and the vicar was again grateful. Some of the parishioners were able to return home, though most were less fortunate and had to wait several days until the waters receded.

Isabelle, too, found that she was exhausted and fell asleep immediately and did not awaken until late morning. Mrs. Fairborough had been very eager to provide her with everything she needed and she was quite comfortable.

At luncheon on the day after the flood, Mrs. Fairborough asked Isabelle countless questions about London society. Her ladyship was eager to answer these questions, thinking it little enough to do for someone who was so generous to her. Still, Isabelle could not help but be amused by the way her hostess's eyes would grow wide at the mention of some important personage, and she did her best to supply anecdotes about the Prince Regent, and the royal dukes and all the great ladies of society.

The Reverend Fairborough was not so interested in society. Yet, he found Lady Isabelle's stories very amusing and wondered, too, what it must be like to be part of London's brilliant social scene. Isabelle, of course, was very weary of that social scene, but knew that the Fairboroughs would be shocked to hear her say so. Indeed, she thought she envied them the quiet of the country, though certainly things in St. Peter's parish had been far from quiet.

That afternoon Isabelle visited the flood victims that remained in the church. She tried to speak to all of them and she was surprised to see the Potters were still there. She had heard that by late afternoon those in the northern part of the county had been able to return to their homes.

"Still here then?" she said. "I'm glad to see you again. I don't think I could ever thank you enough for your kindness."

"Good heavens, m'lady," said Maude Potter. "You've thanked us so many times, and no thanks be necessary at all. 'Tis not often we have a fine lady and a gentleman like his lordship at our house. And if his lordship hadn't been there, my Will would not be here today."

"Aye," nodded Will. " 'Tis true and I be wondering if we might say thank you to his lordship and see how he be feeling."

"I don't know how he is, but if you'll come to the vicarage with me, we can see."

The Potters waited dutifully at the vicarage door as Isabelle went in to confer with Reverend Fairborough. That gentleman went up to the Earl's room and returned with word that his lordship would be happy to see the Potters, though the visit must be short. "And," added the vicar, "the Weaver family was spared. Not a life has been lost. We must be very thankful."

The Potters were rather self-conscious entering the vicarage, for Mrs. Fairborough did not encourage such visits. They followed the vicar upstairs and little Jeremy was constantly reminded where he was. Isabelle smiled and followed them too, for she was eager to see how the Earl was doing.

They all entered the room, and her ladyship was glad to see his color was much improved and he looked relaxed. Aside from his arm which seemed to pain him, the Earl of Biddleton looked quite well.

His lordship looked up at his delegation of visitors and smiled slightly. He was not a man accustomed to smiling and it was always with some effort that he did so.

"M'lord," said Will Potter, "I want to be thanking you for saving my life." Will looked rather embarrassed and Mrs. Potter continued.

"We be so very grateful to your lordship."

"I am glad to have been able to help you," said the Earl. "And I owe both of you many thanks and an apology, too, I think."

"Apology?" said Will with a puzzled expression.

"Yes, for I was not the best of houseguests. I realize it."

"Nonsense, m'lord."

"No, I was uncivil and I regret it. You are good people and very kind to Lady Isabelle and me. I do thank you."

The Earl extended his hand and the Potters each shook it. The Potters muttered that they were the ones who must thank him and that it was an honor meeting him and then the vicar ushered them out of the room.

Isabelle hung back and when the others were gone she walked to the Earl's bedside and sat down in a chair beside him.

"That was very nice of you to tell them that. You amaze me, my lord."

The Earl frowned. "You are amazed that I can be civil?"

Isabelle laughed. "I suppose I am, for this is the first time I have seen you be civil. Now don't get angry, we have a truce remember?"

"Yes," said his lordship with a faint smile, "I do recall it."

"And may we extend the truce a little longer?"

His lordship looked suspiciously at her and wondered if she was serious. She saw his hesitation.

"I swear, sir, that you are a most aggravating man. I believe you want us to be forever enemies. What must I do to convince you that I am in earnest? We do not have to be friends. Indeed I do not see that that is a possibility, but a small truce would not be so bad. I swear I shall be on my best behavior and it would be best if we could be civil to each other. After all, this is a vicarage and a poor place for us to be squabbling."

"Perhaps you are right," he said dubiously.

"Then we will continue the truce?"

"Agreed."

"Good. Now you must tell me of your exploits."

"Exploits?"

"You are a hero, you know."

The Earl frowned. Did he detect mockery in those blue eyes?

"Do not be absurd."

"The truce, my lord, and I am being serious. Your modesty prevents you from acknowledging the fact that you are very courageous. Though I knew this already since I remember how you tried to protect me from that dreadful footpad. And don't look at me like that. You were quite gallant and I did appreciate it and I am serious, I assure you."

"You blow these things up out of proportion."

"Do I, my lord? I daresay, it is no small thing to save a man's life, and though you do not count it as much, I do think saving my honor is something too."

"Now it is you, my lady, who is forgetting the truce."

Isabelle laughed. "Your pardon. But do tell me what happened. I do want to know, but if you are too weary, I will go."

"No," he replied a bit too eagerly, for in spite of his steely reserve he was beginning to enjoy the visit. "I am not tired at all. And if you want to hear it, I shall tell you of this adventure. By the gods, I'd call it a nightmare. I am not adventurous by nature and I know you know it, too. I rode to this Fenwillow and had a devil of a time getting there. The poor horse did his share of slipping and sliding, for parts of the road were flooded and it was mud covered and dashed slick. But I finally arrived and went about shouting like some idiot for everyone to leave."

"And they believed you? That's amazing," said Isabelle with a grin.

"Will you be serious?"

"I beg your pardon," said her ladyship with mock contrition.

"They believed me. They'd have been fools not to, for the rain was still coming down and they knew how the river was. So I saw them all off to the north and one woman told me about some family to the south."

"The Weavers."

"I thought I was telling this story."

"Your pardon again, m'lord."

"And so I rode to the south and again had a devil of a time finding the place. These Weavers are a stubborn lot, too, and I couldn't convince them that the danger was serious. And suddenly I heard the rush of the water and I knew I was too late. The sluice gates were open or the dashed thing had not held and the whole area was suddenly inundated by water. I could not imagine how fast it came."

The Earl noted with satisfaction that Lady Isabelle was listening with a very serious expression. "What did you do?"

"The recalcitrant Weaver family and I scurried up atop their cottage. I must say it was most undignified."

He was surprised when Isabelle did not laugh but stared wide-eyed at him. "What ever did you do?"

"The water rose higher and higher and nearly reached the roof. The poor horse was swept away. Good God, I didn't even tell Potter. Odd he didn't ask."

"What then?" said Isabelle, eager to hear how his lordship extricated himself from this dreadful predicament.

"I thought we would all be drowned and the Weavers

had a little boy who kept crying and an elderly uncle who kept praying very loudly and singing some dreadful non-conformist hymns. I don't know what was worse. I expected us all to go to watery graves at any moment and suddenly our salvation arrived, a timely *deus ex machina*."

"What was it?"

"A boat."

"A boat?"

"Yes, it just came floating by and I was able to grab it, though it wasn't easy, and we all got in. There were no oars of course, but we were able to use a couple of flat planks. And we were able to get to higher land. A place called Watlin Marsh or something and the people there were able to get me back north and I walked the rest of the way here. The Weavers stayed at Watlin Marsh, but I had had enough of their company."

"But your arm. How was it hurt?"

The Earl smiled.

"It must be amusing, my lord. How good it is to see you smile though I cannot imagine how hurting your arm can be so funny."

"It is only funny because I came unscathed through the entire ordeal and hurt my arm as I neared St. Peter's Church. There was no gallantry involved in this injury, I regret to say. I was so tired I could hardly walk and it was dark. I slipped and fell on this arm. It was very painful. Don't you think that is amusing?"

Isabelle shook her head. "No, for once I do not. Does it pain you still?"

The Earl looked surprised at her ladyship's reaction.

"It is nothing at all."

"I do not know that. Let me see it."

The Earl raised his eyebrows and smiled again. "Is this proper?"

"Don't be silly, my lord."

He shrugged and pulled the sleeve of his nightshirt up to reveal an arm covered with black and purple bruises. "Hideous, is it not?"

"It must be painful."

"No, not really if I am careful."

"Then be careful and get your rest. I hope I have not tired you."

"I am not an invalid."

"You are hurt though, even if you are too stubborn to admit it. So I will let you rest." She got up to leave and paused at the door.

"This was not so bad, was it?" she said.

"What?"

"The truce." Isabelle smiled and left the room leaving the Earl to wrestle with a variety of conflicting emotions.

Chapter 9

By noon Biddleton was becoming weary of staying in bed. He was feeling quite well aside from his arm which continued to be painful. He got up from the bed and looked out the window of his room. Water was everywhere. Yet the sun was out and its presence lent an optimistic note to the day.

The vicar's manservant had been expecting the Earl to rise and had been waiting for signs of him stirring. He entered the room a bit apprehensively, for as a local village lad, he was not accustomed to serving the nobility.

His lordship had never been one to consider the feelings of servants and usually regarded them with haughty indifference. Yet somehow he felt far more charitable than usual toward the young man who had entered the room and greeted him with uncommon civility.

The young man, surprised at the Earl's demeanor, was eager to be helpful and soon his lordship was bathed and dressed. His own clothes had been retrieved from the Potters' house. They had been cleaned and brushed and his lordship felt relieved to be finally wearing his own clothes again. The only unfortunate thing was he had to borrow a coat and pair of boots from the vicar and the boots fit a bit snugly while the coat was decidedly unfashionable.

When Biddleton entered the vicar's drawing room it was

empty and a maidservant informed him that the vicar and Mrs. Fairborough would join him soon.

"And where is Lady Isabelle?" asked his lordship, trying to sound disinterested.

"Her ladyship be at the church."

"The church?"

"Aye m'lord," replied the maid not at all awed at speaking to such a distinguished and noble personage. "Her ladyship be assisting the poor homeless."

"Indeed."

"Aye, her ladyship has taken command, m'lord."

"Taken command?" Biddleton was intrigued.

"Aye, so I heard tell. 'Tis her ladyship who's organized everything at the church. 'Tis at the church she is now, m'lord, supervising the feeding of the poor and hungry."

His lordship suspected that the serving woman was daft but decided to go over to the church and see for himself. He left the vicarage and crossed the churchyard trying to steer clear of numerous puddles.

The church swarmed with activity, but the situation was not at all chaotic, as might be expected. Biddleton spied Lady Isabelle in the front of the nave. She was too busy to notice his presence, talking first to one person and then another. The Reverend Fairborough was standing beside her listening intently. The Earl stared in amazement, for it did appear that frivolous, infuriating Lady Isabelle was taking command.

"Now my good people," called the vicar. "Do listen please. Lady Isabelle has suggested that the women and children form a line here down this aisle. Yes, that's right and the men over there. There will be soup and bread for everyone. Yes, that's right. Women on this side. Very good, very good."

Isabelle was still unaware of Biddleton's presence, for she was engaged in talking to the vicar's cook.

Reverend Fairborough, however, caught sight of the Earl and hurried off to greet him.

"Lord Biddleton. Up and around I see. Good, good. You are looking well."

114

"It seems there are still many victims of the flood, Vicar."

"Dear me. It is a pity but so many cannot yet return to their homes. Mostly those from the western part of the parish. It will be a time before the waters recede, though I am grateful that today's weather is so excellent."

Biddleton nodded. "I am sorry to further inconvenience you with my presence."

"Nonsense, my lord. It's rare I get visited by a man of your consequence. Mrs. Fairborough and myself are honored to have you."

"You are kind, sir." Biddleton looked over at Isabelle again who was still engaged in giving instructions to the vicar's cook. The Reverend followed his gaze.

"Ah, Lady Isabelle. Truly, my lord, she has been a godsend."

The Earl's eyebrows raised slightly.

"Oh, yes, indeed, sir. I must admit that I am not accustomed to this type of thing. Organizing things and telling this one to go here and that one to go there and so on. Lady Isabelle has a remarkable way about her, though I suspect it is breeding, of course. As a lady in a ducal household she has much experience in this type of thing. There are so many servants at those ducal homes, to be sure."

Biddleton was finding it hard to keep his amazement from showing on his face. He was certain that no house was less organized than that of the Duke of Fothingham. Yet there was Lady Isabelle handling the difficult situation with apparent ease.

"Yes, my lord, it was an act of divine providence that led Lady Isabelle here. I should have been lost without her."

The lines of hungry people passed by the vicar's servants and received a bowl of soup and some bread. It was all very orderly and Isabelle seeing things going well looked across the nave. There she spied Biddleton and the vicar.

How well he looks, thought Isabelle, strangely glad of the fact. The vicar waved to her and she said a couple of final words to the cook and crossed the crowded nave to meet them.

"You look well, Lord Biddleton," said Isabelle suddenly conscious of the borrowed and not very flattering dress she was wearing.

"And so do you," he replied.

Isabelle laughed. "Good of you to say so, sir, but I fear I look dreadful."

"Dear lady," cried the vicar, "you could never look dreadful."

"Vicar, such stuff and nonsense! But I do appreciate it. And are you feeling well, my lord?"

"Yes, quite well in fact."

"And your arm?"

"Oh, it is a small thing, of course."

"Vicar," cried another voice, and they all turned to see a young man approach. "Might I speak with you sir?"

"Of course, Allen. Do excuse me."

The vicar left them and Biddleton turned to Isabelle.

"It is my turn to be astonished, Lady Isabelle," he said.

"What do you mean, sir?"

"The Reverend Fairborough has told me that you have saved the day for him and taken charge here and I have seen for myself that it is true."

"And that is so astonishing?"

Biddleton paused and smiled awkwardly. "Yes, for I confess I would not have thought it. Pray don't take offense. The truce is still in effect and I want to maintain it."

Isabelle smiled. "And so do I."

"Good. I think I have been a fool."

"You, my lord?"

"Don't gammon me, ma'am. You believe so, too. I have been an ass and have misjudged you from the beginning."

Isabelle looked up at him. "And I you. But in truth, my lord, do not allow this small example of my good works to so influence you. Do not forget my outrageous behavior and frivolous nature."

The Earl saw the mischievous gleam in the lovely blue eyes and smiled.

"I think I have caught onto you, ma'am. Indeed, it has taken long enough. You must have thought me a gudgeon."

Isabelle laughed. "No, I thought you simply dreadful, which is not nearly so bad as you thought me."

Biddleton laughed and Isabelle grew suddenly serious. "I believe, my lord Biddleton, that that is the first time I have ever heard you laugh."

"I confess I do not do so often."

"You must laugh more, sir; for it becomes you."

Biddleton looked slightly embarrassed. At that moment the vicar returned. "And now, my lady, my lord," he said, "let us return to the vicarage. Mrs. Fairborough has luncheon prepared and I am very hungry."

They returned to the vicarage and upon entering were greeted by the vicar's man, Fenster. " 'Tis the squire," said the valet. "He's here in the parlor with the mistress."

"Indeed?" replied the vicar. "I hardly expected him to appear." Mr. Fairborough looked at the Earl and Lady Isabelle. "He takes little interest in local matters. "But I am sure he will be very honored to meet you both."

Mr. Fairborough ushered his two guests into the parlor where Mrs. Fairborough sat conversing with a handsome gentleman who by his dress and manner was obviously a man of fashion.

Isabelle Clairemont viewed this man of fashion with surprise and dismay, for she recognized him as Sir Francis Neville, a man with whom she was well acquainted and disliked heartily.

"If this ain't amazing," cried the gentleman, leaping to his feet. "It's La Belle Clairemont. Mrs. Fairborough told me you were here, but I daresay I found it hard to believe. But here you are and looking as lovely as ever."

"Sir Francis," said Isabelle coolly and reluctantly extended her hand which Sir Francis kissed with practiced skill.

"So you have met Lady Isabelle, Sir Francis," said the vicar.

"Oh, yes, indeed, Vicar, we are well acquainted," said

Sir Francis with a smile, and the Earl of Biddleton found he had taken an inexplicable dislike to the gentleman.

"I should like to present Sir Francis Neville to you, my lord," said the vicar. "Sir Francis, the Earl of Biddleton."

"Biddleton is it?" said Sir Francis, extending his hand. "We've never met, I don't believe. Mrs. Fairborough has told me all about your adventures here. Gad, sir, you have had quite a time of it. And it's usually the dreariest place. Never a bit of excitement. I dread spending time here myself. The country is the greatest bore especially at this time of year and I'd never have left town if it weren't for some awful business I have to take care of. And I am amazed to see you, Belle, in such a place at the height of the season." Sir Francis took an enameled snuff box from his pocket and took a pinch of snuff with exaggerated elegance and the Earl found his dislike of the man increasing.

"Shall we all sit down then?" said Mr. Fairborough.

"Yes, do sit down everyone," said Mrs. Fairborough, who could scarcely believe her luck in having three titled visitors in her parlor. "Sir Francis has come to see how conditions are. Many of those stricken by the flood are his tenants, of course."

"Yes," said Sir Francis, "and I find this flood business a damned nuisance. The main road to London is quite impassable, you know, and I was planning to return to town. Now I shall have to remain here. A damned nuisance if you'll pardon my language, Vicar."

Lady Isabelle remained silent, for she was trying hard to conceal her distaste for Sir Francis.

She had never liked him. He was one of Charles Fensbrook's circle and his superficial charm masked a character of extraordinary meanness. Not only was Neville a notorious rake and gambler but he delighted in malicious gossip and it was said that he never had a good word to say about anyone. This made him extremely popular with the fashionable set who loved to listen to his chatter. It was also said that one could not claim to be part of the most elite society until Sir Francis Neville had added one's name to his catalogue of stories.

Sir Francis looked from Biddleton to Isabelle and a

slight smile came to his face. Odd that a fellow like Biddleton would be in the company of La Belle Clairemont. He'd heard something about that bandied about at the club but had regarded it as nonsense. Charles will be furious, thought Sir Francis with a wicked little smile. I can't wait to tell him.

"You will be glad to know, Sir Francis," said the vicar interrupting the squire's thoughts, "that some of the land north of the church was not flooded."

"How nice, Vicar, but I daresay the only land I am concerned about is the road to London and it is covered with water and I am quite marooned here. Luckily there is such agreeable company here now."

Isabelle frowned. "Your concern for your tenants is very touching."

Sir Francis laughed. "My dear Isabelle, the plight of the rustics touches me deeply. Indeed I believe I have lost a fortune due to this infernal rain. These country fellows were never very productive at the best of times."

"My dear Sir Francis," protested the vicar, "the men of my parish are good, hardworking men."

"Of course, of course," replied Sir Francis wearily. "That is what they are forever telling me. But let us change the subject. I am so very curious as to why Lady Isabelle and Biddleton are here. I should never be found here myself except that my grandfather had the misfortune to receive this wretched land in payment for a gambling debt. But do tell me, Belle, how you came to be here."

"There is little to tell," said Isabelle. "I was on my way to Winterhaven to visit my aunt and cousin."

"Oh, yes, the Balderstons. How very dutiful you are." Sir Francis smiled his little smile and Isabelle felt an urge to slap his face.

"And I expect that you are off to visit relatives, Biddleton," continued Sir Francis. "Dashed bad luck all this rain."

The Earl made no reply and Sir Francis continued. "I hope you have news from London. I do hate to be away even for the shortest time. One misses so much. A year

119

ago I was gone for a fortnight and missed all the excitement about Lady Haverly."

Lady Isabelle looked at Sir Francis in surprise. "Lady Haverly is one of my dearest friends."

"Of course, and it must have been particularly shocking to her friends when she bolted last year. Left old Haverly without even a note. Took off to Italy with young Alex Canfield, and poor Haverly nearly died of the scandal."

Isabelle saw that Mrs. Fairborough and the vicar were looking quite shocked and she replied angrily. "I don't see why you resurrect such old stories. I thought you prided yourself in spreading only the most current gossip. Pray excuse me. I do not enjoy hearing old stories about one of my closest friends told no doubt for my benefit. Good day, Sir Francis."

Isabelle got up abruptly and walked out of the parlor.

"Oh, dear," said Mrs. Fairborough. "Lady Isabelle is upset. I will go to her. Excuse me, too."

Sir Francis seemed delighted at the result of his story. "Oh, dear, perhaps I should not have mentioned the story, but I just happened to think of it."

The vicar looked at Sir Francis. He was a dreadful man, he thought and yet he was the most important man in his parish and he must be tolerated. Biddleton felt no need to tolerate the man and was about to make an uncivil reply when Fenster entered.

"Sorry, sir," he said, "but there be many at the church in need of you, sir. Mrs. Evans be asking for you."

"Oh, do visit your flock, Parson," said Sir Francis leaning back in his chair, "I shall talk to his lordship here."

The vicar hesitated but finally excused himself and left the Earl alone in the parlor with Sir Francis Neville.

"I hope you didn't really think Isabelle was angry with me," said Neville.

"It did appear so."

"We know each other too well for that." Sir Francis smiled knowingly at the Earl who frowned and had an urge to throttle the insolent fellow. "She's a beauty though ain't she? Damned beautiful woman. Getting a bit on in years now of course. Must be six and twenty if she's a day."

"I hardly think a lady's age should be the topic of conversation between gentlemen."

"Of course. But I only mention it since it is interesting that she's not yet wed. Of course no one is too eager to be tied to the Clairemont line, but it's not that Belle didn't have suitors either. She had 'em by the dozen and to my mind she was dreadfully choosy. Rejected old Lord Redgate for one. And he's got plenty of money though he's a dreadful bore. I daresay a woman like Belle would be better off married to an old bore like Redgate. She'd be able to hoodwink him easily. Her friend, Georgiana Haverly, had a fine old time for quite a while. Now it's too late I fear. Not too many would be willing to wed La Belle. At seventeen or twenty perhaps, but at twenty-six never. The young lady's a bit too, how shall I say it, experienced?"

The Earl of Biddleton was suddenly enraged.

"How dare you, sir!" he cried. "If this were my house I should throw you out."

Sir Francis smiled. "I shall go on my own accord, Biddleton. It was an honor to meet you. Give my best to Lady Isabelle. Good day."

Biddleton glared at him and Neville got up and hurriedly left the room. It's true then, he thought gleefully. Old Bore Biddle and La Belle Clairemont. My God, what a story. He looked as if he would attack me. That will add a marvelous touch. I can't wait to see Fensbrook's face.

Sir Francis left the vicarage and climbed into his awaiting curricle. "Damn this flood," he said, whipping the horses. "But I'll get to town somehow even if I must swim." He laughed. "I can't wait to see Fensbrook's face."

Lord Biddleton shook his head. He had never met a more despicable man than Sir Francis Neville. He rose from his chair and looked out the parlor window to see Sir Francis get into his curricle and drive off oblivious to puddles and pedestrians who happened to be in the way of his fashionable vehicle.

"My lord."

The Earl turned to face Fenster.

"The vicar wondered if you'd see Will Potter. He wants to speak with your lordship."

"Will Potter? Of course. Do have him come in."

Will Potter entered the parlor looking rather ill at ease. He clutched his hat tightly in his hands and stood awkwardly.

"You look troubled, Will," said his lordship. "Is something wrong?"

"Aye, m'lord."

"Not your family?"

"Nay, I thank God 'tis not that."

"Come, Will, sit down here and tell me what is wrong. Sit down, man."

Will sat obediently and nervously fingered his hat.

"The squire was just here, m'lord."

"Sir Francis Neville. I met him."

"You see, m'lord, the squire told us we'd get no help."

"No help."

"In paying the debts, m'lord. We're all in debt. Sore bad in debt, m'lord, what with the bad seasons we've had. And the flood has ruined many of us hereabouts. The squire says he needs to be paid and if we can't pay our rents we'll be evicted and the lands sold. You see, m'lord, I've been on the land all my life and so have we all and our fathers and grandfathers afore us. And we'll have no place to go. There be little work in the city in these times."

"Are you sure you are not mistaken, Will? Surely Sir Francis will not expect any payment from anyone this year."

" 'Tis what he said, m'lord, and the squire be a hard man. You being a gentleman and knowing about such things as a man of property, I thought your lordship might know if there be anything poor folk like us could do. We don't want to leave here."

"Don't worry, Will," said the Earl. "There must be something. I shall look into the matter myself. I am sure that you have enough to worry about as it is. Is the water receding now?"

"Aye, m'lord, though leaving a poor mess behind. 'Twill be weeks to get things back to normal."

"Yes," replied the Earl, "and you must concern yourself with that. I shall discuss your problem with my financial adviser and shall send word to you."

"I should be much obliged, m'lord."

"I cannot promise anything but I shall look into it. And, Will . . ."

"M'lord?"

"I did not tell you that I lost your horse. The poor creature vanished in the flood water. I'm sorry."

"Oh, your lordship has no need to be sorry, for though poor old Red be gone, the folks of Fenwillow be saved. And many here have lost animals and though it be a pity, 'tis not so bad. Maude and me and little Jeremy be well and I thank God for it and 'twill think little of poor Red."

"But nevertheless, Will, I feel responsible for his loss and will repay you. But I pray you will wait for such reparation, for I confess I am without a farthing at this moment thanks to your Black Sam, the blackguard, but you have my word that I shall repay you."

Will Potter looked embarrassed. "Your lordship is very kind."

The Earl, who disliked sentiment of any kind, quickly changed the subject. "So I wish you well then and give my good wishes to Mrs. Potter and little Jeremy."

"I will, m'lord. Good day to your lordship."

Will left and the Earl walked over to the window and gazed thoughtfully out at the church. He had little time for reflection, however, for suddenly a man burst into the room.

"I will see her," he cried and Biddleton turned and directed a puzzled and disapproving gaze at the man whom he recognized immediately as Jock, Lady Isabelle's coachman.

Jock was quickly followed by Fenster who looked sheepishly at the Earl.

"Pardon, m'lord," said Fenster. "This person demanded to see Lady Isabelle and I told him to wait and he refused and came barging in. I could not stop him."

"Aye," said Jock in a loud voice. "There's no one who could stop Jock Cameron when he's worried to distraction about m'lady. Where is she?"

"Calm down, man," said Biddleton sternly. "Your mistress is quite well. You have no need to worry."

Jock looked unconvinced. "It's all right, Fenster," said Biddleton. "Please be so good as to inform her ladyship that Jock is here."

Fenster nodded and left and Jock continued to regard the Earl with a distrustful expression. His lordship was glad when Isabelle arrived, though in Biddleton's opinion that lady expressed far too much happiness in seeing her surly Scotsman.

"Oh, Jock," cried Isabelle rushing to meet him. "I have been so worried. Was it dreadful?"

The Scotsman looked from his mistress to the Earl. "No worse than how your ladyship must have suffered."

Isabelle laughed. "I have not suffered at all. But what happened to you? How did you find me?"

Jock folded his arms in front of him. "I went to find a wheelwright and find one I did though the fellow did nae want tae come. I had to persuade him." Jock grinned and Biddleton lifted his eyebrows at her ladyship, who only smiled.

"And persuade him I did, but the rains began to come and the bridge was washed out minutes before we came upon it."

"Oh, dear," said Isabelle. "I hope no one was hurt."

"No one," said Jock, "though 'twas a problem then how to find your ladyship."

"Poor Jock."

The burly Scot smiled. "I made my way to the next village some ten mile east and then was able to cross and also to obtain a vehicle, though 'tis nae fit for m'lady."

"Then we have a way to get to Winterhaven."

"Aye."

"Good. My aunt must be dreadfully worried. We are quite close actually. Mrs. Fairborough said Winterhaven is but an hour's drive from here."

"Aye."

124

"Then I shall inform Mildred and the Fairboroughs and we shall be off. I daresay the vicar has enough to care for without me."

Lord Biddleton had been listening to Isabelle with great interest. "I doubt that either the Reverend Fairborough or his wife will be eager to hear you are leaving."

Isabelle smiled at the Earl and he felt oddly affected by the famous Clairemont smile.

"And what will you do, sir?" said Isabelle.

"I don't know," replied the Earl. "Perhaps I could hire a horse and return to town."

"You'll not get far traveling south," said Jock unconcerned at interjecting a comment into the conversation of his betters. "The roads south are all flooded."

"Then I shall wait, I suppose."

Isabelle looked thoughtful for a moment.

"Come with us to Winterhaven."

His lordship looked surprised and Isabelle laughed. "It is not far and from there you could get to London by way of the main road through Lippingham. Isn't that right, Jock?"

Jock frowned and replied with some reluctance. "Aye, 'tis a good road and would be open."

"I would not want to impose upon you," began the Earl.

Isabelle smiled again. "Or is it that you do not think we can sustain our truce for so long a time? Indeed it is doubtful."

Biddleton laughed. "You could be right, my lady, though we have been sustaining our truce for, let me see, for nearly half a day I think."

"That is most promising then, sir. Surely we can conceal our loathing for each other for a few more hours."

Biddleton smiled again. "If you are willing to try, ma'am, so am I."

They smiled at each other and Jock regarded them both with bewilderment and great uneasiness.

Mrs. Fairborough was quite upset when she was informed of Lady Isabelle's plans. To lose two highborn

125

guests so suddenly was a severe blow and she did her best to persuade Isabelle to stay. However, her ladyship was quite set upon departure and as soon as the luncheon was finished, Isabelle insisted upon leaving.

"I thank you both so much," said Isabelle. "How grateful I am to you, Mrs. Fairborough, for your kindness and the loan of this dress. And I shall only be at Winterhaven after all. I should like to call upon you if I may."

"My lady," cried Mrs. Fairborough, "I should be so honored if you would."

"And you must come to Winterhaven soon. I shall send word to you."

Mrs. Fairborough was thrilled and thanked Isabelle profusely.

Isabelle, Biddleton, and Mildred got into the vehicle which was a small, old-fashioned carriage and were soon off. Mildred gazed out the carriage window and Isabelle, who sat facing Lord Biddleton, gazed speculatively at that gentleman.

"The Fairboroughs were very nice people," she said.

"Indeed," replied Biddleton, "the vicar was most obliging even to loaning me a pair of boots. I count it as divine providence that the Reverend Mr. Fairborough and I share the same boot size. Well, nearly the same boot size."

"That is remarkably fortunate."

Isabelle looked out the carriage window.

"And it is also fortunate that the weather has cleared up. I pray that the flood waters will soon go down and all those poor people can return to their homes. Do you think they will be able to save any of the crops?"

"Perhaps some," said the Earl, gazing out onto the rain-soaked fields. "Though I'm afraid much of the wheat has been destroyed."

"It's all so dreadful."

"Yes. I know Will Potter is worried. He has some doubts that he shall be able to pay his rent."

"But surely the owner of the land . . ."

"The owner of the land is Sir Francis Neville."

Isabelle frowned. "I pity his tenants." She was silent for

126

a time and Biddleton was reluctant to say anything further about the unpleasant topic of Sir Francis Neville.

Finally Isabelle spoke. "You were probably shocked at what Sir Francis said."

Biddleton shook his head. "I was shocked by the man's lack of sensibility."

"And not by his story about Georgianna Haverly? Confess, my lord, you must have thought it shocking. It was a great scandal and Georgianna is my dearest friend."

"I do not pretend that I am not somewhat shocked at such stories. I confess I am not a sophisticated man, nor am I accustomed to the ways of the smart set."

"Which is why you were so shocked about the idea of your nephew and me."

The Earl of Biddleton looked suddenly distressed. "Lady Isabelle, I had hoped that that matter might be forgotten."

Isabelle was surprised at Biddleton's earnestness. "I'm sorry. We have been getting on so famously. I fear the thought of Francis Neville is enough to ruin my day. I had never dreamed to see him."

"It was an unfortunate coincidence, but I assure you, ma'am, I had ample opportunity to determine the man's stamp." Biddleton paused and smiled slightly. "I have learned to be dubious of gossip. Often times one may hear ill of a person and then discover that one was very much of a fool to believe it."

Isabelle smiled at the Earl and his lordship looked back at her with a look that made Mildred feel slightly confused. The worthy servant thought the Earl's attitude toward her mistress had undergone a remarkable transformation. Trying to appear disinterested, Mildred nevertheless listened intently to the conversation.

"I want you to know, sir, that despite all the things that Francis Neville says about her, Georgianna is a good friend and a good woman. I do not excuse what she has done. She did leave her husband. I know it is dreadful, but her situation was intolerable. She did not act out of frivolity or impulsiveness. No indeed. It was out of desperation that she left Haverly and I do not find it right to condemn her."

"Then neither will I do so," said Biddleton. "In any case I could only think well of anyone whom Neville would slander."

Isabelle shook her head. "This will never do at all, my lord."

"What will never do?" replied Biddleton worried that he had somehow given offense.

Isabelle grinned. "The Earl of Biddleton being so agreeable to the infamous Isabelle Clairemont. How will anyone ever know that we are the bitterest of enemies?"

His lordship laughed. "I fear that is a problem. But I am sure that soon enough my disagreeable personality will come to fore and we shall be quarreling energetically."

They both smiled at each other and Mildred, despite her attempts to appear oblivious to the conversation, regarded them both thoughtfully.

Chapter 10

"We are nearly there," said Isabelle looking out the carriage window. "This is Winterhaven."

Biddleton looked surprised. Never had an hour passed so swiftly. Although it made him rather uncomfortable to realize it, the Earl of Biddleton was finding the company of Lady Isabelle Clairemont extremely enjoyable. Biddleton frowned as he thought suddenly of Eudoria Waxwood. Egad, he thought, I have not given one thought to her until now.

"There it is," said Isabelle, intent on their arrival. "Isn't it a lovely house?"

The Earl swept his thoughts of Eudoria aside. "Magnificent," he said eying the house with appreciation.

Winterhaven, the home of the baronets of Balderston, had been built during Queen Anne's time. It was a splendid example of the architecture of that period, its graceful lines expressing a tranquil beauty well suited to its wooded setting.

The carriage soon came to a stop and a liveried footman hurried to open the door.

Following close behind was a very young gentleman who broke into a delighted grin as Isabelle stepped down from the carriage.

"Belle," cried the young gentleman whose tendency toward corpulence did not prevent him from rushing

129

quickly to her ladyship and enfolding her in a hearty embrace.

"Hector," cried Isabelle. "how glad I am to see you."

"By all the gods, cousin," cried the young gentleman. "We were so worried about you. Why, this abominable weather and all these tales of bridges out and floods and other such stuff. By the faith it's good to see you, Belle."

The young gentleman seemed nearly overcome with emotion and hugged Isabelle a second time. Her ladyship laughed. "Hector," she said extricating herself from his embrace, "you must meet someone."

Hector looked puzzled.

"Yes, I am not alone." By this time the Earl had alighted from the carriage and was looking expectantly at Isabelle.

"Here he is. Lord Biddleton, may I present my cousin Hector. Sir Hector Balderston, may I present the Earl of Biddleton."

The gentlemen nodded to each other and shook hands.

"How do, my lord," said Hector. "Didn't know Belle was bringing anyone, but I'm dashed glad to meet you. We're always eager for company."

"You are very kind sir," said Biddleton, "but I do not intend to trouble you for long. I must get back to London as soon as possible."

"Nonsense, sir," said the young baronet. "I won't hear of it. By the great muse, I don't know of a guest coming to Winterhaven and rushing off."

Isabelle laughed. "That's true, my lord. I daresay most of the guests stay at least a month. Some for years, but do not fear, I shall help you to escape to London."

"Really, sir," said Sir Hector, "Belle is the greatest tease. But let us all go in, for Mother will be so relieved to see you and eager to meet you. And I see you have brought Mildred. How do, Millie! Mrs. Doig will be glad to see you, I know." Mildred curtseyed and smiled. The young baronet was always the most considerate of gentleman and although Mildred always approached a visit to Winterhaven with trepidation, she was genuinely fond of its young master.

"Then let us go in," continued Sir Hector. "Oh, Belle, such anguish we have suffered waiting for you. May the gods be praised," he cried and taking his cousin's arm he led them all into the house.

Upon entering the stately manor house, Sir Hector Balderston shouted loudly, "Mother, it's Belle! Mother!"

The Earl, who was not accustomed to gentlemen shouting in such a manner, regarded the baronet with a curious look that Isabelle did not fail to notice. "Mother," called Hector again and then turned to Isabelle.

"Damned if I know where she is," said Sir Hector. "Hemphill!" This cry brought quick response as an elderly white-haired servant appeared. "Where's my mother, Hemphill?"

"Her ladyship is at the rehearsal," replied the white-haired man in a soft voice.

"Of course. Go and fetch her this instant, Hemphill, but don't tell her Belle is here."

The servant looked at Isabelle and a smile appeared on his wrinkled face. "How good it is to see your ladyship."

"Thank you, Hemphill," said Isabelle, "how well you look."

"Of course," cried Hector. "Hemphill is always well. Go on, man." Hemphill hurried off and Hector turned to Biddleton. "Eighty-three he is, Hemphill, and spent every one of those years at Winterhaven. Nearly as old as the building. Remarkable, ain't it?"

The Earl nodded and Isabelle found his expression so serious that she nearly burst into laughter.

"Isabelle," said a forceful feminine voice and a very imposing lady entered the room. This lady embraced Isabelle firmly and then kissed her cheek.

"What a joy to see you, my dear. Indeed this is wonderful."

"And I am so glad to be here, aunt."

The imposing lady bore a distinct resemblance to Sir Hector. Both of them were rather stout and both had very prominent chins that seemed to denote a forcefulness of character. Lord Biddleton noted with interest that neither

Sir Hector nor his redoubtable mother bore the slightest resemblance to Lady Isabelle.

"Yes, we worried about you, dear Isabelle," said her ladyship's aunt. "But here you are." Suddenly she noticed Biddleton. "And you have brought someone with you."

"Yes, Aunt. This is the Earl of Biddleton. Lord Biddleton, my aunt, Lady Balderston."

"Biddleton, you say?"

"Yes, ma'am."

"So good to meet you, Biddleton." Lady Balderston extended her hand and took the Earl's in a firm grip. "I believe I met your mother once. Lady Biddleton. She was Lady Edith then. A very charming girl she was. I remember how much I liked her. That was years ago, of course, and so you are Lady Edith's son. A handsome young fellow you are."

Isabelle smiled at Biddleton's expression. "Thank you," he managed to say, but Isabelle could tell that he was unaccustomed to thinking of himself as a handsome young fellow.

"Well, let us all go into the parlor and sit down," said Lady Balderston, ushering them from the entry hall to a very handsome room furnished tastefully in the latest mode.

When they were all seated, Lady Balderston began. "Do tell us, Belle, what kept you. We were worried."

"Dear aunt, there is so much to tell."

"And we want to hear every bit of it," said Sir Hector.

"It is really nothing so exciting except, of course, when we were robbed."

"Robbed," cried Lady Balderston. "Oh, no!"

"Yes, you see I was traveling in the coach and Lord Biddleton came riding up behind us. He was galloping so fast that we thought he was a highwayman. It seems rather silly now, but Jock whipped the horses and we were going so fast and then the wheel broke."

"But the robbery?" said Sir Hector.

"You see, Jock went to get help and Lord Biddleton stayed with us."

"It was all my fault actually," said Biddleton.

132

"We won't go into that, my lord," laughed Isabelle. "But suddenly this dreadful man came upon us and demanded our money."

"Was it Black Sam?" cried Hector.

"Good Lord," said Biddleton. "Does everyone know of the blackguard then? It was, I suspect, Black Sam."

"Oh, that's quite thrilling," said Hector. "I thought of using Black Sam as the subject of an epic poem. He's very famous in these parts, though by all reports he's an ill-mannered boor."

Biddleton was beginning to feel some irritation. "Ill mannered? Indeed, sir, the fellow should be hanged. He's a damned felon."

"His lordship saved me from him," said Isabelle, a trace of a smile on her lips.

"Lady Isabelle," began the Earl.

"No, you did, sir."

"I did very little and was soundly thrashed by this Black Sam for my pains."

"The devil!" cried Sir Hector, who was relishing every detail of the tale.

"And then we were left without any money and if that were not bad enough, it began to rain and we were soaked and took shelter at a small cottage. But then there was the flood."

"Oh, dear," cried Lady Balderston.

"But we came through unscathed except for Lord Biddleton who injured his arm saving the people of Fenwillow as well as Will Potter. His lordship is quite a hero."

The Earl looked embarrassed. "Lady Isabelle is exaggerating."

"I do not do you enough credit, sir," said Isabelle. "You are too modest." She turned to her aunt and cousin and continued. "There was a flood, you see."

"Yes, we've had much rain here, but we've heard of the disasters to the south," said Lady Balderston.

"It was Lord Biddleton who warned the people of Fenwillow of the impending flood. And he saved one of the farmers, Will Potter. Pulled him from the raging river."

"Lady Isabelle," cried Biddleton, "pray do not exaggerate so! It was hardly a raging river."

Isabelle laughed. "It was a creek then, but I saw it, sir, and it was a swollen treacherous sort of creek."

"You were very heroic, Biddleton," said Lady Balderston, much impressed. "You are to be commended."

"Really, it was nothing."

"Don't sound like nothing to me," said Hector. "Sounds dashed heroic. But tell me more of Black Sam."

Biddleton frowned. He did not wish to discuss the matter any further and to make matters worse he was beginning to feel a slight dizziness. "Forgive me," he said, "I do not wish to discuss it any further."

"Do not plague the man, Hector," said Lady Balderston sternly. "I do not think it fitting to discuss this murderous rogue as if he were some sort of romantic hero. Indeed I shall summon Jennings and have him ride to the village and report this to the constable."

Biddleton smiled weakly at his hostess, for he suddenly felt quite ill. His lordship was of hearty constitution and was seldom bothered by sickness of any kind, yet the dizziness persisted.

Isabelle, who had been watching Biddleton, noticed that he had grown pale. "My lord," she said, "are you unwell? You look very pale."

"A slight dizziness," replied Biddleton. "It will pass."

"Heavens, man," cried Lady Balderston. "You do not look well at all. We must get you to bed."

The Earl looked startled. "I am not so ill as that, I assure you. I did not intend to burden you and I am sure that I will feel better after a while. I intend to return to town this afternoon if you would be so good as to loan me a horse."

"Good God, my lord," said Hector. "You're as pale as a frog's belly. Pardon my language, cousin. We'll not even consider your leaving."

"No, indeed," said Lady Balderston. "You will go to bed this very minute and we shall bring you some of Mrs. Doig's soup. That will put you to rights. Hemphill!"

The elderly servant appeared.

"Fetch Harry and Paul to assist his lordship up to his room. The one that's been readied. Hurry now."

"Lady Balderston," protested the Earl, "I do not . . ."

"I will not hear another word. I shall not have my guests dying at my doorstep. It ain't sociable. Ah, here's Harry and Paul."

Two strapping country youths entered the room and approached the Earl.

"No, I assure you," cried Biddleton, but by now he was feeling even worse and was in no condition to protest further.

"You may as well give in, my lord," said Isabelle. "You must rest. You do look very ill. I fear it must be the result of too much exertion and your experiences with the flood waters. Pray do not argue."

Biddleton looked at Isabelle and saw the genuine concern in her face. "I see I am outnumbered and must submit." Before he could say another word the two rustic youths had him firmly by each arm, and before he knew it he was dressed in one of Hector Balderston's nightshirts and helped into a large and comfortable bed. Barely had his head touched the pillow before he was fast asleep.

After the Earl of Biddleton had been taken to his sickbed, Isabelle and her aunt and cousin resumed conversation.

"It came upon him very suddenly," said Isabelle with a worried look. "He seemed to be quite well this morning though he had been through quite an ordeal with the flood. Do you think it is serious?"

"We shall fetch Dr. Renfrew as soon as possible. Perhaps Biddleton is only suffering from exhaustion. He looked quite tired." Lady Balderston looked at her niece. "You look well enough, Belle, though that gown does not become you."

Isabelle laughed. "I borrowed this from Mrs. Fairborough."

"And who, pray, is Mrs. Fairborough?"

"Wife of the vicar of St. Peter's Church."

"Oh, yes, I believe I've heard our own Reverend Woodbury mention Vicar Fairborough."

"We stayed at the vicarage after the flood."

"Floods and highwaymen," said Sir Hector, "such an exciting time you've had. I'm not sure what to make of your Earl though."

"He is not my Earl."

"Well, you did bring him, didn't you, cousin? He seems a bit stuffy, don't you know, though perhaps it was on account of his illness. But if you like him, we shall endeavor to like him too."

"Indeed," added Lady Balderston. "We shall like him for your sake."

"Good heavens," cried Isabelle, "you may like or dislike him without thought of offense to me. I scarcely know him. In fact when first I met his lordship, I formed a distinct aversion to him and he for me. I thought him the most dreadfully arrogant and self-righteous man."

"And now?" said Lady Balderston.

"And now I'm not sure what to think. We were getting along quite well. It was astonishing actually."

"That is good to hear," said Isabelle's aunt. "I have the feeling he's the steady sort that would make a good husband."

"Not for Belle," cried Hector. "Not at all her type."

Isabelle burst into laughter. "This is nonsense and I would hate to see Lord Biddleton's expression if he heard you two. Although we are no longer enemies, I suspect the Earl still thinks me something of a frivolous miss. And besides that, I am far beyond the hope of matrimony. And yet another matter, I believe his lordship is engaged to another."

"Then it ain't right for him to be running after you," said Hector gruffly.

"He is not! Oh, don't be silly, Hector."

Hector began to make a reply to this but was interrupted by the appearance of a most unusual-looking gentleman.

Lady Isabelle was accustomed to meeting peculiar people when she visited Winterhaven, yet she was not prepared for the remarkable appearance of the gentleman who entered the room. He was exceedingly short and very thin and he was dressed in an extravagant satin coat and knee breeches. The gentleman's clothes were of the style popular some twenty years ago in France and he wore an elaborate powdered wig that had not been fashionable for many years. Isabelle thought he looked as if he belonged to a different era and she was reminded of a portrait of her father, painted when the Duke was a young man of twenty, that hung at Fothingham.

The newcomer entered the room with a graceful air, delicately waving a lace handkerchief. His countenance was that of a man between fifty and sixty years of age and his face was heavily rouged and powdered, giving him the look of a theatrical performer. He was indeed an unusual-looking gentleman, yet his brown eyes and merry smile bespoke a charming and good-natured personality.

"Ah, monsieur," said Hector rising from his chair. "You must meet my cousin."

"It should be an honor," replied the newcomer in a pleasant voice with a strong French accent.

"Lady Isabelle Clairemont, I should like to present the Comte d'Aubusson. *Monsieur le Comte*, my cousin Lady Isabelle."

Isabelle extended her hand and the *comte* took it, and bowing low, kissed it with great elegance.

"I am so completely charmed, Milady Isabelle," said the Comte d'Aubusson.

"But I should know my charming hostess would have a very charming and beautiful niece."

Lady Balderston laughed. "Such flummery, monsieur, but how dearly I love it."

"It is very good to meet you, monsieur," said Isabelle, liking the French nobleman in spite of his odd attire.

"Your aunt has said much good about you, though I am unprepared for such beauty."

Isabelle laughed. "I fear I feel rather disheveled at the moment. I have just arrived and am in an unfortunate state. All of our boxes were left in the other carriage. I have no luggage at all. This is my only dress and I have borrowed it."

"Well, we shall have to arrange to get the other carriage," said her aunt. "I'll have Paul attend to it."

"I think my Jock might do better, ma'am."

"Surely. But in the meantime we had best find you other clothes. Oh, dear, I fear it is not quite possible for you to wear mine."

"If I may be so bold," interjected the *comte*, "perhaps Madame la Comtesse is more like milady in height."

"Indeed," said Lady Balderston.

"And I am certain my wife will have some gowns she could lend Milady Isabelle."

"How kind, monsieur," said Lady Balderston. "Come, Belle, let us be off to find madame. She is in the orangery, is she not?"

The *comte* nodded.

"Excuse us, gentlemen."

Before Belle could make a comment, her aunt had her arm in a firm grip and was leading her forcefully away.

Lord Biddleton awoke feeling much better, though still a bit dizzy. He opened his eyes and looked about the room, unsure at first where he was.

"Good God!" exclaimed his lordship, suddenly catching sight of a heavy inert object positioned on the bed near his feet.

At his lordship's exclamation the object came to life. It moved slightly, regarding the Earl with small bloodshot eyes, and yawned. His lordship, who did not count love of animals among his characteristics, recoiled in horror.

It was a dog but a more grim-visaged creature could not be imagined. Its face was flattened horribly and its lower jaw jutted out giving it a most forbidding aspect. Its forehead was wrinkled with folds of hairy flesh and it had a thick muscular body covered with short hair of a brown brindled color.

"Good God," repeated the Earl envisioning the creature at his throat and uncertain what to do. He lay motionless continuing to regard the creature with horror.

"Orpheus!" cried a voice from the doorway and the Earl looked up in relief to see Lady Isabelle Clairemont.

"There you are! You must not disturb his lordship!" Isabelle entered the room and grabbed the dog's collar. "I'm so sorry, Lord Biddleton. Orpheus is accustomed to sleeping in this room and is a creature of habit."

"I only hope his habits do not include devouring sleeping gentlemen."

Isabelle laughed and looked at Lord Biddleton, surprised at his humorous reply. "I think you look much better, sir. The rest must have helped."

"Oh, I do feel much better, but how long have I slept?"

"Several hours."

"Good God!"

Isabelle laughed. "I was worried but you look so much better. You grew ill so suddenly. I fear it was the result of your strenuous and heroic activities."

"Not that again, I pray you. I do not wish to hear of my heroics ever again." The Earl smiled and Isabelle noted that he looked quite pleasant when he did so and almost handsome.

"As you wish, my lord, I will try but I can't promise that I will remain completely silent on the subject."

Her ladyship tugged upon Orpheus's collar and the dog reluctantly got down from the bed and stared up at Isabelle. "You must find another place to rest, Orpheus. Go find your mistress. Go now."

The dog seemed to think this over for a moment then wagged his stubby tail and sauntered out of the room.

"He is really a sweet dog, though he looks ferocious. Bulldogs are like that, of course. The best-natured dogs they are."

The Earl was relieved to see the good-natured animal leave the room, for its grim, flattened face with its great yellow teeth made him quite uneasy.

"I do not like dogs overmuch," said the Earl, "though it's not the thing for an Englishman to admit it."

Isabelle, who loved dogs, smiled. "I warn you, sir, do not express those sentiments within my aunt's hearing, for she dotes upon Orpheus and the other bulldogs."

"The others?"

"Oh, there are others, sir. There is Eurydice, of course."

"Of course."

"And Argus and Niobe and then the puppies."

"Oh, no."

"Oh, you will love them, my lord. They are lovely sweet things once one gets used to their appearance, of course."

"I'm not so certain I will be able to get accustomed to them. With all due respect to Orpheus and Eurydice and Ulysses or whatever their names are, I have never seen more unfortunate-looking creatures."

Isabelle laughed her usual musical laugh and the Earl smiled again. She looked beautiful, he thought, looking into her blue eyes with their thick blond lashes. Suddenly he noticed the gown she was wearing. He had not seen anyone wear such a dress since he was a child.

The dress was an old-fashioned one of green satin with a great deal of lace decorating a low-cut bodice. The skirt was wide and billowing and though Lady Isabelle looked lovely she looked most unusual.

"Oh, you have noticed my gown," said Lady Isabelle turning around. "Isn't it grand?"

"It is, ma'am, but do not tell me it is the latest thing or I shall be very confused."

"It was the latest thing twenty years ago. And I pray it does not return to fashion for it is rather uncomfortable. But this is one of the gowns belonging to Madame la Comtesse d'Aubusson. You see, my lord, all my boxes were on the carriage and *Madame la Comtesse* was very kind and loaned me this."

"I should think she would have something a bit newer."

Isabelle laughed. "Oh, this gown is not old, sir, simply old-fashioned. The *comtesse* has all her gowns made like this.

"Oh, sir, wait until you meet her and the *comte*. They are the most fascinating people. They were members of the Court of King Louis and fled from France during the revolt. *Madame la Comtesse* refuses to change her gowns, for she sees the new fashions as 'concessions to the rebels.' "

"Good God, and her husband?"

"He too dresses as if he were still attending the late king. It's as if time stopped when they left France. Quite sad really."

"Dashed odd, I'd say," returned his lordship. "But you look very nice, my lady Isabelle. You look like my grandmother."

"Oh!" cried Isabelle in mock indignation. "Though you are on your sick bed you can still insult me!"

Biddleton laughed. "I fear I'm not good at compliments. My grandmother was a very beautiful lady. And you look very beautiful."

"My lord," said Isabelle with a smile, "I do not know what to think of you. We do have a truce, of course, but there is no call for you to be so charming."

The Earl shook his head and smiled. "I, charming? There is no danger of that. I think you know that charm is not one of my characteristics."

"I do not know about that, sir," said Isabelle, "I suspect you do not realize how charming you can be. After all, the Potters thought you were the most wonderful gentleman. Mrs. Potter told me so."

Biddleton laughed. "I was so rude to them at first." He paused. "And I was rude to you, too. I hope you have forgiven me."

"Of course, and I too am in need of your forgiveness."

"Then we are friends?"

"Yes, of course." Isabelle smiled and extended her hand which Biddleton took and pressed warmly.

This amicable scene was interrupted by the appearance of Sir Hector and a man of such excessive stoutness that Isabelle's cousin looked very thin by comparison.

"Belle, is the Earl better then? It would seem so!" Sir Hector gave his cousin a sly wink and she cast a threatening look at him.

"Good to see you looking better, sir. And you'll soon be quite fit, for here is Dr. Renfrew who is devilish clever at the leeching business, eh, Renfrew?"

Dr. Renfrew, who had been nearly winded by the walk up the stairs, was breathing heavily and quite red in the face. He could only manage a nod in reply.

"Renfrew is the best physician hereabouts, studied at Edinburgh or some such place and is one of the best."

Dr. Renfrew smiled gratefully at Sir Hector.

"Good of you to say so, Sir Hector. And now if Lady Isabelle might excuse us, I shall examine the patient."

Lord Biddleton looked dubiously at the physician's rotund form and then at Isabelle, who smiled encouragingly.

"You are in good hands, sir. Dr. Renfrew is well known for his skill."

"You are too kind, my lady," said the corpulent doctor, looking very proud.

The Earl looked still unconvinced but sighed and watched Lady Isabelle leave the room.

Isabelle returned to the parlor to find her aunt.

"Isn't Orpheus looking well?" said Lady Balderston, nodding toward the motionless bulldog who sat in one of her best chairs in the formal sitting room.

Isabelle smiled. "He's looking wonderful as is dear Niobe." Niobe, who bore a remarkable resemblance to Orpheus, turned her brown eyes upon Lady Isabelle and grinned a wide bulldog grin.

"Niobe is looking well. Come here, my darling. Niobe, come to Mama." Niobe stared at her mistress and then got up from the floor where she had been sitting and walked slowly to her mistress, who picked her up and set her on her lap.

Niobe was not the smallest of dogs and Lady Balderston had to exert a good deal of effort to pick her up, but once ensconced in Lady Balderston's ample lap, Niobe looked quite content.

"I think Niobe is getting a trifle large, aunt," suggested Isabelle. "She is a puppy no longer."

"Alas no, but she'll never outgrow my lap." Lady Balderston took a chocolate from a table near the chair and gave it to Niobe, who chomped it greedily, causing Isabelle to understand why the dog was so fat.

"And how is your Earl? Is he better?"

"Good gracious, aunt, Lord Biddleton is not 'my' Earl and he is much better."

"I am glad to hear it. And don't worry, my dear. Renfrew will make him right in no time. But dear Isabelle. We have had no time to talk of your family. Tell me everything. I have not seen any of you for an eternity."

Isabelle was happy to launch into her report of the family. It took quite a long time, for there were so many stories to tell and Lady Balderston had endless questions. Finally the conversation was interrupted by the appearance of Sir Hector and Dr. Renfrew.

"Ah, Hector," said Lady Balderston, "how is Belle's Earl?"

Isabelle wished her aunt would not persist in referring to his lordship in those terms but said nothing as Dr. Renfrew launched into a description of his efforts on the Earl's behalf.

"His lordship is suffering from slight inflammation of the lungs though not serious, I assure you. He is a very stubborn gentleman and refuses to be bled, which is unwise, but there will be no harm in waiting for a while more. He should stay abed for four or five days and then be very careful in his convalescence. In two or three weeks I believe he shall be quite well."

"Good, good," said Lady Balderston. "I am so relieved. How can we thank you Dr. Renfrew? As usual your great skill has saved the day."

Dr. Renfrew bowed as low as his very corpulent frame would allow and smiled, knowing that her ladyship's praise combined with his usual fee would be satisfactory thanks indeed.

The worthy doctor then made his excuses and left.

"So aren't you relieved, Belle, your Earl is going to be well?"

"Hector, I beg you to cease referring to Lord Biddleton as 'my Earl.' I told you I barely know the gentleman."

Sir Hector sighed. "Ah, cousin, you may wish us to believe that but, Mama, when I arrived at the Earl's room with Renfrew, Belle and the Earl were exchanging such looks of devotion. Oh, it was so beautiful. I shall write a poem. Yes, a poem for you two fortunate creatures to be in love."

"Hector!" cried Isabelle. "You are jesting!"

Her cousin looked at her with a peculiar expression and

pressed his plump fingertips together in a thoughtful gesture. "Excuse me, ladies," he said. "I must have pen and paper!" With these words he made a dramatic exit and Isabelle looked at her aunt and shook her head.

"I dearly love my cousin, aunt, but he is acting very strangely. In truth, ma'am, the Earl and I have become friends but that is all."

"My son is a poet," said Lady Balderston, as if no further explanation were necessary, "and is very romantic. He sees things through the eyes of an artist." Isabelle shook her head and got the uncomfortable feeling that Lady Balderston took her son's words very seriously.

"But where are your guests, Aunt Agatha?" said Lady Isabelle to change the subject.

"Oh, the *comte* and the *comtesse* are with the Kingsley-Dunnetts, of course. You have not yet met Mr. and Mrs. Kingsley-Dunnett. They always devote most of the day to their work and cannot be disturbed."

"But you said the *comte* and *comtesse* are with them."

"Yes, but they sit quietly and watch. They say nothing, for that would disturb their creative energies."

Isabelle smiled. "And what pray tell are they creating?"

"An oratorio."

"An oratorio?"

"Yes, and a masterpiece. Mr. Kingsley-Dunnett is a poet. Hector adores him, of course, for he is so brilliant and Mrs. Kingsley-Dunnett writes music. She, too, is brilliant and together they are writing the great masterwork *Paradise Lost*."

"I thought that had already been written."

"Belle! Do not make jokes. Of course *Paradise Lost* was written, but this is an oratorio based on Milton's work. Oh, the parts that are written are breathtaking and you have come at a most fortunate time, for Mrs. Kingsley-Dunnett has said she believes they are near completion of the final portion. Such a monumental work, perhaps the greatest of all musical works. Isn't it thrilling to be here while it is being created?"

Belle nodded with great solemnity. "Indeed, ma'am, I shall be eager to hear portions of this great work."

"And you shall very soon. The Kingsley-Dunnetts usually are most obliging about performing several of the marvelous songs."

"I shall be very eager to hear them," said Isabelle, who knew the caliber of most of her aunt's artistic guests and was not quite ready to place the unfinished oratorio next to Handel's *Messiah*.

"Oh, here are our guests now."

Isabelle looked up to see two ladies and two gentlemen enter the room. She was now acquainted with the *comte* and *comtesse* and was most eager to meet Mr. and Mrs. Kingsley-Dunnett of whom her aunt had spoken so highly.

Mr. Kingsley-Dunnett was a thin man of average height who dressed in a very careless manner. His coat and trousers were loose and ill cut and his neck cloth was tied in a very unfashionable knot around his neck. His thick black hair was long and curly, giving him a wild look that was quite startling. His face was rather thin and slightly wrinkled and though his age was difficult to guess, Isabelle thought he must be at least forty. His most notable feature was a pair of very blue and piercing eyes that looked at everyone with a kind of grim intensity.

Mrs. Kingsley-Dunnett, though far less startling in appearance than her husband, was a most unusual-looking lady. She was exceedingly short, some three inches shorter than Lady Balderston and very thin and therefore looked very tiny beside the other ladies. She had a pale, intelligent-looking face and red hair pulled back into a very severe style. Her dress was very simple though quite respectable looking, and like her husband she had very blue eyes that regarded one with great intensity.

Standing next to Mrs. Kingsley-Dunnett, the Comtesse d'Aubusson looked like a giantess. Though she was a bit shorter than Isabelle, she appeared far taller due to her elaborate hair style that was powdered and adorned with flowers and feathers in the style made popular by Queen Marie Antoinette.

Madame la Comtesse was a very handsome woman who looked far younger than her fifty-three years. She was heavily powdered and rouged and wore a star-shaped

145

patch on her cheek. Her gown was very similar to the one she had lent Isabelle though more elaborate and Lady Isabelle noted that there could be no greater contrast in appearance than that between the Comtesse d'Aubusson and Mrs. Kingsley-Dunnett.

"Here they are at last," cried Lady Balderston, leaping to her feet. "Dear Mr. and Mrs. Kingsley-Dunnett. I am so eager to present my niece, Lady Isabelle Clairemont, to you."

Isabelle found the gaze of Mr. Kingsley-Dunnett rather disconcerting. However, she managed a gracious reply to his polite greeting.

Mrs. Kingsley-Dunnett, a very quiet lady, shook Isabelle's hand and regarded her dress with interest.

"How lovely, Lady Isabelle," she said in a quiet precise voice. "Do you share *Madame la Comtesse*'s sentiments about fashion?"

Isabelle felt rather awkward. "No, I can sympathize with the *comtesse*," she said, smiling at that lady, "but I am dressed in this fashion because my clothes have not yet arrived and *Madame la Comtesse* was kind enough to loan this to me."

"Yes, yes," said the *comtesse* eagerly. "Dear Phoebe, you see the Lady Isabelle had no gown so, yes, I give her mine. So beautiful you look. You must come to Paris and meet the queen after this Bonaparte is removed. You will love Her Majesty. There is no one more charming than Antoinette of France."

Isabelle looked startled for a moment, puzzled that the *comtesse* should speak of the unfortunate Queen Marie Antoinette in the present tense, though she quickly surmised that the *comtesse*'s command of English must be at fault. She managed to smile graciously at the *comtesse*.

"Yes, dear Phoebe," continued the French lady, "poor Lady Isabelle. She tells me of her dreadful experiences with the rascals of the road, highwaymen you would say."

"Oh, Lady Isabelle," cried Mrs. Kingsley-Dunnett, "how vexatious for you!"

"Yes, indeed," said Lady Isabelle. "Though I must be

truthful. Our assailant was a mere footpad, not a highwayman."

"And there is the poor English Milord who is most ill, is he not? A pity," said the *comtesse*.

"Yes," said Lady Balderston, "I have had no opportunity to tell you about all of this, since you were engaged with your work, but Belle brought with her the Earl of Biddleton, who fell ill after their ordeal. But our physician, Dr. Renfrew, is most optimistic about Lord Biddleton's recovery."

"I do not trust physicians," said Mr. Kingsley-Dunnett in a melodious voice. "I myself should attend the stricken gentleman."

"You, sir?" said Lady Isabelle.

Mr. Kingsley-Dunnett turned his steady gaze upon her. "I am chiefly a poet, though I am also greatly interested in the healing powers of nature. If we all led more natural lives, we would none of us have these problems."

"How very true," said Lady Balderston, but Isabelle felt rather uncomfortable as Kingsley-Dunnett continued to stare at her.

"I could do this gentleman much good, I am sure, with some of my herbal medicines," he said.

"Isn't he remarkable?" exclaimed Lady Balderston. "A man of science as well as an artist! Dear Henry is so accomplished."

Lady Isabelle nodded with the others but suddenly wished she were elsewhere because Mr. Kingsley-Dunnett continued to stare at her and Isabelle feared she was blushing. She wished her borrowed gown were not so low cut and tightly corsetted.

Fortunately, a diversion appeared in the form of Sir Hector. The baronet looked triumphant and in great spirits.

"My dear Hector," said Mr. Kingsley-Dunnett, "you look as though you have done something to be proud of."

The baronet smiled. "I should not say that, sir, though I am working on a new poem and it is going splendidly. I am inspired." He looked at his cousin. "Inspired."

"Then we want to hear this poem, Hector," said Mrs. Kingsley-Dunnett.

"Oh, not yet, ma'am. Not quite ready to let anyone see it, but as soon as I am, I will show it to you. I see you have met my cousin, the lovely Isabelle, and she will charm you as she charms everyone. Too bad her Earl isn't able to come down. The Earl of Biddleton is his name and though he is not of an artistic temperament, he can't be so bad if Belle likes him."

The baronet grinned broadly at Belle and all the guests turned and stared at her. Lady Isabelle Clairemont was seldom at a loss for words, but she suddenly experienced a rare awkward moment and managed only to smile at her cousin and hope she was not blushing too much.

Chapter 11

Although Lord Biddleton was not completely well by the next day, he was feeling much better and Lady Isabelle was overjoyed at his quick recovery. She visited him in the morning and found him seated at the desk wearing one of her cousin's dressing gowns.

"My lord," said Isabelle reproachfully, "you should not be about so soon. Dr. Renfrew would not approve."

"I do not care for the opinion of that charlatan, Lady Isabelle," replied the Earl with a smile. "How good of you to visit me."

"Are you writing a letter? I do not want to disturb you. I shall come back later."

"No, do not go. I am finished. It was just a short note to my sister."

"I thought you had already written to her. My aunt said she took a letter you wrote last evening and had it delivered by messenger."

"Did she? I did not want her to take the trouble."

"Town is not so far after all and I'm sure she gave the messenger many other errands to do. He left at dawn and should have arrived at London by now."

The Earl folded his letter and sealed it with wax from the candle on the desk. "There is nothing urgent about this letter. No special messenger is needed at all. Indeed, I

149

need not even have bothered to write since I hope to be on my way back soon."

"I hope you will not depart too hastily."

Biddleton smiled. "I will not. After all, despite this infernal illness which is nearly past, I am enjoying myself."

"You are?" Isabelle looked surprised.

"I do not enjoy being ill, but far better to be ill among such congenial company than at home where Lydia would pester me incessantly."

"But I am pestering you and in time all of us will be. And wait until you meet everyone. I must warn you that my aunt's guests are often unconventional. I might even say eccentric, but they are charming in their way. All except one, but I will say nothing to prejudice you against anyone. You will meet them all soon enough.

"But I do think you must get more rest. I will leave you. Oh, I can take the letter if you wish."

The Earl handed it to her and Isabelle could not help but notice to whom it was addressed.

"Oh, dear," she said, "whatever will Lady Ambrose think when she knows you are here?"

Biddleton broke into a grin. "You know, I believe I am developing a sense of humor. I think the whole thing is very amusing."

Isabelle smiled too. "I suppose it is, but I shall see your letter gets on its way. Now do get some rest, my lord, and I shall see you later."

Isabelle smiled and left the Earl, who watched her go with a disappointed expression and then returned dutifully to bed.

Isabelle spent the rest of the morning with her aunt, who was intent upon discussing Lord Biddleton. Unfortunately, Isabelle did not know enough about the Earl's relatives and fortune to satisfy her aunt and Lady Balderston resolved to find out more information from a neighbor whose hobby was keeping up with London society.

Lady Isabelle and her aunt found themselves alone at luncheon. Sir Hector had closeted himself in his room and had left instructions that on no account should he be disturbed. The Kingsley-Dunnetts were similarly intent upon their project and declined lunch. The *comte* and the *comtesse* likewise declined lunch saying they desired to stay with the Kingsley-Dunnetts. Isabelle thought it all a bit odd, but Lady Balderston explained that the ways of artists were often difficult.

Isabelle spent the afternoon on a solitary ride around the estate, and when she returned to the house she found a stately carriage that bore the crest of the Earl of Biddleton.

"The Earl's valet and a gentleman arrived, m'lady," said the elderly butler.

"They arrived very quickly," commented Isabelle.

"They are with his lordship now," said Hemphill. "They have only just arrived."

Isabelle entered the parlor and found her aunt.

"Aunt Agatha, Hemphill said the carriage arrived with Lord Biddleton's valet and another gentleman."

Lady Balderston nodded. "The gentleman was a Mr. Galbreath. A very quiet man. Biddleton's secretary or something. I'm not sure where to put him if he stays."

"Well, surely there is someplace, aunt, but pray excuse me, I must change my clothes. I fear I'm quite mud-splattered from my ride. I shall return in just a moment."

Isabelle changed quickly and returned to the parlor, where she took up her embroidery and began to discuss family matters with her aunt. After a time two gentlemen appeared at the doorway and Isabelle, expecting to see her cousin, was very surprised to find the Earl of Biddleton completely dressed and looking quite healthy.

"My lord," cried Isabelle. "You should not be up so soon."

"Certainly not, sir," said Lady Balderston sternly. "Dr. Renfrew would be furious."

"I am sure he would be, ma'am," replied Biddleton, "but I feel very well. Perhaps not completely recovered but I could not bear to stay abed any longer. I thought the company of you two ladies would do my health good."

"My lord Biddleton," laughed Isabelle. "You are becoming terribly charming."

Biddleton smiled in return and reflected that indeed he would never have said such things before.

"This is my financial adviser, Mr. Galbreath." Mr. Galbreath bowed to the ladies. "We had a business matter that needed immediate attention, Mr. Galbreath must leave us now."

"Ladies, my lord," said Mr. Galbreath bowing again and taking his leave.

"He's a dashed clever man, Galbreath," said his lordship.

"I pray you sit down, Biddleton," said Aunt Agatha. "I'll not have you dying on me. Do take care of yourself, sir."

The Earl obediently sat down. "Do forgive me for bursting in upon you."

Lady Balderston surveyed his lordship critically. "You look much improved, though a bit pale."

"Your hospitality is greatly appreciated. I know I have been a difficult houseguest."

"You have been ill, sir," replied Lady Balderston, "and under the circumstances a model guest. I am grateful to you for assisting my niece and am honored to have you under my roof."

"You are kind, ma'am."

As he said these words his lordship felt a slight pressure against his trouser leg and was startled to see a brown four-footed creature looking up at him with what appeared to be a ghoulish grin.

"Good Lord!" said the Earl in surprise and Isabelle burst into laughter.

"It's only Orpheus, Lord Biddleton," she said. "He likes you."

Biddleton saw that Lady Balderston was watching him, so he smiled and placed a reluctant hand upon the bulldog. Orpheus looked pleased and turned toward the Earl, lifting a paw to enable his lordship to scratch his stomach.

"Oh, yes, of course," said Biddleton, scratching Orpheus with more enthusiasm than he felt. "A wonderful dog you have here, ma'am."

Lady Balderston was not quite sure if the Earl was sincere, but she saw that Orpheus seemed content and felt that he was a good judge of people.

Two other canine creatures approached. "You have several dogs I see. Lady Isabelle told me you did," said the Earl, continuing to scratch Orpheus and hoping the other heavy-jowled creatures would not want similar treatment.

"I have eight altogether," replied Lady Balderston.

"Eight?"

"Oh, yes. You know Orpheus, of course, and that is Niobe and there," she pointed to a larger white bulldog with brown spots, "is Argus and Eurydice and her puppies are out in the garden."

"How nice," was all the Earl could think to say and Isabelle looked down at her embroidery, trying hard not to laugh.

Finally Orpheus had enough of the Earl's scratching and sniffed and walked away joining the other two dogs. The three of them climbed awkwardly onto the sofa and sat there staring at the Earl.

Biddleton was glad when he heard human voices, and a man and woman entered the room. Isabelle thought she detected a slight rise of his lordship's eyebrows, but he showed no other sign of surprise at the appearance of the Comte d'Aubusson and his lady.

Although he had been somewhat prepared by what Isabelle had said about the *comtesse*'s attitude toward modern fashion, the Earl was startled by her appearance. She was a tall statuesque lady and her dress and hair style took the Earl back to the days of his boyhood.

He rose awkwardly as they approached. The *comte*, he thought, looked like a relic from the past, with his powdered wig, shining blue satin coat, breeches and hose, and high-heeled shoes.

"Lord Biddleton," said Lady Balderston, "I should like you to meet the Comte and Comtesse d'Aubusson."

The *comte* made a magnificent bow and the *comtesse* curtseyed gracefully and Lord Biddleton bowed awkwardly and greeted the *comte* and *comtesse* in French.

"How good to meet you *Madame la Comtesse, Monsieur le Comte*."

Isabelle noted that his lordship's French was excellent, and as he exchanged pleasantries Isabelle could tell that the *comte* and *comtesse* were much impressed with him. The *comtesse* looked from the Earl to Isabelle and smiled approvingly.

They all then sat down and the *comte* switched to English. "I prefer to speak English now that I am here, Lord Biddleton," said the *comte*. "Though one day I will return to France."

"I have heard that Bonaparte is allowing many of the old nobility to return," said the Earl.

"Bonaparte." The *comte* looked disgusted. "That Corsican peasant. Bah! I will not return until he is gone from France."

"*Oui*," said the *comtesse*. "We shall return when Her Majesty the Queen Marie Antoinette is restored to her rightful throne and His Majesty reigns again."

Lord Biddleton tried not to show his surprise but looked over at Isabelle for a clue as to how to react. She caught his look but could only shrug and change the topic of conversation.

"Have you been with the Kingsley-Dunnetts, Madame?"

The *comtesse* nodded. "We do like to watch them. They are so talented. It is so very interesting to be there as they work."

"Oh, yes," said his lordship, "Lady Isabelle has said they are composing music."

"*Oui, monsieur,* but it is a great work, a masterpiece as you would say."

"Indeed?"

"Oh, yes," agreed the *comte*, "Mr. Kingsley-Dunnett is a genius and his wife is a genius, for a woman."

Isabelle smiled at this remark and looked at the Earl who was trying to act interested in the Kingsley-Dunnett's masterpiece.

"But I do think," said Madame la Comtesse suddenly, "that it nears the hour of three o'clock."

"Goodness me," cried Lady Balderston with a look of great agitation, "you are right, madame!"

"Gracious, Aunt Agatha," said Lady Isabelle, "what

does three o'clock signify? Is it some magic hour? Shall we all be turned into pumpkins?"

To her surprise no one laughed and her aunt looked grave.

"It is not only that it is three o'clock, Isabelle, but it is three o'clock and Thursday."

Isabelle was still unenlightened by this statement but waited for her aunt's explanation.

"At three o'clock on Thursday," said Lady Balderston, "the Kingsley-Dunnetts perform portions of the oratorio that have been completed."

"*Oui*," said the Comtesse d'Aubusson, "it is so exciting, no? That we are first to hear the masterpiece. But let us go to the garden."

"The garden?" said Lady Isabelle.

"Of course," replied her aunt, "Mr. Kingsley-Dunnett believes his work is best heard out of doors where he is surrounded by nature."

Isabelle looked over at Lord Biddleton, who was regarding her aunt curiously.

"But Aunt Agatha," she said, "there is a slight chill in the air today and it is quite cloudy. I daresay Lord Biddleton should not go out into the garden."

"Of course not." Lady Balderston looked quite deflated. "The *comte* and *comtesse* must go and we will stay here with our guest."

"I insist you do not stay on my account," said the Earl. "Please go on. I should feel terribly guilty if I knew I upset your plans."

"I don't know," began Lady Balderston, looking from the Earl to the mantel clock with indecision.

"Yes, go, aunt," said Isabelle. "I will stay with his lordship. I can certainly postpone hearing the masterpiece a bit longer."

The *comtesse* looked from Isabelle to the Earl and smiled knowingly. "It is settled then. Come, Jean-Paul and madame. It is soon too late." She rose quickly and the *comte*, who was accustomed to doing as his wife wished, followed, taking the *comtesse*'s arm.

Lady Balderston still hesitated and then as the mantel

clock struck the hour and began to chime she overcame her reluctance to leave her niece alone with the Earl. "All right then. But I do feel quite inhospitable deserting a guest like this."

"I assure you, ma'am, I do not mind."

Lady Balderston nodded and looked over once more at Isabelle and then hurried off.

"I daresay, my lady Isabelle," said the Earl when the others had left, "if you should like to accompany Lady Balderston, do not feel you have to sit here with me."

"My lord Biddleton," said Isabelle with a smile. "I must confess I had no desire to do so. In truth, sir, I am not eager to hear the fabled oratorio, for I have met the Kingsley-Dunnetts, sir."

The Earl smiled. "Then you have not been convinced of their genius?"

"Genius they may have and Mrs. Kingsley-Dunnett is agreeable enough but her husband! Oh, dear." Lady Isabelle made a face and the Earl laughed.

"I see, ma'am, that I am not the only gentleman that you have taken an instant dislike to."

"Lord Biddleton! If I disliked you, and I confess I did when first we were acquainted, it was because of your appalling conduct toward me. And if I recall correctly it was you, sir, who disliked me even before you had met me."

"An injudicious thing to do, disliking persons one has never met."

"I'm glad you think so."

"But I have changed my opinion, I assure you, ma'am. And I hope you have changed yours."

Isabelle smiled. "Changed my opinion?"

"Of me, of course."

"I will say, my lord, that I now find you quite agreeable."

The Earl was slightly taken aback by her ladyship's sincere tone and was disconcerted again by La Belle's famed blue eyes.

"But I am glad your man has come with your things. You do look nearly recovered. Oh, yes, I wanted to tell you that my coach horses have been recovered and the village authorities are watching closely for the ruffian to appear. Unfortunately your horse is still missing."

"Oh, I don't care so much about the horse, Lady Isabelle," said the Earl, "and not overmuch about the money though I am not one to take such losses lightly. But the villain took the Biddleton ring and that I do regret."

"The Biddleton ring?"

"Yes, a ring of great importance to my family. Given to the First Earl by Henry VII and worn by each succeeding Earl and now lost by me. I fear I will never forgive myself for losing it."

"But it was not your fault."

"Perhaps not, but I feel that the six previous Earls are looking down upon me with disgust and shaking their hoary heads. I would have thought that being the Seventh Earl would be lucky."

Isabelle laughed. "Don't tell me you are superstitious?"

"Not really, though as I recall the robbery did occur on the thirteenth of the month."

Isabelle laughed. "Really, sir, you are taking your loss well. I am sorry I did not know the ring's value. Surely it will be restored to you."

"I am not so optimistic, but it is done and as Mr. Galbreath always says, 'Forget the past. Consider only the future.' His advice is very practical. A brilliant man really. A genius at predicting the price of grain. And he's very modern, too. We have made great strides in wheat production at Biddleton Manor. But that is probably a very boring topic."

"Oh, I don't know, sir. I can't remember ever hearing about wheat production."

The Earl smiled. "It is boring. Sometimes it even bores me and I am a man who is known to be a great bore myself."

"Come now, my lord, you do not mean that."

"Oh, yes, I do, for I know what they say of me in town. In fact I fear there are many people in town who are amazed to hear my name is Biddleton, for they are so accustomed to hearing of 'that bore Biddle.' Soon someone will accost me on the street as Lord Borebiddle.

"They call me far worse, I know, and some of it I deserve, for I confess I have never been much for society."

"And society is the worse for that, sir. I have found how charming you can be, my lord. You do not give people enough chance to get to know you, that is all. You must attend more functions and get out more. Why, you have completely charmed the Aubussons. Your French is remarkably good."

"Oh, that is the result of having a French nurse from infancy. The *comte* and *comtesse* are a most interesting couple and very agreeable. But I fear I have not charmed your aunt at all."

"That is only because my aunt is not quite sure what to make of you. Despite my reputation as one of the wild Clairemonts and my aunt, I must mention, is herself a Clairemont, I am not accustomed to bringing gentlemen to Winterhaven every time I visit."

The Earl laughed.

At that moment Hemphill entered the parlor with a letter for Lady Isabelle on a salver. Isabelle took the letter and examined the seal.

"How odd," she said. "A letter from Charles Fensbrook. You know Mr. Fensbrook, of course."

"Yes." The Earl frowned, for he disliked that gentleman intensely though they were only slightly acquainted. Fensbrook embodied every quality the Earl despised. He was lazy, frivolous, and insolent. His morals were reprehensible and the Earl thought him nothing but a fop and a gamester.

Lady Isabelle put the letter aside though she was curious about it, for Charles was not one to write letters, but she was not so eager to read it.

"Would you like to read the letter, Lady Isabelle?" asked his lordship. "I will excuse myself."

"Of course not, sir. Do not think you can escape from visiting with me so easily."

"Lady Isabelle!" The Earl looked horrified. "I didn't mean . . ."

"I was only jesting, sir. Really, I will read it later."

The Earl, who suddenly disliked Mr. Charles Fensbrook more than ever, reflected that Lady Isabelle probably preferred to read Fensbrook's letter in private. She would no doubt cherish every word of the fellow's letter, which would sparkle with wit and charm. Yet, the Earl noted Lady Isabelle was not acting like a woman who had just received a letter from her beloved.

Her ladyship, unaware of the Earl's reflections, asked about his health.

"I feel quite well, ma'am, and should be well enough to return to town shortly."

"I hope you will not be too hasty, sir. Do stay at Winterhaven until you are completely well."

His lordship, thinking suddenly of his sister and Eudoria and looking at lovely Lady Isabelle, felt no urge to return to London.

"But I am sure your family misses you, sir."

"Do not be so sure."

"Lord Biddleton!"

The Earl laughed. "There is just my sister Lydia."

"And Cuthburt," suggested Isabelle.

At the mention of Cuthburt's name the two of them exchanged amused looks. "And Cuthburt is off somewhere as we both know well."

"Yes we do. And is there no one else?"

"Well," said the Earl reluctantly. "There is Eudoria, Miss Waxwood that is."

"Miss Waxwood," repeated Isabelle, having heard the name but not recollecting where she had heard it.

"I am engaged to Miss Waxwood."

"Oh, I did know you were engaged. I think Cuthburt mentioned it, but I did not recall the name of the lady. I believe I have never met Miss Waxwood."

"She is not out much, for her health is not usually good."

"I am so sorry to hear that."

"Yes, it is a pity. But tell me more of the Comte and Comtesse d'Aubusson."

Lady Isabelle was surprised at the abrupt turn of the

conversation and wondered if Miss Waxwood's illness was a subject too painful for the Earl to discuss.

"Oh, they are a fascinating couple," said her ladyship, glad to turn to a less distressing topic, "though in truth, my lord, I am not certain if madame is serious when she speaks of the late queen of France as if she were still living."

"Most odd."

"My aunt has said they fled from France in eighty-nine. Their estates were confiscated but they did manage to escape with the family jewels. Madame was an intimate of the queen and *Monsieur le Comte* was an important man at court. It must be dreadful for them to be away from their country for all these years."

"They seem quite content here at Winterhaven, but I daresay their manner of dress is most unusual. But, Lady Isabelle, tell me of this oratorio that everyone is talking about."

Isabelle laughed. "Do you like Milton, my lord?"

"Milton? As a matter of fact I hold Milton to be one of the greatest of all poets. His work is far superior to the nonsense these modern poets produce nowadays!"

"Heavens, sir, how can you be so enthused about modern agriculture and so antagonistic toward modern poetry? Really, my lord, it does not seem consistent. And pray do not tell my cousin Hector your views, for he is a poet and does not share your sentiments at all. But if you are fond of Milton you will be pleased to know that the Kingsley-Dunnetts have set *Paradise Lost* to music or something of that sort, for the oratorio is based upon it."

"Is it?" replied Lord Biddleton. "It seems a most ambitious and perhaps impertinent idea. I shall be eager to hear this work."

"Let us go and hear it then."

"But I doubt the wisdom of my going out."

A mischievous look appeared on Isabelle's face. "We won't have to go out, my lord. Come follow me." She got up from the chair. The Earl looked puzzled.

"Come on, sir. Follow me."

His lordship got up and did as she said. He followed

Lady Isabelle from the parlor into the hallway and then into a small room with large windows all along one wall.

"This way," said Isabelle in a conspiratorial whisper. "Over here." She moved toward the window and motioned for the Earl to follow. "You see," she whispered, "a perfect view of the garden."

Lord Biddleton looked out and saw the garden with its carefully trimmed shrubs and colorful spring flowers. "A lovely garden," he said in a whisper. Then he paused. "Why are we whispering?"

Isabelle laughed and replied in her regular voice. "Habit, I fear. You see, when I was a girl I used to visit Winterhaven every year and my sister Anne and my brothers and I called this the whispering room. I'm not sure how it got started, but whenever we came in here Burwicke insisted we had to whisper. And we'd all come in here very quietly and watch my aunt and uncle and all the adults in the garden through these windows, and since we were whispering, it was more exciting."

The Earl looked at her strangely and Isabelle laughed. "I know it was silly, but I imagine you did very silly things yourself as a child."

His lordship looked thoughtful. "No, I don't think I did," he said at last.

Isabelle laughed again. "Look, there they are. They are only just coming out. I suppose they were delayed because Mr. Kingsley-Dunnett gave a speech or something of that sort."

They watched as the six people assembled in the garden.

"That, sir, is Mr. Kingsley-Dunnett, the man with the dark hair."

"Odd-looking fellow," said the Earl, studying the gentleman with great interest. "Reminds me of a Latin tutor I once had. A dreadful fellow he was. His name was Baxter and I detested him."

"If he were like Mr. Kingsley-Dunnett, you had good reason, my lord, though I am not being at all charitable. Ah, he is having everyone get quiet now. He is certainly in command. See how important he looks."

They watched with great interest as Mr. Kingsley-Dunnett looked down at a paper in his hand and motioned to his wife who sat down on a stone bench and put the flute she had been carrying to her lips.

Kingsley-Dunnett signaled her again and she began to play.

"I can't hear a thing," said Isabelle. "We must open the window."

"Allow me," said the Earl leaning over her ladyship and pushing open the window. This maneuver put him in a position of dangerous proximity to Lady Isabelle and though his better judgment urged a hasty retreat, the Earl bravely remained at her side and tried to concentrate on the happenings in the garden.

The sound of the flute drifted into the room and its sound was so clear and the melody so lovely that Lady Isabelle labeled Mrs. Kingsley-Dunnett as a most talented musician.

The Earl, standing so close to her ladyship, found himself staring at her soft blond hair that fell in gentle ringlets and noted that Lady Isabelle's perfume was a most delicate and delightful fragrance. The flute's beautiful sound combined with Lady Isabelle's loveliness exerted a strange influence on the Earl and he suddenly felt an almost overpowering urge to take La Belle Clairemont in his arms.

Luckily, the spell was broken when Mr. Kingsley-Dunnett began to sing in a loud tenor voice that was slightly off key. "Oh, dear," whispered Lady Isabelle. "Whatever is he saying? I can't understand the words although he is quite loud. Aunt Agatha seems thrilled, doesn't she?"

Lady Balderston, who was enraptured by Mr. Kingsley-Dunnett's performance, stared at him with great attention. Sir Hector did likewise.

The *comtesse*, who was enjoying the performance, nevertheless found her mind wandering and glanced over toward the house and saw the two figures standing at the window.

She smiled and raised a slender hand to wave at them and Isabelle waved enthusiastically from the window. Kingsley-Dunnett, who caught the *comtesse*'s motion from the corner of his eye, turned for a moment to the window.

"Oh," cried Isabelle as her eyes met Mr. Kingsley-Dunnett's, and though he kept singing heartily, she thought she could detect a change in his expression and suddenly she felt a chill. She managed to nod calmly at him but as he continued to gaze at the window she began to feel most uncomfortable.

Lady Balderston and the rest of the party assembled in the garden followed the direction of Mr. Kingsley-Dunnett's gaze and all saw Isabelle and the tall Earl.

"We are discovered," whispered Isabelle in mock terror.

The Earl laughed. "If you did not want us to be discovered we should have crouched down and peered over the window sill like spies."

Isabelle turned and looked up at him with a broad smile on her face. "Of course, why didn't I think of it?"

She turned back to the window and waved again. "Now, sir, let us return, I would not want to distract Mr. Kingsley-Dunnett any further."

They turned and left the room and Isabelle, though she tried to appear in light spirits, could not get the image of Kingsley-Dunnett's piercing gaze out of her mind.

Chapter 12

While the Earl of Biddleton dressed for dinner, distressing thoughts crossed his mind and he pondered them in grim silence, acknowledging his valet's presence with an absentminded nod whenever that hardworking individual addressed a remark to him.

"Sir Hector's valet is a peculiar man," his valet, Harold, was saying. Harold was a talkative young man, but his master usually silenced him with a look of displeasure. The Earl was not one to encourage servants in idle talk. That evening, however, his lordship seemed so preoccupied that Harold was able to talk as much as he wished. "Of course, his master is a poet which is odd too, but not odd for this household."

The Earl only nodded and Harold was amazed that he had not yet received a stern rebuke in spite of having spoken of his betters. Taking advantage of the situation, Harold prattled on and on and although he knew his master had not heard a thing he said, he received great satisfaction from being able to talk so long without even the slightest reprimand.

His lordship was quite oblivious to his valet, for he was intent upon his own moral dilemma. He was horrified to realize the intensity of his attraction to Lady Isabelle. What was even worse was the realization that in addition to the intense and not unusual attraction a man would feel toward a beautiful woman, he liked Lady Isabelle and enjoyed her company.

His lordship frowned and shook his head. Liked Lady Isabelle? Good God, he thought miserably, I am in love with her.

A sigh escaped the Earl and his valet, Harold, stopped talking for a moment. Never had he seen his master in such a mood, and the valet thought his behavior was very curious indeed.

The Earl sighed again. I am an engaged man, he thought. I am pledged to Eudoria. Eudoria. The thought of his betrothed put him in even worse spirits and he hung his head and had a most doleful expression on his face.

"My lord."

"What?" The Earl looked up suddenly. "You say something, Harold?"

"Yes, my lord. I wanted to say that your lordship is ready now. All finished I am, my lord, and quite fine your lordship looks."

Biddleton scowled at the valet and without a word, Harold bowed and departed. The Earl looked at his reflection in the mirror and frowned. Take hold of yourself, he thought. There is no reason to make a fool of oneself. If Lady Isabelle knew about this, she would laugh. He turned to go. "No," he said, taking a final look in the mirror. "I know her a little better now. She would not laugh." He smiled ruefully and left the room.

Lady Isabelle Clairemont sat at her dressing table thoughtfully studying her reflection while Mildred dressed her hair. It is odd, she though, how different Lord Biddleton is from my original opinion of him. Perhaps he is a bit reserved, but he is not at all the stuffy prig that Charles believes him to be. Charles. Her ladyship suddenly remembered the letter that had arrived from Mr. Fensbrook.

"Mildred."

"M'lady."

"Would you please fetch the letter that is on the bed?"

The maid did so and Lady Isabelle took the letter and broke the seal.

165

"My dear Isabelle," it began, "how dull everything is in town. There is no one of any consequence about at present and the club has become dreary beyond belief."

Isabelle smiled. So, Charles, she thought, it is so dull that you would even write a letter to me. Oh, dear, it must be extremely boring.

Lady Isabelle continued reading. The letter was not long and Charles had little to say except that everything was so dreary and everyone in town so provincial and insignificant. He related an anecdote about a country gentleman's ignorance of fashion that Isabelle did not find amusing. He closed by wishing that her "dutiful stay at that frightful place Winterhaven would be short" and she would soon return "to brighten the dreariness of London."

Isabelle folded the letter and placed it on the dressing table. Perhaps, she thought, if Charles were not himself so dreary he would find life more interesting. She also resented his reference to Winterhaven as "that frightful place," for no place save Fothingham was dearer to her heart.

And if that dreadful Kingsley-Dunnett were not here I would as soon spend the season at Winterhaven as in town. She smiled as she thought of her adventures en route to Winterhaven and of Lord Biddleton.

He must think me very frivolous, she thought, but he is a good man, I think. A pity his fiancée is so ill. I know it grieves him.

A slight frown appeared on Lady Isabelle's face as she thought of Lord Biddleton's engagement. Although she did not like to admit it, she found that the fact that he was engaged was slightly disappointing.

For heavens sake, Belle, she told herself, you hardly know the man.

Yet she felt that she did know him somehow and liked him very much. I fear I like him too well, mused Isabelle. Better that we had remained enemies.

Isabelle was roused from this melancholy thought when Mildred completed her work and asked if her mistress found it satisfactory.

"Oh, yes," replied Isabelle absently. "Thank you, Millie."

Mildred was somewhat disappointed by this faint praise, for her mistress was usually far more enthusiastic. However, Mildred was aware of the unusual mood that had descended upon her ladyship that evening and hoped that the evening's dinner party would restore her usual good spirits.

It was a small intimate dinner with only eight at table and to her great dismay Lady Isabelle found herself next to Mr. Kingsley-Dunnett. That gentleman was dressed in a very worn evening coat that bore the stains of many previous dinners and his dark curly hair fell in wild disarray about his face.

Mr. Kingsley-Dunnett was most attentive to Lady Isabelle, regarding her with his cold blue eyes and trying to engage her in conversation.

"And what did you think of the portion of my greatest work you heard this afternoon, my lady?" he said, watching her intently.

Lady Isabelle felt very uncomfortable, for although she had many times been forced to talk to unpleasant persons and her good breeding usually stood her in good stead, she had never met a more revolting individual than Henry Kingsley-Dunnett. It was difficult to hide her repugnance toward him, but she managed a civil reply.

"I could not hear as well as I may have wished, sir, but I am sure it was excellent."

Kingsley-Dunnett smiled, revealing a set of uneven yellowish teeth. "It is the best thing I have ever done and though some might construe this as vanity, I must say it is perhaps one of the greatest works of our age."

Isabelle nearly laughed. What a pompous ass, she thought.

"I hope you will come and hear us tomorrow," he continued. Then he leaned toward her and said in a low voice, "Perhaps you would walk with me tomorrow. I rise very early."

Isabelle was shocked and stared at him in astonishment, but Mr. Kingsley-Dunnett only smiled in return. "Tomorrow," he said again.

Lady Isabelle replied coldly, "I think not, sir."

He smiled again. "We shall see." The smile had become a leer and Isabelle felt the urge to slap his face. She would have done so but had no desire to create a scene. Instead she gave him a disdainful look and turned to the Comte d'Aubusson who was seated at her right and began to converse with him. Fortunately, Lady Balderston, who was seated to the left of Mr. Kingsley-Dunnett, began to talk to him in animated fashion and he spent the rest of dinner discussing poetry with his hostess.

Lord Biddleton found himself placed between the Comtesse d'Aubusson and Mrs. Kingsley-Dunnett. Mrs. Kingsley-Dunnett acknowledged his lordship's presence with a nod and sat very quietly. She spoke very little and what little she did say was addressed to Sir Hector Balderston. Young Sir Hector was more intent upon his meal than the conversation and was glad that Mrs. Kingsley-Dunnett did not speak very much and he was able to concentrate fully on enjoying the excellent roast duck.

Madame le Comtesse was dressed in all the magnificence of the court of Versailles. Her elaborate powdered hair style rose nearly a foot from her head and was festooned with ribbons and a little flag that bore the *fleur de lis*. Madame conversed with Lord Biddleton, alternating between French and English so quickly that after a time the Earl was not sure which language he was speaking.

"I think Monsieur Kingsley-Dunnett is a remarkable man," she said in French. "Did you not think so? I saw you and Milady Isabelle in the window. Such a beautiful couple. Ah, to be young and in love."

The Earl was startled. "*Madame la Comtesse*," he replied in French, "you misunderstand. I am engaged to another lady in London."

"Oh, milord," laughed the *comtesse*. "I see you not only speak like a Frenchman you act like one, too. Do not fear, I am discreet always."

"But, madame!"

The *comtesse* smiled. "I am discreet, monsieur. Depend upon it."

The Earl was horrified. This Frenchwoman thought he

168

was having an affair with Lady Isabelle. Well, the French were always thinking everyone behaved with the same appalling lack of scruples that characterized their own behavior in such matters. He knew nothing he could say would convince the *comtesse* of her error, so he sighed and tried to change the conversation to a more suitable topic.

The Earl was glad when the last course of dinner was finally completed. The only person with whom he had been able to talk had been the *comtesse* and she gave him such knowing and indulgent looks that it was almost unbearable.

Finally it was time for the ladies to be excused and the gentlemen were left alone to drink Sir Hector's excellent port and to discuss any topics fit only for masculine ears.

The Earl had met Mr. Kingsley-Dunnett only briefly before dinner and had had no opportunity to speak with him. Since his lordship had disliked the poet from the start, he did not regret this lack of opportunity.

Kingsley-Dunnett leaned back in his chair and drained his glass of wine. He then set the glass upon the table and looked over at the Earl. "I hope, my lord," he said, "that you are enjoying your stay at Winterhaven. But one could not help that when there is a beautiful lady like Lady Isabelle present."

The Earl disliked Kingsley-Dunnett's tone and he found his way of staring at him quite insolent.

"I'm a poet, my lord," continued Kingsley-Dunnett, pushing a lock of unruly black hair away from his eyes, "and I appreciate the beauties of nature. Lady Isabelle is a glorious sight, is she not? Like a nymph rising from the sea."

His lordship looked coldly at Kingsley-Dunnett, finding his words impudent and his manner insufferable. Kingsley-Dunnett smiled.

"Oh, yes, my cousin is a beauty," said Sir Hector, entering the conversation. "That is obvious, of course. But, Mr. Kingsley-Dunnett, I want to say again how much I admired the 'Temptation,' which you sang for us today. It was marvelous, a work of true genius."

Mr. Kingsley-Dunnett accepted this praise with a

gracious nod as if he were a sovereign accepting tribute from his grateful subjects.

"Yes, monsieur," said the Comte d'Aubusson. "Beautiful. I was moved nearly to tears. So beautiful!"

Mr. Kingsley-Dunnett smiled again and turned then to the Earl as if expecting another accolade. When none was forthcoming he sniffed scornfully and turned again to Sir Hector.

"And Hector, dear boy, when will you read us this poem you have been talking about?"

"Oh, sir," said Sir Hector sheepishly, "I thought I might this evening when we rejoin the ladies if you think it would be a suitable occasion."

"Certainly, Hector. A splendid time."

The Earl stared sullenly at Mr. Kingsley-Dunnett and made no attempt to join in the conversation. After what seemed a very long time, Sir Hector announced that it was time to join the ladies and they rose and left the dining room.

The ladies had been engaged in discussing a number of topics ranging from Mrs. Kingsley-Dunnett's virtuosity on the flute to the vagaries of fashion.

They greeted the gentlemen warmly and soon everyone was engaged in conversation. The Earl tried to avoid the *comtesse* and he also did not want to be seen talking to Lady Isabelle. This was, of course, difficult, due to the smallness of the company, but his lordship endeavored to remain at the side of the *comte* and urged that gentleman to regale him with tales of life during the *ancien régime*. The *comte* was only too happy to oblige the Earl and talked warmly of Versailles and the king and innumerable members of the French nobility.

Lady Isabelle, who had barely been able to exchange a word with his lordship all evening, was surprised to see that the Earl seemed to be avoiding her. Her suspicion was confirmed when she managed to address him and he replied in a very civil but distant manner. Lady Isabelle was quite disturbed by this, but before she could reflect upon it further, her cousin claimed their attention.

"I should like to announce, my dear friends and guests, that I have completed a new poem."

The statement brought congratulatory remarks from everyone. "Thank you, thank you. If you ladies and gentlemen will indulge me I shall endeavor to recite my newest work which I have entitled 'Two Lovers True.'" The baronet cleared his throat and clasped his hands together in front of him. He then began.

Two lovers true I chanced to spy one eve
When moonlight fell upon the misty lane
The lady fair was crying on her sleeve
"Alas, my love, why must we part again?"

The handsome knight looked sadly at his love
"My lady fair, I fear I must depart
For King and duty beckon from above
And though I go I leave with you my heart."

I saw upon her lovely face a tear
She turned to him and heard I then a sigh
"Dear love, though I will not be very near
My faithful heart to your sweet side will fly."

And I the guilty listener who saw
This touching scene was moved forevermore.

Sir Hector stopped and looked mournfully at the guests who applauded enthusiastically.

"*Très magnifique*," cried the *comte*. "Oh, monsieur, I was so moved."

"Beautiful, Hector," said Lady Balderston, a tear forming at the corner of her eye.

Hector looked at Mr. Kingsley-Dunnett with a mixture of eagerness and fear, for the master's opinion was of paramount importance.

"Hector," said that gentleman after a dramatic pause. "That is the best poem you have ever written."

Isabelle smiled. She was sure it was the best poem her cousin had ever written which only illustrated the lamentable quality of his previous works. She looked over at Lord

171

Biddleton, and noted that he did not seem to be enjoying the evening very much and she hoped that Sir Hector would not regale the company with any more of his poetry.

Fortunately, he did not and instead went to the piano where he accompanied Mrs. Kingsley-Dunnett, who played a Mozart flute sonata. Since Mrs. Kingsley-Dunnett was extremely talented and since Sir Hector was a far more capable musician than poet, this entertainment was quite successful. Lord Biddleton, who loved music found it a welcome respite from the conversation, though he did find himself stealing glances at Lady Isabelle. Try as he would he could not keep himself from thinking about her and how wonderful she looked that evening.

Lady Balderston was not an advocate of late evenings and the party soon broke up and all the guests retired to their rooms.

As Lady Isabelle prepared for bed, she reflected that it had been a most unpleasant evening. She always had the feeling that Mr. Kingsley-Dunnett was watching her and though she tried to ignore him, he was so utterly detestable that his image kept reappearing. Lady Isabelle was also a bit puzzled by the Earl of Biddleton's behavior. He had been very cold and formal and had avoided her and she wondered if she had done anything to offend him. After pondering these thoughts for what seemed a very long time, Lady Isabelle finally fell asleep.

Remembering Kingsley-Dunnett's statement about rising early and walking in the garden, Lady Isabelle was determined to stay in her room for as long as possible. When she finally appeared downstairs, she found her aunt in the sitting room with the Earl of Biddleton. The only other occupant was the bulldog Orpheus.

"Belle," said her aunt reproachfully, "it seems you have brought your London hours to the country. It is very late and we have all been up for hours."

"Oh, it appears I am a slugabed," said Lady Isabelle. "I am not usually so, I assure you, aunt, and will endeavor to rise earlier from now on."

The Earl had risen when she entered the room and Isabelle smiled at him. "Good morning, Lord Biddleton."

"Good morning, Lady Isabelle."

She regarded him curiously, for his tone was again coldly formal.

Isabelle sat down on a chair across from Lord Biddleton. "And how are you feeling this day, my lord? I was afraid you had left your sickbed prematurely and that you would find last evening too strenuous."

"Not at all," said his lordship. "I believe I am completely recovered and shall be leaving for town soon."

"Lord Biddleton, I insist you stay another few days. You should not risk traveling," Lady Balderston said forcefully.

"I assure you, ma'am, I am well enough to travel. The journey is not long."

"But at least you will talk to Dr. Renfrew. He will be calling here to see about you and you must abide by his advice."

The Earl raised his eyebrows slightly at the mention of Dr. Renfrew. He had no faith in that gentleman's abilities, but since his hostess seemed so set in her opinion, he acquiesced.

Suddenly the butler appeared.

"Yes, Hemphill."

"Pardon, my lady," he said, "but Cook would like a word with you. I informed her you were engaged, but she says it's important."

"Very well, Hemphill, I'll see her now." She turned to her guests. "This will take but a few moments. Do excuse me."

Lord Biddleton rose as Lady Balderston left the room and returned to his chair where he faced Lady Isabelle with a very serious expression that was not dissimilar to that on Orpheus's face.

"And where are my aunt's guests, sir? I am sure all of them and my cousin have been up since dawn and are pursuing all sorts of important tasks."

The Earl, who did not like being alone with Lady Isabelle, replied briefly as to the whereabouts of the various

Winterhaven guests and they lapsed into an awkward silence.

Finally Isabelle said, "Good gracious, my lord, what is amiss? You look extremely uncomfortable and last night you were barely civil to me. I had thought we had settled our differences. Have I offended you? Pray tell me, for I did not intend to do so."

His lordship looked at her in embarrassment. "Oh, I didn't mean for you to get that impression. I assure you, you have in no way offended me and I regret that I have given you cause to think otherwise."

"Then what is wrong?"

The Earl got up from the chair, folded his arms across his chest, and looked uncertain as to what to say.

"You see, ma'am," he said awkwardly, "I feel it best that we are not seen together."

Her ladyship looked astonished.

"This is difficult for me to say, but you see, the Comtesse d'Aubusson thinks that you and I are . . . well, she hinted that . . ." He stopped hopelessly at a loss for words.

Isabelle stared at him for a moment and then realized what he was trying to say. She suddenly burst into laughter. "Oh, Lord Biddleton," she cried, "don't look so tortured. Oh, dear, this is too funny." She began to laugh again and could not continue.

Lord Biddleton looked horrified at her reaction.

"You think it funny, my lady?"

Her ladyship was laughing so hard she could only nod. Finally she managed to say, "Sit down, sir, and do not look so tragic. It is funny, don't you think so? Poor madame, how she must miss the intrigue of life at court."

Isabelle then looked up at the Earl, who had made no move to sit down. He was not smiling. He was looking at her with an expression of disapproval.

"Lady Isabelle," he said, "I think you take this matter too lightly."

"And you, sir, take it too seriously," said her ladyship, suddenly irritated. "If I am not upset, I do not know why you should be. Winterhaven, after all, is far from London and your reputation is still safe."

The Earl looked embarrassed. "You misunderstand," he began.

"I think not," said Isabelle coolly. "And you have no more need to worry about scandal, my lord. I shall avoid you like the plague from now on. I shall be as uncivil to you as you were to me last night. Good day to you. Come, Orpheus."

Lady Isabelle got up and left the room very angry at Biddleton. She left the house and entered the garden with Orpheus close on her heels. "That man," she said, "and just as I was beginning to like him he reverts to his former ways. Charles is right. He is a prig and has no sense of the ridiculous."

She shook her head and walked on through the garden, oblivious to the delightful weather and beautiful flowering shrubs. Suddenly Orpheus growled and Lady Isabelle turned around in surprise. There stood Henry Kingsley-Dunnett with a most unpleasant smirk on his face.

"Good morning, my lady Isabelle," he said.

"Good morning."

"I feared, dear lady, you would not meet me here after all."

Isabelle looked shocked.

"Meet you here? You, sir, are mistaken. I did not intend to meet you here and were I not preoccupied by other matters I would have remembered not to come here. I was told you were engaged with your work."

"And so I am, fair lady, for I am an artist and the work of an artist is to appreciate beauty and you, my dear, are a work of art so lovely that words cannot adequately describe your charms. We belong together, you and I, art and artist. And you know it too. Come, madame, there is no need to pretend. I could tell you feel the same attraction to me as I to you. It is natural, inevitable."

Isabelle stared at him incredulously. "You are mad, sir, to say such things and your wife is not far away."

He took a step nearer. "Mad? Oh, yes, maddened by your beauty and my desire for you, fair nymph. And my

175

wife? The bonds of marriage mean nothing to persons like us. Love must be free from the constraints of convention."

He lunged at her and caught her up in his arms and attempted to kiss her. Lady Isabelle, despite her horror and revulsion, was still in command of the situation. A strong woman, she tried to push him away and when this was not sufficient she planted a kick to his shin.

"Oh!" he cried in surprise and released her.

Orpheus was growling menacingly at the ill treatment his beloved Lady Isabelle was receiving. "Orpheus!" cried her ladyship noting that the worthy bulldog was dangerously close to attacking her fervent admirer. "No, Orpheus."

Kingsley-Dunnett looked down at the bulldog and his face turned very white.

"No, Orpheus!" cried Isabelle again, reaching down and grasping the dog by his collar. "You are fortunate, sir, that I was able to stop Orpheus in time. He is of a tenacious breed, sir, and were he to grab hold of that artistic throat of yours, it would be difficult to persuade him to release it. I assure you, Mr. Kingsley-Dunnett, that you are mistaken if you believe I am enamored of you. And should you attempt to force your attentions upon me again, sir, I will not restrain Orpheus."

Mr. Kingsley-Dunnett looked from Isabelle's determined face to the bulldog that continued to growl and regard him with the most ferocious of expressions. He said nothing further but turned and hastened off.

"Lady Isabelle!" Her ladyship, who was still kneeling at Orpheus's side, looked up.

"Lord Biddleton."

"Are you all right, ma'am?" The Earl looked genuinely concerned and extended a hand which Lady Isabelle took and his lordship helped her to her feet. "What has happened? Who was here?"

"Oh, I am fine, my lord. It was nothing."

The Earl frowned. "It was that cad Kingsley-Dunnett, wasn't it? By my honor, that fellow is detestable. Did he offend you? If only I had been here sooner, he would have regretted his insolence."

Isabelle looked at the Earl in surprise.

"Do not fear, Lord Biddleton, Mr. Kingsley-Dunnett had cause to regret his ill manners." She looked down at Orpheus who was looking well satisfied with himself.

"Good fellow," said the Earl stooping down to pat the bulldog's head.

Lady Isabelle looked closely at Biddleton. "I am astonished at your concern and that you should appear. I thought we were avoiding each other."

The Earl looked at her with a pained expression and rose to face her. "Lady Isabelle, I don't want you to dislike me. I did not mean to offend you, for I have nothing but the highest respect and . . . admiration for you." He looked down at the ground for a moment and then continued awkwardly. "I was upset by the *comtesse*'s hints about the two of us, but it is not what you think at all. I am the biggest fool and not good at saying what I mean. I want to apologize for offending you. I deeply value your good opinion of me and perhaps you cannot think good of me now, but I pray that you will not despise me. I would be miserable if you did. I know I am a boor and have no talent for words."

Lady Isabelle was frankly confused, for only moments ago he had been the haughty priggish Earl of Biddleton and now he was genuinely contrite and apologetic. Isabelle shook her head. "I do not know what to think of you, sir. I accept your apology eagerly and admit that perhaps I was too frivolous earlier. After all, you are an engaged man and your sensibility is due to your regard for Miss Waxwood. It is I who should apologize to you."

"No," he replied emphatically. "I am at fault."

Isabelle smiled. "I suppose it really doesn't matter where the fault lies. Let us return to our amicable relationship. I recall we had determined to be friends."

"Yes," said the Earl smiling for the first time. "That we had decided."

"Good. Then, sir, if you are as well as you look, indeed you look completely recovered, allow me to show you my aunt's gardens. That is if you feel up to a walk. I don't want to tire you."

The Earl smiled. "My lady Isabelle, I have been so long confined to the sickbed that being out of doors again is simply marvelous. I assure you I am fit as ever and if you can bear my company, I would be most grateful if you could show me Lady Balderston's garden."

Lady Isabelle grinned and curtseyed and his lordship made an elegant bow and extended his arm.

"Aunt Agatha is fiercely proud of this garden," said Isabelle, taking the Earl's arm, and the two of them walked off on one of the paths.

"She is most proud of the roses," said Lady Isabelle, "though it will be some weeks before they are in full bloom. Oh, you should see them then."

"I am fond of roses," said the Earl and Lady Isabelle looked at him with a trace of surprise, for the Earl of Biddleton had not seemed the sort of man to be overly fond of flowers.

"When I was a boy at Hedgegrow House, which is my house at Biddleton, there were rows and rows of rose-bushes in the garden. I remember how sweet they smelled."

Lord Biddleton's voice had grown wistful and Isabelle felt she was seeing a new side of the Earl's personality.

"Yes," he continued, "Lady Balderston's garden is very much like my mother's garden at Hedgegrow House. Oh, she was very proud of it, too. Poor Bevan, the gardener. How he labored to make sure everything was perfect."

The Earl looked from the rose bushes to Lady Isabelle. "That was a very long time ago." He appeared wistful for a moment then continued, "Yes, I am reminded of Hedgegrow House, though Lady Balderston has a taste for garden sculpture that my mother did not share." His lordship looked across the garden at a very large and peculiar sculpture of what appeared to be a dog with wings.

Isabelle laughed. "They're awful, aren't they? Though my aunt did not have them brought here except for the mermaid on the fountain, that is. She is guilty of that."

The Earl and Isabelle walked toward the peculiar statue. "Is it a dog? It can't be Orpheus."

Isabelle laughed. "Of course not. That is my griffin,

178

though I admit the face is more like a dog than a lion. But the wings are most griffinlike."

His lordship studied the griffin with new interest. "I thought the griffin had the head and wings of an eagle and the body of a lion. This has a dog's face or is it a cat's?"

The creature in question had a strange, unidentifiable head and bore a malevolent scowl captured forever in granite.

"I don't know," said her ladyship dubiously. "I think it is the head of a lion and I thought it was a proper griffin though perhaps not. But I love it in any case."

"And you said this was your griffin."

"Of course. You see, this one was mine and the one across the pond from it was Burwicke's griffin. Anne has a swan. There, you see it over there? And poor Rob. All that was left for him was the fountain mermaid and he didn't like it very much. But we all had our own sculptures or we thought of them like that. But we all loved the griffins. They're perfect for riding."

"Riding?" The Earl's eyebrows lifted slightly.

"Of course. They're the perfect size. We would climb up upon them. I'd sit on this one and Burwicke would take the other and Rob would get up behind me and Anne behind Burwicke and we'd shout across the pond at each other and pretend we were knights at a joust."

"Good heavens."

Isabelle laughed. "Oh, I fear we were a wild lot in those days and I hope I don't shock you with our antics. Riding the griffins was very tame actually. They never moved very fast."

Lord Biddleton laughed.

"What was far worse than that was that Rob and Burwicke would grow tired and get down from the griffins and pretend they were fighting with broad swords. All very harmless, of course, until Rob slipped and fell into the pond one day. Poor Rob, but he wasn't hurt. But how he looked! We called him King Neptune for days and how we were scolded. Aunt Agatha called us dreadful monsters!"

His lordship looked up at the stone griffin and then at

Isabelle. "How wonderful it must be to have happy memories like that."

"But surely you have some silly childhood experiences."

The Earl looked seriously at Isabelle. "No, I cannot say that. I had no brothers and my only sister is Lydia, who is twelve years older than I. I never knew my father. I was still an infant when he died and I was ten when my mother died, leaving me to Lydia's care. She was newly married to Lord Ambrose and I went to live at Ambrose Manor. Lydia was a very stern taskmaster which stemmed from her sense of duty to me of course. And then I went off to school. I never liked it much though I did meet some good friends like Ralston Keith. But in any case, Lady Isabelle, my childhood was neither happy nor carefree and I envy you." Biddleton looked suddenly embarrassed.

"But I am telling you all this about my childhood. Good heavens, I've never told anyone such things. I didn't mean to bore you."

Isabelle, who had gained new insight into the Earl's character, looked up at him and smiled. "You have not bored me at all, sir. But remember too that we got into plenty of scrapes as children, and . . ." She smiled again. "I fear we Clairemonts are still prone to getting into scrapes now and again. Yet it has always been good to have such a family, rambunctious as we are. We were never bored, in any case."

Lord Biddleton looked down into Isabelle's blue eyes and reflected that it would be very difficult to be bored with Isabelle Clairemont around.

"Now tell me," he said, looking again at the griffin. "How did you get up on the beast? It's quite far up there."

"Oh, we were ingenious. You see this small niche on this side? One foot here and then grab onto the tail and take a slight jump." Lady Isabelle illustrated her words by putting her toes into the small niche, grasping the beast's tail, and giving herself a push and then swinging herself up onto the griffin's back.

The Earl, quite astounded by this most unladylike maneuver cried, "Lady Isabelle, do be careful."

Her ladyship, now perched sidesaddle on the sturdy griffin, laughed. "Don't worry at all, my lord. Come up!"

"Come up?"

"Of course."

Lord Biddleton looked up at the grinning lady and then from side to side.

"No one will see you!" cried Isabelle.

The Earl grinned in reply and then shrugged. "As you wish, but I do not usually climb upon rocky griffins." He put one long, booted foot into the niche and was soon up and seated beside Lady Isabelle.

"That was simple wasn't it?" asked Lady Isabelle. "And now we can be off flying on this winged steed to whatever adventures we could wish. We traveled many times to Persia and China and India and all the places our tutor tried to teach us about in our geography lessons."

The Earl looked down. "I hope you traveled to all these places without falling off this creature."

"Of course, though Annie did nearly fall once on a journey to Egypt. And I must admit coming down can be a bit tricky if one is not careful."

Lord Biddleton, who was suddenly finding his closeness to the beautiful Lady Isabelle rather unnerving, decided that sense dictated he quickly return to the ground.

"Well, Lady Isabelle," he said, "though a trip to India would be exciting I think I'd best remain here. I will try to descend from the creature before anyone sees me here and wonders what has happened to stodgy old Biddle."

With these words his lordship swung his long legs down and gracefully descended from the sculpture's pedestal.

"Well done, sir," said her ladyship. She turned and got off the griffin's back.

"Oh, dear," she said, holding onto the sculpture's back and looking dubiously at the ground.

"What is it?"

"I fear I can't get down."

"Nonsense."

Lady Isabelle laughed. "I fear I was always much better at coming up than coming down. Oh, dear, a broken neck would be most inconvenient."

The Earl grinned and shook his head. "It's easy. Come lean down to me and grasp my arm."

Clutching the griffin with one hand Isabelle leaned over and took the Earl's outstretched hand.

"Now the other."

"Are you sure, my lord? I am no tiny creature."

"Don't be absurd. Come, I'll catch you."

Isabelle released her hand and quickly reached for the Earl. Two strong arms caught her around the waist and her ladyship threw her arms around Biddleton's shoulders and was lifted safely to the ground.

This contact with the Earl provoked a totally unexpected sensation in Lady Isabelle, and she found herself clutching his lordship tightly and having no desire to release him. The Earl found having Lady Isabelle in his arms a most dangerous experience and as they stood there together, neither of them moving, he found himself leaning toward her, unable to resist the urge to kiss her full and inviting lips. However, just as their lips were about to meet, a familiar voice brought the Earl to his senses and he released her ladyship quickly.

"So there you are," cried Sir Hector Balderston. "I did expect to find you here, for it's too lovely to be indoors and the garden is marvelous this time of year. I would not have bothered you at all," said Sir Hector, looking very jovial, "but it is time to sing."

Isabelle and Biddleton looked sheepishly at each other, both rather embarrassed yet both thinking Sir Hector's interruption was horribly ill timed.

"To sing?" Isabelle managed to say.

"Yes, the oratorio or the portion called 'Satan's Guile.' It is a brilliant piece. Mrs. Kingsley-Dunnett says it is her favorite and she thought if we all sang the various parts we'd have a fair idea of what it sounds like."

"Really, Hector, I don't know," said Isabelle, looking over at his lordship.

"Come now, Belle, you have a beautiful voice." He turned to the Earl. "And you sing, of course, don't you, sir?"

Lord Biddleton hesitated. He was still slightly unnerved

by his conduct toward Lady Isabelle. Fortunately, that lady showed no signs of being upset by his behavior.

"Of course you do, sir," said Sir Hector. "Come on, you two. It's great fun, you'll see."

His lordship looked over at Lady Isabelle again and was relieved when she smiled at him. He smiled at her and turned to Sir Hector. "Why not?" said Lord Biddleton with a grin. "Come, ma'am, we shall sing for our supper."

Isabelle laughed and taking Sir Hector's arm she left the garden with Biddleton and Orpheus following close behind.

Chapter 13

"Are you a baritone, sir?" asked Mrs. Kingsley-Dunnett as the Earl and Lady Isabelle arrived.

"As a matter of fact, I am," replied the Earl.

Mrs. Kingsley-Dunnett looked very small and yet strangely formidable that day. Her red hair was pulled back tightly from her face and she wore an aged frock of faded blue fabric. "Then you will be the serpent," said Mrs. Kingsley-Dunnett in a soft but authoritative voice. "Is that satisfactory, Henry?"

Mr. Kingsley-Dunnett came forward and looked coldly at Lady Isabelle. "It will have to do," he said "though we shall have to wait and see how satisfactory it is."

Mrs. Kinsley-Dunnett handed Isabelle and Biddleton sheets of music. "And Lady Isabelle, you will sing Eve's part."

Isabelle took the music and looked at Lord Biddleton. He smiled slightly and Isabelle was glad to see he found the situation amusing.

"*Madame la Comtesse* and Lady Balderston," said Mrs. Kingsley-Dunnett, "you ladies and Sir Hector shall have to do as the chorus. We should have a hundred voices to do justice to it, but we shall have to do the best we can. I hope the copies are adequate. I did them myself."

Isabelle looked at the sheet of music in her hand. The

notes were clearly visible, but she had some trouble in deciphering the words of the song.

"Mr. Kingsley-Dunnett shall be Adam, of course," continued Mrs. Kingsley-Dunnett.

The Earl leaned over and whispered to Isabelle. "He should be the serpent, I'd say." Isabelle giggled and Mrs. Kingsley-Dunnett looked sternly at her.

The *comtesse* spoke up suddenly. "Dear Phoebe, I regret that this word I do not know. And this one also. My English is not so good."

Isabelle thought that Mrs. Kingsley-Dunnett's copy was more at fault than the *comtesse*'s English, but Lady Balderston spoke up. "Dear *comtesse*, follow Hector and me. We are all singing the same words."

"Of course," said the *comtesse* with the smile that had delighted scores of courtiers at Versailles. Isabelle smiled at the French woman, for she was growing quite fond of that remarkable lady. Today the *comtesse*'s hair was unpowdered. It was flecked with gray and nearly hidden by an enormous hat covered with white plumes.

"This is exciting," cried the *comtesse* suddenly.

The *comte*, who was standing by Kingsley-Dunnett, waved to his wife. "Will you not sing with us, monsieur?" said Lady Balderston.

The *comte* put up one delicate hand. "No, madame, I fear my voice would not do justice. But I shall be the audience. no?"

"Ladies and gentlemen," said Mrs. Kingsley-Dunnett, "we will get started now if you please." She sat down at the piano. "Do listen carefully," she said and began to play the opening chords of "The Serpent's Guile."

Hemphill the butler opened the doors of Winterhaven to admit two ladies. "We are not expected," said the elder of the two in a stern voice. "I am Lady Ambrose and this is Miss Waxwood."

Hemphill looked at the two ladies. He had no idea who they were, but they were dressed so well and had such an air of importance about them that he knew they were personages of consequence. A quick glance at the expensive carriage that had delivered them to Winterhaven reinforced his conclusions.

"Please announce us," said Lady Ambrose forcefully.

"Pardon, my lady," said Hemphill, "but my master is engaged as is my mistress and all the guests. You may wait for them if you please."

Lady Ambrose frowned but said nothing and looked expectantly at the butler, who hurriedly ushered them inside. As they followed the butler into the house and down the main hallway, the ladies heard the sound of music. It grew louder as they continued on, and suddenly the butler stopped. "I must ask you to wait here until the music is finished, my lady. On no account is the music to be interrupted. The master's orders."

Lady Ambrose shrugged and cast a withering look at Hemphill, who bowed and retired. Miss Waxwood looked about the room, which was a small anteroom of some kind furnished in what was to her a flamboyant and gaudy style. Yet, before Miss Waxwood could comment upon the room's tawdriness or mention that she was beginning to feel slightly faint, a very short and eccentrically dressed gentleman entered the room. The ladies stared at him strangely, for he wore a powdered wig and satin coat and breeches and made a magnificent bow.

"Forgive this boldness," he said. "I am the Comte d'Aubusson. I am not engaged with the music. Is it not splendid?"

Miss Waxwood frowned. "It is rather odd to have musical entertainments with an invalid in the house."

The *comte* looked puzzled. "Invalid, madame?"

"Why, of course. The Earl of Biddleton. We have received word that he is very ill and made haste to come to his side."

"The Earl of Biddleton? *Oui*, Milord Biddleton is here."

"Perhaps we might see him," said Lady Ambrose, eying the *comte* coldly.

"Oh, he is in there with the music, of course."

Miss Waxwood shook her head. "Loud music is not at all conducive to one's recovery. Come, Lady Ambrose." The two ladies advanced toward the door.

"Yes, we go in," said the *comte,* "but do remain quiet. Sir Hector would not want the music disturbed."

Lady Ambrose looked scornfully at the *comte* and opened the door. Her mouth fell open in astonishment, and Miss Eudoria Waxwood felt dangerously near collapsing when she beheld what was beyond the door. A redheaded woman was playing the piano with hearty vigor, and a group of ladies and gentlemen were standing together and singing with the enthusiasm of a village choir.

Suddenly a familiar baritone voice rang out, and Miss Waxwood was stunned to see that the source of this quite melodious sound was the Earl of Biddleton, looking in perfect health and standing beside a radiant blond woman, whom she recognized as Lady Isabelle Clairemont. She stared at the Earl in shock and then noted the rest of the company.

There was a very large red-faced young gentleman and a stout older lady as well as a peculiar-looking man whose appearance was so disheveled as to be quite shocking. There was also a tall woman in a ridiculous dress who wore an enormous and quite unfashionable hat and sang with a shrill unpleasant voice. Finally, there was a pair of grim bulldogs that sat near the piano looking like gargoyles from some gothic cathedral.

"Oh, dear," murmured Miss Waxwood, her hand on her heart.

The singers were so absorbed in their work that they took no notice of the two ladies who had entered the far corner of the spacious room. They continued singing, and the red-headed woman kept nodding in time to the music. Finally, the singers joined together in the final notes of the song and Mrs. Kingsley-Dunnett triumphantly hit the final notes on the piano. There was silence for a moment and then the *comtesse* cried out, "Oh, Phoebe, so beautiful, so marvelous!"

Mrs. Kingsley-Dunnett rose from the piano bench with a look of great satisfaction on her face. The Earl had enjoyed himself immensely despite his difficulty, which was caused by Mrs. Kingsley-Dunnett's poor copying, in reading the music. He grinned at Mrs. Kingsley-Dunnett. "It was very good, ma'am," he said. He looked down at Isabelle, who was standing beside him. "You have a lovely voice," he said softly.

"Thank you, sir, and you were a splendid serpent." They both laughed.

Lady Ambrose, who had listened to the concluding strains of "The Serpent's Guile" with dismay, viewed her brother with a look of horror. There he was, acting as if he were on the most intimate terms with the notorious Isabelle Clairemont, who was undoubtedly playing up to her brother with her oft-practiced skill.

Miss Waxwood was still clutching her heart and looking very pale. Lady Ambrose, who despite her affection for Eudoria had no time for such displays of weakness, grasped Miss Waxwood's arm and forcefully led her toward the group. The singers, who had begun to drift apart, stopped and stared at the newcomers. Lord Biddleton gaped at them in astonishment. "Lydia," he cried. "Eudoria!"

Lady Balderston, who was not unaccustomed to strangers walking into her house unannounced, walked toward them with a gracious smile. "How do," she said. "I am Lady Balderston. Welcome to Winterhaven."

Lydia looked at her hostess with the cool hauteur that characterized her personality. "I am Lady Ambrose and this is Miss Waxwood."

"So good of you to come," said Lady Balderston without much conviction. "It appears you know the Earl of Biddleton."

His lordship had come forward by this time and was enduring his sister's looks of disapproval with equanimity. "Lady Ambrose is my sister," he said, "and Miss Waxwood is the lady to whom I am betrothed."

"Well, you are very welcome here," said Lady Balderston.

"Yes, of course," chimed in Sir Hector, his round face still flushed from his exertions during the singing. "Good to have more guests. Splendid. I hope you sing."

Lady Ambrose gave him one of her famed withering looks. "I think not, young man."

"Lady Ambrose," said Lady Balderston, noting her new guest's haughty demeanor and resenting her strongly, "allow me to present the others to you. My son, Sir Hector." Sir Hector bowed with civility but hoped that this dragon of a lady did not stay long. "And this is the Comte and Comtesse d'Aubusson." The *comte* bowed again and the *comtesse* made a grand curtsey.

Lady Ambrose stared at them coldly, studying the *comtesse*'s dress with undisguised amazement. "We met this gentleman earlier," she said and to the *comtesse* she addressed a short, "How do?"

"And this is Mr. and Mrs. Kingsley-Dunnett. They are artists. Mr. Kingsley-Dunnett is a poet and his dear wife is a musician."

Lady Ambrose, who loathed artists, nodded grimly. Mr. Kingsley-Dunnett smiled at her with what Lydia perceived to be great impudence and he then looked at Miss Waxwood with keen interest.

"And, of course, this is my niece, Lady Isabelle Clairemont."

"It is very good to meet you, Lady Ambrose, and you, Miss Waxwood," said Lady Isabelle with her famous charm. Lady Ambrose, however, was impervious to Isabelle's charm and regarded her with disapproval.

"I am quite astonished to see you here," said Lord Biddleton, noting his sister's alarming lack of good manners.

"I don't know why you should be surprised, Biddleton," she replied and the Earl winced at hearing her call him by that name. He was always "Lucius," except when he had fallen from her good graces, and as a boy, hearing that stern "Biddleton" was enough to make his blood run cold.

"You said that you were ill. What sort of a sister would I have been if I did not drop everything to rush to your side? Yes, I dropped everything, even attending what was probably going to be the most amusing party of the year to visit you in your sickbed. But I see I needn't have bothered. You have made a remarkable recovery."

Biddleton, who was becoming increasingly embarrassed by his sister, frowned. "As you have said, it was quite unnecessary for you to come. I remember I wrote and told you there was no need for it. I daresay, it was unwise for Miss Waxwood to travel so far."

Miss Waxwood, who had remained very quiet, looked at the Earl. Her dark eyes had a mournful expression and she spoke accusingly. "How good of you to worry about my health. I am not so well as I could wish, and no doubt this journey has not been good for me. You, however, look quite well and I congratulate you on your recovery."

Lady Isabelle observed Miss Waxwood's demeanor toward his lordship with surprise. There was no trace of affection between them and Miss Waxwood seemed angry that she did not find Biddleton on his deathbed. Of course, thought Isabelle, I suppose she feels he was never ill at all. Oh, dear.

All the guests stood looking at each other and finally Lady Balderston spoke up. "You ladies must be fatigued from your journey. I shall have a servant take you to rooms where you may rest. Do follow me."

"You are kind, I'm sure," said Lady Ambrose. "Poor Eudoria does need some rest."

When Lady Balderston and her new guests were gone, Sir Hector looked at the Earl with new sympathy. He was sensitive to Biddleton's embarrassment and, therefore, changed the subject, referring again to the oratorio and perusing the sheets of music.

"I think," said the *comte*, "I would like to stroll in the garden." He turned to his wife. "Madame?"

The *comtesse* nodded and took her husband's arm. "Excuse us please. We shall walk in the garden."

Biddleton watched them leave the room and turned to Isabelle. "By my honor, I am sorry they came. Lydia is not one to endear herself to most people."

Isabelle smiled encouragingly. "Oh, I expect Lady Ambrose is fatigued from her journey. And one must admit, my lord, that it would be unsettling to find you looking so fit when they expected to see you very ill."

"I would hope Lydia would be glad to see me well, but no, she would sooner see me suffering miserably in bed."

"Lord Biddleton!"

"Well, it is true. I am sorry I was so disobliging. Had I

known of her visit, I would have had a relapse. By the gods, Lady Isabelle, I believe she thinks I was never sick at all."

"I think you may be right." Lady Isabelle suddenly smiled that mischievous smile that Biddleton was now beginning to appreciate. "Perhaps Dr. Renfrew could come and sign an affidavit as to the deplorable state of your health when first you arrived at Winterhaven."

The Earl laughed. "Perhaps that would be worth attempting. I do hope my sister does not offend Lady Balderston. Your aunt has been so very kind to me."

"Don't worry, sir. Aunt Agatha is not one to take offense without giving it back measure for measure. Come, my lord, let us go to the drawing room and wait for Lady Ambrose and Miss Waxwood to return."

Lady Ambrose's disgust at finding her brother in perfect health was not at all lessened by finding him sitting in the drawing room smiling at Lady Isabelle Clairemont. "Oh, Lydia," said the Earl getting quickly to his feet. "Where is Eudoria?"

"Miss Waxwood is feeling slightly indisposed and is resting. You know how delicate she is."

"I am sorry that she is not feeling well."

"Yes, I am sure you are." Lydia looked coldly at her brother.

Lady Isabelle was highly amused by Lydia's expression, yet she felt rather sorry for the Earl, reflecting that his youth under his sister's humorless and watchful eye could not have been pleasant. "I do hope, Lady Ambrose," said Isabelle in a cheery voice, "that your journey was not unpleasant. The weather has been very nice, which is so fortunate since we have had so much rain."

Lady Ambrose raised her head haughtily and replied in a condescending tone, "Some may think so, though I found it rather hot." Isabelle found Lydia's manner of speaking so pompous that she had a difficult time refraining from laughing.

Lady Ambrose gave Isabelle a disdainful look and then turned to her brother. "You said in your letter you had

191

had some problems on the journey and Lady Balderston had graciously allowed you to stay here. You did not elaborate and I was quite worried. What, pray tell, were these problems?"

His lordship, who was growing increasingly irritated with his sister for her ungracious behavior and rude manner toward Lady Isabelle, frowned. "I shall tell you then. I was on my mission . . ." At the word "mission" Lady Ambrose gave her brother a warning look. "Oh, don't look at me like that. Lady Isabelle knows of my mission. Anyway, I was riding like some accursed Hun and when I came upon Lady Isabelle's carriage, her coachman whipped on his horses thinking I was a highwayman."

"Good heavens!"

"Well, I daresay, Lydia, I looked like one."

"You did, sir," said Isabelle with a smile.

"Yes, and then the carriage hit a rock or some such thing and the wheel broke."

"How unfortunate," said Lydia with a hint of sarcasm in her voice.

"And that was only the beginning. A damned footpad came upon us and stole everything I had. Curse the fellow. A wretched blackguard he was."

"And Lord Biddleton was extremely brave, Lady Ambrose," said Isabelle, glancing at the Earl. His lordship met the glance with a look that alarmed Lady Ambrose, who decided her brother had lost all sense of propriety.

"Come now, Lady Isabelle," said the Earl. "I was not brave at all."

"Nonsense, sir. Lady Ambrose, you have reason to be proud of your brother. He risked his life in standing up to the footpad, who was armed with a pistol."

"Humph," sniffed Lady Ambrose. "Standing up to an armed ruffian indicates a lack of good sense, I should think."

Isabelle laughed. "Really, ma'am," she said, but noting Lady Ambrose's unpleasant expression, she thought it best to say nothing further.

"So the fellow stole everything from you?" said Lady Ambrose. She shook her head and then suddenly had a thought. She looked down at her brother's hands. "Not the family ring, Lucius?"

"I am afraid so, Lydia."

Lydia looked shocked. "But you didn't tell me. Oh, how could you, Lucius? How could you be so careless? The ring has been in the family for centuries. Oh, Lucius!"

The Earl grew increasingly pale at his sister's words and stood up suddenly. "I have had enough, Lydia! The ring is gone and no one could feel worse than I do about its loss. There is no need for you to say any more about it. I'll not have you accusing me of carelessness as if I were some pathetic schoolboy."

Lady Ambrose stood up and faced her brother. "You have never before spoken to me in such a manner! I refuse to listen to you if you are going to scream at me in that way!" With these words Lydia cast a furious look at the Earl and another at Lady Isabelle and flounced out of the room.

Isabelle, who had witnessed this altercation with dismay, sat very quietly. Biddleton watched Lydia leave the room and then looked over at Isabelle. "I am sorry." He sat down looking extremely miserable. "I do not usually make horrible scenes like that. I do apologize."

"There is no need for you to apologize to me. I am only sorry Lady Ambrose is so angry."

"She had no right to act as if I lost the ring," said the Earl angrily. "And I do not think she has any right to treat you so insufferably."

Isabelle smiled. "I can understand how she feels, I think."

"You can?"

"Do not forget, my lord, she thought I had schemed to marry her son."

"My God, I'd forgotten about Cuthburt."

"And now she sees you here with me. I daresay she knows where Cuthburt is by now, and since she hasn't said anything about him, I suspect he did go off to Fothingham with Rob. That is not the sort of news to put Lady Ambrose in good spirits. Indeed, if one considers the matter, your sister is showing remarkable restraint."

Biddleton looked at Isabelle and smiled, his anger fading. "I should not say that, but perhaps you are right. She has been concerned with Cuthburt. I shall try to be more understanding, but I will not have my sister acting with such bad manners."

Isabelle smiled. "I hope you two can make things right, for I hate to see brothers and sisters quarreling. Indeed, it reminds me a little of my sister Harriet and brother Lindsay, who are always so busy fighting with each other, that they do not realize how terribly fond they are of each other."

The Earl shook his head thoughtfully. "I don't think Lydia and I have ever quarreled before. I rather like it actually."

"Lord Biddleton!"

His lordship laughed. "I am only joking. You see, I can now make jokes. Perhaps not good jokes, but jokes nevertheless. Don't you think I'm improving?"

Lady Isabelle looked into his lordship's eyes and the rather dangerous feeling she had experienced in the garden when his arms were around her returned. There was a silence as they gazed at each other and Isabelle was finally able to gain control of herself. "I hope Miss Waxwood is feeling better," she said.

"Oh, yes," said the Earl absently. "Of course." He felt again the urge to take the beautiful Lady Isabelle into his arms and thought of that moment in the garden. Neither of them had spoken of it, though his lordship had thought of it so many times.

"Have you known Miss Waxwood long?" asked Isabelle, who was also thinking of the moment in the garden but thought it best to put aside such thoughts.

"Yes, quite long." The spell was broken and the Earl returned to reality. "The Waxwoods have been friends of my family for a very long time. I have known Eudoria since childhood." The conversation was taking a direction that his lordship did not particularly like and he was glad when the Comte and Comtesse d'Aubusson entered the drawing room. Each of them carried a small white object that upon closer inspection proved to be a bulldog puppy.

194

"Eurydice will be looking for her puppies," said the *comtesse*. "I do not know where she is. Do you?"

Lord Biddleton stared at the *comtesse*, not knowing at all what she was talking about. Isabelle smiled. "No," she said, "I have not seen her."

"Could you take them?" asked the *comtesse*, and without waiting for an answer, she dropped the small bulldog into Isabelle's lap. "We must go back to see Phoebe. We are late and you English are much opposed to lateness, no? Be good, Castor."

"Yes, here, monsieur," said the *comte*. Following his wife's example, he dumped his bulldog into the Earl's lap. "*Merci.*"

The *comte* and *comtesse* then left the room, leaving Isabelle and Biddleton with slightly bewildered expressions on their faces. One of the small white dogs turned and looked up at Isabelle with a rather mournful expression and she began to laugh. "Oh, dear, sir. It looks as though we are now to be nursemaids to Eurydice's puppies." The little dog in Biddleton's arms seemed quite content and began to lick the Earl's hand.

"Good God," said his lordship.

Isabelle got up and held the bulldog close to her. "Let us take them outside and find Eurydice."

"Indeed, though I don't know who this Eurydice is or why she should want them."

"Heavens, my lord," Isabelle said. "She is their mother."

The Earl looked closely at the pup in his arms. "Then she is probably the only one who would want them." Isabelle laughed and the Earl continued. "Then let us return these to her before she misses them and decides I am responsible for the loss. Indeed, ma'am, this Eurydice, if she resembles the esteemed Orpheus, is not one with whom I would want to tangle."

When they got outside, they put the puppies down, but the one Biddleton had been holding stayed by his lordship's side and refused to move. "He has grown so fond of you, my lord," said Isabelle highly amused at the Earl's expression.

"Good Lord," said the Earl.

A large white animal appeared on the heels of Lady Balderston, and his lordship, noting the family resemblance between the pups and the large dog, concluded rightly that this was Eurydice. The pups barked and ran to meet her, though after a short greeting they rushed back to Isabelle and Biddleton.

"Oh, they are clever, aren't they?" cried Lady Balderston, looking fondly at the puppies. "So like their father, Orpheus. How I shall hate to part with them."

"Part with them?" said Isabelle.

"Yes, they are growing larger now and no longer need their mother. Eight bulldogs are a few too many. Hector thinks so, in any case. I thought I should find them good homes."

"I'm sure that would be nice, Aunt Agatha, though it is a shame to have them leave you."

Lady Balderston looked rather sad. "Yes, yes. I wanted to surprise you later, Belle, but I will tell you now. I want you to have one of the puppies."

Isabelle looked surprised.

"Yes, I know how you love them and I'm sure Castor will be happy, though you must watch that Lindsay takes care and does not get into mischief."

Isabelle, who despite her love for dogs had no desire to bring home a bulldog, did not know what to say. Her aunt acted as if she were bestowing the crown jewels upon her and there was no way to refuse without offending her aunt.

"Aunt Agatha," she said finally, "I am overwhelmed. But I hope you are certain you can bear to part with him."

"I shall have to bear it, that is all," said Lady Balderston.

The puppy that Biddleton had been holding continued to sit at his feet and gaze up at the Earl with undisguised admiration.

"He's taken to you, Biddleton," said Lady Balderston. "Never seen such a thing before."

His lordship looked down at the puppy and then at

Lady Balderston. "I don't understand it, ma'am. Animals don't usually take to me."

"Never have I seen such a thing," repeated Lady Balderston, ignoring the Earl's remarks. "But Pollux has made his choice and I'll abide by it. You may have him, sir. I know you'll give him a good home. I'll admit, Biddleton, I was not at all sure of you when first we met, but you're a good man and one to be trusted."

The Earl looked down at the little bulldog that was staring up at him with his tongue hanging out. His lordship knew that his hostess was conferring great honor upon him by the gift and there wasn't anything he could do but accept with good grace. "I'm honored," he said. "Quite honored."

Lady Balderston was quite satisfied with this response. Although she had been worried that the Earl, an engaged man, was toying with her niece's affections, she was much more sympathetic to Biddleton after seeing his sister and Miss Waxwood. A realist in spite of her seeming eccentricities, Lady Balderston knew that alliances between persons of rank and wealth seldom included love or even affection. After talking to Miss Waxwood, Lady Balderston could not grudge the Earl his harmless flirtation with Isabelle. She knew well that her niece was not a silly girl on her first season and could certainly take care of herself. Lady Isabelle, had she known her aunt's thoughts, would have smiled, for she was becoming dangerously fond of the Earl of Biddleton and was beginning to question her ability to handle the situation.

"Then it is settled," said Lady Balderston. "Let us leave Castor and Pollux in their mama's care, for I think it is time for luncheon." The Earl was only too glad to leave his new canine admirer and escorted the ladies into the house.

Miss Eudoria Waxwood did not feel very well and would have preferred to stay in her room rather than join the others for luncheon. However, Lady Ambrose had insisted firmly that she steel herself and attend, for as her ladyship put it, she "should not leave Biddleton in the hands of that scheming female."

So Eudoria reluctantly changed her dress, patted her pale cheeks, and dutifully followed Lydia to the dining hall. There Lady Ambrose made sure Eudoria was seated next to Lord Biddleton and with herself sitting on his other side, Lydia was certain that her brother was protected from the dreaded Isabelle Clairemont.

Lady Isabelle found the luncheon quite unpleasant, for Lady Ambrose was still furious with her brother and refused to speak to him. She sat directing frowns alternately at Isabelle and Biddleton.

Eudoria was also perturbed at his lordship and met his attempts at conversation with short answers and reproachful looks. No one else at the table said much. Sir Hector was too intent upon the cold mutton and Lady Balderston was unwilling to exert the effort to try and converse with such unpleasant guests.

The Kingsley-Dunnetts were very quiet, Mrs. Kingsley-Dunnett because of her usual quiet nature and Henry because he was still somewhat upset by what he considered his very shabby treatment by Lady Isabelle. Even the *comte* and *comtesse* were rather subdued and though madame began to direct some questions at Lady Ambrose, she was soon silenced by her ladyship's disobliging answers.

Lord Biddleton was miserable and was relieved when the unpleasant luncheon was over. As the guests got up to leave, Lady Ambrose turned to her brother. "Poor Eudoria looks as though she could use some air. Biddleton, I think you could escort her to the gardens."

The Earl, who had had enough of Eudoria's reproachful looks, had hoped that she would retire to her room again, but he recognized his duty and replied with great civility. "Yes, Eudoria, I think that would be very good for you. Shall we?"

Miss Waxwood nodded and took the Earl's arm and the two of them left the dining hall. Lady Ambrose watched them with some degree of satisfaction, for despite her brother's seeming lapse in his sense of propriety, he was a very staid and sober gentleman and doubtless all he needed was Eudoria's presence to jolt him back to reality.

"And now," said Lydia with an imperious look, "I hope you will all excuse me. I think I will rest in my room." With these words she was off, leaving the guests quite relieved to see her go.

"That's a bad-tempered female," said Sir Hector. "She doesn't fit in at Winterhaven. I hope she leaves soon."

"Now, Hector, I am appalled to hear you say something like that," said Lady Balderston. "Though it is true, I'm sure it's not polite. She is a dreadful woman. Not at all like Biddleton."

"I don't know," said Mr. Kingsley-Dunnett malevolently, "I see the resemblance quite clearly."

Isabelle gave Kingsley-Dunnett a look of disgust. How I detest you, she thought.

Mrs. Kingsley-Dunnett suddenly spoke up. "I think, Henry, we must beg to be excused, for there is much to do. I have been thinking about the 'Flight from Eden' and am eager to get back to work."

"May I come, too?" said Sir Hector eagerly. "I won't be a bother."

"Dear Hector," said Mrs. Kingsley-Dunnett fondly. "You are never a bother."

"I think," said Isabelle, "I will write some letters. Do excuse me." With these words Isabelle left and reflected that her visit to Winterhaven had taken a most unsatisfactory turn.

Isabelle stared at the blank sheet of paper. She was not in the mood to write letters, though she had managed to write a short and not very amusing letter to her family. Now she was attempting to write to Charles Fensbrook and found she had little to say to him.

She was glad when there was a knock at the door and in walked the *comtesse*. "Do I disturb you, Lady Isabelle?" she said.

"Oh, no, madame, I am glad to see you. I am afraid I was not doing so well with my letter writing."

"Letter writing," said *Madame la Comtesse*, "is not an

easy thing. I do not write so many letters except, of course, to Her Majesty and to Louis-Claude."

"Louis-Claude?"

"Oh, he is my son."

"Madame, I did not know about your son. Do tell me about him."

The *comtesse*'s eyes grew bright. "He is the dearest boy. So handsome. So like his father when he was young. I am so proud of him. He is very young and in the King's Service. A soldier and so handsome in his uniform. I do not like this soldiering so much, but Louis-Claude said he must serve the King and so he is aide to the Duc de Belleville. I am such a proud mother."

"Is your son still in France then, madame?"

"*Oui*, he must do his duty."

Isabelle was puzzled at this information and wondered what the *comtesse*'s son would be doing in the army of France now that Napoleon Bonaparte was so firmly established as emperor. She did not pursue the matter and the *comtesse* changed the subject. "Such a lovely day," she said, walking to the window and looking out. "Oh, I do not like to see it."

"See what, madame?"

"Your Biddleton and that sickly lady. Oh, what is her name? Oh, yes, Miss Waxwood."

"Heavens, madame, he is not my Biddleton and he is engaged to Miss Waxwood."

"Yes," said the *comtesse*, turning away from the window and sitting down in a chair beside Isabelle. "I did not like him so much at first, your Biddleton. Too much the Englishman I think when first I see him, but then he speaks such excellent French. And then I see how much in love with you he is."

"Madame!" cried Isabelle, turning very red.

"Dear Isabelle, of course he is in love with you. He does not love this Miss Waxwood at all. What an unhappy marriage. Why does he not marry you? I cannot understand it."

"Dear madame," cried Isabelle, "he hardly knows me and he has been engaged to Miss Waxwood for some time.

And I think you are mistaken. I am sure he must be very fond of Miss Waxwood." Isabelle spoke without conviction and the *comtesse* smiled sympathetically.

"But you love this Biddleton, do you not?"

Isabelle looked uncomfortable. "Good heavens, madame!"

"See, you do not deny it!" said the *comtesse* triumphantly. "And there is no reason why you do not marry him. You have beauty and rank. Your father is an English *duc*, a great lord, is he not?"

Isabelle laughed. "My father is indeed a duke, madame, but he is not so grand I assure you. He is a dear man and very kind, but I must explain that despite my father's rank, few are eager to make alliances with my family. I am surprised you have not heard of us. We are quite infamous, we Clairemonts. I must tell you a fact that is widely known among society. We are not at all wealthy. My father is heavily in debt and I have little dowry. At six and twenty years of age I am an established spinster and not what is known in society as a good catch."

"Such nonsense. You are beautiful and good and kind and very charming. And you are still very young. *Sacré bleu!* I am twice your age."

"Are you?" Isabelle was surprised, for she had thought the *comtesse* not a day over forty.

"I myself married very young," continued the *comtesse*. "I was but sixteen when I married my first husband and eighteen when I married the second. I was nearly thirty when I married Jean-Paul and," the *comtesse* paused and winked at Isabelle, "it is the best of my marriages, though we have been through unhappy times Jean-Paul and I. And fortune is not so important especially if one person is rich. When I married Jean-Paul I was very wealthy and Jean-Paul was not so wealthy. It did not matter at all.

"But it is good to be fond of one's husband, and to be in love with a husband is unusual but most convenient. I did not love my first two husbands in the least, though they were not bad men in their way. Her Majesty was the one who thought I should marry Jean-Paul. 'Henrietta,' she said to me one day, 'marry this lover of yours, for His

201

Majesty is tired of his friend, Monsieur le Comte d'Aubusson, thinking of nothing but you and he is sure marriage will change him.' "

The *comtesse* laughed. "But it did not change anything. And you are not so unlike me, dear Isabelle. You would be happy with this Earl."

Before Isabelle could reply, the *comtesse* rose abruptly. "But it is dinner time now. How fast the time is going. Hurry and dress." And then she was gone, leaving Isabelle to shake her head and smile.

Dinner that evening got off to an even less auspicious start than did the day's unpleasant luncheon. Although Lady Ambrose had softened a little toward her brother since he had dutifully entertained Miss Waxwood throughout the afternoon, she was still angry with him. Her anger, combined with the natural unpleasantness of her disposition, made her a most disagreeable dinner partner.

Sir Hector, who was sitting next to Lady Ambrose, was able to ignore her by concentrating on the numerous courses of the meal and he only took some interest when she announced, "We shall be off to town early in the morning. We can impose upon you no further."

Lady Balderston made a feeble attempt at assuring Lydia that she was welcome to stay longer, but Lady Balderston was actually relieved to hear her difficult houseguest was leaving.

"You have been so kind to Biddleton," said Lady Ambrose. "We are so grateful." This remark was made in a cold sardonic manner and Lady Balderston muttered an acceptable reply and was silent. Biddleton, too, kept very quiet and the meal passed very slowly.

Isabelle longed for the evening to end and was glad when the last course was finished and the ladies retired. However, she soon found that being in a room with Lady Ambrose and Miss Waxwood was most awkward.

"I suppose," said Lady Ambrose, after seating herself stiffly on the sofa, "that you, Lady Isabelle, have heard from your brother Robert."

Lady Isabelle was surprised at being addressed by Lydia

202

after being so pointedly ignored most of the evening. "Robert? Oh, I have not heard from him directly," she said.

"My son Cuthburt is with him at Fothingham," said Lady Ambrose stiffly.

"He is? I'm sure they are enjoying themselves. Fothingham is so beautiful."

"Yes," replied Lady Ambrose, who did not particularly like to think of her son enjoying himself. "I was relieved to find he had gone there. He had not left word and I was worried."

Isabelle smiled, knowing well what had worried Lady Ambrose.

To Isabelle's relief the *comtesse* joined them.

"Ah, so beautiful it is here in the evening. This is a lovely place. I am reminded of Paris or Versailles in the spring."

"I have never been to France," said Lady Ambrose coldly. "I think England is the place for Englishmen."

"Yes," said the *comtesse* with the trace of a smile. "I have thought so too."

Isabelle smiled and Lady Ambrose regarded her coldly.

"Ah, yes," continued the *comtesse*. "Such grand *fêtes* there are in the spring. How Her Majesty loves them. Queen Antoinette is so charming and so gay and always planning amusing entertainments."

"You refer to Queen Marie Antoinette of France?" asked Lady Ambrose with a puzzled expression.

"Of course," said the *comtesse*.

"I was confused," said Lady Ambrose, "for you spoke as if she were still alive. The late Queen of France was a frivolous woman they say. But such a barbaric fate. We were all quite appalled to hear it. To die as she did as a common criminal with all the rabble watching. But so many met the same fate at the hands of *Madame la Guillotine*. Monstrous."

Madame la Comtesse heard these words and her face grew very pale.

"Please, Lady Ambrose," cried Isabelle, but it was too

late. The *comtesse* stood up and raced from the room. Lady Ambrose and the other ladies looked astonished.

"Whatever has happened?" cried Lady Balderston.

"I assure you I have no idea," said Lady Ambrose.

Isabelle rose. "Don't worry. I'll go and see if she is all right." She hurried out and found the *comtesse* in the garden sitting on a stone bench. She was very still and staring up into the darkened sky.

"Madame," said Isabelle very concerned. "Are you all right?"

The *comtesse* managed a rueful smile. "Sit down, dear Isabelle."

Isabelle did so and the *comtesse* took her hand. "You have thought me eccentric."

Isabelle began to protest, but the *comtesse* cut her off. "I am, I know. I do not like these times. I wish always for the old days." She stopped and paused a moment. "Those days are gone. You and your aunt and cousin and your Biddleton, too, have been kind to me. I know I talk as though the Queen were alive. Sometime I think she is. I wish it so. No one has said to me, 'Henrietta, you are mad. The Queen of France is dead.' You are all too kind to me. Lady Ambrose is not so kind but she is right to say these things. The Queen is dead. My dearest friend.

"I too wanted to die, for Louis-Claude was dead also. Yes, Louis-Claude my only child. A traitor to the Republic they said. The criminals! He was Marquis de Bourbonnais and a wealthy man but only eighteen. And he was a soldier devoted to the king. They took his estates and then his life."

"Oh, madame," cried Isabelle.

"No, I am fine. I think I will retire. Please tell Agatha I am fine. No, do not come with me. I would like to be alone."

Isabelle watched her go and sighed. How tragic was the *comtesse*'s life. Isabelle reflected and hoped that Lady Ambrose's tactless words had not done irreparable harm to the French woman.

"Lady Isabelle?"

It was Lord Biddleton standing very tall and looking

very worried. "Tell me what has happened. The house is in chaos. My sister and Eudoria have retired and Lady Balderston is very angry. What has happened? Whatever it was it was Lydia's doing, wasn't it?"

Isabelle nodded. The Earl sat down on the bench. "What did she do?"

"She remarked that Queen Marie Antoinette was dead."

"Good God."

"She didn't know how the *comtesse* was, I suppose, but she could have been more sensitive."

"Lydia, sensitive?" said Lord Biddleton. "I am afraid that is quite impossible. So was the *comtesse* very hurt? Did she think the Queen still alive? She is eccentric, though I never knew if she really believed the Queen to be alive or not."

"I think she really knew, but she liked to pretend otherwise. You see, her son too was killed by the rebels."

"I didn't know."

"She only just now told me. He was only a boy of eighteen."

"Poor lady. I wish that Lydia had never come. What a muddle she has made of everything."

Isabelle got up from the bench and Biddleton rose, too. "I am sure the *comtesse* will be better tomorrow," said Isabelle. "She is a strong woman. Perhaps it is better for her to face reality. Yes," she looked meaningfully at the Earl, "I think it is best for all of us to do so."

"Yes," he said and though it was very dark she could see that he was frowning.

"You will leave tomorrow very early. I think it best we say farewell here."

"Lady Isabelle," said his lordship. He paused as if searching for the right words. "I have enjoyed it here. I know I can be a dreary bore and I was, but your company was delightful. I'll cherish these memories."

Isabelle smiled. "Then it has not been so bad?"

He laughed. "I enjoyed everything. No, not everything. Not that Renfrew fellow or Kingsley-Dunnett, though the singing was great fun. And I certainly regret Lydia's arrival and that is the only reason I shall be glad to leave, for I do not want to inflict my sister on you any longer than necessary."

Isabelle smiled and looked up at his lordship. "I was glad you recovered so rapidly and I do regret that incident with the footpad though I'll never forget it and will always be grateful to you for your courage."

"Nonsense."

"No, it's true. And then of course there was the flood. We have had some adventures, you and I. We didn't get on so well at first. I know you thought me brazen and I'll admit I thought you a bit of a prig. I confess it. But I am glad, my lord Biddleton, we have become friends. And we will part friends. So I will say good-bye to you, sir, and safe journey and I wish you happiness on your marriage."

She extended her hand and he took it and held it for a time until she pulled away and quickly returned to the house.

Chapter 14

The morning after his return to London, Biddleton awoke feeling tired and depressed. He winced as he remembered the miserable journey home. Throughout this seemingly interminable journey his sister, Lydia, and Eudoria Waxwood had remained silent, refusing to answer his attempts at conversation with anything but curt one-word answers and disapproving looks.

He then thought of Isabelle Clairemont and felt even more miserable. To think that he might never see her again. The thought was unbearable. The Earl forced himself to put aside these thoughts as he dressed and then went down to breakfast.

As he neared the dining room, he was approached by his butler. Mills looked distressed and Biddleton looked questioningly at him.

"Lady Ambrose is here, my lord. In the dining room."

"My sister here now?" asked Biddleton, frowning.

"Yes, my lord. She arrived an hour ago but she said you should not be disturbed. She said she would wait."

"I see, Mills." He hesitated and then walked through the dining-room doors. Mills watched his master sympathetically. He could well understand his lordship's reluctance to see his sister. Lady Ambrose was a most unpleasant female indeed.

Lord Biddleton entered the dining room and found his

sister drinking a cup of tea. She looked up at him and he found the same disapproving stare that he remembered from the day before. "Lydia," he said, advancing toward her, "you are here early."

"I was here earlier, brother, but your man informed me you had not risen. I suppose you were exhausted after all that strenuous singing at Winterhaven."

The Earl sat down across from her. "I see, Lydia, you are still displeased with me. May I remind you that I was at Winterhaven because of you?"

"Because of me?" repeated Lady Ambrose.

"You sent me after Lady Isabelle, don't you remember? She was supposedly eloping with your son."

"Yes, and thank heaven she was not! But that don't signify, Lucius. You did not have to stay at that house!"

"Oh? What should I have done? Walked back to London? You know that I was hardly in any condition . . ."

"Yes, yes, I know. You were ill."

"I was ill even though you prefer not to believe me."

His sister shook her head. "All I know is that I found you in that room singing with those dreadful people."

"There is nothing dreadful about them, except for Kingsley-Dunnett, of course. I found Lady Balderston and her guests quite charming."

"Yes, especially Lady Balderston's niece!" cried Lydia angrily. "I could see you thought her very charming."

Lord Biddleton flushed but answered calmly, "Lady Isabelle is a fine woman . . . intelligent, kind . . ."

"And beautiful," said Lady Ambrose archly.

The Earl frowned but said nothing.

"I refuse to believe it! I send you to rescue my Cuthburt from that woman and you become ensnared in her net."

"Her net? Come, Lydia, this is outrageous."

"I am not a schoolgirl, Lucius. I saw how you looked at her. No doubt she decided you were a much bigger prize than Cuthburt."

"That is enough!" shouted Biddleton.

Lady Ambrose was startled by his fury. "I am quite disturbed by your behavior, Biddleton. You acted quite shamelessly with that Clairemont female and now you speak to me in this shocking manner."

The Earl shrugged. "You may think what you will. Lady Isabelle and I did nothing improper."

"Hmmpf . . ." muttered Lady Ambrose. She eyed him angrily. "And what of Eudoria? That poor child. You must make amends with her before it is too late. Tell her you want to set your wedding date immediately."

Biddleton frowned and, as usual when the subject of his approaching marriage came up, remained stubbornly silent. Lady Ambrose stood up in exasperation. "I see you are still of a rebellious mind. I can't understand it. With your upbringing and all the trouble I went through to raise you . . ."

"Please, Lydia, I have no desire to hear of your sacrifices this morning."

She stared at him in horror and Biddleton felt guilty for his intemperate words. He said quickly, "I am sorry, Lydia, but I am upset. You have been quite unjust."

Lady Ambrose looked at him coldly. "Perhaps you will come to your senses in a few days now that you are away from that dreadful place."

"Perhaps," murmured Lord Biddleton.

"And I thought you could set an example for Cuthburt! I never imagined that you would be susceptible to that woman's devious charm."

"There is nothing devious about the lady's charm," replied Biddleton. "It is quite genuine."

Lydia sniffed, "The lady is quite notorious."

"Yes, you have said that before."

"She is a Clairemont! The family is infamous! It is well known that Lady Isabelle is frivolous and runs with a fast crowd. She has no sense of propriety. Why, do you know she was quite uncivil once to the Duchess of Huntley?" The dowager Duchess of Huntley was one of the matrons who presided over the elite assembly of Almack's.

"Really?" asked Biddleton, who was acquainted with the pompous and ill-tempered duchess, "I have often wished I could be uncivil to that lady myself!"

"Biddleton! Ignore that if you will, but can you ignore

the fact that Isabelle Clairemont is still on intimate terms with the notorious, adulterous Georgianna Haverly, who left her husband for another man and caused a great scandal?"

The Earl smiled. "I know of that and I do not care at all about it."

"Biddleton!"

His lordship smiled again and his sister fumed, "Oh, you are dreadful. I shan't stay here any longer." Her brother, far from being upset by this news, seemed relieved. He rang for the butler and Mills quickly appeared. The butler immediately observed her ladyship's obvious anger. However, to his surprise his master was smiling.

"Do see Lady Ambrose to her phaeton, Mills."

"That is unnecessary," said the lady, hurrying toward the door. She turned back, ready to deliver a parting speech, when she apparently changed her mind and proceeded out the door.

Lord Biddleton turned to his astonished butler. "Mills, would you see about my breakfast?" he asked calmly.

"Of course, my lord," replied the butler, and as he left he gave his master a quizzical look.

Lady Ambrose angrily contemplated her brother's conduct as she rode home. "He has never acted like this. It's all because of that Clairemont woman." The Clairemonts. Lydia was heartily sick of them. First her son and now her brother, Lucius, was entangled with the Clairemonts. She had been quite displeased to receive Cuthburt's letter that informed her that he was staying with Lord Robert at Fothingham. However, she was at least glad that Cuthburt was not in the company of one of the female members of the Clairemont family.

A few days after Lord Biddleton's departure from Winterhaven, Lady Isabelle left her aunt's house to return to London. Although she was sorry to leave her aunt, she felt strangely eager to return to town. Isabelle was surprised to find how keenly she missed the Earl's company and wondered whether she would see him when she was back in London. No, she decided. It was extremely unlikely. Lord

Biddleton lived quite apart from the Clairemonts' circle of friends. Besides, it was only a matter of time before the Earl married. As she thought of Lord Biddleton's betrothed, a slight smile formed on Lady Isabelle's lips. "Poor Biddleton," she said, shaking her head.

After bidding her aunt and cousin Hector and the Winterhaven guests farewell, Isabelle climbed into the carriage, followed by her maid. Mildred was carrying her mistress's new pet. Castor yawned and seemed rather blasé about his first journey to London.

The ride back to town was uneventful, far different from the journey to Winterhaven. Isabelle mentioned this to her maid and Mildred detected a note of regret in her mistress's voice. "Surely, my lady, you wouldn't want a repeat of that ride!" said the maid in horror.

Isabelle laughed and playfully patted her dog on the head. "No, Millie. I am not eager for that! But you must admit it was quite an adventure. I daresay, at least we have some diverting tales to tell when we return."

Mildred smiled. She was, in fact, looking forward to recounting their adventures in the servants' hall. Isabelle remained silent for a time, watching the passing countryside. When they reached the stretch of road near where they had been accosted by the footpad, Isabelle remembered that incident in detail. She then spotted the Potters' humble cottage and smiled. She turned to her maid. "There's the Potters' cottage, Millie!" Isabelle leaned out of the carriage window and shouted, "Stop here, Jock." The carriage came quickly to a stop. "I must see the Potters. Here, Millie, put Castor down and take this." She handed her maid a parcel tied in cheesecloth. "And I shall take this."

Isabelle and her maid got down from the carriage and made their way to the Potters' cottage, which Isabelle decided looked unaffected by the flood.

Mrs. Potter greeted them with exclamations of surprise and delight. "M'lady," she cried, "I did not expect you to visit!"

"I am sorry to come upon you without warning and I

211

cannot stay. Mildred and I are on our way back to London."

"Do come in, m'lady." Isabelle and Mildred entered the cottage and sat down upon two sturdy chairs. Little Jeremy Potter stood beside his mother, clutching her skirts, and looking up at Isabelle with wide eyes.

"Good day to you, young Jeremy," said Isabelle.

"Good day, ma'am," said the lad.

"How polite you are. I have brought you something, Jeremy." Isabelle took a parcel from Mildred and handed it to the child. An expression of delight came to Jeremy's face as he took the bundle.

"M'lady," said Maude Potter, "your ladyship had no need to bring him something."

"But I wanted to. Open it, Jeremy."

Jeremy pulled the wrapping from the object. "Ma!" he cried. " 'Tis a soldier and a horse, too."

It was indeed a toy soldier sitting upon a white horse. Both horse and rider had been carved from wood and painted with painstaking attention to detail.

"Oh, m'lady," said Mrs. Potter, " 'tis too fine a gift for folk like us!"

"Nonsense, Mrs. Potter. And it is a sturdy toy, I assure you, for my brother Lindsay had one very like it and it survives still, which is quite an accomplishment. And this is for you. It is a cake made by Mrs. Doig at Winterhaven. Mrs. Doig is known for her cakes."

"I thank you, m'lady."

"You are very welcome, but I fear it is small payment for the kindness you showed us when we came to your door that dreadful night. I am grateful that your cottage survived the flood."

"It was providence that saved us. The water come very near, but not to the cottage. All was saved, but for some of the crops. Will be in the fields now. Oh, he should like to see you, m'lady." As Maude Potter said these words, her husband entered the cottage.

"M'lady," said Will with a grin, "I saw the carriage and come a'running." He looked about the cottage. "Is his lordship not here?"

"I am afraid not," said Isabelle. "Lord Biddleton returned to London earlier."

Will looked disappointed. "Would your ladyship be seeing him in London?"

Isabelle colored slightly. "I am not sure, Will."

"I be asking, for I should like to thank him. First for the horse."

"The horse?"

"Aye, he said that he lost old Red in the flood, though 'twere no fault of his to be sure. And his lordship sends me a new horse and a finer animal was never seen in these parts. A fine strong mare she be, and never will be a better horse for pulling a plow."

"Aye," said Maude Potter. "A fine horse she be, but 'tis even more cause to be grateful to his lordship. There's the new shoes his lordship sent Will, but 'tis even more!"

"Is there?" said Isabelle curiously.

"Aye," said Will, "his lordship has canceled our rent payments for the year."

"Indeed? But how is that possible?"

"I thought your ladyship knew," said Will. "Lord Biddleton be the new landlord. He's bought all the lands in the county owned by Sir Francis Neville. Saved many a poor man like myself from ruin, though Mr. Galbreath, his lordship's man, has said we had best make good with next year's crops. And we will, too, for there will be no danger of flooding, for his lordship is seeing that the sluice gates be repaired. So if your ladyship could tell Lord Biddleton how grateful we are."

"Aye," said Maude, "and also that we hope he comes back to his new lands. A kinder gentleman never lived." Will Potter nodded and Isabelle smiled thoughtfully.

"Pa," said little Jeremy, taking advantage of the temporary lull in the conversation, " 'tis a gift from m'lady." He held the wooden soldier up.

"A fine gift," said Will, taking the wooden soldier. "I hope you thanked her ladyship proper."

Jeremy looked slightly startled. "Oh, I thank you, m'lady," he said eagerly.

Isabelle laughed. "You are very welcome, Jeremy. I am

213

so glad to see you all well and that things have worked out very nicely. I do not know if I shall see Lord Biddleton very soon, but if I do, be assured that I will convey your thanks to him. And now I fear Millie and I must leave you. Good day to you and farewell."

The Potters thanked her ladyship for her condescension, and Isabelle and Mildred returned to the carriage. Throughout the rest of the journey Isabelle was deep in thought. How good of him to help the Potters and the others. Why did he not tell me of it? Isabelle smiled to herself. Of course, he would not say a word about it. So lost in these musings was Lady Isabelle that she was surprised when they arrived at the familiar brick townhouse in which she and her family lived when in London. Mildred took the sleeping Castor from her mistress and Lady Isabelle was assisted from the carriage by one of the Clairemonts' footmen.

As soon as she alighted from the carriage, she was greeted by joyous shouts as her brother Lindsay and sister Harriet raced out to greet her.

"Belle!" cried Lindsay, giving his sister a quick but nonetheless enthusiastic hug. "I didn't think you'd ever get here! Tell us about the footpad! It must have been famous, getting held up and all. Although," he added with a grin, "I should have preferred a highwayman!"

Isabelle burst out laughing and Harriet shook her head. She looked scornfully at her brother. "Really, Lindsay, you are dreadful! Belle was in the gravest danger and you call it famous!" She looked over at her sister and asked somewhat eagerly, "Did you fall into a faint, Belle, at the sight of the villain? What did he look like? Was he dark and handsome? All villains in novels are dark and handsome."

Lady Isabelle's eyes sparkled. "I'm sorry to disappoint you, Harriet, but the rogue was neither dark nor handsome . . . just an unpleasant bully and I did not fall into a faint, I assure you. But I see I shouldn't have mentioned the episode in my letter. You two have much too vivid imaginations. It really wasn't all that exciting."

214

"Oh, Belle," said Lindsay despairingly. Both he and Harriet were regarding her with disappointed faces.

Isabelle laughed. "All right! Actually, it was dreadfully exciting and I shall tell you all about it. But let's go in. I want to see Mama and Papa." She suddenly remembered something and turned back to the carriage.

"Millie, hand me Castor."

"Castor?" Lindsay and Harriet repeated in rare harmony.

Lady Isabelle took the bulldog puppy from her maid and both Lindsay and Harriet let out shrieks. "A puppy!" cried Lindsay in excitement. "Aunt Agatha gave you one of Eurydice's puppies!"

"Oh, look at it," exclaimed Harriet. "It is so ugly!"

The bulldog gazed at her with its brown eyes and appeared offended by this remark.

"Don't mind her, old fellow," said Lindsay, patting the dog on the head. "Harriet ain't too fond of animals." He paused and added, "Or people either!"

"You little devil!" cried Harriet angrily. "I do too like animals." She gave Castor a tentative pat on the head. "And I like most people, although I can't abide a certain little brat."

"It is so good to be home," said Isabelle dryly, watching her sister and brother. "Come, you two. Declare a temporary truce and let's go in." Harriet and Lindsay glared at each other but quickly followed after their eldest sister.

Lady Isabelle was met at the door by Marston, who welcomed her back while gazing rather comically at the small bulldog. "A gift from Lady Balderston, my lady?" he inquired, looking at his mistress.

"Yes, Marston, this is Castor. No need to announce us. I shall introduce him to Mama and Papa."

The Duke and Duchess were in the drawing room and both jumped up with cries of delight at the sight of their daughter. "Belle, dear!" cried the Duchess, kissing her daughter and then regarding her with maternal pride. "You look wonderful."

"You are a welcome sight, m'dear," cried the Duke, following his wife's example and kissing his daughter resoundingly on the cheek. He looked at the bundle in her arms and asked jovially, "What's this? Belle and the Beast?"

"This, Papa," said Isabelle smiling, "is Castor, son of Orpheus and Eurydice. Aunt Agatha wanted me to have him."

The Duke shook his head. "Aggie and her bulldogs! She's always been besotted with those dogs of hers. I think it is because they resemble my late brother-in-law."

"Giles!" cried the Duchess. "Don't say such things. It is quite ridiculous."

The Duke smiled at his wife's reprimand, but he continued, "Did Agatha have her usual house full of lunatics, my girl?"

Isabelle smiled. "Aunt Agatha's houseguests were rather interesting, Papa."

The Duchess quickly entered the conversation. "Belle dear, tell us about Biddleton. I was so surprised to hear about your meeting him upon the road. Most unusual."

"Yes, Belle," chimed in Harriet, "tell us about Old Bore Biddle."

"Old Bore Biddle?" said Isabelle, looking strangely at her sister.

"Yes, Belle," laughed Lindsay, "that's what Papa calls him."

Isabelle looked over at her father. "Just a nickname the Earl has acquired, my dear," said the Duke, grinning. "He ain't the most popular fellow, you know. Rather dull and a miser, too, from what I hear. Damned odd, ain't it? A fellow with all his money? But I guess sometime that's the way it is with such gentlemen."

"Really, Papa," replied Isabelle, irritated at her father's condemnation of the Earl. "Just because Lord Biddleton does not frequent the gaming tables, you think him a miser."

"It ain't only that, daughter," replied her father, surprised at her tone, "they say Old Biddle spends all his time building up his estates and adding to his fortune. It just ain't natural for a gentleman to be so concerned with money."

Isabelle reflected that her father could use some concern

for money himself, but she merely smiled. "Well, I assure you, Papa, the Earl is not some old gudgeon who sits and counts his coins all day. For one thing, he is not that old. He is about Burwicke's age."

The Duchess had watched this exchange between her husband and her daughter with considerable interest. Although the Earl did not sound like the type of man her daughter would favor, the Duchess noticed Isabelle's quick defense of him. "I quite agree with Belle, my dear," she said to her husband. "I am sure the Earl is a fine man. After all, he is Cuthburt's uncle and Cuthburt is a very dear boy. But we musn't keep Belle any longer. She must be tired after her journey and needs to rest. We will hear all about her trip at dinner."

Isabelle smiled and nodded. "I fear I am a bit weary." She looked down at the bulldog in her arms. "Castor is tired too. Perhaps, Lindsay, you and Harriet could take him and ask Cook to give him something to eat." Her brother and sister happily agreed and quickly left the room, Lindsay proudly carrying the newest member of the household.

A few hours later the family was sitting around the dining-room table enjoying an excellent supper of roast duck. The conversation was dominated by Isabelle's account of her trip to Winterhaven. They all listened with rapt faces to the tale of the footpad and laughed at her recounting of the Potters' hospitality. They were horrified at the story of the flood and much impressed with Isabelle's account of Lord Biddleton's heroism. After a detailed description of all her aunt's houseguests and happenings at Winterhaven, Lady Isabelle decided she had talked enough and asked for some news of the family.

"Have you heard from Anne?"

"Oh, yes," said the Duchess, "she is having a wonderful time at Lucy's. She should be home in two days."

"And Rob has been staying at Fothingham?"

"The rascal. He left town without so much as a by your leave and sent us what appeared to be a hastily scribbled note concerning his whereabouts." The Duchess shook her head. "He is so impulsive, your brother Rob. He and Cuthburt Ambrose, who accompanied him to Fothingham, have been frequent visitors to the Cummings estate."

"I am sure they are enjoying themselves."

"I should say so," said the Duke. "Dashed odd leaving town during the season. Oh, not for you, Belle, or Annie, for you two have always loved the country, but Rob always wants to be in the thick of things. I expect we'll see him soon enough though. And really, things have been quite dull lately, haven't they, my dear?"

The Duchess nodded. "They have indeed, but after all, there have been so many Clairemonts out of town." She paused and smiled at Isabelle, who smiled in return. "But I should like to hear more about the Earl of Biddleton. It is strange that we have never met him. I wonder . . ." She left the sentence dangling and sat with a thoughtful expression on her face. Lady Isabelle glanced at her father and they smiled.

"Mary dear," said the Duke, "what great scheme are you planning now?"

"Scheme, Giles? I wasn't scheming. I was only thinking that since Cuthburt is such a good friend of Rob's and Lord Biddleton has become acquainted with Belle, why, we should invite the family over for dinner."

"Mama," began Isabelle, "I really don't think . . ."

"Yes," said the Duchess, ignoring her daughter, "it is time that we met Cuthburt's mother and uncle. Why, Cuthburt is like one of the family."

Isabelle burst out laughing. Her family looked at her strangely and she said in an unsteady voice, "I'm sorry, Mama. Really, I think I am still tired and feeling a little silly. If you want to invite them, by all means do, but I fear you will find Lady Ambrose a difficult dinner guest. And since you are asking the Earl, I think you might also invite his fiancée."

The Duchess's face fell. "His fiancée? Lord Biddleton is engaged?"

"Yes, Mama. I did not tell you that I met Lord Biddleton's fiancée and his sister at Winterhaven. When they heard he was ill, they rushed to visit him."

"And who is this fiancée?" asked the Duke, who, unlike

his wife, was not at all disappointed to hear of the Earl's engagement.

"Miss Eudoria Waxwood, Papa."

"Oh, yes," said the Duchess, "I believe she is the daughter of Sir James and Lady Samantha Waxwood."

"Sir James Waxwood?" cried the Duke. "By God, I know the fellow. Rather unpleasant. Met him at Drake's. A sour fellow he is."

"Giles!" warned the Duchess.

"Well, he was, m'dear," replied the Duke. "Frightfully rich, too, so I was told. I suppose Biddleton was looking for a large dowry."

"Really, Papa!" cried Isabelle.

The Duchess shook her head. "Then we must, of course, invite Miss Waxwood, too." However, Isabelle noted that her mother's enthusiasm had quickly vanished with the mention of Miss Waxwood, and she decided it was quite unlikely that the Earl of Biddleton would be receiving a dinner invitation to the Clairemonts after all. Oddly enough, she found this very disappointing.

The next afternoon Lady Isabelle was in the garden watching her youngest brother and sister playing with Castor. Harriet and Lindsay had already become devoted to the puppy, they refused to let it out of their sight for a moment. Castor seemed unconcerned by their excessive devotion and nonchalantly waddled around the garden sniffing at the flowers.

"Oh, dear, I hope that beast ain't uncivil to strangers," came a lazy voice from behind the hedges.

Harriet and Lindsay laughed and hurried over to the visitor. "Ain't he something, Mr. Fensbrook?" asked Lindsay with pride.

"Yes, Lord Lindsay, he is *something* indeed. But what?" replied the gentleman comically studying the bulldog.

"Oh, Mr. Fensbrook," said Harriet, "Castor is a bulldog, of course. Aunt Agatha gave him to Belle."

Mr. Fensbrook glanced over at Isabelle and smiled. "I should think, Lady Belle, your aunt could have found something more your style, not this ugly brute."

219

"He is not an ugly brute," cried Harriet, forgetting her first assessment of the dog. "Castor is the sweetest dog in the world." She patted the dog fondly and it wagged its stubby tail.

"Then perhaps Castor is the perfect dog for the Lady Isabelle then," said Fensbrook, "since, like his mistress, he appears to capture hearts so easily."

"Do quit your nonsense, Charles, and sit down," replied Isabelle smiling. He positioned himself on the bench next to Isabelle and continued to observe the bulldog.

"I must thank you for your letter, Charles," said Isabelle. "It was quite unexpected."

"Well, my dear Belle, I thought you'd be frightfully bored out among the provincials."

"No, indeed, I was not bored at all."

Lindsay quickly burst into their conversation. "Haven't you heard about Belle's adventure, Mr. Fensbrook? She was robbed by a footpad and then she and the Earl of Biddleton were caught in a storm and had to stay at a cottage and there was a flood and . . ."

"Not so fast, Lord Lindsay," said Fensbrook, "what's this about a footpad and Biddleton?"

"The footpad robbed the Earl, too," said Lindsay. "He even took his coat and boots!"

"Yes, the villain!" added Harriet dramatically.

Fensbrook looked over at Isabelle. "I had heard a tale about you and Biddleton together in some Godforsaken country place, but I could scarcely believe it. Odd that you did not mention it in your letter to me."

"In any case, Charles, it hardly matters, since you appear to be so well informed. I suppose Sir Francis had the club quite entertained with the story."

"I was not entertained," said Fensbrook coolly. "And what the deuce were you with Biddleton for? Or perhaps it is none of my business." The last question was asked in a mocking tone and Isabelle reddened. Instead of answering him, she turned to Lindsay and Harriet.

"Would you two please take Castor in for a while?"

"But Castor likes it out here, Belle," began Harriet who

220

was quite interested in her sister's conversation. However, Lindsay was already tugging at the puppy's collar.

"Come on, old fellow. Let's go in and see if Cook has a treat for you."

"Don't you dare," said Harriet. "He'll get fat!"

"Oh, Harry, a little treat ain't going to hurt him," replied Lindsay. The two continued this argument as they went off toward the house with the bulldog.

"What is more delightful than childish prattle?" Fensbrook commented dryly, as Harriet and Lindsay could be heard arguing in the distance. Isabelle frowned and Fensbrook shook his head. "My dear Belle, don't look so forbidding. Although I suppose anyone might appear so after being with that prig Biddleton for a time."

"Lord Biddleton is not a prig, Charles, and please don't refer to him as such. You are not acquainted with him well enough to make such a judgment."

"And you are, I see." His voice was again mocking, but Isabelle replied casually.

"I do know that I misjudged him at first."

"As he misjudged you?" suggested Fensbrook smiling.

"Yes."

Fensbrook leaned back and merely watched her for a few moments. He suddenly pulled himself forward. "You haven't told me, Belle, how you and the Earl happened to be together. You must admit it is rather strange."

Isabelle smiled and answered lightly. "Perhaps it is odd, but I assure you it is not worth discussing."

"Then you feel it is none of my business."

Lady Isabelle was becoming irritated by Fensbrook's mocking tone, but she remained silent.

"So that tale Neville told about you and Biddleton is true?"

"I do not know what tale he has been telling, Charles, but knowing Sir Francis, I doubt there was any truth in it."

"Oh? Neville said you and Biddleton seemed on quite intimate terms, waylaid together at some country vicarage of all places. Not exactly my idea of a romantic rendezvous, but I suppose it's Biddleton's style."

"A romantic rendezvous?" cried Isabelle in astonishment. "That is too absurd. We were stranded there together quite by accident. That is all."

"That was all? Not according to Neville. He said Biddleton is quite devoted to you and even flew into a jealous rage when he innocently mentioned the number of suitors you've had."

"Sir Francis Neville has never done anything 'innocently' in his life and you well know it, Charles. I am amazed you could believe such a story."

"Oh, I admit Neville likes to embroider his tales a bit, but I do suspect that Biddleton has fallen quite hopelessly in love with you."

"Don't be ridiculous."

"Then don't make me appear so, Belle."

She regarded him with surprise. "I don't know what you mean."

"I mean, my dear, I do not like to be made a fool. What will people think when they see you and Biddleton together?"

"Really, Charles! For one thing it is very unlikely that Biddleton and I will ever see each other again. And even if we did. I don't see how it would concern you!"

"How? I'll tell you, Belle. Everyone will think you've tossed me aside for that boorish prig!"

"Tossed you aside!" exclaimed Isabelle angrily. "I don't recall that there was any understanding between us. You have never been at all serious about me. The only reason you're concerned now is because you fear a blow to your vanity."

Fensbrook stood up angrily. "I see, ma'am, that you no longer wish for my company and quite frankly, I have no desire for yours!" He bowed and gave her one last mocking smile. Isabelle watched him go and wondered why she had not realized before now how shallow and conceited he was. At one time she had fancied herself in love with Charles Fensbrook, thinking him very charming and droll. However, for some time she had been disillusioned with him. As she sat in the garden and thought of Charles

Fensbrook, the image of Lord Biddleton appeared in her mind. He was so very different from Charles.

She suddenly wished beyond everything that the Earl were in love with her. What a dreadful thing to wish, she thought guiltily. He is to be married. It would be quite infamous of me to hope to steal him away from Miss Waxwood. She smiled ruefully and decided she had best forget the Earl of Biddleton.

Chapter 15

Lady Ambrose would have been relieved to learn that her
son had scarcely given a thought to Lady Isabelle Clairemont during his weeks at the Fothingham country estate.
However, she would have been far from pleased to know
that her son's thoughts were increasingly centered on Lady
Isabelle's sister Anne.

Cuthburt Ambrose had never spent a more enjoyable
week in his life. He and his friend Rob appeared at the
Cummings house every day to visit Anne and Lucy. The
foursome spent the days riding, feasting on the meals of
the Cummings' admirable cook, and enjoying quiet after-
noons playing cards or lawn games. Lord Robert, like his
friend, was also enjoying himself immensely. He was
pleased to see his friend and sister on such excellent terms
and also to discover that his old childhood friend Lucy
had become a very captivating young woman.

On the evening before they were to return to London,
Mrs. Cummings had planned a small dinner party. As
Anne was finishing dressing for the party, Lucy knocked
and entered the room.

"Oh, Anne, that dress is lovely."

"Thank you, Lucy. Yours is lovely, too."

Lucy sat down on the bed and watched her friend.
"These two weeks have been such fun," she said suddenly.

"Yes," said Anne, "it has been wonderful."

224

"And Mama had to spoil it by having this dreadful dinner party tonight."

Anne looked curiously at her friend. Lucy was quite fond of society and usually looked forward to even the smallest affair. "Why do you think it will be dreadful?"

Lucy gave a slight smile. "Oh, I don't know." At her friend's questioning look, Lucy laughed. "All right, Anne, I shall tell you the reason. Percival Dunston, the Marquis of Suthersby."

"Lord Suthersby?" Anne appeared confused. She was, of course, familiar with the marquis. In fact, all of society was familiar with the Duke of Wigby's foppish son Percival.

"Yes, Lord Suthersby is coming in all his magnificence," said Lucy, smiling at her friend's perplexed look. "Aren't I lucky to have such a suitor?"

"A suitor?" said Anne in astonishment. "Lord Suthersby? But surely, Lucy . . ."

Her friend giggled. "Can't you imagine me as Lady Suthersby?"

"Indeed, I cannot!" laughed Anne. "It is ludicrous!"

"You and I may think so, Annie, but I assure you, Mama does not. After all, Lord Suthersby is to be Duke someday and he is very rich. Although I wonder if he will remain so with the shocking amount he must pay his tailor," she added with a smile.

"But Lord Suthersby?" cried Anne, still rather astonished. "You really can't mean to marry him!"

Lucy shook her head. "I don't want to marry him, but being an heiress does have its disadvantages. Mama thinks every young man a fortune hunter." She looked at her friend and sighed. "But really, Anne, I think I should prefer a fortune hunter to Lord Suthersby!"

"Have you talked with him?"

"Oh, yes. He called on me twice before we left town. I fear he may make an offer tonight."

"But surely you'll refuse."

"Well, Mama made me promise not to refuse him right away, but to give serious thought to his offer. But I ask you, how can one be serious when thinking about Percival Dunston?"

Anne laughed.

"Come now," said Lucy, also laughing, "I must become composed if I am to get through this evening." She sat stonefaced and then suddenly burst into laughter. "I don't think I shall make it, Anne! But we had best go down. The guests should be arriving soon."

The two friends left the room and went downstairs. As they descended the staircase, they found Lord Robert and Lord Cuthburt Ambrose being ushered through the front door. Lucy feigned surprise as the two gentlemen greeted them. "How astonishing! Lord Robert has become a model of punctuality!"

Rob grinned. "What fellow wouldn't be punctual when visiting such lovely ladies."

Lucy smiled. "Come, Lord Robert, practice your skills of flattery on my mama." Rob offered her his arm and they went toward the drawing room, followed by Anne and Cuthburt.

Mrs. Cummings was standing with her husband and smiled graciously at her daughter's guests. She had always been fond of the Clairemonts despite the Duke's well-known excesses. She greeted Rob and young Ambrose and, as usual, was quite pleased by Lord Robert's compliments.

"Rob, you have inherited the Duke's charm as well as his good looks," she said smiling at that gentleman.

"Oh, Mama," cried Lucy, "don't make him any more conceited than he already is!"

Lord Robert shook his head sadly. "Mrs. Cummings, your daughter, as usual, misjudges me. I am not in the least conceited, although I admit few have more right to be than I!" They all laughed and Mr. Cummings claimed Lord Robert's attention by asking about the Duke and Duchess. His wife, always the perfect hostess, felt it her duty to engage Anne and the young Lord Ambrose in conversation. As they talked the other guests began to arrive.

It was to be a rather small dinner party and in a short time all but one of the guests had arrived. However, as the evening wore on, that one guest, Lord Suthersby, had still not appeared and Mrs. Cummings kept glancing furtively at the doorway, anxiously awaiting the marquis's arrival. In the meantime, her now-hungry guests were stealing glances at her, wondering when dinner would be served. Finally, the butler entered and announced Lord Suthersby. A much-relieved Mrs. Cummings hurried over to greet the young marquis.

Lord Robert, who had been talking to an elderly gentleman of jovial disposition, turned around at the announcement of Lord Suthersby. The marquis strolled into the room, absently waving his quizzing glass and peering about him.

Rob's companion gave a snort. "What the devil is that popinjay, Percival Dunston, doing here? Didn't know he was a friend of the Cummings'."

Lord Robert was also rather surprised, but he watched the marquis with an expression of amusement. As Lucy had predicted, Lord Suthersby had arrived in all of his magnificence. There was nothing remarkable about Lord Suthersby himself. He was a fair-complexioned young gentleman of average height and undistinguished features except for a rather long, sharp nose. However, the marquis's flamboyant clothes always called attention to him. That night he was wearing a waistcoat of an outrageous shade of green. His coat was even more gaudy than the waistcoat, for it was made of a glittering brocade and it was offset by a neckcloth tied in an extravagant fashion. Numerous fobs and seals hung from the waistcoat and Suthersby's fingers were bedecked with glittering rings. His lordship also sported a modish hair style—his light brown hair curled precisely to frame his face.

"Mrs. Cummings," he droned nasally as he took that lady's hand, "so——ooo delightful to be here." Lucy Cummings glanced over at Anne and made such a comical face that her friend had to quickly look at the floor to control an urge to laugh.

"Lord Suthersby," said Mrs. Cummings, "I am so glad you could come." She quickly looked around and, spying her daughter, motioned to her. Lucy dutifully walked over to her mother and the foppish young lord.

227

The marquis, still flinging his quizzing glass absently at his side, bowed as Lucy approached. "Miss Cummings," he crooned, giving that lady a heartfelt glance, "you look as enchanting as ever." Lucy managed a polite reply and quickly looked down at the floor. However, her effort to retain her composure was made more difficult when she saw Lord Suthersby's evening slippers were decorated with small gold tassels.

The conversation in the room had been arrested by the arrival of Lord Suthersby, and Lord Robert excused himself from the company of the elderly gentleman and approached his sister and friend Cuthburt. He leaned toward them and said in a low voice, "Gad, I feel like an absolute dowd in the presence of Suthersby." He looked down wistfully at his coat. "If only I could afford the fellow's tailor."

"Really, Rob," said Anne in warning.

Cuthburt smiled. "The marquis is a difficult fellow to miss in a crowd."

"No matter how hard one might try!" remarked Rob, grinning. "What is the fellow doing here, anyway?" He looked at his sister. "Come, Annie, I see that expression. What is Suthersby doing in the country at this time of year? Why has his lordship graced this dull company with his brilliant presence?"

"Hush, Rob," said Anne, looking about her. "Someone will hear you."

"Then tell me, Annie dear, and I'll be quiet as a mouse. I promise."

Anne gave a sigh. "Well, you see, Lord Suthersby is going to offer for Lucy."

"He what?" shouted Rob, quite forgetting his pledge. The other guests looked over at them in surprise.

"Rob," whispered Anne in embarrassment.

Her brother smiled and continued in an undertone, "That fool Suthersby thinks he's going to marry Lucy? What a farce!"

"But surely Lucy don't intend to marry the marquis," suggested Cuthburt.

"I don't think so, but Lucy says her mother is quite set

228

on the match," said Anne. "Lord Suthersby will be Duke one day and he is very wealthy."

"You forget, dear sister, that the man is also a complete and utter ass."

"I was not approving of the match, Rob," Anne protested. "It is quite unthinkable. But Lucy's mama . . ."

"I see," interrupted Rob, watching Mrs. Cummings and her daughter with the marquis. "Mama Cummings appears quite smitten by dear Percival." He frowned and Anne and Cuthburt exchanged glances. However, they did not speak, as Mrs. Cummings was propelling the marquis and her daughter in their direction.

"Lord Suthersby," said Mrs. Cummings, "you do know our neighbors here, the Clairemonts, don't you? Lord Robert and his sister Lady Anne. And this gentleman is Lord Ambrose."

Lord Suthersby lifted his quizzing glass and peered over his long nose at them. "Ye—ees, of course, Fothingham's children and . . ."

"Ambrose," said that gentleman, seeing the marquis's blank look.

"Dear me," said the marquis, "I don't believe I am familiar with the name."

Mrs. Cummings quickly said, "Perhaps you know Lord Ambrose's uncle, Lord Biddleton?"

"Biddleton?" said the marquis, distastefully dropping his quizzing glass. "Yes, I've met the fellow." Lord Suthersby considered the Earl a very dull fellow indeed. His tone was so insulting that Cuthburt, despite his recent fight with his uncle, was about to make a heated reply.

Mrs. Cummings, however, saw this danger and abruptly maneuvered the marquis away to greet some other guests. Lucy looked back at her friends with an impish smile.

The rest of the evening continued to be rather trying for Mrs. Cummings. Because of the tardiness of Suthersby's arrival, the dinner was overcooked and far below the Cummings' usual fare. She had also found it necessary to keep a constant watch over the marquis since he seemed to have a talent for offending her guests.

After the meal Lucy was persuaded to sing and Anne

229

accompanied her on the pianoforte. Lord Robert was uncharacteristically grim as he watched Lord Suthersby direct adoring gazes at Lucy. Cuthburt, however, seemed quite happy watching and listening to Anne's accompaniment. After a couple of uninspired ballads Lucy, to the relief of most of the company, refused to sing any more. With the entertainment over, the guests began once more to congregate in small groups to talk.

The marquis, keeping his eye on Lucy, leaned over to Mrs. Cummings. "Your daughter is so—ooo very delightful, ma'am, and such a voice!" He lowered his own voice and continued, "You and your husband have given your approval of a match between me and your delightful daughter, but I should like an opportunity to speak to her alone."

Mrs. Cummings nodded. The strain of the evening had taken away much of her enthusiasm about a match between her daughter and the eligible marquis. However, she instructed his lordship to wait in the garden and she would send her daughter out to him. She approached Lucy and whispered to her. Lucy appeared somewhat reluctant, but obediently left the room. Lord Robert had watched these maneuvers with interest and disapproval.

Lucy entered the garden and found the Marquis of Suthersby sitting on a bench, gently patting his side curls. Lucy held back a smile and approached him. When his lordship spied her, he suddenly stood up. "My dear Miss Cummings," he said bowing low.

"Mama said you wished to speak to me?"

The marquis smiled and pointed at the bench. "Do—ooo sit down, my dear."

Lucy went to the bench and hesitantly sat down. The marquis remained standing before her. "I think, Miss Cummings, that you are positively delightful." Lucy smiled but felt most uncomfortable. She looked down at her hands and wished she were inside.

"You are aware, perhaps, of my intention in coming here tonight?" Lucy said nothing and he continued in his droning voice. "My dear Miss Cummings! Lucy! I shall get right to the point. Will you be my wife?" As he said this, he was about to get down on one knee, but remembering his spotless britches, apparently changed his mind. Lucy, despite her embarrassment, observed this and almost laughed. The marquis sat down next to her and grabbed her hand. "What do you say, Lucy, my dear?"

Her promise to her mother flew quickly out of her head as the marquis fervently pressed her hand. "I am sorry, sir, I am flattered, truly, but I cannot marry you."

"What?" cried the marquis in considerable astonishment. "You refuse me?"

"Yes, I am sorry, but I must, my lord."

"What nonsense!" cried Suthersby, his face growing quite flushed. Thinking all she needed was a masculine demonstration of his great passion, the marquis pulled her to him and attempted to kiss her. Lucy avoided him as best she could and gave a distressed cry.

"Suthersby!" cried a voice from the darkness. "Let go of the lady or I'll bruise that beautiful face of yours!" The marquis quickly released Lucy and looked about him in alarm.

"Who is it?" he cried.

Lord Robert walked out from behind some bushes and grinned.

"Clairemont!" shouted Lord Suthersby. "How dare you! Eavesdropping on us!"

"I know, Suthersby. Always been terribly nosy. But in this case I'd say it was damned fortunate I was."

Lord Suthersby glared at him and said indignantly, "I have offered for the lady, Clairemont . . ."

"And she had the good sense to refuse you. Now I think you had best leave, old man."

The marquis looked at Rob and then at Lucy. He patted a curl into place and angrily stalked off. Lucy watched him go and then burst into laughter. "Oh, Rob, really, it was all too funny."

"Funny, ma'am?" said Rob smiling. "I save you from that fop's embrace and you find it funny? But forgive me, Lucy, perhaps you were about ready to change your mind."

Lucy continued laughing. "Poor Lord Suthersby. The look on his face when you threatened him."

"Poor fellow," agreed Rob sympathetically.

"Oh, dear," said Lucy suddenly, "I told Mama I would take some time to consider his lordship's offer."

"I think that half a second was more than enough time to consider it," remarked Lord Robert, grinning again.

Lucy looked at him and smiled. "And what were you doing spying on us like that, Rob?"

He shrugged. "I saw you leave after the marquis and, well, I just don't like the fellow and . . ." He looked at her and blurted out, "Oh, hang it, Lucy, I'm dashed fond of you and I don't want you marrying some damn fool like Suthersby!"

"Oh? And shall I have to get your approval, Lord Robert, before I can marry?" she asked playfully.

He nodded. "And I'm afraid, Lucy, I can only approve of one fellow for you. Me!" In spite of his light tone, she could see that he was serious.

"Rob!" she cried happily.

He quickly took her hands in his. However, just as he was about to speak, he was interrupted by a distraught Mrs. Cummings.

"Lucy, Rob! What has happened? The marquis left in such a huff. He didn't even say anything. Just walked out!"

Lucy and Robert were embarrassed by the unwelcome intrusion of Mrs. Cummings and looked guiltily at each other. Lucy spoke up first. "Mama, the marquis was quite horrible. He asked me to marry him and when I refused, he . . . grabbed me. Luckily, Rob heard me and came to my rescue."

Mrs. Cummings now appeared even more distressed. "That dreadful man! Oh, Lucy dear, I am sorry that your father and I allowed him in our house. To think of that man as my son-in-law." Mrs. Cummings sat down wearily on the bench. "Oh, what an evening this has been."

Rob looked over at Lucy and then spoke, "Mrs. Cummings, I wonder if you might consider a replacement for the marquis?" She looked at him as if he had lost his senses.

"What?"

"Me, Mrs. Cummings! I love Lucy and I want to marry her. I know I haven't got Suthersby's title or fortune, but I'm a dashed sight more agreeable!"

"And I want to marry Rob," said Lucy. Her mother looked astonished.

"When did this come about?"

"Now, Mama, although I've always wanted to marry Rob." Lord Robert looked rather disconcerted by this information.

"I don't know," said Mrs. Cummings uncertainly. She looked kindly at Rob. "You know how fond I am of you and your family, Robert, but . . ."

"But," said Rob sadly, "Rob Clairemont ain't the sort you'd want as a son-in-law?"

"You must understand, Rob. I must think about Lucy's future and I have heard that you . . . well . . ." Mrs. Cummings paused in embarrassment. Her husband had just mentioned the other day how he feared Robert was following in the Duke's footsteps.

"There is no need to explain further, ma'am," said Rob. "Oh, God, what a muddle I've made of things." He smiled at Mrs. Cummings. "I do understand, Mrs. Cummings. I ain't much of a prize. I am a second son with no fortune, although I will inherit a modest sum from my mother. I know my affairs are dreadfully tangled at the moment, but if I were to get them in order, would you perhaps reconsider?"

Mrs. Cummings looked at her daughter's pleading face and sighed. "Yes, Robert. I would reconsider."

He smiled gratefully at her but wondered how the devil he could ever get his muddled affairs in order. "Thank you, Mrs. Cummings, and now I will take my leave." He bowed politely to her and then to Lucy. He directed one last hopeful glance at that lady and returned to the house to find his friend Cuthburt.

* * *

233

The following day Mrs. Cummings declared she had a frightful headache and so the Cummings family decided to postpone their return to London for a couple of days. However, Lady Anne had promised her mother to return by the end of the week, so she arranged to return with her brother and Cuthburt Ambrose. Neither Lord Robert nor Lucy had disclosed the events of the previous evening to Cuthburt or Anne. But they both noticed Rob appeared to be in an uncommonly reflective mood. Lord Robert was not so distracted by his own problems that he could not see the ride back to London as an additional opportunity for his matchmaking. As he helped Anne into the carriage, he said he thought he would drive for a time. At her look of concern he laughed.

"Don't worry, my dear, I shan't be driving fast!" His sister did not appear convinced of this, but smiled. Lord Ambrose seemed quite pleased by his friend's suggestion. The prospect of riding back to London with the sole company of Lady Anne was quite agreeable to him.

As they set out, he and Anne easily fell into conversation. They discussed the previous night's party and laughed over the Marquis of Suthersby. Already they were reminiscing about their days in the country, recounting the fun they had had. After a time Cuthburt smiled and said somewhat wistfully, "I wish we could have stayed longer. The time went so quickly!" He looked at Anne. "Were you sad to leave too?"

"Yes," she replied smiling, "it was wonderful. But I will be glad to see everyone at home. I wonder if Belle has returned from Aunt Agatha's yet."

Cuthburt realized that he had not even thought of Lady Isabelle in the past few days. He spoke uncertainly. "Anne, did your sister, I mean, did she say anything about me that day I came to visit?"

Lady Anne looked at him with her frank blue eyes. "She said she feared she had made you unhappy." Anne paused and then continued, "I know you care for Belle and I do understand."

"Do you, Anne?" He paused and smiled at her. "No, I don't think you understand how I really feel. Oh, Anne,

I've been such an idiot! I only fancied myself in love with your sister like a silly schoolboy. It's you I love!"

She looked into his serious dark eyes. "Oh, Cuthburt, are you certain?"

"Absolutely certain!" he cried. As if to prove this statement, he leaned over, took her in his arms and gently kissed her. "Will you marry me, darling Anne?"

She smiled and replied, "Oh, yes, Cuthburt!" They sat quite happily then, holding hands and smiling at each other. However, reality suddenly presented itself unpleasantly before Anne.

"But Cuthburt, what will your mother say? I don't think she will approve and your uncle . . ." She looked at him despairingly. "He will think me a fortune huntress."

"Don't worry, Anne. I'll go talk to my uncle and . . ."

"Oh, no, Cuthburt!" she cried. "You mustn't. Not yet! Let us wait a while and not tell anyone. Please Cuthburt?"

He looked at her and smiled reassuringly. "All right, Anne. First, I will try to mend things with Uncle Lucius. Don't worry, it shall all work out, you'll see." However, he did not feel the confidence he expressed. Lord Ambrose knew his mother and uncle would be far from pleased by his plans to marry one of the wild Clairemonts. Wild? He looked at Lady Anne and smiled. No one could ever think of describing his beloved Anne with that term. "Yes, Anne darling, things will be fine." He smiled again, pulled her to him, and once again kissed her.

Chapter 16

The Earl of Biddleton took Pollux's leash from the footman. "Thank you, Dennis. Would you inform Mr. Galbreath I'm going out?"

Pollux looked very excited and pulled at his leash, but just as the Earl was about to exit from the parlor his butler arrived.

"Yes, Mills?"

"Sir Ralston Keith to see you, m'lord."

"Wonderful!"

Mills disappeared and returned followed by a very dapper Sir Ralston.

"Lucius," cried Sir Ralston, shaking his friend's hand vigorously and slapping him on the shoulders. "You look well. I've heard you were ill and was worried." Suddenly the baronet stopped and noticed the small white dog.

"What's this, Lucius? A new pet?

Biddleton laughed. "I suppose it is. I don't think I've had a pet before actually. This is Pollux."

Sir Ralston knelt down and patted a very amiable Pollux.

"Friendly one, isn't he?" said Sir Ralston.

"Too friendly, I should think. If he hadn't been so dreadfully agreeable to me I would not have received him as a gift."

"A gift?"

"Yes, from Lady Balderston. It's all a very long story, but I'll tell you everything about it." Pollux gave a short bark.

"Oh, dear, I promised the little fellow I'd take him to the park. Looks like Dennis will have to go in my stead though Pollux won't mind, will you old fellow?"

Pollux looked up at his master with an expectant look. "Oh, Lucius, he'll be heartbroken. I can see how he adores you. Come, let's both go. Its a splendid day for walking and I need the exercise."

"Well, if you don't mind?"

"Of course not and you can tell me how you acquired this worthy beast."

The two friends left the house and walked briskly down the street. By the time they reached the park Sir Ralston had heard the entire story of Biddleton's trip to Winterhaven. The baronet was astonished at his friend's changed attitude toward Lady Isabelle and thought he detected an unusual, wistful note in his friend's voice when the Earl mentioned that lady's name.

As they entered the park, the two gentlemen continued their conversation. Suddenly Pollux began to bark and strain on his leash. "What is it?" cried his lordship.

"Look, Lucius. Another dog running toward us. Good heavens, it could be Pollux's twin!"

As the other dog approached, Lord Biddleton began to laugh. "By God, Rolly, it is Pollux's twin."

The two dogs greeted each other excitedly, for the newcomer was indeed Pollux's twin brother.

"You don't mean Pollux has a twin? Named Castor of course."

"Of course, Rolly, and if Castor is here can some of the Clairemonts be far behind?"

The Earl looked eagerly across the park and saw a very young gentleman running toward them.

"Castor," he shouted and in a few moments arrived breathless.

"I say, young man," said Sir Ralston. "Here is your dog. Come to meet his brother."

The young gentleman grinned and looked at the two

young dogs. "This is famous!" he cried. "It's Pollux isn't it? Then one of you is the Earl of Biddleton."

"I plead guilty to being Biddleton," said the Earl with a smile. "And this is Sir Ralston Keith and you are Lord Lindsay Clairemont, of course."

"Good of you to know my name," said the young lord, quite impressed.

"Well, your sister has told me all about you."

Lindsay grinned sheepishly. "And she's told us all about you, sir," he said. "Said you were a nice gentleman and not at all a prig."

Sir Ralston burst into laughter and the Earl grinned. "Thank you, Lord Lindsay."

Lindsay looked embarrassed. "Oh, I said the wrong thing. Belle will be furious if I've offended you."

"You haven't at all. Now where is Lady Isabelle or are you alone?"

"Oh, I never go out alone. Belle and Harriet are following. Castor broke loose from me and I ran after him. Harriet started to run but Belle called her back. She said it wasn't proper for a lady to be running across the park, though Harry's a dashed good runner and can beat me any time, but please don't tell her I said so."

"Certainly not," said the Earl. "Come, shouldn't we walk along and meet the ladies? They must be wondering where you are."

"Yes, sir." Lindsay stooped down and patted both dogs. "They are alike, aren't they, sir? But I do know you, you naughty fellow." He took the leash. "Come on, Castor." Castor was quite happy at being reunited with his brother and the two bulldogs walked side by side.

"There they are," cried Lindsay pointing across the park. "Oh, how slow they are." Suddenly Lindsay turned his attention to Sir Ralston. "It's an honor to meet you, Sir Ralston. Rob said he met you. Burwicke says you're a real hero and if Burwicke says it, it must be so. How I'd love to be a hero."

Sir Ralston laughed. "I'm hardly a hero, though who am I to argue with Captain Lord Burwicke?"

Lindsay grinned again. "Is Burwicke a hero?"

Sir Ralston laughed. "I'd say so and I'll tell you, my young Lord Lindsay, your brother is probably the best captain in the King's Navy."

"Is he?" Lindsay beamed.

"Of course he is."

"I thought so," said Lindsay.

By this time they had neared the ladies and Harriet could no longer restrain herself but hurried ahead. "Lindsay!" she cried. "Did you find him?"

"Of course I did. He's here and this is his brother Pollux."

Harriet was delighted. "How wonderful. Why they are identical! They're so adorable!"

The Earl of Biddleton smiled at Harriet but looked past her at Lady Isabelle. How lovely she looked, he thought, and how glad he was to see her again.

Isabelle was very surprised to see the Earl again so soon and was slightly disconcerted at finding him there in the park.

"Lord Biddleton," she said, "I see you have met my brother Lindsay."

"We have had that pleasure. And this must be Lady Harriet."

Harriet smiled and dropped a much practiced curtsey. "How do you do," she said.

"And Sir Ralston Keith, how nice to meet you again."

Harriet's eyes grew wide. "Sir Ralston? Oh, dear! Are you really Sir Ralston?"

"Don't be silly, Harry," said Lindsay. "Of course he is. Ain't he got red hair and don't he look like a hero?"

Harriet gave her brother a warning look for calling her Harry but smiled at Sir Ralston, who she suddenly believed must be the handsomest man in the world.

"Your fame has certainly preceded you, Rolly," laughed Lord Biddleton.

"I fear my captain exaggerated a bit about my deeds, though it is certainly wonderful to have everyone think one is a hero."

"Will you tell us how you saved Burwicke?" said Harriet. "Please tell us."

"Yes," cried Lindsay.

"Oh, dear. I'm afraid poor Lady Isabelle and Lord Biddleton have heard this tale, but come you two, let's walk the dogs a bit. See, there's a bench over there and I'll sit and tell the entire story. And I promise you I'll embellish it enough to keep it interesting."

Isabelle and Biddleton laughed as Keith led the two young people off.

"Sir Ralston is a charming man," said Lady Isabelle and then she smiled her mischievous smile. "What did you say his yearly income was?"

Biddleton laughed. "Don't throw that one in my face again. I know you're not scheming to get poor Rolly, though if you were my old friend would be ecstatic."

"Lord Biddleton! Now let us be serious. I am glad to see you. It looks like Pollux is in good form. I hope your journey back to town was pleasant."

"Pleasant?" The Earl smiled ruefully. "Well, I am back in town and I already miss the fair countryside of Winterhaven."

"Nonsense."

"I do. But tell me. How is *Madame la Comtesse*? I have worried about her."

"Fortunately she is well. Aunt Agatha was concerned and so was monsieur, but next day she seemed quite cheerful though perhaps a bit subdued. She's ordered some new dresses. Modern ones."

"I think that's good, or is it? She always looked so splendid."

"Well, I think it is for the best. And now they are even talking about returning to France. The *comte* has written to a friend who has some influence with Bonaparte. Of course, one should not mention Bonaparte's name to monsieur."

The Earl smiled. "I do not much like hearing of him either."

"And the Kingsley-Dunnetts were hard at work when I left."

"Were they? God, what a fellow. His wife is not so bad

240

though. Actually she's quite talented. Pity she's shackled to someone like that."

"I think she misses you."

"Misses me? You mean Mrs. Kingsley-Dunnett?"

"Of course. After you left I heard her say, 'Henry, we'll never find another baritone as good as that fellow Biddleton.'"

"That fellow?"

"I'm afraid she did say 'that fellow,' my lord, and though she certainly did not show the proper respect for your rank, she did compliment you."

"And I am gratified. It is rare to hear compliments. Oh, I did hear another one, though Lindsay would probably not like me to mention it."

"What did Lindsay say?"

"He said that you said I was a nice gentleman and not at all a prig."

Isabelle blushed. "That Lindsay!"

"Oh, don't tell him I told you. I'm flattered, of course."

Isabelle laughed. "But I must give you a message, sir."

"A message?"

"From the Potters."

Lord Biddleton looked slightly embarrassed. "You saw the Potters again?"

"Yes, on my way back to town, and they want to thank you for the horse."

"That was only just recompense for the one I lost."

Isabelle smiled. "But I have it from Will Potter that his replacement horse is the best ever to pull a plow and so it is no mean horse you sent them."

The Earl laughed. "I am glad they like the horse."

"They do." Isabelle paused and regarded the Earl with her blue eyes. "You are a very generous man, sir."

Biddleton blushed. "Nonsense, Lady Isabelle, it was but a plow horse."

"I don't mean that, my lord. The Potters told me that you have bought the lands of Sir Francis Neville and are their new landlord."

"Neville was mismanaging his lands and was glad to be

241

rid of them. I bought the property for a very good price. Galbreath says it will turn a tidy profit in no time."

"So you would have me believe you bought this property to turn a tidy profit?"

"Of course. You know my reputation, after all."

Isabelle shook her head. "Do not fear, my lord. Although I do not believe you for one instant, I will not betray your secret."

"My secret?"

"That you are a very generous and extremely kind man."

Biddleton smiled and gazed into the magnificent blue eyes. "You speak nonsense, my lady Isabelle."

Isabelle smiled back at the Earl and felt again the impulse to throw herself into his arms. Fortunately she did not yield to this impulse but began to speak of other matters.

While Sir Ralston entertained Harriet and Lindsay with tales of the sea, a portly gentleman happened to be walking through the park. He walked rather slowly, for excessive exertion never failed to bring a pain to his side or distress to his respiratory system. Suddenly the portly gentleman stopped abruptly.

Why, it's Biddleton, I think, he said to himself. I think it is. My word! That's Lady Isabelle Clairemont, I think. Good Lord, I've come upon an assignation, I think. The cad! Poor Eudoria! He's a dashed bad one, I think and I think I've a duty to tell Eudoria. Yes, I think I do.

And the portly gentleman turned around and hurried off in the direction he had come.

"You really didn't have to escort us back, you know," said Lady Isabelle as they neared the fashionable townhouse that was the London dwelling of the Duke of Fothingham.

"It was a pleasure," said Sir Ralston Keith. "It's not so often that I get to escort two lovely ladies through town."

"Sir Ralston, don't say such things," cried Lindsay, noting that Harriet blushed with pride. "Harriet will be impossible to live with if she thinks she's lovely."

Harriet glared at her brother and Sir Ralston laughed.

"Lord Lindsay, I expect you had better behave like a gentleman to your sister Lady Harriet."

"You should indeed," said Harriet.

Lindsay frowned but did not want to make any ungentlemanly remarks while his hero, Sir Ralston Keith, was there.

"I hope you gentlemen will both come in for tea," said Isabelle.

"I think that would be most welcome," said Biddleton, glad to have more time with Isabelle.

"Good," cried Lindsay, who went rushing into the house to announce their arrival.

The Duke of Fothingham looked up as his youngest son burst into the room.

"Oh, it's famous, Papa!" he cried.

"What's that, my boy?" said the Duke.

"We're having Sir Ralston Keith to tea! And the Earl of Biddleton, too," he added.

"When will this be?" said his Grace of Fothingham.

"Now, of course," cried Lindsay. "Where's Mother?"

The Duchess entered the room just as her daughters entered with two tall good-looking gentlemen.

"Mama, Papa," said Harriet, "we have brought two guests for tea and also Castor's brother."

The Duchess laughed to see the two young bulldogs who were alike in every way. "Dear me," she said. "Not another one."

"Oh, this is not for us," explained Harriet. "Lord Biddleton owns Pollux."

The Duchess was relieved to hear this news, for she considered one bulldog more than enough. She looked at the Earl with great interest. Not exactly handsome, she thought, though a good strong face and not so unlike Cuthburt. Since her Grace was very fond of Cuthburt Ambrose, she was already favorably disposed toward his uncle.

"Oh, come in, gentlemen," cried the Duchess. "You must think us quite ramshackle. Please, Harriet, take the dogs to the yard. Let Edward watch them."

Harriet was reluctant to leave Sir Ralston even for a moment, but she hurried off and quickly handed the two leashes to a surprised footman and returned quickly.

"Now let me make the introductions," said Isabelle. "I know you have met Sir Ralston Keith." The Duke and Duchess nodded and looked fondly at that gentleman. "But now I should like to present the Earl of Biddleton. My parents, the Duke and Duchess of Fothingham."

Biddleton bowed, and as soon as the necessary amenities had been dispensed with, all of them sat down.

"Odd we've never met, Biddleton," said the Duke, studying him carefully. "I did know your father slightly. He was a good man."

"Lord Biddleton," said the Duchess, entering the conversation, "we are all grateful for how you protected Isabelle from that horrible highwayman."

"Footpad," said Harriet. "Belle said he did not have a horse, so he's not a proper highwayman."

Biddleton smiled. "He stole my horse and is probably now a proper highwayman." They all laughed.

"I hope the ruffian is caught," said the Duke, "and is hanged without much ceremony."

"Giles," cried the Duchess, "I really don't like talk of hangings in my drawing room." Lindsay, who was eager to hear of them, was disappointed when his father dropped the subject.

"Lady Balderston said the local authorities are looking for the blackguard," said Lord Biddleton, "but I doubt the constabulary of the village of Henley Green will have much success. The villain has probably fled the area."

"I hope he's caught," said Lindsay, but before he could make a remark about potential hangings, the Duchess silenced him with a warning look.

The conversation then turned to Sir Ralston, who informed them all that he was enjoying London but was forced to leave town to return to his family estate in the north to see to business.

"You must promise to call on us when you return."

"I will indeed," said Sir Ralston and the Duchess looked from the baronet to her daughter and decided they would make a handsome couple. Unfortunately, Lady Isabelle was paying little attention to Sir Ralston and the Duchess noted that she and the Earl of Biddleton kept exchanging glances.

The Duke noted this, too, and was glad to see that the Earl of Biddleton was not nearly so bad as he had been reputed to be. He is not at all a sporting gentleman, thought the Duke, but quite pleasant and a great deal better than that fellow Fensbrook.

Lord Biddleton was finding that he enjoyed the Clairemonts very much. They were a warm and vital bunch and it was impossible not to like them. Perhaps the Duke was a gamester and spendthrift, but he was a most amiable man and the Duchess was very charming. Their lack of pretension was refreshing and their conversation pleasant and amusing.

While Lady Isabelle, her parents, and youngest brother and sister were sipping tea and eating scones with Lord Biddleton and Sir Ralston, a carriage arrived at the townhouse. It was a familiar, much-worn vehicle that bore the crest of the Clairemonts and when it came to a stop out stepped three young persons just arrived from the country.

"Do come into the house, Cuthburt," said Lord Robert Clairemont.

"I should be getting home," said Lord Ambrose. He paused and looked fondly at Anne. "But I don't want to leave."

Anne smiled at him.

"And I won't just yet. Mother will be angry, but an hour or two won't make much difference."

"Fine, old boy," cried Lord Robert slapping his friend on the back. "Let's go in. I'm famished. We'll have Cook find us something. Come in."

Anne took Cuthburt's arm and the three young people entered the house through a door opened by a smiling Marston.

"Welcome home, my lord, my lady," he said, "and welcome to you, my lord Ambrose."

"Is Lady Isabelle home, Marston?"

"Yes, my lord. Her ladyship and their Graces are in the

drawing room with Lord Lindsay and Lady Harriet and two guests."

"Guests? Who are they?"

"I don't know, m'lord. I didn't announce them. Two gentlemen."

"Hmmm," said Rob, "Let us meet these mysterious gentlemen. We'll just go in. No need to announce us in our own house. Come on."

Lord Robert followed by Cuthburt and Anne entered the drawing room. Noting that one of the gentlemen in question was Sir Ralston Keith, Robert broke into a grin.

"Well," he said, "a crowd here to greet us after our long journey from Fothingham."

"Rob!" cried the Duke, getting up to greet his son with a hearty handshake. "And Annie dear." He kissed Anne and then turned to Cuthburt. "And Cuthburt, always a pleasure. And this is especially fortunate, your coming in, for your Uncle Biddleton is here too."

Cuthburt shook the Duke's hand but was so astonished to see his uncle sitting in the drawing room of the Duke of Fothingham that he could say nothing but stood gaping at the Earl. Lord Biddleton was equally astonished to see his nephew appear. They had parted on such bad terms that he had not looked forward to their next meeting.

"Cuthburt," said the Earl rising to his feet and extending his hand which Cuthburt took warily. "I didn't expect to see you."

"Nor I you, sir."

"How good this is to have you both here," said the Duchess. "Now, let me see, I certainly don't need to introduce you two gentlemen. And Sir Ralston, you have met Rob though perhaps not Anne and I don't know if Lord Biddleton has met Rob or Anne. Oh, dear. I will just say this is Lord Biddleton. This is Sir Ralston Keith. This is my son Robert, my daughter Anne, and Lord Ambrose."

Cuthburt was very confused by his uncle's presence. He had first suspected Biddleton had come to make some ridiculous scene but he noted that all the Clairemonts were smiling and happy and at least until his uncle had recognized him, Lord Biddleton had been smiling and acting as

246

if he were among his closest friends. It was all very odd, thought Cuthburt as he was ushered into a chair and offered a cup of tea.

"You must be tired."

"Yes," said Anne, who was regarding the Earl of Biddleton with keen interest and speculating about his presence there. "It was a rather long journey and we are all tired. I think I shall have to excuse myself soon and get some rest."

"Right," said Robert, "the old carriage ain't the easiest vehicle to travel in. Though I was driving and I daresay that made it a bit easier."

"Oh, yes," said Isabelle, "if Rob drove, be sure he hit every hole in the road. Poor Anne and Cuthburt. How you must have been jostled unmercifully."

Anne smiled and thought that they had been jostled quite a bit, but since she and Cuthburt had been the coach's only occupants, it had been great fun.

"I daresay," said Cuthburt. "It wouldn't do to comment on Rob's driving." The two friends smiled at each other. "But I do think Wilkins the coachman's hair is several degrees whiter."

"Cuthburt!" laughed Rob. "It is a very rough road!"

Everyone laughed and Cuthburt said, "It is good to see you all, but I must be getting back home."

"And we too must go," said Lord Biddleton.

"Rob was going to drive me to Paxton Court."

"That won't be necessary," said Lord Biddleton. "Ralston and I walked here. I've discovered it's not so far to my house and from there I shall drive you myself. We have had little time to talk in recent days." The Earl got up from the sofa. "I must say I enjoyed meeting all of you. I hope to see you all again soon."

The Clairemonts expressed the same sentiments with a sincerity that amazed Cuthburt Ambrose, who was so amazed by the whole thing that he did not notice the way his uncle's eyes met those of Isabelle Clairemont as he said farewell.

When the Earl of Biddleton, his nephew, Sir Ralston, and Pollux arrived at the Earl's townhouse, Cuthburt was still confused and a bit apprehensive. His uncle was still in an uncommonly good mood, doubtless caused by the presence of Sir Ralston Keith, who was a very good-natured and agreeable gentleman. Cuthburt was also surprised to see Pollux, for he had never thought his uncle to be fond of dogs.

"I say," said the agreeable Sir Ralston as they turned in at Biddleton's house, "I must be going, Lucius. I'm late as it is."

"Won't you come in for a moment?"

"I'm afraid not, my friend. I will leave you at your doorstep, for I must be off on some calls. I'll come again, Lucius, before I leave for the north." The two friends shook hands. "And you, Lord Ambrose, jolly good to see you again. Good luck to you." He shook Cuthburt's hand and was off.

Biddleton and Cuthburt entered the house and the Earl handed Pollux over to his footman and led Cuthburt to the drawing room.

"I say, sir," said Cuthburt, worried that now that Sir Ralston was gone, his uncle's good mood would vanish. "I should be going too."

"Nonsense, Cuthburt, I should like to talk to you."

Cuthburt felt some misgivings at this statement but entered the drawing room and sat down on the sofa and awaited the worst.

"We have not always been on the best of terms," said Biddleton, sitting down in a chair near Cuthburt.

"Yes, sir."

"There, that is an example. You call me sir."

"You are my uncle."

"Good lord, Cuthburt, I am not so much older than you after all. Nine years at most."

Cuthburt considered this. He had always thought of Biddleton as being far older than he.

"I don't want you to call me sir or even uncle. I hope you will call me Lucius and I hope we can be friends." Cuthburt looked amazed. "I know I have treated you badly, Cuthburt," continued Biddleton. "I shall be trying to improve, though I can't promise I shall be completely changed overnight, for I have been too long a cold fish and all those things people have rightly called me." Cuthburt could only stare at his uncle and marvel at his transformation.

"You probably thought I would lecture you about your hasty departure and spending time with Robert Clairemont."

"Yes, sir," nodded Cuthburt.

"Lucius."

"Yes, Lucius," said Cuthburt with a faint smile.

"Well, I am not going to do so. You did cause your mother a severe fright though. But I discovered I had been too hasty in my support of your mother against the Clairemonts. You see, I came to know Lady Isabelle and now realize that I misjudged her. I can well understand your regard for her."

Cuthburt felt uncomfortable. "I am glad sir—Lucius, I mean. But I have also discovered that my regard for Lady Isabelle was but a boyish infatuation. Lady Isabelle was always kind to me but never took me seriously. She tried to set me down easily, but I'm afraid I acted like a foolish schoolboy. I'm sure Lady Isabelle thinks me a complete ass."

"Come now, Cuthburt, the lady is far too perceptive and generous to think that."

Cuthburt looked at his uncle curiously. He had certainly changed and his newfound respect for Lady Isabelle was most odd.

"I suppose so. But, Lucius, you mean to say you no longer disapprove of my association with the Clairemonts?"

"Yes, that is what I mean. I think society has been too hard upon the family. And I will trust that you are old enough and well bred enough to be your own man and choose your own friends. You've always had a level head, Cuthburt. I've known it for some time but still treated you like an infant."

Cuthburt smiled broadly.

"I want to be friends now, Cuthburt. I truly do."

"I can't tell you, sir, Lucius, I mean," said the young Lord Ambrose, "what this means to me." Cuthburt paused and looked thoughtful. "Lucius," he said finally, "I was not going to tell you this." He paused and Biddleton waited for him to continue.

"I would like to marry Lady Anne Clairemont," he said suddenly and looked warily at Biddleton.

To his surprise his uncle smiled. "Is this not rather sudden?"

Cuthburt blushed. "I know I seem ridiculous and shallow, having transferred my affections so easily from one lady to her sister. But if I had not been so blind, I would have realized Anne and I were suited. I could not see that at first, for I was so blinded by Lady Isabelle's beauty. Anne is just as beautiful though in a quieter way and she is a very sweet and gentle girl. I know we should be happy."

"And how does Lady Anne feel about this?"

Cuthburt looked slightly embarrassed. "Anne loves me," he said, "as I love her."

The Earl looked sympathetically at his nephew. "But you are very young."

"I shall be one and twenty in the fall and Anne is just turned twenty. Many have been younger."

Biddleton looked thoughtful and Cuthburt waited fearfully for his reply.

"We shall have a time convincing your mother of the suitability of the match," said the Earl with a smile.

"You mean you approve, sir? I should say Lucius? After all, Anne has little money."

"Did you want a rich wife then, Cuthburt?"

Lord Ambrose laughed. "I do not care in the least about the money, for I have enough, but I thought you would say it foolish not to consider money at such times."

"And it is foolish. But as you say, you can easily support a wife on your income and you reach your full majority in a few months. Lady Anne appears to be a very well-bred and charming young lady. No, my dear Cuthburt, I do not object. If Lady Anne will have you, I will give you my full support in convincing Lydia."

"Lucius," cried Cuthburt, impulsively grasping his uncle's hand and shaking it enthusiastically. "What a lucky

250

fellow I am to have such an uncle! I can never thank you enough. And I'm sure Mother will come round when she knows Anne and if you put in a word for us. Mother always follows your advice."

The Earl lifted his eyebrows at this and smiled, for he had never known Lydia to be receptive to his advice.

The Earl rose. "Well, Cuthburt, I am glad we are finally friends now, but I think it's time for you to see your mother. When you need my help, it will be there. Now I will have Maxwell bring round the curricle for you." He extended his hand again and Cuthburt shook it gratefully.

"Thanks awfully, Lucius," he said and departed, thanking whatever forces, be they natural or supernatural, that had transformed his uncle.

The Earl smiled at his nephew's elated expression and watched him go. It was a novel experience to part so amicably and it would be good to have a nephew whom one could regard as a friend rather than as a meddlesome schoolboy.

Biddleton smiled at the thought of Lydia's reaction to Cuthburt marrying one of the Clairemonts. He became suddenly serious. A pity that it is not her brother who is marrying into that family. The Earl shrugged and went to find his secretary, Galbreath.

Chapter 17

Miss Eudoria Waxwood was alone in the parlor when the butler announced the arrival of Mr. Garfield Chalmers.

"Oh, please do send Mr. Chalmers in," she told the servant. When the butler left the room she hurried to the mirror over the mantel and anxiously glanced at her reflection. Miss Waxwood decided she looked quite pale and wan. Thus reassured, she retreated to the sofa and eagerly waited for the gentleman's arrival.

Mr. Chalmers entered the room a moment later. His face was redder than usual and he appeared out of breath.

"Miss . . . Waxwood," he puffed, taking a few steps into the room.

"Mr. Chalmers!" cried Miss Waxwood in alarm. "Whatever is the matter?" She quickly got up and solicitously escorted the gentleman to the sofa.

Garfield Chalmers continued taking gulps of air as the lady patted his arm reassuringly. Finally his breathing returned to normal and his face also returned to its natural color. He mopped his forehead with a handkerchief and looked apologetically at Miss Waxwood.

"Do forgive me, Miss Waxwood. A bit winded, I think. Walking here too briskly, I think. Yes, too briskly."

"Think nothing of it, sir. But you shouldn't overexert yourself."

"Yes, yes. You are quite right. Quite right, yes." Mr.

Chalmers shifted his rotund form uncomfortably and his face bore a pained expression.

"Mr. Chalmers, is there something wrong?" asked Eudoria, noting Mr. Chalmers's look of distress.

He looked at her and briskly nodded his head. "I fear it is. Yes, most definitely I fear so, Miss Waxwood."

"Tell me then. Perhaps I can help."

Her offer made him appear even more miserable. "You are so good, Miss Waxwood. So very good. And Biddleton don't deserve you."

Miss Waxwood was in agreement with his estimation of the Earl and said plaintively, "Yes, but I am pledged to marry him." She looked tragically at Mr. Chalmers. "My engagement to Lord Biddleton has been a severe trial."

"Dear lady!" cried Mr. Chalmers. "You cannot marry the fellow. He is a cad and a bounder, I think. A scoundrel, I think."

Miss Waxwood seemed surprised by the gentleman's vehemence. "Why, Mr. Chalmers . . ."

"I tell you, Biddleton ain't a fellow to be trusted."

"Have you . . . do you have some information on the Earl?" asked Miss Waxwood curiously. Mr. Chalmers gave a reluctant nod.

"Please tell me, sir," pleaded the lady.

Mr. Chalmers sighed. "It pains me to tell you, dear lady, but it is my duty, I think. Yes, my duty." He looked at her and she nodded encouragingly at him to continue.

"Well, you see, I was walking in the park just now and I saw Biddleton." He paused, his face growing redder again.

"Yes? You saw Biddleton? Was he alone?"

"No, dear lady. He was not. He was with another lady."

"Oh, I see."

"My dear Miss Waxwood," cried Mr. Chalmers in a concerned voice. "I fear you look ill. I shouldn't have told you this, I think. Too disturbing, I think."

She weakly put her hand up. "No, sir. It is quite good of you to tell me this." She hesitated. "Did you recognize the lady, sir?"

"Yes. She was the Lady Isabelle Clairemont, I think. Yes, quite definitely the Lady Isabelle."

Miss Waxwood flushed. "Lady Isabelle and Lucius! Humiliating me like this. It is quite infamous."

"Yes, dear lady, quite infamous. Quite infamous indeed."

She looked meaningfully at Mr. Chalmers. "You know, sir, I never really wished to marry Biddleton. Even as a girl I thought him quite unpleasant. But our families were quite set on the match . . ."

"I do understand, of course," murmured Mr. Chalmers sympathetically.

"But I don't care. I shan't marry him! It would be quite intolerable."

Mr. Chalmers brightened. "Yes, yes, intolerable. Quite intolerable to be sure."

She looked at him and suddenly smiled. "I must thank you, sir, for coming here today and telling me this. You have saved me from a most horrible mistake."

"I, my dear lady?"

"Yes, you have convinced me that I could not marry a man such as Biddleton. A . . . a cad, didn't you say?"

Mr. Chalmers looked thoughtful. "I did call him a cad, I think. A cad and a bounder."

Miss Waxwood nodded and said distastefully, "That is exactly what he is. And you, sir," she added in a much different voice, "are quite good and noble."

Mr. Chalmers blushed and stammered a protest.

"No, sir," said Miss Waxwood with conviction, "you are too modest. I recognized your good and noble character from the beginning. I . . . I often wished Biddleton was like you."

"Miss Waxwood . . ." he began in a choked voice.

"Eudoria," she corrected him.

"Eudoria," he said, "dear lady! I am devoted to you. I think I mustn't say this. Haven't any right, I think."

"Oh, Garfield," she returned, "what nonsense! You have every right, you dear and noble man."

His round face brightened. "Do you mean? Could you

mean, Miss . . . Eudoria, that you would consider marrying me?"

"I shouldn't have to consider it, Garfield, I would say yes immediately." Mr. Chalmers appeared elated and with some effort he knelt down in front of her.

"Will you marry me then, dear Eudoria?"

"Yes, Garfield, I will." He grasped her hands in his and they gazed adoringly at each other.

It was unusually quiet at the residence of the Duke of Fothingham and Isabelle savored the rare silence. She was the only one left at home that day. The Duke and Duchess, Anne and Harriet were paying a call and Rob and Lindsay were off somewhere with Castor.

Although the Duchess wanted Isabelle to accompany them, Isabelle had begged to be excused saying she did not feel up to visiting anyone. Actually Isabelle wanted some time to herself and the Duchess, sensing her daughter's mood, did not press her.

Isabelle spent the time in her sitting room but soon found she could do little but think of Lord Biddleton and began to wish she had accompanied her parents. If only he were not engaged, she thought. She smiled. Or not so honorable. Heavens, Belle, she told herself with a laugh, you are dreadful.

Her ladyship felt suddenly restless and left her sitting room and decided to go downstairs. Just as she reached the staircase, she heard loud voices. It was the butler, Marston, and a loud man who was talking angrily.

"I demand to see him," cried the man.

"His lordship is not in!" said Marston forcefully.

"You've said that, but I believe his lordship is in and I will see him."

Isabelle hurried down the stairs to aid Marston. "What is this," she said angrily. "Who are you, sir, to speak so?"

The stranger regarded Lady Isabelle with an appreciative eye. "Pardon, your ladyship," he said. "I don't mean to upset your ladyship, but I'm here to see Lord Robert, who I expect is your ladyship's brother, you being Lady Isabelle I'd warrant."

"You have the advantage of me, sir."

"Arthur Grilling at your service, my lady."

The man made an awkward bow and Isabelle studied him. He was not very tall but powerfully built and dressed with care. He looked much like a prosperous merchant, but there was a hardness to his features and an insolent air about him despite his outwardly subservient manner. He was perhaps about fifty years of age and Isabelle decided he was altogether a most unpleasant fellow.

Marston looked helplessly at his mistress. "This person would not leave though I have told him that Lord Robert is not at home."

"It is all right, Marston, I shall see Mr. Grilling myself."

"You, my lady?" said Grilling.

"Yes, do come into the drawing room, sir." Marston looked reluctant to allow Grilling into the house but he frowned and stood aside. Grilling gave the butler a scornful look and followed Lady Isabelle into the drawing room.

"Do sit down, sir," she said.

Grilling looked pleased. "Very kind of you to condescend so, my lady," he said.

Isabelle smiled. "Let us get to the point, sir. I know you are here about my brother's debts."

Grilling smiled. "I see his lordship has taken his sister into his confidence, but this is men's business and if your ladyship could fetch Lord Robert. . . ."

"He is not here and if you won't believe Marston, I hope you will believe me."

"Of course, my lady. I wouldn't doubt a lady's word."

Isabelle smiled. "Now I pray you tell me why you are here. I shall inform my brother."

Grilling sat back in the sofa and rubbed his chin thoughtfully. "I suppose I could, your ladyship being a lady of obvious perception, a right clever lady and all. Aye, I'll tell your ladyship. Lord Robert is in debt, m'lady, and has been too long in paying. He borrowed from my establishment to pay off some rather embarrassing debts and now the debts are due. We've waited far too long already, being sensitive to his lordship's rank as we are. But we can't wait much longer and I fear, my lady, that it could be rather unpleasant if Lord Robert don't pay up."

Grilling smiled and Isabelle shuddered, for he reminded her for a moment of Henry Kingsley-Dunnett. Although she was revolted by Grilling, she did not want to anger him.

"Pray, sir, give me the exact amount of my brother's debts."

Grilling frowned.

"I would be grateful if you did so, Mr. Grilling." She managed a charming smile.

"Eight thousand pounds," he said.

"Eight thousand pounds?"

"A tidy sum, m'lady, and you can see why I've got to collect. It's not only me, of course, but I've got a business and associates to think of."

Isabelle was shocked at the sum, for she had no idea the amount was so staggering but she tried to remain calm.

"Do not worry, Mr. Grilling. I assure you you will have the sum in full. I shall see to it myself. You have my word."

"Then that's good enough for me, m'lady. I won't take any more of your ladyship's time."

"Good day to you, Mr. Grilling."

Grilling bowed. A very cool lady she is, he thought. And ladies like her have ways of getting some blunt together.

He smiled as he left the house, feeling that his talk with Lady Isabelle would be likely to bring some results.

Her ladyship sat for a time in the drawing room pondering Grilling's visit. What a detestable man, she thought. Oh, Rob, how shall we get you out of this? Isabelle knew her father's affairs were so tangled that it would be impossible to find eight thousand pounds anywhere. "If only Burwicke were here." Yet her brother Burwicke had little money himself, and she doubted if he would know what to do.

There is only one person to whom I might go for advice, she thought. No, I couldn't. Isabelle got up and paced across the drawing room. Yes, I could. If anyone will know what to do it will be Biddleton. She nodded and left the room.

Chapter 18

The Earl of Biddleton was having a difficult time concentrating on Mr. Galbreath's sage advice concerning some of his western properties. "And I should recommend certain improvements at Tildondale," the able Mr. Galbreath was saying. "I think a few modest steps might enable your tenants there to increase their wheat production." Biddleton nodded. He did not care at that moment what Galbreath wanted to do, for he was thinking only about Lady Isabelle Clairemont and how she had looked when they met at the park the previous day. Mr. Galbreath, having concluded his business, bowed and left Biddleton to his thoughts.

The butler, Mills, entered a few moments later and his lordship looked up. "Sir Ralston Keith to see you, my lord."

"Oh, good, do show him in, Mills." The Earl was happy to hear his friend had come again, though he was a little surprised, for he had not expected another visit so soon.

"Rolly," said the Earl as Sir Ralston entered the library, "so good to see you."

"Well, I can only stay a short while. I'm afraid I'm off to the North sooner than I expected. It seems there is a bit of trouble with some of the tenants."

"I hope it is nothing serious."

"So do I." Sir Ralston smiled. "But it's best I'm off today. I only wanted to stop and see you first."

"I'll miss you, Rolly. God, it's been good having you back."

"It's good of you to say so, Lucius." Sir Ralston looked closely at his friend. "I say, old man, you do look in rather low spirits. It's certainly not my hasty departure that's got you blue deviled."

The Earl laughed. "I'm not at all glad you're going, but it is something else."

"Do you want to tell me about it?"

"I should hardly think I should burden you with more problems."

Sir Ralston laughed, "Burden away, old friend. I do want to hear about it if you wish to tell me."

Biddleton hesitated. "Yes, I should like to tell you. You've never thought me a romantic, have you?"

"Hardly."

The Earl smiled. "And I am not a romantic, or I didn't think so anyway. I have always been very pragmatic and practical about things and now . . . ." His lordship looked embarrassed. "I have fallen in love for the first time in my life, and I am nearly thirty and engaged to be married besides." Biddleton looked at his friend to see his reaction, but Sir Ralston did not look at all shocked. "You aren't astonished, Rolly?"

"Not really, Lucius," said Sir Ralston. "I mean I was there yesterday when we met Lady Isabelle."

"What?"

"Oh, Lucius!" cried Sir Ralston, laughing, "I would have been blind if I hadn't noticed how you looked at Lady Isabelle. And it's not so unusual. She is one of the most beautiful and charming ladies I have ever met."

The Earl frowned. "So I am so very obvious. Good lord. She probably thinks me a terrible gudgeon. How could she ever have any affection for someone like me?"

"By my honor, Lucius," said Sir Ralston, "Lady Isabelle may not think you a gudgeon, but I certainly do. I have never heard such ridiculous talk. Are you blind, my friend? It was so obvious to me that Lady Isabelle Claire-

259

mont is much attached to you. Indeed, my friend, I envied you."

"What?"

"Oh, Lucius, don't you remember how happy she was to see you? My God, man, she is dashed fond of you."

"Nonsense. She is in love with Charles Fensbrook."

"That coxcomb? I should hope you'd give Lady Isabelle more credit than that."

"Do you really think she is not in love with Fensbrook?"

"I know it. Lady Belle ain't one to hang after an idle fellow like Fensbrook especially after she's seen my friend Biddleton."

"Don't be absurd, Rolly!"

"Don't you be absurd!"

"Then you are serious?"

"Of course, Lucius."

Biddleton sat down on the sofa and looked at his friend mournfully. "But I am engaged to Eudoria."

"Engaged, not married, and I thank Heaven you are not, for Miss Waxwood would have made you miserable and you her."

"But I am honor bound to marry Miss Waxwood."

"Would you make both of you miserable because of your devotion to your honor? Think, Lucius."

"What can I do?"

Sir Ralston smiled. "You could either murder Miss Waxwood, though I do not recommend it, or you could cry off."

"Cry off? A gentleman would not 'cry off' as you put it."

"Hang it, Lucius, forget your infernal gentlemanly honor. Think of Lady Isabelle Clairemont."

The Earl looked thoughtful. "You're right, of course. I will break the engagement. I must. I don't know how I thought I could go through with it. What would I do without you, Rolly?"

"I don't know," said Sir Ralston Keith with his usual smile. "I really don't know."

*　　*　　*

Sir Ralston Keith's visit had left the Earl of Biddleton in a hopeful mood and he resolved to visit Eudoria immediately. He was usually a cautious man and was more inclined to listen to his head than his heart. Perhaps it was quite ludicrous that Lady Isabelle could ever be in love with him. She was a beautiful, vivacious woman, while he was a stodgy bore. He thought of Sir Ralston's words and smiled.

He had made his decision. Perhaps Lady Isabelle had no real feeling for him, but he had to find out. He knew most definitely that he could never marry Eudoria Waxwood. If he could not have Lady Isabelle Clairemont for a wife, he would have no one. He would go and see Eudoria and break off the engagement.

Lord Biddleton hesitated. Breaking off his engagement to Eudoria would not be easy. It was quite unthinkable for a gentleman to cry off and most awkward. Yet there was no choice. I will explain to Eudoria and hope for the best, he thought. That is all I can do. Having made up his mind, he rang for his butler and instructed him to have his phaeton readied.

A short time later, Lord Biddleton entered the Waxwoods' drawing room where he found his betrothed. As he entered she looked up from her embroidery and stared at him. Biddleton noticed that Eudoria had a touch of color in her usually sallow cheeks, and her eyes appeared animated. He walked over and took her hand.

She nodded coolly. "Lucius, it is quite convenient that you chose to visit me today."

"Convenient?" asked the Earl raising his eyebrows.

"Yes, you see, I wanted to speak with you."

"Oh?"

She looked down at her embroidery and made a few jabs at it with her needle. "I needn't tell you, Lucius, that I have been disturbed by your behavior of late."

"Yes, I have been aware of that."

She glanced up at him. "I was never so shocked as when I went to that . . . house. I expected to find you dreadfully ill and instead, there you were, looking quite healthy and singing some horrid song!" She paused and

Lord Biddleton was amused by her opinion of what the egotistical Kingsley-Dunnett considered a masterpiece.

Miss Waxwood seemed to catch the amused look in the Earl's eyes, for she suddenly bristled. "I really don't know what has come over you!" She eyed him coldly and Lord Biddleton frowned. Miss Waxwood added spitefully, "Or perhaps I do know." Biddleton began to speak, but Eudoria put up a thin hand in a gesture of dismay. "Please do not say anything until I am finished. I shan't discuss your behavior any further except to say that it has been quite shameful. And so, Lucius, I will get to the point. I do not wish to marry you."

At this fervent declaration, Lord Biddleton was filled with elation, but he attempted to retain an appropriately sober expression on his face. "You see," continued Eudoria, "we are quite unsuited. I never especially wanted to marry you, but since it was my duty . . ." She trailed off but then continued, "But in the past few weeks the idea of marrying you has become quite . . . abominable to me!" Lord Biddleton could have expressed mutual accord with this, but tactfully remained silent. Eudoria looked down at her embroidery. "What if we did marry? No doubt you would be keeping that female or another."

"I should be *what*?" cried the Earl incredulously.

Miss Waxwood blushed. "I know a lady is not supposed to mention such things, but I, for one, would not tolerate such a situation. Many wives do, I suppose, but I will not!" She looked at him and said sarcastically, "Oh, do not take on that self-righteous expression. You cannot delude me any longer."

"Delude you? Please explain yourself, ma'am. Such monstrous accusations must be explained."

Both of them were now quite angry. Miss Waxwood put a hand to her forehead. "Oh, I am getting the most frightful headache." Biddleton seemed unsympathetic and she glared at him. "All right, I shall explain, but I blush to do so, for it is really quite scandalous. You and Isabelle Clairemont have been most brazen, going off together like you did."

"Going off together? You are quite mistaken, ma'am. I

262

was following Lady Isabelle because . . ." He stopped. The Earl had no wish to discuss his earlier suspicion about Isabelle with Miss Waxwood. He was at a loss as to what he could say.

"Please go on," said Eudoria, quite pleased by the Earl's obvious discomfiture.

"I . . . we . . ." began Lord Biddleton in confusion, but he suddenly said hotly, "you are quite wrong about Lady Isabelle and I shan't hear such slander against her!"

She shook her head. "As I said, Lucius, I will no longer be deluded. I know you now for what you are."

"And what, pray, is that, ma'am?"

She looked at him and her face was solemn as she passed her judgment. "A rake."

The Earl stared stupefied at her and then quite surprisingly burst into laughter. The situation had suddenly seemed quite ridiculous even to the Earl of Biddleton.

"Really, sir!" cried Eudoria. "You are insufferable!"

"An insufferable rake," commented Biddleton, still laughing. He decided that Lady Isabelle would appreciate the joke. That he, Lord Biddleton, known in society as a priggish bore, was suddenly considered a womanizer, a despicable rake, was quite absurd. He finally regained his sense of decorum, although he almost lost it again at the sight of Eudoria's shocked face. "Do forgive me, Eudoria. I have acted badly, but believe me, I am no rake. It is true that I have developed a very high regard for Lady Isabelle. But I assure you that your view of that lady is completely distorted and unfair."

"Please do not continue," replied Eudoria coldly. "You need not sing the lady's praises to me." She went on somewhat hesitantly. "You see, in my distress over you I found a friend and sympathetic supporter in . . . Mr. Chalmers." She glanced at the Earl but he showed no great surprise. "Mr. Chalmers was so kind and supportive. I became quite fond of him and I am going to marry him!"

"Marry Chalmers?" repeated Lord Biddleton and he suddenly smiled. "I am glad, Eudoria. I think Chalmers is just the man for you."

She was somewhat irritated by the evident relief on his

face, but she nodded. "So, Lucius, I suppose this ends the thing."

"Yes," he replied, trying to look grave. "I regret, Eudoria, that I may have caused you any embarrassment or distress."

She waved a hand of dismissal. "It does not signify. I am quite happy. And now, Lucius, I do have the most frightful headache."

"Of course," the Earl said. He bowed and departed.

As Lord Biddleton stepped out of the Waxwood house, he felt not only relieved but hopeful. He began humming a tune and then realized it was "The Serpent's Guile" from Kingsley-Dunnett's remarkable oratorio. The Earl suddenly smiled. "No doubt Eudoria would think me well cast for the part of the serpent." He continued humming as he climbed into his phaeton and rode briskly away from the Waxwoods'.

Scarcely an hour after his master had returned to the house, the Earl of Biddleton's butler was quite astonished to answer the door and find a very beautiful and unescorted lady standing there. "I must see the Earl of Biddleton," she said and the butler was much surprised at the sense of urgency in her voice. His master did not often have beautiful ladies coming to his door unescorted and it all seemed most improper and not at all the sort of thing Mills was accustomed to.

"Do tell his lordship it is Lady Isabelle Clairemont," said the beautiful lady and Mills tried not to show his surprise, for that lady had been often discussed in the servants' hall, despite Mills's attempts to keep his subordinates from gossiping about their betters.

Since his return from his meeting with Eudoria Waxwood, Biddleton had been in the best of moods. When the butler entered, his lordship smiled. This slightly disconcerted the worthy servant for his master was seldom so agreeable. "A lady to see you, my lord. Lady Isabelle Clairemont."

"Are you sure?" cried the Earl leaping to his feet. "Show her in immediately!"

The butler looked at his master with a surprised expression but hurried off and returned with Lady Isabelle. Biddleton smiled as she entered and suddenly had the urge to rush to her and declare his feelings. However, he quickly saw from her expression that there was something wrong and so he restrained himself.

"What is it?" he cried. "Lady Isabelle, do sit down." Isabelle sat down obediently on the sofa and the Earl sat beside her.

Her ladyship smiled gratefully at the Earl. "I suppose this is irregular, my coming here like this. I know everyone will think it quite shocking."

Biddleton smiled. "I don't care what anyone thinks."

Isabelle smiled in return. "Of course, you would say that. You are very kind."

"Nonsense. Tell me why you are upset."

"I know it's dreadful of me to come to you with my problem. It is a family matter, really, and I do not wish to trouble you with it, but you are the only man I know whose judgment I know I can trust."

"I am flattered. But tell me of this problem."

"It's my brother Rob. He has got hopelessly into debt. He borrowed money from some dreadful man whose name is Arthur Grilling and I am so worried. The man is obviously a criminal and a ruffian and I'm afraid Rob is in danger. You are a man skilled in financial matters, a sensible man. Is there anything I can do to save Rob from this person?"

Lord Biddleton frowned. "Is it quite a lot of money?"

"Eight thousand pounds."

"Good Heavens!"

"I know it is a great sum, but isn't there something that can be done?"

"Does the Duke know about this?"

"I don't know, but Father is severely in debt and he has never been good with money. There is little I can think to do except sell my grandmother's necklace, which she gave to me before she died." Isabelle took a small object wrapped in tissue paper from her reticule and handed it to the Earl. His lordship unwrapped it and found a lovely emerald necklace.

"It's lovely."

"Yes, and very valuable and I thought that if I could sell it and pay at least part of the sum back to this Grilling, it could buy some time to raise the rest. But I don't know how to go about this type of thing. I wondered if you could sell it for me and find Grilling and convince him to wait for the rest. I know it is a lot to ask of you."

The Earl looked at Isabelle and noted the concern in her blue eyes. He longed to take her in his arms and comfort her. However, he only smiled encouragingly and said, "You have no need to worry about anything, Lady Isabelle. I will deal with this matter."

"Thank you," said Isabelle. "You are a good friend. I shall always be grateful."

Biddleton smiled and reflected that it was not Lady Isabelle's gratitude that he wanted. Indeed, he thought it would be dreadful if gratitude were the only feeling she could have for him.

The Earl would have been astonished to know that Isabelle, though indeed grateful, was dangerously close to throwing herself into his arms and declaring that she had loved him from those early days at Winterhaven. Yet, to prevent herself from doing anything so scandalous, she stood up quickly, murmured her thanks again, and hurried away.

After Lady Isabelle left, the Earl of Biddleton called for his secretary. "What do you know of a fellow called Arthur Grilling?" his lordship asked abruptly.

"Grilling?" said Mr. Galbreath with a thoughtful look. "I have heard the name. Yes, of course, a moneylender and a rogue."

"Do I have eight thousand pounds I can obtain quickly?"

"Eight thousand pounds, my lord?"

"Do I have it accessible?" said the Earl impatiently.

"Yes, of course, my lord." Mr. Galbreath tried hard to hide his astonishment, for never before had the Earl expressed the need for such an enormous sum, and since the need was somehow connected with an unsavory person like Arthur Grilling, Mr. Galbreath was even more amazed.

"Good," said the Earl. "I want you to come with me to see this Grilling. Where would I find the fellow?"

"Indeed, my lord, these persons have offices on a common street. It should not be difficult to find him but, I assure you, my lord, he is a very disreputable man as are most of his colleagues."

"Then I must make haste to see him."

Mr. Galbreath could not find any logic in his employer's statement, but decided it was not his place to comment. He shrugged and followed the Earl out of the room.

Mr. Arthur Grilling was going over some notes in his small cluttered office. "Damn," he muttered as he looked at one paper and he muttered again as he perused another.

Suddenly a young man appeared at the back door of the office and entered with a grin. "Well, don't you look the proper gent? A banker I'd guess. Most respectable."

Grilling looked up from his desk and scowled. "Good God. Not you, Sam. By Heaven, I thought I was rid of you. Are you mad to come here?"

The young man laughed sardonically. "Is that a proper greeting for your only son, Father? I thought you'd be overjoyed at my return."

"Overjoyed? You young puppy. Damn your eyes. I've never had a day's rest since you entered the world. And you return to plague me. I thought you'd be in Newgate by now. By God, I'll not have you bringing the police to my door!"

"Come, Father," said Sam Grilling. "I suspect the police will be at this door whether I come or not. You ain't trying to make me think you're an honest businessman are you? God, I expect you're still sucking money from those unsuspecting souls."

"At least I'm not out robbing coaches and murdering people."

The young man laughed. "And you think I am?"

"I heard as much from many people. Why are you here anyway? I'll not hide you."

"Come, Father," said Sam, "you always have."

"I'll not do it again."

As he said these words, in walked two distinguished-looking gentlemen. One looked very much the haughty aristocrat. He looked scornfully at Arthur Grilling and then at his son. Suddenly a look of astonishment came to the gentleman's face.

"Good God!" he cried. "It's you!"

Sam Grilling at first did not recognize the Earl of Biddleton but then a look of horror came to his face. He turned to flee, but before he could escape, the Earl pounced upon him and managed to grasp one of his arms in a painful grip.

"I've got you, you villain," cried Biddleton. Mr. Galbreath stared openmouthed at his employer and had no idea what to do.

"What is this?" cried Arthur Grilling.

"This fellow," cried the Earl, holding on to the young Grilling despite the young man's attempts to elude his grasp, "stole my money and my ring at the point of a pistol and I'll be damned if I won't see him hang."

Galbreath was still standing staring at his employer as if he were a circus performer. "I'll call a constable, my lord," he said finally and began to rush from the room.

"Wait!" cried Arthur Grilling. "Don't, sir. Don't do that!"

Galbreath hesitated and looked at the Earl. Sam Grilling had ceased his struggles, for the Earl had his arm in such a painful hold, the movement was unbearable.

"What is the fellow to you?" said Biddleton. "Or are you his accomplice?"

"God forbid," cried Arthur Grilling. "He is my son, I regret to say, and if he has wronged you, sir, I'll try to right it. Please, sir!" Grilling suddenly had a thought. "Your honor has come to me for money, I'm sure. I'll pay you if you let Sam go. He deserves what he would get, sir, but his poor mother would die if her son was hanged."

"Wait, Galbreath," called the Earl. "Maybe we can

settle this without the authorities. I want to know, my good fellow, if you have the ring you stole from me."

"The ring?" said Sam. "How can I think about some damned ring if you're pulling on me arm so?"

The Earl loosened his grip. "Do you have the ring?"

"I got it," he gasped. "It's bloody hard to sell. It's in me purse."

"Duncan, get the purse."

Mr. Galbreath took the purse and opened it, pouring the contents into his hand. "It's here, my lord, the Biddleton ring." Galbreath hadn't even known the ring was missing, but he was, of course, well acquainted with it.

"Thank God." Biddleton released Sam Grilling and the young man rubbed his arm and looked menacingly at his lordship.

"Get out of my sight," said Biddleton in a threatening voice that Galbreath had never heard before. "I'll deal with your father." Sam Grilling seemed to pause as if he contemplated a counterattack.

"Get out!" cried his father and the young man left.

"Your son is a damned footpad, Grilling," said the Earl, "and you're not much better. But I will make a deal with you if you value your son's life, or your own for that matter. Hiding felons is a capital offense, Grilling."

Arthur Grilling looked pale. "If it's money you need, I have money. I'll give you one hundred pounds."

Biddleton looked at him with disgust. "You count your life cheaply, don't you? What I want are some notes in your possession, the debts of Lord Robert Clairemont."

"But he owes eight thousand pounds," cried Grilling.

"Your son is an armed robber. He nearly killed me and he stole my horse. You were hiding him here."

Grilling bit his lip and looked from the Earl to Mr. Galbreath. He frowned and then went to his safe and extracted some sheets of paper from it, which he reluctantly handed to the Earl.

His lordship handed the papers to Galbreath and kept his eyes on Grilling. "Are they all there, Duncan? Eight thousand pounds?"

"Yes, my lord."

"Good. Come, Duncan." They began to leave. "And Grilling," he said, pausing at the door, "you have been most cooperative." Grilling gave him a furious look, but most of his anger was directed against his errant son, whom he vowed to deal with if ever that young man had the poor judgment to return.

Biddleton and Mr. Galbreath left the dingy office and quickly entered the awaiting carriage. When they were safely on their way back, Duncan Galbreath sat silently, regarding his employer with a strange look.

The Earl smiled triumphantly and placed the family ring once more on his finger.

"That was the man who robbed you, my lord?" said Galbreath.

"Yes, and I will tell you all about it later." Biddleton smiled. "I should not have been so hard on the villain, or Black Sam as he is called," he said, "had he not had the poor sense to insult the future Countess of Biddleton."

Mr. Galbreath looked bewildered and his lordship laughed.

Chapter 19

Lady Ambrose sat at a table in the home of her friend, Lady Billings. Lady Billings had invited five other ladies for luncheon and Lady Ambrose sat listening with alternating interest and boredom to the conversation at the table. However, her disapproving look was replaced by one of keen interest when the ladies turned the conversation to the subject of finding suitable wives or husbands for their children.

"I tell you, my dears," confided Horatia Grigsby, a plump, chatty woman, "I only wish my James were a few years older because I have met a most charming young lady and quite eligible."

"Well, who is the girl?" asked Lady Ambrose in her abrupt fashion.

Mrs. Grigsby looked at her and smiled. "Lydia, I see that calculating look. You're thinking of Cuthburt."

"Nonsense. Cuthburt is too young to marry."

"Oh, I don't know about that. He is much too charming a young man to remain a bachelor for long."

"Come, Horatia," replied Alice Whitcombe impatiently, "tell us who this eligible lady is. Perhaps she would be suitable for my Humphrey."

Mrs. Grigsby looked dubious of this but finally divulged the lady's name. "Lady Anne Worthington."

"Of course, the Worthington girl," said Lady Billings.

271

"I've met her, too. Such a pretty creature and such charming manners."

"And an heiress. Why I've heard Lord Worthington's fortune is enormous."

"'Worthington?" asked Lady Ambrose. "Do you mean the Earl of Worthington?"

"Yes, his family's estate is way up north," replied Lady Billings. "The family seldom stays in London. They keep quite secluded out in the wilds."

"But Lady Anne is quite well schooled, none of the country miss about her" said Mrs. Grigsby.

"Well, I admit, Horatia, that Lady Anne does sound like a prize," said Mrs. Whitcombe. "But is she in London?"

"Yes, she is staying with her aunt, Lady Thackery. And, of course, she is also a second cousin to the Cummingses and with no doubt be staying with them for a time."

"How old is the girl?" asked Lady Ambrose.

"I believe she is eighteen. Not much younger than Lucy Cummings. This will be her first season."

"From the way you talk, Horatia," said Mrs. Paxton-Carrington with a smile, "it will also be her last."

As the other ladies continued to talk around her, Lady Ambrose sat considering. Although she felt Cuthburt too young to marry, she began to wonder if perhaps it would be wise to arrange a suitable match. A wife would keep Cuthburt away from the Clairemonts. Yes, Lady Ambrose decided, a wife like Lady Anne Worthington was precisely what her son needed.

After departing from Lady Billings's house, Lady Ambrose and her son drove to Hampstead where Lady Ambrose said she wanted to buy a new reticule. Cuthburt helped his mother out of the phaeton and offered his arm. As they neared the corner, Cuthburt suddenly spied his beloved Anne walking with her friend Lucy Cummings. He glanced apprehensively at his mother, who appeared in an oddly reflective mood. As the two young ladies neared, Anne also caught a glimpse of Cuthburt and his mother and gasped.

272

Anne and Lucy stopped as Cuthburt and his mother came face to face with them. Lady Ambrose was quite surprised when her son halted before two young and very pretty young ladies.

"Mama," said her son, who despite his discomfiture was overjoyed to see Anne, "I don't believe you are acquainted with the ladies." His mother shook her head and craned it down at the ladies.

"This is Lucy Cummings. Miss Cummings, my mother, Lady Ambrose. And," he continued smiling at Anne, "this is Lady Anne . . ."

Before he could finish his mother broke in. At the mention of Lucy Cummings she had immediately remembered the conversation at Lady Billings's house. Lady Anne Worthington was a cousin of the Cummings girl. Extremely eligible, they had said, and an heiress. This pretty, well-mannered young woman was, of course, Lady Anne Worthington.

"Lady Anne!" exclaimed Lady Ambrose in such a friendly manner that all three looked at her in considerable surprise. "I am so pleased to meet you, my dear." She extended a long, thin hand toward the lady.

"Thank you, Lady Ambrose," replied Anne, her timidity departing her with this friendly greeting. "I am also happy to meet you. Cuth . . . Lord Ambrose has often spoken of you, so I am glad we have had this chance to meet."

Lady Ambrose glanced sideways at her son. She was quite surprised, but nonetheless pleased to find that her son and the Worthington girl were so well acquainted.

Cuthburt and Lucy were exchanging curious glances and he gave her a slight shrug as if to say he had no idea of what was going on. "Lady Anne," said Lady Ambrose regarding her approvingly, "how is your father? I hope he is in good health."

"Oh, yes, ma'am. Papa is well, thank you."

"Unfortunately, my dear, I am not acquainted with your father but I have heard he is a fine man and he must be to have raised such a lovely daughter."

Cuthburt Ambrose appeared even more startled by this

remark. He was well aware of his mother's opinion of the Duke of Fothingham.

Cuthbert continued to listen in astonishment as his mother and beloved continued their conversation. Lucy also entered the conversation occasionally but almost laughed at the irritated expression on Lady Ambrose's face whenever her attention was drawn away from Anne. Finally, Anne and Lucy declared they had best be on their way and after an amiable farewell they continued in opposite directions down the street.

"Really, Anne," cried Lucy in muffled laughter. "I daresay no one has made such an immediate success with Lady Ambrose. A few brief moments and she acted as if you were her daughter."

Anne blushed but she was pleased by the meeting. "I don't believe it, Lucy. I feared Lady Ambrose would quite disapprove of me."

Lucy smiled at her friend. "Well, it is hard not to approve of you, Anne. Does this mean, Anne, that you and Cuthburt will marry now?"

Anne looked startled. "Lucy, how did you know?"

"We are friends, Anne, and don't think I didn't see how famously you two got on. Rob and I agreed you are perfectly suited for each other."

Anne suddenly laughed. "Oh, Lucy, I do love Cuthburt and he did ask me to marry him, but we thought it best to wait until he could get his mother's and uncle's approval."

"Well, his mother appears to be no problem. How about his uncle?"

Anne smiled. "I don't know. It is funny, Lucy, but I was quite afraid of Lord Biddleton. You see, I heard he didn't approve of my family and well, then when we returned home last week there he was in our parlor having tea! In any case, Lucy, I am quite happy now. I thought it was impossible that I should ever marry Cuthburt and now, Lucy, everything seems possible."

Cuthburt Ambrose did not know what to think about his mother's surprising reaction to Lady Anne Clairemont. After they had parted company from the two young ladies, Lady Ambrose continued to lavish praise upon Lady Anne. "That young lady," she said with emphasis, "is what every mother hopes for."

"She is?"

"Yes, I would quite approve of your marrying a girl like that."

Cuthbert blinked and stared at her.

"You approve of her then?"

"Of course! I approve of any Worthington."

"Worthington?" asked Cuthbert in surprise.

"Why, yes. As I told that dear child, I never met her father, Lord Worthington, but I have heard he is an excellent man."

Cuthbert suddenly looked deflated. "Yes," agreed her son grimly. "Lady Anne Worthington, of course." He remained silent for the rest of the journey. He was quite certain that his mother would not remain so fond of the young woman she had met if she knew her name was not Worthington but Clairemont.

When Lord Robert and his brother Lindsay returned to the house after taking the puppy Castor on a walk, Rob was surprised to see the house so deserted. "Where is everyone, Marston?" asked Lord Robert. "I thought everyone would be home by now. It seemed we were gone a dreadfully long time. I never walked so far in my life though Lindsay could have walked farther."

Marston smiled as Lord Lindsay greeted him and then was off with Castor. "A most energetic young gentleman," said Marston, who was very fond of the youngest of the Clairemonts.

"Indeed," said Rob. "Far too energetic. So what has been happening here? Did anyone call for me?"

Marston appeared reluctant at first to reply. "There was a person named Grilling, m'lord."

"Grilling! How dare he call on me here. I hope you sent him on his way."

"I tried to do so, m'lord, but he was a determined person."

"Egad! Damn his impudence. Did you and Edward have to toss him from our doorstep?"

Marston looked embarrassed. "No, m'lord, Lady Isabelle spoke with Mr. Grilling."

"Belle? Oh, no! Where is she, Marston? Where is Belle?"

"Her ladyship is in the drawing room I believe, m'lord."

Rob nodded and entered the drawing room to find his sister sitting in a chair with her embroidery. However, Isabelle was not concentrating on her needlework. Instead, she was staring absently out the window. She looked up as Robert entered the room.

"Rob."

"What's this about you talking to that fellow Grilling? Really, Belle, I don't like the idea of my sister talking to a man like that."

"He was quite civil."

"Civil? Come, Belle, he is a bully and a low fellow. How dare he talk to you!"

"Really, Rob, I was quite capable of talking to him and it was most illuminating."

"Was it?"

"I learned your debts stand at eight thousand pounds."

"Damn Grilling."

"I am glad he told me. Why didn't you tell me yourself?"

"Come now, Belle, what could you have done in any case?"

"Sold my necklace. The emerald one."

"Good God, that would be ridiculous."

"I don't think so. I have already done so."

"You what?"

"I have sold the necklace."

"How could you? Where did you go?"

"I didn't actually sell it myself," said Isabelle. "I asked someone to assist me."

"Oh, no! Whom did you ask?"

Isabelle hesitated. "Lord Biddleton."

"Biddleton?" Lord Robert stared at his sister with a look of incredulity. "He is nearly a stranger and from what Cuth-

276

burt says, a damned cold fish. How could you do such a thing, involving a stranger in family matters?"

"He is no stranger to me, Robert," said Lady Isabelle with some irritation. "I trust him completely and whom else would I ask?"

"But the Earl of Biddleton?" Lord Robert shook his head and was about to say something more when Marston arrived. "The Earl of Biddleton to see you, m'lady."

"Biddleton!" cried Rob looking at his sister. "I see he's done his deed for you. Very quickly, too. Belle, I can never forgive you for involving him in this."

Marston looked uncomfortable and Lady Isabelle replied, "Please show the Earl in, Marston."

Lord Biddleton looked very happy and smiled eagerly at Lady Isabelle. However, when he noted Lord Robert, whose expression was none too hospitable, he stopped. "Lord Robert," he said, "very good to see you."

Lord Robert frowned. "I think you have come to see my sister," he said. "I shall leave you."

"Pray, do not," said Lord Biddleton. "This involves you, sir."

"Yes," said Robert, "though I do not see why it involves you, sir."

Biddleton smiled. "I have something for you." The Earl reached into his pocket and produced some papers and handed them to Robert.

"What is this?" asked Robert, taking the papers and examining them. He then looked at the Earl in astonishment. "How did you get these?"

Biddleton laughed. "You have your sister to thank."

"That necklace could not have been worth eight thousand pounds," said Robert.

"No," said the Earl, "but I persuaded Mr. Grilling to accept less."

"But how?"

"It doesn't matter."

Robert looked suspiciously at the Earl. "Why have you done this? You have no reason to help me or my family."

The Earl smiled at Isabelle. "But I do. For one thing

my nephew Cuthburt is going to marry your sister Anne, that is, if Lady Anne will have him."

Rob and Isabelle looked astonished. "Is this true?" cried Isabelle.

"Yes, indeed."

"And you approve?" said Rob.

"With all my heart."

"You're not a bad fellow after all, sir," said Robert with a grin. "Then we'll be related, won't we? So I suppose it's all right that you helped me. Forgive me for being such a fool. You've saved my life, Biddleton."

"Surely not!"

"You have." Robert turned to Isabelle. "I thought it was hopeless. You see, I want to marry Lucy."

"Oh, Rob," cried Isabelle, "you are getting married too? And to Lucy? Oh, that's marvelous. I know you'll be happy." Isabelle embraced her brother and kissed him on the cheek. "You'll be so happy."

"I think I will be very happy," said Rob, smiling. He looked gratefully at Biddleton. "Because of Biddleton taking care of these debts I am free. And I swear by my honor, I'll not game even one farthing away ever again. Oh, I'll be dull, I suppose, but I think I can convince the Cummingses to accept me. Thanks awfully, Biddleton." The Earl shook Rob's hand.

"I'd thought I'd given up lecturing," he laughed, "but I hope you will be careful. Do not hesitate to call upon me for advice or assistance."

"I swear to you, sir," declared Rob, "you shall never have to aid me in such a fashion again! And now if you will excuse me, I want to see Lucy. She's arrived in town, you know. Good-bye." Robert eagerly left and Isabelle laughed.

"You have saved the day, my Lord Biddleton," she said, looking fondly at the Earl.

His lordship smiled in return and sat down beside Isabelle. "I did nothing really."

"Come, sir, I should not call it nothing. How did you reclaim his debts? My necklace did not bring so much, surely."

The Earl looked serious. "Oh, the necklace. Let me see." He reached into his coat and produced a small bundle. "You mean this."

"You didn't sell it!"

"How could I have done so? It is your necklace after all."

"But Rob's debts? You did not pay them yourself? Biddleton, you didn't!"

He laughed. "No, my lady. Certainly not. I am far too parsimonious a fellow to do any such thing." He took her hands in his. "I would have done so, but it wasn't necessary. It was dashed odd, really. Look here." He held up his hand.

"Your ring," cried Isabelle, "not your family ring!"

"The very one! And I will tell you the entire story after one short question."

"And what is that?"

"Marry me?"

"My lord! You can't mean it! Surely you could not wish to ally yourself . . ." The Earl smiled and stopped Isabelle's protests by placing his arms around her, pulling her close, and gently pressing his lips to hers.

Isabelle returned his kiss with surprising fervor. "Oh, Biddleton," she murmured, hugging him tightly. "You don't know how much I love you."

"My darling," he said, "I don't know how it could be possible that you could love me, but I will thank the gods for it. My dearest Isabelle, I am the luckiest man alive and no one could love you more."

Isabelle gazed at the Earl adoringly, then suddenly pulled away. "But Miss Waxwood? Oh, dear, what will we do?"

Biddleton laughed. "That lady has had the good sense to break our engagement. Alas, she is going to marry another."

"Then she is very foolish," said Isabelle, throwing her arms around his lordship and kissing him joyously.

Chapter 20

When the Duke and Duchess and their two daughters returned home from their visit, Marston greeted them and announced in a confidential tone. "The Earl of Biddleton is in the drawing room with Lady Isabelle."

"Is he?" said the Duchess. "We will see him, of course, but, Anne and Harriet, I want you to go up to your rooms. We've had a long day and you must make ready for dinner."

"But I would like to see the Earl," said Harriet. "Perhaps Sir Ralston is here, too."

"No, m'lady," said Marston, "the Earl is alone."

"Oh." Harriet was quite disappointed. "Then I will go up."

"Indeed you will, miss," said the Duke.

"You see, Harriet, Papa is getting stern," laughed Anne. "Come on, let us not provoke him further."

The Duke laughed. "You're a sensible girl, Annie."

When their two young daughters had ascended the stairs, the Duke and Duchess walked to the drawing room.

"I wonder what Biddleton could want," said the Duke.

"I wonder indeed," said the Duchess.

When they entered the drawing room their Graces of Fothingham were quite astonished to see their daughter Isabelle and the Earl of Biddleton sitting together on the sofa. They were smiling at each other and seemed to be on the most intimate terms. The Earl was holding Isabelle's hand and speaking softly to her. He rose quickly when the Duke and Duchess entered.

"Good day, Biddleton," said the Duke.

"Duke, Duchess," said the Earl with a broad grin.

"We have been waiting for you," said Isabelle with a smile. "We have something to tell you."

The Duke and Duchess waited expectantly.

"Lord Biddleton has asked me to marry him and I have accepted."

"Oh, Isabelle!" cried the Duchess, rushing to embrace her daughter. "Oh, I am so delighted."

The Duke smiled too and shook Biddleton's hand. "I'm surprised, of course, Biddleton," he said, "but delighted. Belle is dear to us but it's time she married."

"More than time, you mean," laughed Isabelle.

"Isabelle!" said her mother.

Lord Biddleton laughed. "I hope you will accept me as a son-in-law. I will provide for her well," he said gazing adoringly at Isabelle and taking her hand.

"I'm sure of that, sir," said the Duke. Suddenly he looked embarrassed. "I should like to talk privately with you, Biddleton."

"Of course."

"We will leave you gentlemen then to talk," said the Duchess.

"Yes," said Isabelle smiling encouragingly at Biddleton. He returned her smile and watched her go. It was, he thought, the happiest day of his life. His lordship then turned to the Duke.

"Biddleton," said his Grace of Fothingham, "I shall get to the point. Two points actually. I thought you were engaged."

"And I was but my engagement is off. It is Isabelle I wish to marry."

"You show good sense in that," said the Duke. "But there is a small matter we must discuss." His Grace looked quite pained and at a loss for words.

"If it's about the financial arrangements," said the Earl, "I am a wealthy man, sir."

281

"By God, everyone knows that, sir. I am talking about Isabelle. She has no money, though I'd hoped to bestow some of the property upon her, but I confess, Biddleton, my affairs are sorely tangled. Belle will have nothing."

"My dear Duke. It does not signify in the least. I do not need to marry a rich wife. It is the greatest luck that Isabelle would even consider me. No, Duke, I want only Isabelle."

"You're a good man, Biddleton," said the Duke.

"But I do have a request."

"A request?"

"I am known as a man who attends very carefully to managing his own affairs. This is true, but I have a most able assistant. His name is Duncan Galbreath and he is a genius. My request is this, sir. That you allow my assistant to oversee your affairs for a time. Indeed to give him free reign and do as he suggests."

The Duke frowned.

"I do think it would insure good relations between us, Duke, and I assure you it will be quite painless."

"Painless, you say?"

"Of course."

"Then I will do it. By God, sir, this fellow will have his work cut out for him. I never did understand much about money except for spending it."

The Earl smiled. "Well, sir, if Galbreath is successful there will be more for you to spend."

"Capital. My hand then, sir, and welcome to the family." The Duke shook his prospective son-in-law's hand vigorously and called for Marston to bring the port.

Lady Ambrose was furious with her brother when she heard the news. The bearer of the bad tidings was Lady Waxwood, who had announced in her stentorian voice, "I pity Biddleton and had hoped we would be related, Lydia, but Mr. Chalmers is the man for Eudoria. I hope Biddleton will recover from his disappointment."

Lydia was appalled and had a hard time remaining calm but she was able to listen to Lady Waxwood for nearly an hour, exhibiting remarkable restraint. When I see Biddleton, she thought as Lady Waxwood took her leave, I will make him regret that his stupidity lost him a bride like Eudoria. I worked so long to arrange the match and he has no right to ruin everything.

Her ladyship was in this unfortunate frame of mind when her butler announced her brother's arrival. Lydia stared at him as he entered her drawing room and was further incensed by the happy expression on his face. He could at least be miserable, she thought.

The Earl ignored his sister's formidable expression and greeted her warmly. "I suppose," he said, "you have heard that Eudoria has broken the engagement."

"I had heard," said Lady Ambrose bitterly, "and I am shocked, Biddleton. You seemed to want the engagement broken. You did everything to antagonize Eudoria."

"I did want the engagement broken," said his lordship. "I would have broken it off myself actually. I was quite happy when Eudoria put an end to it herself."

"You are dreadful," cried Lydia. "You do not wish to marry and do your duty."

"But you are wrong," said the Earl, smiling. "I am eager to marry. But Lydia, I want to tell you that you have no need to fear that Cuthburt will become entangled with Lady Isabelle."

"And why is that?"

"Because the Lady Isabelle and I are to be married as soon as possible."

"What!" cried Lady Ambrose. "You can't marry into that family. This is outrageous! Biddleton, have you lost your senses?"

"I have not. Indeed, marrying Lady Isabelle is just about the only sensible thing I have ever done."

"I will never speak to you again."

"Lydia, that is your choice. I hope you will reconsider but it is your choice. I am marrying Lady Isabelle."

Lydia stared sullenly at her brother. She could think of nothing to say. Biddleton was acting very strangely, she thought, and it was the Clairemont influence that was the root of the problem.

"Lucius," cried a voice. "How good to see you!" Lord

Ambrose entered the room and shook his uncle's hand. His mother regarded them both with suspicion, for never had she seen them on such good terms.

"Have you heard," said Lydia, "your uncle's engagement is broken off?"

"Oh, I am sorry."

Biddleton laughed. "No need to be sorry, I am very happy about it."

"Yes," said Lydia, "and he has lost no time in finding another bride, a lady well known to you."

Cuthburt looked puzzled. "Indeed?"

"Yes, I am going to marry Lady Isabelle Clairemont."

"The devil," cried Cuthburt and then broke into a grin. "Of course I should have known that something had changed your attitude toward the Clairemonts."

"I hope it doesn't bother you, Cuthburt."

Young Lord Ambrose laughed. "Not at all. Lady Belle was not for me. I know it now, but you and she will be happy. You are a lucky man."

"I know," said Biddleton, beaming happily.

Lydia could bear this display of joy no longer. "You both are horrible!" she cried. "At least it means I will not have a Clairemont for a daughter-in-law and I should be grateful I suppose."

Cuthburt and his uncle exchanged glances.

"What is this? A conspiracy?" cried Lady Ambrose. Cuthburt smiled.

"No, Mother, but I have something to tell you. You won't like it at first."

"Oh, no."

"I am going to marry Lady Anne Clairemont."

Lady Ambrose stared incredulously at her son and then at her brother. "You knew of this, Biddleton?"

"Yes, and I approve. You and I both misjudged the Clairemonts. There's not an older family in England and Lady Anne is a very nice girl. I can say it though I only met her once. She is Isabelle's sister."

"You'll grow to love her, Mother," said Cuthburt.

"I do not think so."

"You will," said Cuthburt with a forcefulness that amazed his mother, "if you will but give her a chance."

Lady Ambrose looked from her son and frowned. She was outnumbered and she knew it. She was completely powerless. She was not one to concede defeat easily, but neither was she one to pursue her goal when the chance of victory was so slight. Better to say nothing, she thought, and pressed her lips together in a bad-tempered pout.

The Biddleton carriage pulled up to the Duke of Fothingham's townhouse and stopped. The footman hastened to open the door.

"I don't want to go in," said Lydia crossly.

"I insist," said her brother. "Cuthburt and I are marrying into this family. If you choose to be part of our family, you will be civil to the Clairemonts."

"I do not like coercion," said Lady Ambrose. She gave her son and brother another of her withering looks and then got out of the carriage. Cuthburt and Biddleton exchanged amused looks.

"Never fear, Lucius," whispered his nephew, "I can tell she is softening. She'll come round."

Biddleton, who was not so certain of this, hoped it was true and got out of the carriage. The Duke and Duchess were overjoyed to see them and Isabelle and Anne were there, too, both of them looking radiantly happy.

"Cuthburt, my boy," said the Duke, "Anne has told me the happy news. By God, to have two daughters married at once. I don't know if I can take the strain of it."

"Nonsense, Papa," laughed Isabelle. "You'll be glad to be rid of us."

Lydia was determined to be only barely civil and she regarded Isabelle coldly. Then she saw Anne. "You are Anne Clairemont?" she asked.

Anne blushed. "Yes, ma'am," she said.

Lydia looked from Cuthburt's smiling face to Anne, who was also smiling, and then shook her head. "Lady Anne," she said, capitulating in the face of the insurmountable odds and deciding to accept the inevitable. She reluctantly extended her hand to Anne and then turned to Isabelle. "And Lady Isabelle," she said.

Isabelle smiled. "Lady Ambrose," she said and then looked at the Earl and saw that he was smiling triumphantly.

"This is all so marvelous," cried the Duchess. "How happy to have two children married to such wonderful men."

"Mama," cried a voice and the Duchess looked up and saw her son Robert with Lucy Cummings in tow.

"Robert," cried her Grace, "where did you come from? And, Lucy, dear, how nice to see you."

"We came in the back way to surprise you," said Rob, "and we have an announcement." Lord Robert looked from his parents to Cuthburt and Anne and Biddleton and Isabelle. "I'm afraid yet another Clairemont is heading to the altar."

"Rob" cried the Duchess. "You and Lucy!"

"Yes," said Rob gaily. "It's a miracle but Lucy said she'd have me and Mr. and Mrs. Cummings agreed." He winked at Lord Biddleton.

"Oh, Lucy," cried the Duchess, embracing Miss Cummings and then all the ladies took turns embracing that young lady and wishing each other all the happiness in the world.

Lindsay and Harriet stood surveying the scene and Lindsay shook his head. "It's all so wonderful," cried Harriet.

"I don't know," said Lindsay thoughtfully, "but at least Castor shall see more of his brother."

The adults were all talking and a mood of gaiety prevailed. Marston felt it too and was smiling in spite of himself when he heard a knock on the door. He opened the door and looked in astonishment. There stood two fashionable strangers with a familiar gentleman in naval uniform.

"My lord Burwicke!" cried the butler, forgetting his place momentarily.

The naval gentleman laughed. "Marston, good to see you, old man. What is happening here? Not a party at this time of day?"

The butler smiled. "A party of sorts it is, m'lord."

Just when the Duchess thought she could know no further happiness in walked a handsome young gentleman to disprove her theory.

"Oh!" cried the Duchess. "It's George!" She rushed to that young man and fell upon his neck, tears forming in her eyes.

Isabelle uttered a delighted cry and then noted the two other newcomers. She stared at them for a moment and suddenly the light of recognition came to her. "Biddleton," she said, taking his hand. "It is monsieur and madame! I don't believe it. They've arrived with Burwicke. Oh, what a day this is!"

Burwicke's arrival caused such a commotion that it was impossible to get near that gentleman for a time. Isabelle and the Earl rushed to greet the Comte and Comtesse d'Aubusson, who were now dressed in the height of English fashion and looked quite stunning. The *comte* and the *comtesse* each embraced them both. "So," said the *comtesse*, "your Earl is here. He will marry you, no? You see, I was right." She turned to Biddleton. "You speak such good French, monsieur, I knew you must have good sense. See, I am right." They all laughed.

"But how did you come to arrive with Burwicke, madame?" cried Isabelle.

"The strangest coincidence! We were not so sure where to find your house and we saw the handsome naval gentleman. We stopped to ask directions and he is your brother! Such a charming man, too. And so here we all are!"

Isabelle embraced the *comtesse* again. "There has never been a day so happy!" She released the *comtesse* and turned to Biddleton, "Never," she repeated softly.

It was some time before Isabelle and the Earl were able to sneak away to the garden for a moment alone.

"You know, my love," said her ladyship, leaning on the Earl's arm. "I never thought I could know such joy."

"Nor I, my darling," said the Earl, leaning down and kissing the lady.

"I was so glad to see Burwicke. If only he could stay.

And the *comte* and *comtesse*. They are marvelous. I shall miss them when they go back to France."

"I, too, will miss them," said the Earl, "for they remind me of how we met."

Isabelle looked up at him and smiled. Suddenly there was a loud noise and they looked over to see Lindsay come rushing from the house, Castor and Harriet close on his heels. They shouted merrily as they passed the Earl, and Isabelle laughed and shook her head.

"My lord Earl of Biddleton," she said looking up at his lordship. "Are you certain you know what you are getting into?"

The Earl smiled down at her. "I think I do, my love," he said and pulling her to him he kissed her smiling lips.